SONS
OF WAR

OTHER BOOKS BY NICHOLAS SANSBURY SMITH

SONS OF WAR

NEW YORK TIMES BESTSELLING AUTHOR

NICHOLAS SANSBURY SMITH

BLACK
STONE
PUBLISHING

Printed in the United States of America
Originally published in hardcover by Blackstone Publishing in 2020

First paperback edition: 2021
ISBN 978-1-79996-144-4
Fiction / Science Fiction / Apocalyptic & Post-Apocalyptic

1 3 5 7 9 10 8 6 4 2

CIP data for this book is available
from the Library of Congress

Blackstone Publishing
31 Mistletoe Rd.
Ashland, OR 97520

www.BlackstonePublishing.com

For my wife, Maria, for encouraging me to write the story I always wanted to tell. For my agent, David Fugate, for all the early feedback. And for Josh Stanton of Blackstone Publishing, for believing in my stories and bringing them to readers around the world.

"Underdogs have turned empires into ashes. We're going to build ours from the embers."
—Don Antonio Moretti

"Sometimes, you have to use evil to fight evil."
—Marine Sergeant Ronaldo Salvatore

PROLOGUE

November 2011

NAPLES, ITALY

The black Mercedes pulled up in front of one of the oldest basilicas in Naples, built with remnants of a far older Roman temple.

Antonio Moretti imagined how soldiers might have looked back then: the leather armor, muscular bodies, short swords gripped in callused hands. His own soldiers concealed their weapons beneath black suits. The difference in appearance was striking when he pictured it, but he supposed their minds were not so different. They had the same worries: protecting leader and family, making a living, surviving. In that regard, not much had changed over two millennia in the ancient city.

A Moretti soldier opened the back door, and Antonio stepped out, ignoring the demonstrators shouting across the street, and the signs insulting his family. He turned instead to the towering basilica of San Paolo Maggiore.

The exterior facade blocked the waning sunlight, but he kept his sunglasses over his eyes as he got out of the car. He didn't want his family or his comrades to see him like this. He was respected as a hard man, and on these streets, respect was the currency that mattered most.

Growing up in the slums not so far from here had made a man of him early in life. Four tours of duty with the Italian Fourth Alpini Paratroopers Regiment in Afghanistan and Iraq further toughened and tempered his character. And working for the Moretti family organization had strengthened it with blood.

But tonight, he was going in blind. Nothing had prepared him for burying his father, gunned down by a rival mafioso outside a local café.

Antonio did a quick scan for threats, though he was surrounded by men who would take a bullet for him and his family. That hadn't been enough to save his father, however, and they still didn't know which of the rival families was responsible.

"Antonio," said a rough voice.

Another car had pulled up, and several men in tailored black suits got out. At the lead was his younger and only brother, Christopher, also a veteran of the Fourth Alpini. They both had left their home as younger men to fight in a war, only to come home to another war.

They embraced with a kiss on the cheek, and Christopher turned back to the car to let out his wife, Greta, and their ten-year-old son.

"Help your mother, Vinny," Christopher said.

Raffaello Tursi, a quiet soldier with a rosary in one hand, walked over. He was one of the Moretti family's most loyal soldiers, a man who had never married and had given himself to the business and to God.

"Area is secure," he said.

"Thank you, Raff," Antonio said. He reached inside the Mercedes and took his wife's hand.

Lucia, the embodiment of elegance and grace, stepped down onto the street. She leaned in and unbuckled their three-year-old son, Marco.

He smiled, revealing two rows of perfect little square teeth.

Antonio kissed his son on the forehead, just below his thick black hair, which matched Lucia's dress and every article of clothing Antonio could see.

Raff instructed the other Moretti soldiers, who formed a phalanx around the two families as they walked toward the stone steps. Antonio helped his wife up the flights to the basilica's massive front door.

The guards accompanying them weren't the only armed men here. A pair of police officers stood sentry near the two ancient Corinthian columns that had survived wars from Roman times to twentieth-century aerial bombardment.

Inside the historic church, candlelight danced over the front foyer as Antonio stopped to dip his finger in holy water and make the sign of the cross. It had been a long time since he stepped into a holy place. The same guilt he always felt was with him today. Part of him believed he didn't deserve to be here after all the things he had done, all the men he had killed for his country and for his family.

The beauty of the ancient frescoes depicting the lives of Saints Peter and Paul helped ease his troubled mind as two police officers checked him for weapons.

He held up his arms and gave them each a glare. Today, he was in no mood to deal with these assholes.

"You're clear," said one of the guards. He motioned for Antonio to continue to a table where three more officers watched the guests.

"Sign here," said a policewoman with sharp green eyes.

Antonio had expected this type of security, but it was still frustrating even though he knew it was for their own good. This was the first time in as long as he could remember that the entire Moretti family had gathered in one place. It was also why they had to break Roman Catholic tradition and have funeral home employees move the body into the church.

There would be no final ride across the city for the family, and no pallbearers for the casket of Stefano Moretti. With all the violence among the other crime families in the city, it was just too dangerous. No one was safe, and the escalating war was going to get a lot worse now.

Little Marco looked over at his father with eyes full of wonder and curiosity. Antonio had long ago decided he would protect the boy's innocence and give him a childhood and a future away from all the bloodshed and crime.

A future unburdened by worries of war.

Christopher and his family were cleared through security, and together the two families set off down the central nave decorated with golden archways, carved marble columns, and a vaulted roof of magnificent frescoes. Passing through the transept, they gazed up at the polygonal apse covered in ornate paintings. Even little Marco seemed impressed, staring at the dazzling semidome above them.

The splendid art and the tone of hushed awe in the basilica, and the sight of his beautiful family already sitting in the row of reserved seats near the altar did nothing to mollify Antonio's indignation at the closed casket. The bastards who did this hadn't stopped with a bullet to the heart, but had riddled his father's face as a further insult.

An image of the corpse surfaced in Antonio's mind, filling him with another hot wave of rage, which he managed by letting out a discreet sigh. He would string them up by their guts when he found them.

The macabre thought seemed blasphemous in this holy space, but Antonio didn't care. He had long given up any ideas of getting to heaven. Only endless fire and pain awaited his soul.

"Antonio," said a gravelly voice.

The words came from cousin Lino De Caro. At first glance, standing there in his bespoke suit—if you ignored the gold hoops in his ears—he might almost pass for a banker or financial advisor, but the expensive drapery hid the ropy muscle, tattoos, and scars that reflected Lino's violent past.

He was the Moretti family assassin, and his well-honed skills would soon be put to work. Sitting to his right was another seasoned killer, their husky cousin Zachary Moretti. Both were made members of Antonio and Christopher's crew, much higher in rank than the grunt associates who had escorted them inside.

Raff ushered Antonio and his family to their row of seats.

"Be good, little man," he whispered to Marco as Lucia carried him past.

Antonio shuffled over to make room for Christopher and his family while Raff knelt to pray.

Soldiers Frankie Trentino and Carmine Barese sat with their Moretti wives on Antonio's left. The rough-looking men both had long hair, slicked back to-night, and weathered faces. They scooted down the row, the scent of cologne and cigarettes drifting off their suits.

"*Ciao*," Antonio said.

Carmine, also a Veteran of the Italian military, forced a smile across his droopy, scarred face—the result of a grenade that had nearly killed him.

The two Moretti made men embraced Antonio in turn, giving murmured condolences. Then they, too, knelt for their prayers. More guests arrived to pay their respects, filing into the basilica, slowly making their way through security.

A small commotion pulled Antonio's attention to the back of the nave.

"This is a disgrace!"

Antonio knew that deep voice the way a baby knew the voice of its mother. The man who had been a second father to him walked into the church, wearing a three-piece suit and a coat draped like a cape over his wide shoulders. Don Giuseppe Moretti, Stefano's older brother and the leader of the Moretti family, was already arguing with the cops.

Two bodyguards flanked Giuseppe. After a moment of heated conversation, the husky old don lifted his arms, allowing them to check him for weapons. He continued to speak under his breath, no doubt uttering words unsuitable for this holy place and solemn occasion.

Antonio sat back in his seat, trying to relax. The gentle touch from Lucia helped calm his nerves, and she reached up to take off his sunglasses.

They locked eyes, sharing the strength that had gotten them through other difficult times.

Giuseppe took a seat with his wife across the aisle. They were childless now, having lost their son and daughter ten years earlier in a fire meant to kill them all, and now he was about to bury his only brother.

Antonio nodded when Giuseppe looked his way. He glimpsed a deep pain in his uncle's eyes—a moment of weakness that he had never seen in the rock of the family.

The don's eyes rested on the casket housing his younger brother. Stefano was a respected man, but he had been the muscle of the Moretti family, not the brains. The true titan was Don Giuseppe, who also served on the city council. His background in organized crime was well known throughout the city, and so was his ambition to run for mayor, which made him an even bigger target than Stefano.

Now, with Stefano dead, it was up to Antonio and the other Moretti captains to protect their leader and their family's honor.

As the final guests were seated, the holy congregation entered through the back doors. The choir started in hymn, and the presiding priest, a short man with a gray beard and thinning hair, started down the central nave with his entourage of altar boys.

He swung a censer on a chain, back and forth, spilling fragrant smoke over the congregants.

Antonio looked over his shoulder to scan the faces. Many people, all of them carefully vetted by the family, had come to show their support and pay their respects tonight.

There were also men from other families, including the allied Sarcone family. Enzo Sarcone, a capo and brilliant entrepreneur, sat near the back of the basilica.

Their eyes met, and Antonio nodded, but Enzo looked away after only the briefest acknowledgment. Antonio turned again to the front of the basilica. Everyone here was nervous about the financial implications of his father's death.

The priest raised his arms, his robe hanging loosely.

"Tonight, we are here to pay respects to Stefano Moretti, a man whom many of you loved deeply," he said. "His life was cut short by the violence that plagues this city—violence that I pray will end."

Lucia gripped Antonio's hand.

The priest continued his appeal for peace and empathy for several minutes. Antonio wanted to tell him that his hollow words meant nothing, that the church had its own problems and, moreover, that the Moretti family was one of the biggest donors in the city.

Marco climbed onto Antonio's lap, resting his head on his father's shoulder. As Antonio shifted to get comfortable, he noticed that Enzo had gotten up from his seat and was walking out of the church. Four more police officers walked through the open door and closed it behind them.

But why would Enzo leave right *now*? What emergency could possibly …

Movement caught his eye. Across the basilica, on the other side of the rows where Don Giuseppe sat with dozens of highest-ranked men and their families.

In the glow from hundreds of candles, Antonio spotted three other cops walking in the shadows near the marble columns and statues.

Something was wrong …

Antonio whispered to his wife, "Get ready to move."

"*What?*"

"Do as I say."

Antonio jerked his chin to Christopher, who had already sensed that something was off. The cops continued in the shadows.

"Let us pray," said the priest.

As the guests bowed their heads, Antonio turned toward the back of the church, where the officers pulled out their handguns. One man pulled a submachine gun from a duffel bag under a table.

Another officer looped a chain through the handles of the front door and secured it with a bicycle lock.

"*Dio mio,*" Antonio whispered, realization hitting him like a bullet.

While everyone had their heads bowed, the choir broke into hymn. The heavenly voices stopped with the raucous din of automatic gunfire directed at Don Giuseppe.

His body jerked spastically as the rounds hit him. Bullets lanced into the pews, and the Moretti associates and soldiers who stood up were cut down. In seconds, ten of the men Antonio had grown up with were slumped dead, their blood pooling on the holy ancient floor.

Tuning out the screams and the chaos, Antonio focused on the one thing that mattered most: his family. He had to get them out of here.

They were already moving left out of the pew, with Christopher in the lead, but when he started toward the front foyer, Antonio grabbed him and pointed toward the altar, where the priest had taken cover.

A cop was waiting for them there.

Not a cop, Antonio realized, pulling back on Lucia's hand.

He recognized the assassin's face: a midlevel soldier from the small but aggressive rival Canavaro family. A shock wave of disbelief ripped through Antonio.

The *underdogs* were behind this?

Most families wouldn't dare do this in a church, of all places. Not on holy ground. The very idea was monstrous. There were rules in La Cosa Nostra, and killing in a church—especially killing women and children—was a cardinal sin.

But the Canavaros apparently didn't care about burning for eternity if it got them ahead in their mortal lives.

Antonio watched the demon in the flesh raise a gun.

"Christopher!" he yelled.

The soldier raised his pistol and fired as the scream echoed through the halls. The bullet meant for Christopher struck Greta in the chest. Christopher turned toward the gunman as his wife crumpled to the ground next to young Vinny, her hand still in his.

Christopher bolted toward the assassin, screaming at the top of his lungs. The man shot him in the arm and then the chest, but the bullets only slowed Christopher down; they didn't stop him.

He slammed the Canavaro soldier into the altar. Then, grabbing him by the throat, Christopher slammed his head into the wood once, twice, and once more just to be sure.

Antonio pulled Lucia toward the back door as she held a crying Marco close to her chest. She wailed as they walked past Greta's limp body.

"Vinny, you have to go with your aunt," Antonio said.

The boy hesitated.

"Go!" Antonio yelled.

Lucia grabbed the boy with her free hand, and Antonio rushed over to pick up the revolver that had killed his sister-in-law. He looked for targets as his wife carried Marco toward the back exit, with Vinny in tow. Christopher ran over and collapsed near his wife's side.

Antonio pulled the hammer back on the gun and backpedaled as he covered their retreat. All across the open room, the other assassins were hunting down Moretti soldiers, shooting them as they tried to escape with their families. The death and chaos happening all around him made his heart sink, but habit and the killing instinct took control.

He aimed and pulled the trigger, striking a "policeman" in the neck. Lino picked up the fallen man's gun. Zachary had taken down another of the cops and beaten his face into mush.

Antonio fired at a Canavaro soldier who took refuge behind a column.

"Christopher!" Antonio yelled. He looked over his shoulder to see his brother carrying Greta. Blood spread outward from the two bullet holes in his suit.

"Go, go!" Lino shouted.

He hopped over a pew, and Zachary followed. Frankie and Carmine joined them with their wives, and the group ran to the back doors, where the choir had already fled.

In the back hallway, they found the assistant priest sprawled on the tile floor, hit in the back by a stray bullet.

While his family slopped through the blood of their loved ones, Antonio trained his gun on the door that had opened behind the altar. Sure enough, one of the assassins emerged into the rear hallway. Before he could bring up his submachine gun, Antonio put a bullet through his eye.

The man dropped, providing a narrow view through the doorway to the massacre in the church. Screams and moans filled the space, some of them cut off by gunshots as the assassins continued to execute his family.

"Antonio!" Lucia yelled.

He hesitated, torn between saving his wife and child and saving his friends and fellow soldiers. The gun had two or three shots at most—heading back into the nave would be suicide.

Antonio swore and ran after his family. He raced down the back passageway and past an alcove with the statue of an angel holding a sword and wearing armor, its features tense and hard with the burdens of a warrior protecting the innocent from evil.

Gunshots echoed behind him, heralding the deaths of more Moretti soldiers. Ahead, at the end of the hallway, he saw Lucia clutching Marco against her breasts, tears streaming down her perfect face. Only a handful of family members had made it out alive.

The realization struck Antonio like a bullet. The reign of the Moretti family had all but ended here in the basilica.

The only future, and only hope for his boy, was away from Naples, in a country where they could raise him without fearing for his life.

Fleeing their home to find a safe place was a sad but necessary reality. But the Morettis would return to Naples, stronger than ever before, when the time came to take their revenge.

-1-

Eight years later

Dominic Salvatore pinched his bleeding nose and walked to the side of the basketball court in Hollydale Regional Park. The game continued as though nothing had happened. Bloody noses, black eyes, and scraped knees were common on these courts, where basketball was war dressed as sport.

As a mixed martial artist, he was accustomed to athletic injuries, and if not for the flow of blood, he would have stayed in the game. But he had to stop the bleeding if he wanted to get back on the court.

Taking a seat on the bench between two sweaty players, he eyed the dark-skinned young man who had elbowed him in the face. Ray Clarke aimed a sharp grin at Dominic.

"Just an accident, Dommie boy," he said.

"You're a better hooper than you are a liar," Dom called out. "And you're really not all that good at shooting hoops, either."

Ray laughed and went up for a shot. The ball nicked the rim and landed in an opponent's hand.

Dom didn't waste any more time arguing. That wasn't his style. When he got back out there, he would give it right back to Ray, but twice as hard.

"Dom, let's go!" shouted Andre "Moose" Clarke, Dom's teammate and best friend and Ray's younger brother.

"Gimme a few," Dom said. He grabbed a towel from his gym bag, keeping his thumb and forefinger clamped above his nostrils.

"You good?" said a female voice. Camilla Santiago walked over from the end of the bench and sat down beside him. She was his age, not quite eighteen, and also a senior at Downey High School, where they had met in Spanish class. Now she was practically his Spanish tutor, and a good friend on the courts.

"Fine," Dom replied.

She brushed her long ponytail over one shoulder. Her dark eyes studied him for a moment, then flitted back to the game. She loved to play with the guys, but some of their friends were dicks and preferred she stay on the bench. It made sense—she was better than some of them, and they had fragile egos.

He toweled sweat off his lean body and welcomed the refreshing breeze that whipped the palm fronds on the other side of the fences.

According to scientists, this summer was the hottest in recorded history. Droughts in the American Southwest, floods in the Midwest, and hurricanes on the East Coast had devastated an entire season of crops.

Dom tried not to worry about all that. He was here to have fun—and to win.

Moose went up to dunk the ball. All six feet, two

inches and 220 pounds of him rose into the air, slamming into the guy guarding him.

The ball sank through the chain net, and Moose landed back on his Nikes. Unlike his older brother, he reached down to help the opponent he had knocked down.

"Nice!" Camilla called out.

"Give it to 'em, Moose!" Dom shouted.

"Get some, baby!" Moose yelled. He flexed his massive biceps, lowered his head, and gave a loud snort. His Afro, sculpted low in the middle and sticking up and out on the sides, did indeed look a lot like moose antlers. The distinctive 'do and his imposing size had led to a nickname that stuck.

Camilla grumbled about wanting to get back into the game and then stood, cheering her teammates on. Dom grinned. She was a firebrand, almost as competitive as he.

He looked out across the park. Not as many joggers as usual, and only a few families grilling. The hot wind carried the scent of barbecue, but there was something else in the air, so palpable it almost had a smell. Fear—the same kind that crept up on him before he entered the ring to fight an opponent. A messy combination of adrenaline and anxiety that made him feel as if he might puke.

But the complete absence of fear made men weak. That was what his dad always said. Marine Sergeant Ronaldo Salvatore had a lot of great quotes and sayings.

Today, Dom saw fear in the uncertain gazes of parents who had brought their kids to the park for a picnic, trying to enjoy what normally would be a perfect Saturday. He also saw it in the emptiness of the park—all the missing families that normally would be playing on the slides or eating at the picnic tables.

As much as Dom tried to focus on having fun, he couldn't ignore what was happening in America. Extreme weather events had displaced millions of people and bankrupted the biggest insurance companies and factory farms.

Government bailouts had finally resulted in a default on the $30 trillion in debt the country had accrued, creating a trickle-down effect across the globe. Currencies crashed, inflation rose, and a perfect storm roared through the global economy.

The federal government had all but shut down, and people were in the streets, rioting over skyrocketing prices of gas, food and water, and utilities.

But it wasn't just the general population that had taken to the streets. The gangs were also adding to the chaos. Even here, today, a group had gathered outside the new skate park, smoking joints and laughing over the thump of Mexican gangster rap.

It looked like a small clique, probably affiliated with the Norteño Mafia, like most of the Latino gangs. From here, he couldn't tell what clique, and there were plenty to pick from.

Downey, a dozen miles southeast of LA, was once the mother of modern street gangs, but the police had worked tirelessly with the community for years to rid the city of them; forcing out MS-13, the Sureños, the Crips, the Bloods, and a score of smaller gangs.

Until now. The crashing economy drew violent opportunists back out into the light, and it added to the opioid epidemic already ravaging the city.

"Hey, check that out!" yelled Camilla.

Dom rose to his feet beside her to watch a group of National Guard Humvees speeding down the highway on the other side of the dry concrete ditch that was the Los Angeles River. It didn't surprise him, not with all the rioting these days.

"Wonder where they're going," Moose said.

"Who cares?" Ray said. "Let's play."

The trucks made their way through the slow-moving traffic, and Dom thought of his father. He would be back from Afghanistan soon, his company recalled to help deal with the civil unrest here at home.

It wasn't just his dad's unit. Other marines and soldiers were coming home from hot spots around the world, and Dom feared they were returning to fight on American soil. Whispers of a second civil war were everywhere. People blamed the government, and some states, including California, were already talking about seceding from the union.

"Hurry up, Dom," Moose said. "We're getting our asses kicked."

"I'll go in," Camilla said.

"I'm coming," Dom replied.

She grumbled again and sat back down. Dom took the towel away from his nose and looked up at a news helicopter crossing the skyline.

More shouts came as Moose went up for another dunk and slammed it home. Dom tucked the bloody towel away and ran back out to the court.

"About time, baby," Moose said.

Ray gave him the million-dollar pearly-white grin that was infamous for getting girls to drop their panties.

Dom wiped the last bit of blood from his nose with his forearm and dribbled the ball down the court, using his speed and agility to get around Ray.

They were about the same size: six feet, and two hundred pounds of mostly muscle. A perfect match on the court when playing fair, but then, Ray wasn't much for playing fair.

See how well you stack up against me in the ring, Dom thought.

Moose held up a hand for a pass, and Dom faked one to him, then maneuvered around Ray, dribbling in for a layup. He jumped and gently tossed the ball. It hit the backboard and dropped through the net.

"Attaboy," Moose said. "Back in the game, baby. Twelve–ten."

Ray snorted and reached for the ball as it sailed through the air. He caught it and started dribbling as Dom moved into position to guard him. As Ray got closer for the shot, Dom blocked his body with his own, moving his arms up and own. Ray was fast, but not as fast as Dom or even his younger brother, Moose, a skilled soccer player who had caught the eye of scouts from the Los Angeles Football Club.

Ray, on the other hand, wasn't on anybody's radar except the academic probation committee at UCLA.

The ball shot across the court back to Ray, and Dom bolted to intercept. He missed, and Ray caught it. He launched the ball, but Dom jumped higher, deflecting it and coming back down on top of Ray, knocking him on his ass.

Camilla snickered and nodded at Dom from the bench.

"What the hell!" Ray shouted.

Dom shrugged. "Defense, man."

He reached down, extending a hand, but Ray slapped it away and pushed himself up. Glaring, he came face-to-face with Dom.

"Easy, guys," Moose said.

"I ought to knock your dumb ass out," Ray said.

Dom smiled. "See how that works out for you."

Moose tried to wedge an arm between them, but Ray pushed up against Dom, knocking him slightly backward.

"Watch it," Dom said.

"Or what? You think you're some kinda badass fighter, don't you?" Ray said, chin raised as if asking for a punch. "I heard you ain't *shit*."

Ray spat on the ground to the side, but Dom didn't take the bait. Everyone on the court knew that Dom was 5-and-0 in the Octagon.

Ray pushed Moose back just as a rumbling sounded in the distance. It quickly grew in volume, drowning out even the thumping bass of the gangbangers' boom box. Dom looked to the eastern skyline. He knew that noise from his time living on military bases.

"What is that?" Moose asked. He and Ray joined Dom, forgetting their argument to stare at the squadron of fighter jets that came roaring over the skyline.

"Dude, what are they doing so close to the city?" Ray asked.

He was right. Dom had never seen jets come in this low, so loud the scream hurt his ears.

"Get down!" Moose yelled.

Dom crouched with everyone else as the jets

rocketed over, heading away from the city. The low rumble continued in their wake. Families had already deserted their half-eaten meals and were running to their cars as the sound faded.

"What the hell was that about?" Moose asked.

"I don't know, but it's not good," Camilla said.

Dom stood slowly, shaking his head. She was right, and he had a feeling something dire was about to happen. He just hoped men like his father could stop the tide of violence before it was too late for America.

* * *

Marine Sergeant Ronaldo Salvatore drowned out the radio chatter and the conversations in the Humvee. Normally, he would have been shooting the shit with the other marines, especially today. The platoon known as the Desert Snakes was freshly back from deployment in the barren, dangerous mountains of Kandahar.

Lance Corporal Callum "Tooth" McCloud, youngest of the four, sat behind the wheel, and Staff Sergeant Zed Marks rode shotgun. Ronaldo sat in the back with Corporal William "Chaplain" Bettis, the eldest of their small team.

Tooth's deep Irish brogue filled the Humvee, rapping the lyrics to one of the newest American chart toppers. The freckle-faced kid with green eyes didn't always speak with a brogue, but when he did, he could usually make Ronaldo and everyone else laugh. Today, though, he was just annoying.

"Will you shut your trap, Tooth," Marks hollered. "Please?"

Tooth grinned big, exposing the prominent upper incisors that earned him the nickname. "Ah, ya don't like my tunes, Sarge?" he said in the thickest accent he could muster.

Corporal Bettis frowned and scratched his salt-and-pepper hair. Then he went back to doing what he usually did in his spare time: reading his well-worn pocket Bible. The "chaplain" had been a seminary scholar until 9/11. He kept to himself, but he always had an ear to lend a brother marine who needed it.

Today, Ronaldo needed an ear.

The convoy sped away from its forward operating base, toward downtown Atlanta. Normally, Ronaldo could ignore other worries when he was heading out on mission, but today his mind was focused on his family back in Los Angeles.

For almost two decades, his wife, Elena, had raised their son Dominic and his sister, Monica, mostly on her own. She was a strong, smart woman, and although they had their share of problems as a couple, he could sleep well at night knowing they were safe with her.

But today he wasn't sure how safe they were. The situation continued to deteriorate, with riots and violence in every major city. In LA, the gangs were rising to power, and any teenager who couldn't find a job was ripe for recruitment.

There would be more junkies, more violence, more ruined lives.

When he arrived home from Afghanistan six days ago, Elena had begged him not to go to Atlanta. Instead of the joyful homecoming he had imagined, they had gotten into an argument in front of the kids.

Now, all the way across the country, he was kicking himself for not controlling his temper. At least, he could count on his boy to look after them. Dom was smart, brave, and fit, and Ronaldo had entrusted him with a shotgun and pistol to protect his mother and sister.

He tried to get his family out of his thoughts, but seeing all the residents fleeing Atlanta on the opposite side of the highway wasn't helping any.

Maybe I should have gotten them out …

Ronaldo was the only one in the Humvee who had a wife and kids—well, kids he knew about, anyway. Tooth couldn't keep it in his pants and quite possibly had offspring somewhere.

Bettis was a loner, and Marks, like so many of their brothers, had gone through a terrible divorce. All the men had struggled with relationships, thanks to the horrors of war that they couldn't help bringing home with them after each deployment.

"They must think they'll find jobs out that way," Marks said, looking across the interstate at the stalled line of cars topped with bundles and suitcases. "Reminds me of the refugees leaving Baghdad."

Ronaldo lifted his helmet long enough to wipe the sweat off his buzz-cut head. While he found it hard to accept that America was in such dire straits, it wasn't hard to see how things had gotten to this point. The combination of severe weather, economic collapse, and social breakdown had the country coming apart at the seams.

In the back seat, Bettis made the sign of the cross above his wrinkled brow to start a quiet prayer. His features were hard, and Ronaldo suspected that prayers wouldn't be enough to see them through this time.

"This shit is fucked," Tooth said, all business now. He had said it a hundred times since they stepped back onto US soil, and in his normal voice.

It occurred to Ronaldo that maybe the rapping hadn't been so bad, after all.

Tooth changed lanes to avoid a car with smoke coming from its engine. Marks looked over his shoulder, scrutinizing Ronaldo.

"You good?" Marks asked, cocking an eyebrow.

"Yeah, bro, I'm good."

"No, you aren't, man."

Ronaldo frowned. He and Marks had fought insurgents and terrorists in hellish, isolated hot spots around the world for almost two decades. As a result, they could read each other like an open book.

Marks sighed. "I got no family to worry about, brother, but you do." He paused as if searching for the right words. "Dom's a good kid. He's got instincts like his old man and will look after Elena and Monica."

Radio chatter filled the Humvee as they sped toward downtown, weaving in and out of lanes once they pulled off the highway. At stop signs, they paused only to make sure the path was clear.

The rioters were growing more brazen, destroying storefronts, tipping cars, and setting fires.

"This shit is really happening in *every major city*?" Tooth asked.

"Sure sounds like it," said Marks.

"So we're going to sit on the sidelines and play babysitter?" Tooth paused to inspect the toothpick he'd been chewing on. "I'd rather be out there—"

Another transmission came over the radio. This one chilled Ronaldo to his core.

"*Dirty bomb ... San Francisco port ... Mass casualty event ...*"

"Holy shit," Tooth said. "Turn that up."

Ronaldo fiddled with the radio, his mind back on his family. They would be safe from the radiation in Los Angeles, but what if more attacks came?

"Buncha' pussy terrorists, I bet," Tooth said. "Hittin' us when we're weak. Goddamn asshole cowards."

He continued to mutter profanities as they followed the convoy deeper into the chaos.

"Stay frosty," Marks said, "and when we get out there, you keep your finger off the bang switch, Lance Corporal. Got it?"

Tooth nodded, but his face was set with grim conviction. "Sergeant, you heard the radio—"

"Yeah, I heard it, and we're here to help civilians, not make things worse. Do you hear and understand the words coming out of my mouth?"

"Loud and fucking clear, Sergeant."

"Good."

Ronaldo and Marks exchanged a glance. First the assassinations, now a dirty bomb ...

"Who is doing this?" Ronaldo said, incredulous.

"Somebody that wants a reset," Bettis replied.

"Reset?"

No longer in his praying voice, Bettis said, "These domestic or international terrorists, whoever they are— they haven't taken credit for the attacks, because their goal isn't just to spread terror. It's to take our country down while we're weak. That's why the assassins wore masks."

"That's what *I'm* trying to say, man," Tooth said, cinching his body armor a little more snugly.

"Two years away from retirement, and our country is falling to pieces," Marks said.

A pair of Black Hawks thumped overhead. As they crossed the skyline, Ronaldo watched the crew chiefs manning the M240 machine guns mounted in the open doors.

"That army?" he asked.

"I can't tell," Tooth said, craning for a better look.

"Not army," Bettis said. "That's the new Corps."

The marines all studied the Black Hawks. Ronaldo glimpsed the symbol of the new American Military Patriots (AMP): the head of a raven. He wasn't a big fan of the name, since *all* marines, sailors, soldiers, and guardsmen were patriots. But some young Harvard grad working in the White House had probably thought it sounded catchy, and the "Always on Watch" slogan was a good pitch to citizens that the government and military had their back in these difficult times.

In response to the civil unrest, the administration had reorganized the National Guard under the AMP banner, and the move had gained traction with surprising speed.

"Vice President Elliot must be behind this," Marks muttered. "He's a four-star freaking general, and he's dangling POTUS like a puppet on strings."

Tooth chuckled nervously, but Ronaldo didn't find it funny. "It's brilliant and ironic," he said. "The marketing campaign of a government and military looking out for civilians is exactly what people want right now: to feel their government cares."

"Yeah," Marks said, "but it's also another excuse for the Coleman Administration to take troops away from the states so they can't rebel."

"And grab all the best equipment while they're at it," Bettis said. "I heard the Air Force is being transferred under the AMP banner, which means they'll have access to all those new F-Thirty-Fives. I thought those were supposed to be for us."

"They're welcome to 'em" Marks said. "Fucking boondoggle waste of money, with all the problems they've had."

Tooth muttered, "It's a disgrace to let anyone else have *anything* made for the Corps."

"Guys, just be careful who you say that around," Bettis said.

Ronaldo acknowledged the older marine with a nod. He was right, of course, and with all the talk of civil war, they needed to watch their expression. The army, navy, and marines had yet to be absorbed by AMP, but Ronaldo's gut told him it was just a matter of time.

As the convoy reached the edge of downtown, Ronaldo made the sign of the cross and prayed. For his family. For his country. And for all the people who were going to die in the aftermath of the dirty bomb in San Francisco.

"Good to see you putting your faith in God," Bettis said. "We all should do that more often." He looked pointedly at Tooth, who grinned.

"Much respect to you, old man, but I just don't think God has anything to do with what happens on this planet."

Ronaldo prepared for yet another theological debate, but this time, he was spared. Instead, another radio transmission distracted the group. Their convoy was being rerouted to Centennial Olympic Park, in the heart of downtown. Traffic on the opposite side of the freeway had come to a stop, and people were standing outside their cars in the midafternoon heat.

Emergency lights from police cars and state troopers flashed along the shoulder as officers did their best to keep the flow moving, but several stalled cars bottlenecked the mass exodus.

Ronaldo shifted his rifle against his shoulder. The thought of actually using it crossed his mind for the first time since he arrived back stateside. Could he do it? Could he really fire at Americans?

If they're terrorists, hell yes.

What about rioters, though? Average people driven to do crazy shit out of desperation.

He shook away the thoughts as the convoy turned down a street that paralleled a railroad. Hundreds of people were marching across a bridge over the tracks.

Tooth took a left at the next turnoff, following the convoy's path. Storefronts on the intersecting streets were already shattered, and the hull of a burned-out car smoldered where a city truck with a snow blade had pushed it off to the side.

On a side street, a line of cops in riot gear held their ground against a mob of civilians wearing masks and carrying backpacks. They were chanting something he couldn't make out.

Ronaldo checked his gear one last time as they drove toward the gate blocking off the marshaling area. Sandbags were stacked in front of the entrance, and he nodded back at an AMP soldier who raised a hand as the Humvee drove into a parking lot.

FEMA; the Red Cross; and local, state, and federal agencies had sent people to a massive lot on the west side of the railroad tracks.

The local greeting wasn't the one Ronaldo had expected. He got out to the angry shouts and screams of several thousand disgruntled civilians on the other side of the fences. Most of them jobless and hungry—of course they were mad.

"All right, listen up!" shouted Lieutenant Tom Castle. The platoon leader's commanding voice and presence even turned the heads of several police officers.

Marks, Ronaldo, Bettis, and Tooth stood side by side, rifles cradled as the other marines in the platoon gathered around.

"We got supplies coming in from the rail," Castle said. "Our job is to protect those supplies and make sure they get to the people that need them. We're not here to poke the hornets' nest, so stay frosty."

Ronaldo's mind turned to his family. If the government didn't turn things around, his children's future would be postapocalyptic, like the books he had read during the long, lonely nights of his deployments.

"No one shoots unless I give the order," Castle said. "I don't care if you're getting punched in your nut sack. Everyone got that?"

"Oo-rah!" the marines all yelled.

Castle went to work, splitting the men into teams. The Desert Snakes followed Marks toward a police officer who was busy barking orders at a group of cops who looked dog tired.

It was like being transported back to Baghdad, 2003.

The Black Hawks that had flown over the interstate earlier crossed the skyline again. Two more birds, both news choppers, hovered above the city.

"They want us up on that rooftop," Marks said, glancing at a low-rise office building. He directed them across the staging area, stopping for a flatbed trailer. The truck crossed in front of them and rumbled onward.

At the top of the stairwell, the marines accessed the roof through an unlocked service door. Marks flashed hand signals, and the team split up, with Marks and Ronaldo moving to a ledge to set up position. Tooth and Bettis took the opposite corner, giving them an overview of several city blocks, including the tide of civilian protesters and rioters.

"Jesus Christ on a pogo stick," Tooth muttered.

"Watch it, kid," Bettis said, shooting him an angry glare.

"Sorry. How about—"

"How about you shut your mug and *focus*," Marks called over.

To the east, a train hissed and squealed to a stop on the tracks, and crews lined up to start unloading the supplies from FEMA warehouses. Ronaldo doubted that the rations were going to calm these people down.

He pushed his scope up and zoomed in on the riot police they had passed on the way in. They were being pushed back into an intersection, closer to the entrance of the marshaling area.

"We got trouble," he said.

Marks lifted a pair of binoculars.

Teargas canisters sailed away into the mass of rioters, swirling and billowing. But this just seemed to further enrage the mob. Several people wearing bandannas and masks charged through the line, throwing rocks and bricks.

The entire area was a tinderbox, and the rioters were doing their best to ignite it.

"Shit, this is jacked," Tooth said. He raised his rifle, and Bettis put his hand on the barrel.

"Take it easy," he said.

One of the officers in riot gear crumpled in the street, and his comrades pulled him to safety.

"Everyone, keep calm," Marks said.

A gunshot came from the south, and Ronaldo turned to zoom in on the bridge, where people were using ropes to climb down.

"We got a security breach," he said.

More gunfire came from the west, and three more riot police went down. Nonlethal deterrence had failed. The rioters were marching full steam ahead toward the gates. The tinder was alight.

Over the noise came the whoosh of a news chopper, coming in for a better view of the area. The two Black Hawks crossed over to intercept and chase it away.

The cops in riot gear retreated with their injured toward the armored vehicles. Ronaldo was impressed by their weapons discipline, especially after some of their own had been severely hurt. If they could maintain that kind of restraint, then it was just possible they could stop this from escalating.

A police loudspeaker sounded, telling the rioters to get back and that aid was on the way. This seemed to mollify some of the crowd, who began to disperse, but hundreds continued toward the staging area.

The Black Hawks circled the news chopper, but the civilian pilot wasn't following orders. The bird continued to hover over the crowds, recording the entire thing.

A transmission from Castle crackled over the comms. "If those crowds hit the gates, we have permission to fire at hostiles to keep them back."

He paused, as if questioning his orders, but then added, "Everyone, pick your targets cleanly if it comes to it."

Ronaldo looked over at Marks, who couldn't hide the shock on his normally stoic face.

"We really doing this, bro?" Ronaldo asked.

"God have mercy on our souls," Bettis said.

Before anyone could question the orders, another round of gunfire cracked in the distance.

"Oh, shit!" Tooth yelled, pointing at the news chopper. Ronaldo watched in horror as it began to spin after taking several rounds.

The pilot fought to control the descent, but the tail rotor was dead, and the bird swirled and came crashing down at the west side of the staging area, exploding on impact. Marines, cops, and civilians dived for cover, but several were enveloped in the fireball.

The deafening blast forced Ronaldo down. As he ducked, automatic gunfire fire rang out. He glanced to the sky, where one of the Black Hawk crew chiefs had opened up with the M240. He fired right into the crowd, mowing down men and women, rioters and peaceful demonstrators.

"Tell that dumb motherfucker to hold his fire!" Marks yelled, waving both hands.

The AMP crew chief continued to rain hell down on the civilians, casually taking lives as if these weren't real human beings. Screams of horror sounded from inside and outside the staging area, where the injured lay on the concrete, bleeding and crawling.

"Stop that gunner!" Marks yelled again.

The crew chief kept right on shooting at the crowd, cutting down more civilians as they fanned away from the gates.

Ronaldo knew there was only way to stop the bloodshed. He raised his rifle and put the AMP gunner in his crosshairs.

God forgive me, he thought as he squeezed the trigger.

-2-

While the world burned, Don Antonio Moretti sat in his office in Compton, just southeast of Los Angeles, working into the night to build a new empire. He and his brother had dreamed of it since growing up in the slums of Naples, Italy, long before the Morettis rose to power, and long before that power was stripped away in the ambush that left most of his family dead.

Christopher stood in front of the TV, puffing a cigar and stroking his graying goatee.

They both had a long way to go in achieving their dreams, and Antonio was starting to question whether coming here was the right move. Just over three hundred thousand Italian Americans lived in Los Angeles, yet the Mafia presence was almost nonexistent. But the Morettis and another Naples transplant family were changing that.

Sipping his espresso, he reflected on his life while the wall-mounted TV streamed the dire news reports from America and all over the world. He was no stranger to war, political upheaval, or crime. Tragedy was part of the Moretti family history, and the blood-bath eight years ago, at their father's funeral in Naples, had left wounds that never healed. Escaping to America had seemed like running. But running was the only way to keep his wife and son alive.

Things weren't all bad here. After fleeing Naples, they had managed to keep in place their Colombian deal with the González family. The operation was small—mostly cocaine, pharmaceutical opioids, and marijuana—but the high-quality product made them a decent return on their investment. It helped keep them afloat while they dabbled in credit-card fraud and fencing the stolen merchandise they got in from Europe.

But things were hard, and the competition with the deeply rooted criminal gangs had them living off scraps. Breaking into the drug business in a big way was dangerous when every corner was owned by a rival organization.

Christopher stared at the only decoration in the room: a poster from the movie *Raging Bull*, a 1980 flick about a middleweight Italian boxer who lost everything. Antonio kept it there as a reminder of what he could lose if he wasn't careful.

He had already lost much. Most of his family. His birth city. The gated compound they had called home, his luxury suits, the cars …

I'll have my revenge. In this life or in hell.

"Have a seat, Chrissy," Antonio said, looking at his watch. He would find out soon whether Lino and Zachary had succeeded on their mission to take out the rest of the Canavaro family.

He got up and closed the door to protect the dozens

of racks of clothing brought in from the UK, which sat covered in plastic wrap. He didn't want them smelling like smoke before he put them out on the black market.

Christopher sat down at the card table. "We survived the slums, war in the Middle East, and the war on our family in Naples for *this* shit?" he said in his deep Neapolitan accent.

Antonio looked at the ledgers spread out on the card table. For the past few years he, too, had worried about the future, but where his brother saw a threat to their growing business, Antonio saw opportunity.

"What's happening out there is going to help us achieve our dream," Antonio said.

"You said it yourself," Christopher reminded him. A dream without a strategy behind it is just that: a dream." He took a puff from his cigar and blew the smoke toward the ceiling. "This isn't Naples. There's more competition, more gangs. More threats. We narrowly survived the last attack, and I lost my Greta."

"I know, and I'm eternally sorry, brother."

"We're weaker than we were then, Antonio. We have to grow before we can expand."

"I know, but I'm asking for your trust."

"You have it," Christopher said. "I'm just waiting to hear your brilliant plan for how we're going to get rich here and not get ourselves killed. Because we've been here six years, and I'm starting to worry, especially with the news."

"That," Antonio said, gesturing toward the screen, "is a good thing for us, and in a few hours you'll see why."

He cracked a rare grin. A good player showed his cards only when he had to. He didn't like giving away information, but it was time to share some things with his brother and his most trusted confidants.

Christopher leaned forward and flicked his cigar ash into a glass dish. The news switched to the dirty bomb in San Francisco.

"Aren't you worried about this?" Christopher asked.

Antonio took another sip of his espresso. "I'm worried for my family, yes."

"I am too," Christopher said. "I don't want to lose my boy like I lost Greta."

"We've survived far worse, and I've been preparing for this war."

Christopher picked up the remote and turned up the TV. Images of the reorganized National Guard came on screen. But the story wasn't about the arrival of AMP troops in Los Angeles; it was about the recruiting stations.

"*AMP centers like this are popping up all across the country, attracting jobless men and women who desperately need a paycheck,*" said the announcer. She stood near the long line of people outside a recruiting center with a banner sporting AMP's raven logo.

"*Noncommissioned officers from other branches are enlisting, and so are mercenary guns for hire. Tens of thousands of National Guard members have been deployed to the streets.*"

"Jesus," Christopher said. "These news anchors are starting to sound like the state crap we had in Italy—basically a propaganda wing for the government."

Antonio steepled his hands, but he wasn't praying. He prayed only when he needed to, and his plan would work without an assist from God.

"This is all good for business," he said. "The police are already distracted with the looters and rioters. This could be the chance we've been waiting for. We know how to make money in the slums, and we know how to organize in situations like this. Don Giuseppe and our *papà* taught us well."

"God rest their souls," Christopher said, crossing himself.

Antonio pulled out the necklace of the Moretti family's patron saint, Francis of Assisi. He kissed the gold charm, saying a prayer for all those they had lost.

Thinking of the ambush at the basilica filled Antonio with rage. Feeling his thumping heart reminded him he was still alive, and as long as it continued to pump blood through his veins, he would get his revenge on the rest of the men responsible.

Next on his list was Don Enzo Sarcone. The *bastardo* who helped betray his family had also moved to Los Angeles, when the other families turned on him a few years back. It was the other part of the reason Antonio had come here: not just to grow his business, but to kill Enzo and poach his customers. That day was soon coming.

He pushed thoughts of revenge aside and walked over to the bulky safe on the floor behind his desk. Punching in his code, he reached inside to grab what remained of their reserves—just shy of sixty thousand dollars. Returning to the table, he set down the stacks of hundreds.

"The police, AMP, and the rest of the military branches are out en masse," Christopher said. "It's a bad time to be making a move in the drug trade. Besides, we're just small fish …"

"That's exactly *why* it's time. The police and soldiers are too preoccupied to bother with—what did you call it?—'small fish.' They're focused on all the rioters and the established gangs."

"We don't have enough men to expand," Christopher said. "We're hardly making ends meet as it is. We got the Norteño Mafia controlling dozens of Latino gangs. We got the Crips. We got the Bloods. We got the Southeast Asian Boys, the …" He puffed on the cigar. "Hell, we can't even take out Enzo."

Antonio heard the anger and struggled to manage his own. "Patience is the virtue you never had, brother," he said. "You must remember, life is long, and to achieve success requires patience and planning. I've had plenty of time to plot our revenge, and the time is almost here."

Christopher did not reply.

"Los Angeles is like Naples with the gangs," Antonio continued. "Which is another reason why I decided to settle here of all places. We understand how this environment works, and that gives us an edge. In Italy, the government is corrupt, and so are the police and the army. Same thing is starting to happen here, and the other gangs you just rattled off don't know how to deal with the cops—or with AMP. I do."

Christopher leaned forward to flick ash into the bowl. "So what if we know how to deal with dirty cops, dirty soldiers, and dirty politicians?"

"Because now is our chance to start working with them."

Christopher sat back in his chair, considering the words.

A knock came at the door, and Raffaello Tursi opened it.

"Don Antonio," he said. "Your guests have arrived."

"Thank you. Send them in," Antonio said.

Raff nodded and backed away, but Antonio told him to hold up.

"I need you to watch over Lucia and Marco tonight," he said. "I'm not sure when I'll be home."

"Of course, sir," Raff said politely.

The soldier was a lonely, quiet man who Antonio often thought belonged in a different line of work. Antonio had never asked Raff to kill anyone, and that was exactly why he was looking after the family tonight instead of coming with them.

The door opened again, and their much younger cousin Zachary Moretti stepped inside the room, wearing a cocky grin. Since that fateful day in Naples, he had turned his extra weight into muscle. And today he had added a blond Mohawk to his presentation.

"Don Antonio," he said in a thick accent. "Christopher."

"What the hell kind of animal you got on your head?" Christopher asked. "You better knock it off there before it shits on you."

Antonio laughed, but Zachary just shrugged. "I kinda like it."

"Where's Lino?" Antonio asked.

"On his way."

Zachary walked farther into the room, his chest muscles bulging beneath the big gold cross hanging out of his open track jacket.

"Well, you gonna tell us what happened?" Christopher asked.

Zachary looked to Antonio for permission.

"Wait till Lino is here," Antonio said. After the eight years he had already waited for his revenge, what were a few more minutes?

"What's it like?" Christopher asked. "Our home—what's it like now?"

"Not the same as it was," Zachary said. "Things are changing there, and not for the better, I don't think."

His English, like Christopher's, wasn't the best, which was partly why Antonio insisted they speak in their second language. He never wanted to be in a position where people, especially enemies, could speak and he not understand. For the same reason, he was also learning Spanish.

Shoes clicked on the tile floor outside. They could only be the Italian leather shoes of Lino De Caro. The wiry, rail-thin man entered wearing a suit, two gold hoops in his ears, and sunglasses propped up on his head.

"You got a haircut too," Christopher said.

Lino ran a hand over his shaved head. Looking at Zachary, he said, "Thanks for waiting, Yellowtail."

Zachary shrugged. "Sorry, man."

"*Yellowtail?*" Christopher said. "Who the hell is ... Oh."

"My new nickname," Zachary said. "I didn't ask for it. Guess it's going to stick, though."

"Cut the shit," Antonio said. He gestured toward the card table and the six bank-wrapped stacks of bills piled in the center. Someday, they would have a real war table, where they would discuss multi-million-dollar operations. But getting there was going to entail some major risks.

Yellowtail and Lino sat down.

"Is it done?" Antonio asked.

They both nodded.

"Every last one of our enemies is in the ground or has fled and won't be coming back," Lino said. "We can return to our home whenever we want, and tell our relatives to come out of hiding."

Antonio sat back in his chair, his body numb and on fire at the same time. "Not *all* our enemies," he said.

All three men looked at him, but none spoke.

"There's a reason I didn't come with you to Naples," Antonio said. "I've decided the Morettis' future is here in Los Angeles, where we can expand. I've already put things in motion. Soon, cousin Vito and our other surviving relatives will make the journey to the Stati Uniti, to join us."

"But—" Yellowtail began to say, running a hand through his blond spikes.

"I've made up my mind, and the wheels are in motion," Antonio said. "I didn't come to America just to escape the bloodshed. I came here to destroy the Sarcone family. Nor did I come here just to make a decent living. I came here to make a *fortune.* The crumbling economy is providing us with an opportunity to do just that, and I need the help of every blood member of our family."

Yellowtail looked wide-eyed at Antonio, but Lino remained calm as usual, while Christopher wore his perpetual frown.

"Naples is no longer our home," Antonio said. "We must accept that." He glanced at his watch and then handed Christopher a bag to put the cash in. "Time to put my money where my mouth is, as the Americans like to say. Follow me and get ready."

"Ready for what?" Christopher asked, rising from his chair.

Antonio stopped in the doorway, avoiding his brother's gaze. "Either you trust me or you don't."

They left the office and passed the small rooms that served as living quarters during long nights, and into the open warehouse stuffed with racks of plastic-wrapped designer clothing.

Vinny Moretti and his best friend, Daniel "Doberman" Pedretti, were taking inventory. Both young men turned and stood side by side, stiff and respectful to the older men.

Doberman dropped his heavily inked arms. He stood a good four to five inches taller than Vinny, who was short, like his father.

"I want that stuff all sold off in bulk," Antonio said. "I want it moved fast."

The order got him a sharp look from Christopher. Antonio didn't blame his brother. They would make far less selling in bulk, but for his plan to work, he needed the cash now.

"Right away, Don Antonio," Vinny said.

He was a good boy. Strong like his father, and smarter. Antonio hoped Marco would turn out as smart and strong as his older cousin. But he had a long way to go. Not even twelve yet, he cared only for video games and music. Girls hadn't even caught his eye yet.

Next, the group moved through an open door into the connecting garage, where they stored a Toyota van, an early 2000s Mercedes-Benz C-Class sedan, and a three-year-old Cadillac Escalade. Two low-level Moretti associates, neither of them made men, were standing guard in the garage. They watched Antonio move to a wall of lockers where they kept gear and weapons.

"Load up, gentlemen." He took off his jacket and put on a bulletproof vest, cinching down the sides. The other men followed suit. Yellowtail grabbed his AR-15, Christopher his Mossberg twelve gauge, and Lino loaded an extra magazine into his MP5.

Antonio tucked his pistol into his concealed waistband holster and put his jacket back on. Then they all piled into the Escalade, with Yellowtail behind the wheel.

The two Moretti soldiers holding security opened the garage door to a dark sky and a deserted street. Most people were off the streets long before the nine o'clock curfew went into effect. It was being monitored by both the police and AMP.

"Where to?" Yellowtail asked.

Antonio pulled out his cell phone, brought up the directions, and handed the phone up to the front seat. Yellowtail zoomed in on the address and laughed.

"Good one, Don Antonio," he said.

"What's funny?"

Yellowtail's forehead creased under the strip of bleached hair. "You want me to drive to *Don Sarcone's house*?"

Antonio nodded. "I want to see where the snake curls up at night."

The other men said nothing as Yellowtail pulled out of the garage, and barely a word during the drive through Long Beach, most of which was controlled by the Bloods and the Norteño Mafia.

Several AMP Humvees met them. In the turret of each truck, a soldier swept the barrel and spotlight of an M240 machine gun back and forth over the government housing projects.

"That curfew starts in just over two hours," Christopher said. "And if we get pulled over, how we gonna explain the weapons and cash?"

"Don't get pulled over," Antonio replied, gazing out the window at one of the roughest neighborhoods in Compton.

It was always the impoverished who got trapped in bad situations. Childhood memories surfaced from when his family lived in a place like this, before his father and uncle got into the drug business and made millions.

Things were tough when he was a boy, and things were tough now. The things that Antonio and Christopher had done in their lives would haunt most older men, but Antonio was grateful for the events that built his character, and he lived without regrets. Not only had he broken the chains of poverty, he had survived two wars and made it to America.

The time of struggle was almost over. The time to rebuild the Moretti family was finally upon them.

Yellowtail moved over to avoid a line of cars waiting at a gas station. An AMP Humvee with the black raven's-head insignia pulled into the parking lot, and armed soldiers jumped out, yelling at the people waiting their turn.

"Fuck me!" Yellowtail said. "Petrol is twenty bucks a gallon!"

"Did you see the price on water?" Christopher said. "*Ten bucks* for a bottle."

Antonio scanned the haggard faces waiting for gas. Many were parents with children in their cars, fueling up to make a run for wherever they deemed safer than here.

They turned down an expensive strip of houses in Los Cerritos, the Long Beach neighborhood where the head of the Sarcone family lived.

The area had avoided most of the street crime because families hired their own muscle to protect their estates. Yellowtail parked under a coral tree, out of view of several armed men patrolling the sidewalks. But Antonio wasn't here to make trouble. He was here for motivation, to see the house of the last man alive who had betrayed the Moretti family.

Antonio spoke to his men in Italian, something he rarely did, calling the Morettis *perdenti*—underdogs. This much they had in common with Canavaro and Sarcone, the two families that had conspired to bring them down. "Underdogs have turned empires into ashes. We're going to build ours from the embers."

Part of being a leader was learning from one's enemies. It was time to use their underdog status to their advantage.

"Take a good look," Antonio said. "This is where we will live soon. But before we cut the head off this *serpente*, we must prepare."

Glancing at his watch, he saw they were about to be late for their real mission.

They drove another fifteen minutes, to a parking lot behind an abandoned Walmart. Plywood covered the broken windows and shattered doors. Several fast-food restaurants and chain stores were also boarded up, and there wasn't a moving car in sight. A lone AMP Humvee was parked in the middle of the lot.

The view reminded Antonio of the slums in Naples.

"Looks clear, but there's lots of places people could be hiding out," Christopher said, clutching his shotgun.

His brother was right, and Antonio felt the trickle of anxiety that came with uncertainty. But it wasn't enough to deter him from the mission.

"Park over there," he said, pointing toward the middle of the parking lot. That would give them multiple escape routes if they needed to leave in a hurry. Yellowtail parked a few hundred feet from the Humvee and shut off the lights.

"Who's that?" Lino asked.

"A friend from AMP," Antonio said.

He kissed the medal on his gold necklace and said a short prayer. This time, it was called for. Then he grabbed the bag of money and got out of the Escalade.

"Stay here and keep it running," he said to Yellowtail.

Christopher and Lino followed him toward the Humvee, where two soldiers cradling M4A1 carbines stood in front of the grill guard.

"You're late," said the bulkier one, a corporal with the beginnings of a gut hanging over his belt.

The other AMP soldier was his opposite, trim with a square jaw. He reached out his hand.

"Good to see you, Sergeant Rush," Antonio said.

"You got the cash?" said the heavyset one.

Antonio directed his gaze at the corporal.

"Relax, Craig," Rush said.

The corporal gave a snort. "I don't like dealing with these guineas."

"What the fuck did you say?" Christopher said, stepping forward.

Craig walked out to meet him, and Antonio held up the bag to defuse the situation.

"Here's the cash," he said.

That stopped Craig in midstride.

"You know what you're doing?" Christopher murmured.

"Where are the guns?" Antonio asked.

Rush walked around the Humvee and opened the back, revealing several crates of M4A1 carbines. "Fifteen of 'em, just like you said. Plus twenty thousand rounds of ammunition. Enough for a small war."

Antonio gave a thin smile. *Exactly.* He and Lino looked into the back of the vehicle while Christopher watched the husky corporal.

"You going to tell me what you want these for?" Rush asked.

"Security," Antonio said.

"How do I know I'm not selling guns to someone who's going to use them on American soldiers?" Rush asked. "I'm seeing too many reports of my brothers being gunned down at checkpoints and in the streets."

Antonio held the sergeant's gaze. "Because I fought with American soldiers in the Middle East. We both did." He nodded at Christopher. "You're not our enemy; you're our friends."

Craig chuckled. "You guys fought with Americans? Why do I not believe that?"

"Corporal, shut your face," Rush snapped.

Craig stiffened, though his drooping gut lessened the effect.

Rush scrutinized Antonio, looking for the lie.

"Where did you boys fight?" he asked.

"We spent six months in Afghanistan in 2006, on a special op to take out a 'terrorist cell,' as you call them."

Antonio left out a few details. The sergeant didn't need to know that the guns were for more Moretti soldiers coming over from Italy. He looked at Christopher's shotgun. What they had to arm themselves with now was pitiful.

"Fifty thousand," Antonio said, handing the bag over.

Rush rifled through it and smiled. "Nice doing business with you, Mr. Moretti."

"And with you." After shaking hands, Antonio waved at the Escalade, and Yellowtail drove over and parked behind the Humvee.

"I'll help you load 'em," Rush said. He and Lino moved the crated weapons and ammunition into the back of the Escalade while Antonio glanced at his watch. Still forty-five minutes to curfew—just enough time to get home.

Lights swept across the parking lot, and a diesel engine clattered. Both Rush and Lino looked over at the approaching Humvee. Christopher brought up his shotgun, but Craig had his rifle trained on Christopher's beak of a nose.

"Don't even think about it, you guinea prick," Craig said. He flitted the barrel to Antonio, who had started to reach for his Glock. "I wouldn't if I were you."

"What is this?" Rush asked, stepping away from the truck.

"A business transaction," Craig said with a cocky grin.

Rush glared. "What the fuck did you do, Corporal?"

"Took an opportunity," Craig said.

The second Humvee pulled up, and four men jumped out, all wearing face masks and black AMP uniforms.

"You son of a bitch," Rush said, reaching for his holstered M9.

"Don't do anything stupid," Craig said. He pointed his carbine at the Escalade. "Get out of the vehicle." Then he trained the weapon back on Christopher, who had already set his shotgun on the ground.

Yellowtail looked at Antonio, and Antonio nodded for him to obey the order.

The four new AMP soldiers fanned out, rifles up.

"Weapons down!" one shouted.

"That means you too," Craig said to Rush.

The sergeant gently pulled his hand away from his holstered gun as the AMP soldiers closed in, guns on Antonio, Yellowtail, Lino, and Christopher.

None of them saw the two muzzle flashes from the Walmart rooftop. Two AMP soldiers slumped to the ground. The other two turned, probably in time to see the muzzle flash right before they each got a bullet in the forehead.

Antonio brought up his Glock and shot the bewildered Craig twice in the chest. Craig slumped to his knees, gurgling from a punctured lung. His wide eyes roved and then locked on Antonio as he walked over and picked up the M4 the corporal had dropped.

"A fine weapon," he said, handing the M4 to Lino.

Then he bent down in front of Craig. The corporal struggled to breathe, his lungs crackling.

"You and I aren't all that different," Antonio said, "in the sense that we're both opportunists. Unfortunately for you, I am also a paranoid son of a bitch." He cracked a sly grin. "It's the guinea golden rule."

Craig tried to talk, but only blood came out of his mouth. He toppled onto his side, and Antonio used the toe of his shoe to nudge him onto his back. Then he raised his Glock and fired four shots into the man's ample gut. The impact from the rounds made his belly shake like Jell-O.

Rush kept his hands in the air. "I had nothing to do with this," he said. "I swear."

"I believe you," Antonio said, pointing the Glock at Rush, "but you're a witness now, and you know my name."

"You said you wouldn't use those guns on soldiers," Rush said, taking two steps back.

"You're right," Antonio said. "I'm not, but I didn't say anything about this one."

"Please," Rush said. "I have a wife and kids."

"Cap him and let's go," Christopher said.

The two snipers from the rooftop jogged over. Both men carried scope-mounted Remington 700 bolt-action rifles. Frankie and Carmine had also survived the night of the ambush almost eight years ago with their Moretti wives. They weren't blood, but they had served Antonio well since moving to Los Angeles.

Frankie had a wooden match in his mouth—a habit he had used to quit smoking.

Antonio nodded at him and went to Carmine. The former sniper had also served in the Alpini and had put his skills to good use tonight.

"Nice shooting," Antonio said.

Carmine spat a wad of tobacco juice on the ground and grinned proudly. He had one dimple; the other had been erased by grenade shrapnel that almost killed him and left a nasty scar as a memento.

Antonio's eyes flitted to the US flag on the back of the Humvee, and he recalled the pride he had felt when fighting with American soldiers in the Middle East. The sergeant in front of him was like the men he remembered over there.

"You want a new job?" Antonio asked. "A better one?"

Rush didn't need to think it over. "Yes, sir."

"Good. I have a spot for a man like you, but cross me and you will end up like that fat fuck."

Antonio turned to his men and gave an order. Working quickly, they stripped the dead AMP soldiers of their weapons and gear.

Frankie pulled up another car and opened the trunk. A muffled voice escaped, and Antonio walked over to see the squirming gangbanger in the back, with a bandanna tied around his mouth.

"Get him up," Antonio said.

Frankie and Carmine reached in and hauled the guy out while Christopher watched.

"Who the hell is that?" he asked.

"Sureño dirtbag," Carmine replied.

The Latino banger jerked and fought in their grip, blood dripping from his battered face. Frankie had done a number on the guy.

"What are you doing now?" Christopher asked.

"Starting a war," Antonio said. He raised the M4 again and fired a shot into the Sureño's gut. Frankie and Carmine let go of him as he crashed to the pavement.

Antonio let him crawl away. It needed to look real. The setup would work only if AMP believed it had happened, which meant Rush had to play along too.

The gangbanger made it all the way across the parking lot before finally collapsing. Frankie ran over, took the bandanna from his mouth, and tossed it to the ground.

Antonio jumped in the Humvee with Rush and Christopher while his other men piled into the other vehicles. It felt odd riding in a military vehicle again, especially one with a flag other than the Italian green, white, and red. But only one flag mattered to Antonio now: the Moretti banner.

"Why didn't you tell me this is what you had planned?" Christopher asked.

"Because you would have told me not to do it."

"You're right about that," Christopher replied. A half grin told Antonio his brother was finally starting to understand.

"When this is all over, we'll have a house in Los Cerritos like Enzo Sarcone, and a lot more." Antonio clapped Christopher on the shoulder. "You'll see, little brother. You will see."

-3-

Dom watched the sky from the deck of their house in Downey, southeast of Los Angeles. The humble living conditions were a step up from being on a military base, and he loved having his own room.

Having a backyard was also great. He stood there listening for the rumble of fighter jets. Ever since the squadron flew over the park, he had worried they would come back, and this time he feared they would drop their payloads on the innocent population in the City of Angels.

And the not so innocent …

The situation continued to crumble nationwide, with more people being injured or killed in waves of violence. Gangs murdering rivals, and civilians getting killed in the cross fire. Junkies overdosing and dying on the streets. People fighting over food and water, rioters taking out their rage on cops and soldiers.

Over the past week alone, a team of AMP soldiers had been ambushed by a clique of Sureños. The mutilated corpses were found wrapped in black raven flags and hanging like bats from a highway overpass. Then a platoon of marines were shot at a checkpoint outside the Port of Long Beach by a group affiliated with the Norteño Mafia, who took their weapons, stripped them naked, and set them on fire.

Men like Dom's father, who were simply trying to help the government regain control of the United States.

The distant *pop* of gunfire sounded as the sun slipped over the horizon—a reminder that control was slipping out of the government's grip.

It was especially bad in Los Angeles. The gangs were becoming more powerful and continued to organize, especially the Norteños, who thrived in anarchic situations like this.

Dom sipped his bottled water and turned to check on his mother and sister. Just inside the door, Elena was cooking dinner—something involving a delicious-smelling pasta sauce. It wasn't the same quality of noodles and homemade marinara sauce they had in the past, but it still smelled great.

Monica sat at the kitchen table, reading a book. Behind them, a TV streamed the news on mute.

Aside from the rationed food and missing their dad, it wasn't all that different from how things used to be on a school night. His parents had done their best to make life "normal." Buying the humble house away from base, teaching them to study and play sports. But Dom wasn't sure things would ever go back to their version of normal. So much had changed over the past year.

Instead of thinking about college, studying for exams, or training at his local gym, he was standing in his yard, with a shotgun slung over his back, and a pistol holstered on his belt. He would have much preferred to be playing basketball with Camilla and Moose or training for his next fight in the Octagon, but here he was, standing watch in his own backyard.

A month ago, when Ronaldo arrived home from Afghanistan, he had looked Dom in the eye and told him the guns were his now and that he was the man of the house. As much as Dom didn't want to accept it, he knew he would be put to the test sooner rather than later.

How would he react if forced by circumstances to take a life?

It was a question most young men never had to ask themselves, but one that Dom found himself pondering more than ever. The city continued to slip into anarchy, and until his father returned, it was his duty to protect his family.

The sliding door whisked open, and Monica poked her head out.

"Whatcha doin', Dom?" she asked.

"Nothing, just thinking."

She walked outside, all five feet two inches of her, a book tucked under her arm. Brushing back her long brown hair, she sat on the wicker couch and sighed. "When's Dad coming home?"

Dom took a seat in a chair across from her so he could talk and watch the sky at the same time. A new flurry of gunshots popped in the distance.

Monica stiffened, her brown eyes wide. "Are those fireworks?"

"No, but it's okay," Dom said. "Those shots are pretty far away."

Elena moved to the open doorway. She nodded but remained there, her black hair rustling in the fall breeze.

He gave her a confident smile.

Ever since Ronaldo had left, she seemed … different. The fight between the two of them the day of his departure had her rattled. Dom wasn't used to hearing his father yell, especially at his mom, but the threat of the apocalypse rattled even the strongest.

"I'm a marine—I can't just decide which orders to follow and which ones to disobey!" Ronaldo had yelled when Elena told him not to go.

Orders. Duty. Respect.

Dom's father had taught him about all these things. But Dom also understood why his mom didn't want him to go. Selfishly, he, too, had wanted his father to stay in Los Angeles. Not because Dom was afraid to look after his sister and mother, but because he was worried his father wouldn't come home.

The riots, the terrorist attack in San Francisco, the desperation of everyday citizens. The entire country was going mad. Dom was used to violence in the Octagon—indeed, he craved it—but this was a different type.

This wasn't a sport. It wasn't a *game*.

Sirens wailed in the distance—officers and emergency crews responding to more chaos. The sounds of violence were no longer sporadic; they had become more of a continuous rumble.

"At least, the police are still showing up to calls," Monica said.

"Yeah, but for how long?" Elena whispered it, as if she didn't want her kids to hear her.

Dom did hear his mom, though, and he didn't disagree. The military and police were losing the fight. When the National Guard first showed up almost two months ago, before they were reorganized into AMP, there had been a strange calm in Los Angeles, and for a while Dom was optimistic.

The schools were still open, and people who still had jobs went to work. The police were managing the best they could, but they didn't have enough men and women on the force to push back the rioters and outlaws who had seized the opportunity to loot.

Everything had spiraled out of control when terrorists hit San Francisco. A ship packed with fertilizer and low-grade radioactive material exploded in its berth just as military and port officials closed in. The government still didn't know who was behind the terrorist attacks, but whoever was doing it was getting the result they wanted: half the nation hiding in fear. The other half were out fighting each other for dwindling resources while the military—most of it, anyway— tried not to add to the violence.

Since the attack in San Francisco, hundreds of thousands had left Los Angeles, and more were streaming out every day to stay with family members in what were considered "green," or safe, zones.

He gripped his shotgun, feeling the burn of anxiety that came with uncertainty. It wasn't a matter of *if*, but of *when* he would have to use the weapon.

Monica went back to reading her book, and Elena walked back inside to finish dinner.

"What is that?" Dom asked his sister. "Astronomy?"

"Kind of ..."

He leaned forward to read the cover, but she pulled it back.

"It's science fiction," she said, grinning.

"Ah, your guilty pleasure?"

"I just finished a book about SETI." When he didn't respond she added, "SETI equals 'search for extraterrestrial life.' It's really interesting to read about the hunt for aliens, but sometimes I'd rather read about fictional ones."

She turned the book over to show him the cover: an insectoid-looking alien, and a space marine in body armor.

"*Starship Troopers*," he said with a grin. "That's mine."

"Figured you wouldn't mind if I borrowed it."

He sat back down and leaned the shotgun against the chair, still smiling at his sister. She spoke at a college level, but she was only thirteen years old. She also talked far too much, in his opinion. In first grade, her teacher had to move her desk away from the other kids because she wouldn't stop yapping.

"I wonder when they're going to let us go back to school," she said.

"I think you might be the only kid your age who actually misses it."

She went back to reading. She wanted to be an astronaut someday, and Dom had no doubt she would, as long as their country recovered.

While his sister was far beyond her years in education, she was still too young and naive to understand the implications of what was happening to their country. Dom wasn't sure *he* understood. What he did know was that things were getting worse, and other countries weren't coming to help them.

Canada, Mexico, Europe, much of Asia and Africa—everyone was suffering from consecutive seasons of failed crops. The droughts and floods had destroyed billions of dollars' worth of food, and half the world was starving. The countries that hadn't collapsed were well on their way.

Dom closed his eyes to daydream about better times and the simple things he missed. When his family was together and happy. Drives down the coast to hidden beaches, trips to the Santa Monica pier, chocolate shakes and french fries, and visits to Monica's favorite place, the Griffith Observatory.

She had been begging Dom to take her there for months, but it wasn't safe. Nowhere in the city was safe right now. Angry shouting down the street confirmed that.

The angry male voices were coming from this block. Standing on a ladder propped against the fence, Dom spotted two guys standing on the corner.

"Get out of here!" yelled Nate Chavez, the forty-year-old car salesman who lived three houses down.

Dom jumped down off the ladder.

"Get inside," he said to Monica.

He moved to the drapes covering the living room windows and pulled them open a crack.

"What's going on?" Elena asked.

"Not sure." From inside, Dom had a better view of the guys. They wore red bandannas around their necks, and tank tops that exposed tattooed flesh.

Definitely Bloods.

But Nate wasn't just some used-car salesman. Like many of the residents in this area, the guy had served in the military. He pushed up his sleeves, exposing lean muscle and army tattoos.

"Mr. Chavez is about to get into it with some gangbangers," Dom said.

Elena walked over to look. She carried the Glock 19 that Ronaldo had taught her to fire. She was a good shot, and Dom had no doubt his mom would shoot if put to the test. He remembered seeing her act crazy only a few times over the years, and they all involved when Dom or his sister was at risk or being bullied.

"Nate can handle his own," Elena said. She leaned closer to the window, squinting.

"You see that?" she asked.

Dom looked toward the house Lucinda Kent owned with her husband, Samuel, a vet who had lost a leg and part of his arm in Afghanistan ten years ago. Two men crept around the side of the house and into the backyard. Both wore red ball caps.

"Oh, shit," Dom said. "I better go warn the Kents."

Elena put a hand on his arm.

"Mom, I have to warn them."

"No, you stay here," she said, grabbing his arm.

"And leave them? Mom, we have to do something. Let's at least talk to Nate."

He unlatched the three locks on the door, then stepped back out into the warm evening air. Nate remained in his front yard, arms folded across his chest. He watched the two bangers with the bandannas walk around the corner and out of view.

"Everything okay, Mr. Chavez?" Dom asked.

Nate nodded and walked over. Elena stepped outside with them.

"You better be careful with that, kid," he said, looking at the shotgun.

"I saw some guys sneaking around Mrs. Kent's house," Dom said. "Looks like Bloods."

"Shit, I better check it out." Nate eased a pistol out of a concealment holster at the small of his back.

"I'll come," Dom said.

"No, you won't," Elena said.

"Listen to your mom," said Nate. "I got this."

He set off across the street and moved around the left side of the house. Dom strained for a better view, gripping the shotgun in sweaty hands.

A gunshot cracked, and Dom took off running, ignoring his mom's cries behind him. He moved around the garage and stopped at the fence.

The backyard had an empty pool, some broken-down outdoor furniture, and a rusted grill—a flashback to barbecues and pool parties in happier times.

He opened the gate just as the two tattooed men bolted out the back door. One of them carried a wooden box; the other had a backpack.

It was almost dark, but a quick glance inside the glass door confirmed they had just robbed Lucinda and her husband Samuel. He lay on the carpet in front of his wheelchair.

"Stop!" Dom shouted at the men. He shouldered the shotgun and followed them with the sights as they ran toward the alley. One of them slowed at his command, but only to pull out a handgun.

Dom centered the barrel on the gangbanger's head, moved his finger to the trigger, and froze.

His target didn't hesitate.

Someone slammed into him and knocked him to the ground just as a gunshot cracked. Dom hit the concrete hard, stars breaking across his vision.

The weight lifted off him, and he rolled over to find Nate on his knees, firing his handgun. He had knocked Dom down, saving him from a shot that would likely have killed him in his moment of hesitation.

Nate fired off several more shots. The men jumped into the back of a pickup, one of them taking a round to the arm. The passenger in the front seat was one of the men standing on the curb earlier—a distraction, Dom realized.

"Stay down!" Nate shouted when Dom tried to get up. He kept his Beretta M9 pointed at the alley.

The truck peeled away, and Nate finally lowered his pistol. He helped Dom to his feet.

"Jesus Christ," he growled. "You just about got us both killed."

"I was just trying to help."

"I had 'em both on my own." Shaking his head, Nate looked Dom over. "You sure you're okay?"

"I'm fine," Dom said. The only thing hurt was his ego. He should have taken the shot when he had the chance and taken a dirtbag off the city's streets. Instead, he had locked up and nearly gotten himself killed. Now the crew of bangers would be back on the streets, free to rob or kill someone else.

Nate went into the house with Dom and found Samuel lying in front of his wheelchair, gripping his bleeding face. Lucinda was trying to help him up, and he was waving her away.

"You hurt, brother?" Nate asked. He and Dom

helped Samuel off the floor and gently set him back in his wheelchair.

"Ten years ago, I'd have wiped pavement with their faces," Samuel grumbled. "Fucking punks."

Lucinda wiped a tear from her face.

"Did they hurt you?" Nate asked her.

"No, but they took all my jewelry, even my engagement ring." She directed her red eyes at Dom. "You should have taken that shot, sonny."

"I'm … I'm sorry, Mrs. Kent."

Nate put a hand on Dom's shoulder. "All that matters is that everyone's okay. Jewelry can be replaced; lives can't."

"He's right," Samuel said. "Most kids would have run, but you didn't. You should be proud of that. Now, go home before your mom gets to worrying."

Nate put a hand on Dom's shoulder. "It's okay, go on home."

Dom lingered a moment and apologized once again. On his way out, he noticed a bare kitchen. Not so much as a box of cereal or a can of soup in sight.

Dom hurried back to his house, where his mom was waiting. Her anger melted for a moment, and she hugged him hard. Then she went back to yelling.

"Never, *ever* do that again, Dominic Thomas Salvatore! You hear me?"

"Yes, Mom, I'm sorry—"

"What would have happened if someone came into our house when you were gone, and hurt your sister?"

"But, Mom, the Kents—"

"Your dad told you to stay here and watch over your sister with me," she said, her voice softening.

Monica ran over and gave him a hug.

"Ah, Mom, give it a rest," she said. "It's time to celebrate!"

Elena wiped something from her eyes and looked at the table, where she and Monica had set out a tray of cupcakes with candles sticking out of the centers.

"It's not much, but it's all I could do this year," she said, sniffling. "Happy birthday, Dominic."

He had all but forgotten: today was his eighteenth birthday.

"Oh, wow," he said.

"Did you not remember what today is?" Elena asked.

"Totally forgot," he admitted.

A rap on the door distracted them, and Dom made his way over to the window to check the front porch. Seeing that it was his best friend, Andre "Moose" Clarke, and Camilla Santiago, he leaned the shotgun against the wall and opened the door.

"Hey, guys, what are you doing here?" Dom asked.

Moose lumbered in, ducking slightly to let his antler 'do clear the low doorway. "You didn't think I was going to skip out on your birthday party, did you?" He winked at Elena, who smiled warmly.

"Hi, Mrs. Salvatore," Camilla said politely.

"Good to see you both," Elena said, returning to the kitchen. "Make yourselves at home."

Monica slid over and looked at Camilla quizzically. "Are you my brother's girlfriend?"

"Monica, go back to your book," Dom muttered.

Camilla snickered. "No, definitely not his girlfriend."

Moose pulled an envelope out of his windbreaker and handed it to Dom.

"What's this?" Dom asked.

"Just open it."

Dom knew that birthday cards weren't really Moose's thing, and he wasn't surprised to see that it wasn't a card. But the contents of the envelope did surprise him. He pulled out a pamphlet with the insignia of the Los Angeles Police Department.

"Now that you're eighteen, you can join up," Moose said. "Maybe we can be partners. You should join too, Cam."

Dom looked up at his friend, studying his face for any hint of a joke.

"I'm joining next week," Moose said. "I know it sounds crazy, man, but ain't no way I'm going to be an actor or a pro soccer player now."

"I've thought about joining too," Camilla admitted. "There isn't much else for us now."

Elena brought dinner to the table. Her eye was on the pamphlet, but she didn't say a word. She set the food down and then wiped at her eye.

"You okay, Mrs. Salvatore?" Moose asked.

"Yeah," Elena replied. "We just had a slight incident before you got here."

"What happened?" Camilla asked, suddenly all ears.

Seeing his friends staring at him, Dom couldn't just shrug it off, and he told them about the gangbangers.

"Another reason to join up, baby," Moose said, slapping Dom on the shoulder. "The city needs us, man. Even my brother is joining."

"*Ray?*" Again Dom checked Moose's expression for some hint of a joke. His brother had always hated cops.

Camilla looked just as surprised. She snorted. "Yeah, right, your bro, a cop, pul-*leeze*."

"I'm serious," Moose said.

"How about we eat," Elena suggested in an attempt to shift the conversation.

"Looks delicious," Camilla said with a hungry smile.

They sat around the table, enjoying the home-cooked rigatoni with Parmesan sauce, one of Dom's favorite meals.

The to-do across the street made for a subdued dinner conversation, but by the time they were finished, everyone had begun to relax. After Elena took away the plates, she lit the candle that Monica had stuck in one of the cupcakes.

"Thanks, Mom," Dom said.

"Make a wish."

Dom looked at the flame and blew it out after wishing for strength the next time he was aiming a gun at someone who wanted to kill him.

His family and two best friends sang "Happy Birthday," and Dom finished off the cupcake in two bites.

"Have another," Elena said.

Dom picked up the plate. "Actually, I was thinking I could take these over to the Kents' house."

"That would be very sweet of you," Elena said.

Moose and Camilla said goodbye and joined Dom outside.

"You really almost got shot?" Camilla asked.

Dom nodded, not mentioning his moment of indecision. "Maybe we can get a game of hoops together after this," he said, changing the subject.

"I'm down," Camilla said.

"Me ..." Moose stopped on the sidewalk and listened to the sirens. "God, things just keep getting worse. We got to do something, guys."

Dom kept walking to the Kents' house.

When they got to the door, he knocked and held out the cupcakes to Lucinda. "We had a few left over," he said. "Thought you might like some."

A smile cracked on her weathered face. "Thank you, Dominic. I'm sorry for getting mad earlier. It's just ..."

Shouting came from inside the house.

It was Samuel, and he wheeled down the hallway to the door.

"They brought us some treats," Lucinda said.

"Is your head okay?" Dom asked.

"Hurry, come look at this!" Samuel said, ignoring them. He turned his wheelchair and moved back into the living room.

"Sorry, he got hit kinda hard," Lucinda said. "Come on in."

Dom and his friends followed her into the living room.

Samuel looked away from the TV. "You see this?" he said, eyes wide. "There's been another attack. A nuclear power plant this time."

The three teenagers crowded around and watched the report.

"Holy shit!" Moose said as the lights flickered and went off. So did the TV.

Dom stepped over to the broken sliding glass door to the backyard and watched as lights winked off across the city. This was one birthday he would never forget.

"That's the rest of 'em," Vinny said.

He shut the van door and slapped Doberman on the back.

"I can't believe your uncle wants us to sell all this shit in bulk," Doberman said. "We'd make more if we hustled it out to our contacts the regular way."

"He must have a reason," said Vinny.

"Probably low on cash, is my guess."

"Like the rest of the country." Vinny walked over to check the row of red five-gallon gasoline containers. They were down to their last ten. Maybe that was why they needed the cash.

But despite the odds stacked against him, Don Antonio seemed unshaken. He had gotten them to safety in Los Angeles and taken care of them since they fled Naples.

Footsteps echoed, and Yellowtail walked into the garage, shaking his head. "I get the privilege of playing babysitter with you little shits today," he said, unslinging a new M4 rifle and walking over to the lockers.

Vinny and Doberman exchanged a glance.

"What are you guys lookin' at?" Yellowtail said. "Grab your guns."

Vinny stood there, puzzled. Normally, they did their runs on their own and carried only one gun, in the glove compartment.

"Get moving, shits," Yellowtail said.

"Chill, man," Vinny said. He was used to verbal abuse from the older guys. Until he took the oath and became a made man in the Moretti family, the others could call him whatever they wanted.

"Why are you coming with?" Vinny asked.

"'Cause we're making a second stop, and I need the van; that's why."

Vinny grabbed a Ruger SR9 and stuffed it in the holster beneath the elastic strap of his blue track pants. Doberman loaded several shells into his sawed-off shotgun, then pumped one into the chamber.

They all walked to the van.

"Who's got the keys?" Yellowtail asked.

Doberman tossed them over as the garage door opened.

Christopher pulled the older Mercedes inside and got out with three sharply attired Italian men. There was fit, wiry Lino with his shaved head and expensive sunglasses, battle-scarred Carmine with his slicked-back hair, and Frankie with his long dark hair and that cheesy-looking matchstick in his mouth.

"Anyone got a Red Bull or some Advil?" asked Doberman. "After the night Vin and I had, I could use both."

"Did you get a headache from the cock-sucking conference?" Carmine asked. He flashed a yellow-toothed grin and spat tobacco juice in the general direction of the floor drain.

"I'm not the one with white stuff on my lip," Vinny said.

Carmine brought a finger to his scarred lip, and the men laughed even harder.

"Gotcha, old man," Vinny said.

In a rare display of emotion, Frankie actually chuckled. Then he walked away with the other men, bantering and shooting the shit.

Only Christopher lingered. He walked over to Vinny and murmured, "Be careful today. Things are bad out there."

"I will."

"Don't worry, I'll watch the kids," Yellowtail said.

"Make sure you do as Zachary says," Christopher said.

The Morettis' Escalade swerved into the driveway, disgorging Antonio, the quiet Raff, and a big, hefty guy Vinny didn't remember ever seeing.

Christopher and crew all came to attention as Don Antonio approached.

"Ah, Vin, got someone I'd like you to meet," he said. "This is your cousin Vito."

The husky man looked old for a cousin.

"Second cousin," Vito said in a gruff voice. He was big, at least two fifty, with long hair, and a large mole on his right nostril.

Vinny remembered him suddenly from his youth. "Vito, good to ... Jeez, I haven't seen you since I was a kid!"

"Been in South America with some of our other

relatives," Vito said. He patted his gut. "Great food down there."

The men all laughed, even Raff.

"Is there any food left there?" Christopher asked.

Vito grinned, but it didn't look friendly, and Vinny recalled stories about his second cousin. Like Carmine and Frankie, Vito had a temper, especially when he drank.

"Good to finally join you all here," Vito said. "And nice to see you, Vin."

The newly arrived men followed Don Antonio to the offices.

"Later, you two pussies," Carmine called out to Vinny and Doberman.

Vinny walked over to the van, shaking his head. He was sick of taking crap from the older men, running errands, and doing the scut jobs. He wanted in on the drugs and the "big stuff," whatever that actually was.

He got into the back of the van, sitting on the seat next to the clothing racks, while Doberman climbed up front. Yellowtail pulled out of the garage, turning up the music as he drove.

"Man, I hate American music," Doberman said. He held out a cord that was connected to his phone. "Let me hook this up. I'll play some *real* music."

"Nah, you won't," Yellowtail said. He turned up some gangsta rap that Vinny had heard as a kid.

"Some California lovin' is what I need right now," Yellowtail said. "You two virgins pop your cherries finally?"

Vinny laughed.

"Come on, did ya get a dime piece, Vin?" Yellowtail flashed Vinny a look in the rearview mirror, then cut his eyes at Doberman. "We know *you* got some skanks."

"You really shouldn't learn English from this music," Doberman shot back.

Yellowtail grinned. "Got to learn somehow, right?"

"If you don't want to piss off Don Antonio," Vinny replied. His uncle required his men to learn English, but some were still struggling with it. Vinny and Doberman, on the other hand, were fluent from attending American schools.

The drive to North Long Beach reminded Vinny of how good things had been when they first got here. Even with the shattered economy, he still loved Los Angeles—the bars, the music, the *girls*.

He grinned as they passed a group of girls on the corner of a park, wearing shorts that showed off their tan legs, and crop tops showing a lot of pushed-up cleavage.

He wasn't a fan of girls showing off too much, which was why he didn't like strip clubs. He liked to be surprised when it got down to business, like last night, when he finally got with Carmen, a girl he'd been chasing for a year.

The steamy memories surfaced, but he buried them and focused on the dangers of today. The gangs were coming out of the woodwork like cockroaches after the lights go out.

Police and military were everywhere, trying to curb the violence, but they were barely keeping up.

"Just up here," Doberman said, pointing.

They pulled off the highway and drove to the truck stop, right across the street from a fenced-off storage business.

"This the place?" Yellowtail asked.

Doberman nodded. "This is where we normally meet Lil Snipes."

"'Lil Snipes'—what a dumb-ass name," Yellowtail said.

"I mean, I like it better than 'Yellowtail,'" Doberman said. "I don't know whether to think of a fish or blond pussy."

Yellowtail glared at him.

"Sorry," Doberman said.

A grin told him Yellowtail liked the joke.

"Better not ever call me a blond pussy, though, or I'll break your neck, bitch," Yellowtail said as a purple Cadillac with twenty-inch rims pulled up.

The bass boomed so loud, it rattled the trunk.

This was the problem with gangsters in Los Angeles, Vinny mused. It seemed they *wanted* to get caught. He appreciated his uncle's under-the-radar approach. No flashy cars or flashy houses.

Maybe that would change when they could afford it, though. He recalled the compound they had shared in Naples. The thought made him think of his mom again.

Stay strong, Vin. You got business to take care of.

Lil Snipes rolled down his window, letting out a cloud of skunky smoke, and waved for them to follow.

They got back into the van and drove across the street to a lot full of shipping containers. Vinny wasn't too worried. Lil Snipes was an asshole, but he was a businessman, and he was about to get a hell of a deal.

When they got to an isolated area of the lot, four African American guys were waiting there, pants hanging off their asses, red bandannas or baseball caps on their heads. Bloods.

"Hold up," Vinny said.

Yellowtail slowed the van. "I can't believe Don Antonio makes us deal with these fucking *cazzi*."

"Lil Snipes isn't all that bad," Vinny said. "But something feels off about this."

Doberman reached down to the sawed-off shotgun.

"Stay here and watch my back," Vinny said.

"What, bro?" Doberman said, twisting around in his seat.

"Just do it."

Vinny opened the van door and hopped out into the hot morning sun. He brought his sunglasses down over his eyes and walked over.

"'Sup, Lil Snipes?" he said.

The Cadillac door opened, and Lil Snipes got out, flicking away the butt of a joint.

"'Sup, Vin, my man?" He held up his muscular arms and grinned, his gold grill and gold-rimmed Armani aviator shades sparkling in the sun.

They slapped hands and did a shake followed with a fist bump.

"Yo, what up with your boys?" Lil Snipes asked, flipping his glasses up to look at the van.

"Albinos, man," Vinny replied. "They don't like the sun. I told 'em to stay put."

Lil Snipes chuckled. "I thought you Sicilians loved the sun."

"We're not Sicilian, bro. We're from southern Italy. Big difference."

He said, "I still don't get the entire Italian gangsta thing, my man. It's not a thing in these parts, feel?"

No, I don't feel. "Guess we're trying to make a comeback."

Lil Snipes's gold grin widened. "By selling me a bulk load of stuff at a discount. A'ight, my man."

"So, we gonna do this, or just shoot the shit all morning?"

"My boys got the cash," Lil Snipes said. "They'll hand it over once we take possession of that *fine* Italian wardrobe you wops got."

"*Wops?*" said a voice.

Vinny heard the click of a van door and cringed.

Yellowtail walked over, looking like a bull about to charge. The gold cross necklace dangled out over his square pecs.

"Who the fuck *you* s'poseta be?" Lil Snipes asked. He chuckled and shook his head. "You look like the Eye-talian version of Cartman."

The other four Bloods broke out laughing.

Vinny half expected Yellowtail to pull out his pistol and blast them all where they stood, but he managed to keep his cool.

"That's pretty funny," Yellowtail said. "But if I look like Cartman, that'd make you Mr. Hankey, the Christmas Poo."

Ah, fuck two ducks, Vinny thought. He raised his hands in the air and stepped between the two men just as Lil Snipes's nostrils flared.

"We're all friends here," Vinny said. "No need to bust each other's balls. This is business, nothin' else."

Lil Snipes and Yellowtail stared daggers at each other over Vinny's shoulders.

"Don't forget about AMP and the cops, guys," Vinny said. "They're everywhere. Quicker we get this shit done, the better."

Both men seemed to hear that. Logic won the day, and they backed down.

"We'll do the trade at the same time," Yellowtail said. "Bring the money, and we'll open the van."

Lil Snipes gestured for his men.

Ten minutes later, Vinny breathed a sigh of relief and reached out his hand.

"Nice doing business with you, bro," Vinny said.

"You too, my man. But next time, leave Cartman back in South Park."

Yellowtail was already back in the van, sitting behind the wheel, eyeing them both.

Vinny held back a laugh.

"Keep dodgin' them bullets, man," he said.

"I don't dodge, I dance," Lil Snipes said, doing a smooth little Crip walk.

Vinny got in, and they pulled out of the lot, eyes back on the Bloods.

"I don't like that guy," Yellowtail said.

"I'd say the feeling is mutual," Vinny said. He relaxed in his seat and smiled as Doberman hooked up his phone to the stereo, blaring Andrea Bocelli.

Yellowtail winced. "This shit makes me want to puke."

"So does your gangsta music," Doberman said.

Reaching over, Yellowtail turned off the radio. "Don't fuck with me, kid."

Doberman sulked, and Vinny looked out the window, tired from the drama of what should have been an easy day.

They drove another hour across the city, sitting in stop-and-go traffic. Protests and a riot had shut down parts of the highway, and they took a detour to Long Beach.

Vinny pulled back the drape and looked out. The sidewalks were crowded. It was odd to see, but with public transportation mostly down and half the city unable to afford gas, it made sense.

"All right, here we go," Yellowtail said.

"Why the hell are we outside a school?" Doberman asked. "They're supposed to be out for the summer."

"Not this one," Yellowtail said. "This is a Valley Christian High School, and they're doing summer classes, which is why we're here."

"Uh, why is that?" Vinny asked.

"You'll see."

As they sat watching, a group of kids filed out the front doors and headed toward expensive cars waiting out front.

"Must be nice," Doberman said. "These people are so rich, they don't have to worry about shit."

"One of 'em has to worry." Yellowtail held his cell phone up and clicked on the Facebook profile of a girl, then handed it back to Vinny. "Don Antonio wants us to find her and nab her as soon as we can. So, for the next few days, I'll be tagging along so you two don't screw it up."

Vinny had no problem with drugs, stolen merchandise, or violence, but kidnapping a schoolgirl?

He looked at the face, then the name. "Carly Sarcone," he said.

"Well?" Yellowtail said. "You up for this shit or what?"

Vinny swallowed. "Yeah, man, we're in."

* * *

The perfect storm, Ronaldo thought. That was what experts were calling the storm front rolling toward the Midwest. The supersystem carried more than swollen storm clouds. It also carried the radioactive isotopes dispersed into the atmosphere from the damaged nuclear power plant in Palo Verde, Arizona.

He was on his way to Phoenix now, in the back of an enclosed flatbed truck with half his platoon. Fresh off the C-130, he thought he would be glad to leave behind the hellhole that Atlanta had become, but leave it to the Corps to find someplace worse.

Terrorists had managed to penetrate the Palo Verde nuclear facility and set off bombs in the central reactors, blowing through the containment vessels and setting up a chain reaction. But it wasn't just the release of radiation that had Ronaldo worried.

Losing power meant that densely populated parts of southern Arizona and southern California, including Los Angeles, were dark, adding to the volatile conditions in both places.

Ronaldo couldn't help but wonder whether California was being targeted. First the attack on San Francisco; now a plant that provided power to LA. The only saving grace had been talking to Elena before he left Atlanta. She was safe, and the kids were fine, but she was beside herself when he told her he was heading to Arizona.

He had never been to Arizona before and never really wanted to go—Iraq had scorched him with enough heat for two lifetimes. And he certainly didn't want to be here today. But new orders had come down the pipeline, and his platoon boarded a plane at the forward operating base in Atlanta. Four hours ago, they had landed at a new FOB a hundred miles from ground zero.

Ronaldo took a deep breath, knowing how lucky he was to still be in uniform. After shooting the AMP soldier in the helicopter back in Atlanta, he had faced an almost certain court martial, maybe even a dishonorable discharge and prison.

The nation was barreling headlong toward a second civil war, between the federal government and states that wanted to secede and govern themselves.

Governor Jim McGehee of California had refused to reorganize the state's National Guard under AMP, and the rumors were flying. One of the more credible sources said that President Coleman was preparing to deploy more AMP troops to those states and arrest the governors who refused the order.

Stories abounded of soldiers being shot for desertion and others being locked away for even the most trifling infractions. The country was going down the shitter. Ronaldo was just trying to do his duty, not get killed, and make it home to his family.

Fortunately, Lieutenant Castle had his back for shooting the homicidal AMP door gunner, and was able to pitch Ronaldo's unblemished record and Purple Heart from Afghanistan to the AMP colonel who wanted Ronaldo's nuts on a satay skewer.

"If you ask me, you're looking to try the wrong man," Castle had argued. *"The one standing to my right is a hero. Your man, on the other hand, murdered dozens of innocent civilians. When he gets out of the hospital, he's the one who should go on trial."*

The colonel said he would push for a tribunal, and Castle mentioned that he would be making the same plea with the Marine Corps brass—but to try the AMP gunner on thirty counts of second-degree murder.

"*They'll probably forget all about it until things calm down,*" Castle had said as they were leaving the colonel's office. "*And that'll be a long damn time from now.*"

If they ever calm down, Ronaldo thought as the truck bounced over another pothole.

The dozen marines with him were sweltering inside camouflage CBRN suits just like his. Ronaldo couldn't see their faces behind the visors, but he would bet they all had the same grim look.

Back at Parris Island almost twenty years ago, when he was just a grunt, Ronaldo had seen pictures of radiation burns, but nothing was going to prepare him for what they would see when they got to Phoenix. Reports of people with radiation sickness had been included in their briefing on the plane. According to the radiation charts, everything within a ten-mile radius of the nuclear power plant was already considered a dead zone.

Thank God the marine platoon wasn't going there. That job was left to people who knew what they were doing.

The comm line crackled—a message from Lieutenant Castle.

"All right, ladies, we're thirty miles from Phoenix. Check your gear, check your buddy's gear, and then check it again. There are still over 1.6 million people in the area, and our job is to help get them out before it's too late."

Ronaldo and Marks checked each other as the

lieutenant spoke over the channel. His voice was more strained than normal—gravelly, like a chain smoker's. Part of that was from weeks spent screaming at rioters in Atlanta.

"This shit ain't gonna be pretty," Castle said. "As you know, those core explosions released significant quantities of radioactive materials and airborne isotopes. A good portion of the population within a twenty-five-mile radius of the plant is going to have acute radiation syndrome, so get your head screwed on tight. We have a job to do, marines, and I expect you all to do it with competence and dignity."

The men finished their gear and suit preps without any of the usual side banter. They were all business now. Innocent American lives were on the line.

Ronaldo glimpsed the command Humvee next to their truck. Castle sat shotgun wearing a CBRN suit.

The men all respected their lieutenant. He was a smart, brave marine who had saved their platoon several times by making quick decisions in dicey situations. Ronaldo alone owed him a couple of lives.

"How do we still not know who's doing this shit?" Tooth asked as he checked Bettis's ruck. "Somebody tell me how these attacks keep happening without us catching a single terrorist."

"Easy," said the lance corporal everyone called Timmy. "They have people on the inside. It's the deep state, man. Think about it. Who can sneak into a power plant, set off explosives, and get away?"

"How do we know *they* did?" Bettis asked.

"I may not be honor roll material," said Tooth, "but I don't believe in *all* that deep-state conspiracy horseshit. Some of it might be real, but if you ask me, this was al-Qaeda, or maybe ISIS."

"Maybe," Marks said, "but they're not shy about claiming credit. And we haven't seen any of that."

"Well, whoever it is, they won't be hitting another power plant," Ronaldo said. "Every last one'll be on lockdown."

Marks shook his helmet wearily. "Y'all don't get it."

"What don't we get, Sarge?" said Timmy.

"They don't need to hit another power plant. You saw the charts. You heard what they said about the clouds carrying the radiation."

All the other CBRN visors were turned toward Marks.

"Palo Verde is the biggest nuclear power plant in the country. The fallout will poison any crops in the Midwest that made it through the drought. It'll be the coup de grâce for our economy."

The other marines considered his words in silence. It wasn't just talk about the deep state or Islamic terrorists that had the men on edge. Rumors were rampant about North Korean or Russian sleeper cells. Some people were even saying it was one of the Mexican cartels.

Not knowing fueled paranoia and anger. Fear had the nation by the short hairs. The newly formed AMP and the rest of the military were up against more than rioters now. Gangs, organized crime families, and the cartels were taking over in cities like Los Angeles— where Ronaldo's family lived.

The flatbed came to a stop, and Ronaldo checked his suit one last time. The marines emptied out the back, jumping onto Interstate 10. They were on the outskirts of Phoenix, with a view of downtown and the billowing plume of smoke rising from the power plant's ruins.

"Holy shit," Marks breathed.

Ronaldo fell in with the rest of the platoon. The highway's westbound lanes were almost completely clear of vehicles, while a steady train of cars and trucks crawled eastward away from the dead zone.

The marines got to the first roadblock, where AMP soldiers in CBRN suits had already set up concrete barriers and a gate. One of the men spoke to Lieutenant Castle, explaining that they had shut the road down and that they needed help getting people out of an assisted living community two miles away.

Castle nodded and moved back to his men to relay orders.

"Staff Sergeant Marks, your team is with me, but Corporal Bettis stays here," he said.

A few minutes later, Ronaldo was in the command Humvee, heading toward the dead zone.

"We're looking for elderly and anyone else who might not have made it out over the past twenty-four hours," Castle said. "Anyone in this area is going to be very sick when we find them, but it's possible we can still save them if we get them medical support."

"What about the people in the dead zone?" Marks asked.

Castle shook his head. "Anyone there is going to die—nothing we can do for 'em."

Tooth drove the command Humvee down the abandoned streets, toward the drifting smoke on the horizon. The invisible airborne isotopes continued to escape unchecked.

Two other Humvees and the enclosed flatbed truck followed them into the residential area. Swirling trash drifted across the road. They drove in silence, listening to the howling radioactive wind.

A small suitcase lay in a driveway, its contents spilled out on the concrete. Ronaldo pictured the family running out of their house, and a child stumbling, dropping the bag. He, too, would have told his kids to leave it there instead of wasting time to gather it up.

The low rumble of fighter jets drowned out the whistle of the wind. Seconds later, a squadron of F-16s streaked across to the east.

The rumble subsided, and the first sign of life darted across the street. Tooth slowed to avoid a golden retriever. The dog stopped in the middle of the road, tail between its legs, then ran into a yard.

"Pull off," Castle said.

"Sir?" said Tooth.

"I said pull off."

"But, sir, it's just a dog."

"'Just a dog,' my ass," Castle said. "That's someone's family member." He got out of the Humvee as it rolled to a stop. Ronaldo also got out, with his rifle slung over his back. The dog stood in a yard, watching them both, eyes roving between them.

"Sir, we're here to rescue people, not animals," Tooth said out the window.

"You must never have had a dog, Lance Corporal Numb Nuts," Castle replied. "Now, shut it."

Ronaldo smiled. He appreciated that Castle was a hard-ass with a soft heart.

The convoy passed the command truck while they chased down the dog.

"Come here, boy," Ronaldo said.

The dog darted away as they approached, clearly frightened. Not that he blamed it; in their CBRN suits, they looked like something almost—but not quite—human.

Marks got out to help, and the three of them finally managed to surround the dog. When it tried to run past Ronaldo, he dived and tackled the snarling, yelping dog to the ground.

The other marines helped him get it into the Humvee.

"Now what do we do with him?" Marks asked.

"Put him in the truck," Castle replied. "We'll take him back with us."

They shut the dog in the back and rejoined the convoy. The trucks had stopped outside a church. From what Ronaldo remembered of the map at their briefing, they were near the edge of the dead zone.

"Looks like we have a situation," Tooth said.

Ten other marines waited on the lawn outside the church, and two more stood on the stoop leading to red double doors. Ronaldo saw something strange as he approached: a chain wrapped around the handles.

"Are those voices coming from inside?" Marks asked.

Ronaldo stopped to listen, and over the wind he heard cries for help.

They were coming from inside the church.

"Get that door open!" Castle ordered.

One of the marines used bolt cutters to break the chain. He pulled it through the handles, then pushed the doors open. A man staggered into the sunlight, a hand raised to shield his eyes from the sun and wind.

Ronaldo glimpsed multiple bodies on the floor behind the man, and a woman crouching with a rosary clutched in her hand.

"What the hell are they doing locked inside?" Marks asked. He stood next to Ronaldo, staring in horror at the sick people who stumbled out of the church.

"Corpsmen!" Castle shouted.

Several marines and the navy corpsmen who had accompanied the convoy moved to help the survivors. Ronaldo walked over to see what he could do to help. He mounted the steps to the church, where he found a woman sitting on a bench.

"Miss?" he said. "I'm here to help you."

She slowly tilted her head toward him as if confused—one of the symptoms of radiation poisoning. But when she saw his uniform, the confusion turned to fear and she scooted away, falling off the bench.

"It's okay," he said, holding up a hand. "I'm here to help."

She crawled away down the aisle of pews.

"Ronaldo."

He turned to find Marks standing in the aisle

"They said *soldiers* locked them in here," he said.

"What!"

Ronaldo turned back to the woman, who cowered behind the far end of the pews, trembling as she whispered a prayer.

-5-

Antonio made love to Lucia in the darkness of their shitty apartment in western Anaheim. Normally, he looked forward to sex with his bride, but tonight, his mind was distracted. She knew him well enough to notice his heart wasn't in it tonight.

"What is it?" Lucia asked.

He rolled off and sighed, embarrassed to admit the truth: that hatred for his enemies had poisoned his mind, and the toxic anger was interfering with one of the things he always looked forward to.

Embarrassed or not, he didn't keep things from his wife.

"It's Enzo," he said.

"I thought you would feel better now that Lino and Yellowtail obliterated the rest of our enemies in Naples," she said. "But I guess you won't be free of this poison in your heart until Enzo is dead too."

His wife didn't miss much.

He slid off the bed and walked over to the window. A blood-orange sky hung over the hilly neighborhood.

Not a single person walked down the sidewalk, and only a few cars moved on the street. Several miles across the city, Moretti soldiers were preparing to take down a small crew of Sureños.

In a few hours, the residents who hadn't left Los Angeles would endure yet another night without power, thanks to the attack on the Palo Verde Nuclear Power Plant. While they slept, Antonio would shake on a major deal that would help his family expand, and soon, very soon, he would deal with Enzo Sarcone.

He turned back to Lucia and admired her naked body in the dim light. *God, you are beautiful.*

More beautiful than the day he met her twenty years ago, when he was just a young soldier preparing for a different war and she was a waitress serving beer to drunk patrons. But it wasn't just her beauty that made her the one. Like Antonio, she had risen from poverty, clawing her way to the top, and had helped him build his business. She was a warrior at heart and a wonderful mother.

"What are you looking at?" she asked in her sharp Italian accent.

"Only a goddess."

Her brown eyes met his, and her dimples framed a widening smile. She brushed her dark hair over her shoulder and beckoned him back to bed.

"Relax, my love," she said.

Antonio let out a long sigh and then made love to his wife until they both melted in grunts and cries of pleasure. After a shared cigarette, he walked over to their closet to look for his new suit, an Armani he had taken from the hoard of stolen merchandise before Vinny sold it off in bulk.

Lucia joined him, grabbed the coat, and held it out so he could slide his arms into the sleeves. Then he turned, and she fixed his collar and kissed him on the lips. He reached up and fixed his wavy brown hair, brushing it backward.

"Very handsome," she said.

He returned her smile and then reached inside the closet to pick a tie from the rack. He selected a silver one and stepped over to the window to see who was honking.

Christopher had pulled up in the old Mercedes, and Raff jumped out and walked up to the front stoop. Unlike some of the other guys, who might have shouted, he waited politely for Antonio to buzz him in.

"I'm not sure when I'll be back tonight," Antonio said to Lucia.

"I'll be up waiting for you. You know I can't sleep while you're away."

He kissed her goodbye, and she followed him down the hall, where he stopped to say good night to his son.

Marco lay on his bed, large red headphones covering his ears, the music playing so loud Antonio could hear it from where he stood.

"Marco." He said it twice until his son heard him and peeled off his headphones, beaming his perfect white smile.

"Nice suit, *papà*."

Marco spoke better English than any of them and occasionally spoke Italian. Antonio was fine with that. Going on twelve years old, the boy had spent most of his life in Los Angeles, and he didn't want him to forget his heritage.

"Good night, Marco," he said. "Be good, okay?"

"You going to work? Can I come?" Marco swung his legs off the bed.

Antonio appreciated his ambition, but Lucia's hand on his shoulder reminded him that they had decided against a life of crime for their only child.

He shook his head, and Marco lowered his in disappointment.

"Vinny gets to go help. Why can't I?"

"Because your cousin is old enough, and you aren't," Lucia said.

"Be good and listen to your mom."

"Is Raff going to be here?"

"Yes."

"Okay, good," Marco said. "He likes to play games with me."

Antonio wondered whether that was a dig at him for being absent, but right now he didn't have time to worry about that. He left his son's room and went outside to speak to the man now responsible for his family's safety.

"Raff," he said, looking him in the eye, "you make sure nothing happens to them, okay?"

"I would give my own life for them, Don Antonio."

Antonio held his gaze. Raff's loyalty was unwavering and absolute, which was why Antonio always asked him to watch over the two lives he valued more than his own.

"I'll take good care of them," Raff said.

Antonio patted him on the shoulder and walked to the car. Cigar smoke drifted out of the Mercedes's open window as Antonio approached. His brother sat behind the wheel, wearing a silver suit that matched the gray streaks in his goatee.

"Last one I've got," he said, holding up the cigar. "Got to enjoy it."

Antonio got in and looked at the shabby apartment building as they drove away. Someday, he would own another compound, from which he would rule the Moretti empire.

"Have you heard the news?" Christopher asked. He turned up the radio. An emergency broadcast played from the speakers.

"The following message is transmitted at the request of the president of the United States. This is not a test. Executive Order One-Oh-Nine places all US states and territories under martial law, effective 6:00 p.m. Eastern Standard Time on September twentieth, 2020."

"Well, shit," Antonio said.

Christopher changed stations, playing a local alert.

"State and city officials, under the instruction of the president of the United States and Executive Order One-Oh-Nine, have placed Los Angeles and the entire state of California under martial law, to be enforced by the American Military Patriots. A regiment comprising AMP battalions from the loyalist states has been sent to Los Angeles, to put down insurrectionist elements. Curfew has changed to 8:00 p.m. Anyone evacuating the city must do so before the curfew or be subject to detention by AMP personnel."

Christopher switched stations again, to a live report.

"Mexican and Canadian officials are reporting an influx of illegal crossings at their borders," said the announcer.

Ironic. Antonio had never thought he would hear about Americans trying to escape to Mexico.

"Naples is sounding better by the minute," Christopher said, "especially now that Lino and Yellowtail took care of the rest of our enemies. Or Rome. I told you we should have moved there."

Antonio sucked in a breath to manage his anger, but this was crossing a line. Reaching over, he yanked the cigar out of his brother's mouth and then tossed it out the window.

"What the hell!" Christopher said.

"I told you, we're staying in Los Angeles, and I don't want to hear anything else about going back to Naples or Rome, or anywhere else. Got it?"

Christopher gripped the wheel tighter and kept his eyes on the road. "Yeah, I got it."

"Do you think we would have been able to get our new men into the country from Italy *before* any of this shit happened?" Antonio asked. "It would have been impossible, but now the government has bigger problems than trying to monitor every crossing."

Christopher pulled onto the highway, quiet but clearly enraged.

"We came here to rebuild and to fly the Moretti flag, and your lack of respect is grating on my nerves, brother."

"I'm sorry if you took it as a lack of respect," Christopher replied. "I'm just on edge about what's happening here."

"You didn't trust me the other night, and look what happened. We took out five AMP soldiers, kept our fifty grand, and added fifteen machine guns and twenty thousand rounds to our armory."

"Things have changed slightly since then."

Antonio didn't disagree, but it didn't matter.

Christopher slowed as they came up on a check-point with the raven's-head flag of AMP, and a banner that read, "Always on Watch."

The slogan was everywhere now, and so were the AMP soldiers, adding new recruits from other branches, as well as mercenaries, to their ranks every day. The men ahead were likely from other states, deployed here when Governor McGehee refused to hand over the state's National Guard to the reorganization authorities.

His brother saw these people as foreign threats, but Antonio saw them as potential customers and allies.

Antonio rolled his window down for an AMP soldier with a pair of dark sunglasses, who ducked down to look at him and Christopher. A second officer walked a bomb-sniffing German shepherd around the car.

The officer tipped his aviators up. "Where are you two headed?" he said in a Brooklyn accent. Antonio was right; these men weren't from California. And they might have fewer compunctions about killing Californians.

If he told the truth, they would be questioning him for the next hour, so he did the natural thing. "To pick up my son from Long Beach and bring him back to Anaheim," he said.

The soldier asked for their IDs, and Antonio handed them over. A quick glance at the cards and then their faces, and the guard motioned them through the open gate.

"Better hurry," he said. "Curfew's been moved to eight o'clock."

"We will," Antonio said. "Thank you ... sir."

They continued north to Los Alamitos Joint Forces Training Base, where a C-130 touched down on the tarmac, no doubt bringing in another load of AMP soldiers.

"Here we go," Christopher said, pulling into the mostly empty parking lot at the Los Alamitos racetrack.

Christopher parked, and Antonio got out of the car. He walked over to the Cadillac and opened the back door. Sergeant Rush sat in the back seat between Lino and Yellowtail.

"Well?" Antonio asked.

"We're good to go," Lino said. "One of the Humvees is ready to move, and we have two of the M4's inside it."

Carmine twisted from the front seat, the wrinkles and scars on his middle-aged face emphasized by the dome light.

"And you?" Antonio said to the AMP soldier.

"I've got the meeting set up with my CO," Rush said. "We just need to go to the base."

"Base?" Antonio said. "That wasn't part of our deal."

Rush sighed. "I know, but you got nothing to worry about. My CO authorized the mission you guys ambushed the other night, but he has no idea it was you guys. He thinks—"

"Hell no!" Christopher interjected. "You think we're *stupid*?"

"He never knew who my contact was, I already told you," Rush said. "He believes the story about the Sureños being behind the ambush. Hell, he saw their dead cholo with his own eyes. You're golden, I promise."

Antonio exchanged a glance with Christopher,

who chewed nervously on a toothpick. He snorted and shook his head when Antonio gave a nod.

"Rush, you ride with us," he said.

The sergeant got out of the Cadillac and slid into the back seat of the Mercedes.

"Remember, if we don't come back tonight, your family dies," Antonio said.

Rush swallowed. "I understand, sir, but you can trust me."

"We will see about that."

They drove to the Los Alamitos base and entered through a barricade after Rush showed his ID. Inside the gates, the base teemed with activity. Soldiers loaded vehicles, and others headed out for patrols beyond the fences.

It had been a long time since Antonio set foot on a military base, and a part of him missed how all the cogs seemed to mesh so perfectly.

A well-oiled machine, like the Moretti organization.

"Park over there," Rush said.

Christopher pulled up to a brick building, and Rush got out.

"Wait here," he said. "I'll be right back."

Christopher looked over at Antonio, who nodded back.

As the sergeant entered the building, they listened to the beating rotor blades of a Black Hawk preparing to take off from a pad behind the building.

"You sure you can trust him?" Christopher asked.

"I don't trust *anyone*, brother."

A few minutes later, Rush returned with a tall, fit man with a pencil-thin silver mustache. They spoke outside the building for a moment; then Rush motioned for Christopher to repark next to a line of Humvees.

"Stay cool," Antonio told his brother.

They got out and waited for Rush and his CO to walk over.

"Welcome to Los Alamitos," said the taller man. "I'm Lieutenant Colonel Marten."

"Antonio Moretti."

"Christopher Moretti."

"Brothers?" Marten asked.

"Yes," Antonio said.

After shaking hands, Marten looked them over with the gaze of a commanding officer. Then he grinned and said, "You got balls coming here to try and make a deal, I'll give you that."

Rush stood as stiff as a board.

"So, the question is, why should I trust you?" Marten asked.

"Because we know where one of your stolen Humvees is, and the men behind the ambush that claimed the lives of several of your men," Antonio said. "And because we're not a gang; we're a professional organization that follows a strict code of honor."

Marten ran his fingers over his mustache, just a quick swipe, as he considered the words. "Okay, give me the address, and if you're right, then *maybe* we can do business."

"Follow us," Antonio said.

He turned to get into the Mercedes, but Marten called out after them. "No, you two are coming with me."

Antonio and Christopher got into the command Humvee with Marten, Rush, and a young man who got behind the wheel. It took only a few minutes for a dozen men decked out in body armor and night-vision goggles to emerge from the barracks.

Half of them climbed into the back of two sand-colored M-ATVs, while the rest piled into another armored Humvee. The convoy rolled out and headed toward the address in Compton that housed the leadership of one of the biggest Sureño crews in the city. The location was only about three miles from their warehouse, and it was a hot spot for gang activity—so dangerous that Antonio and his men hadn't driven through there in months.

Taking them out would be a huge win for the Morettis, but it would cost him too many men. That was why he needed AMP.

Behind armored doors, Antonio rode with the foreign soldiers he had deceived into thinking he was their friend, when in reality they were customers, nothing more. A marriage of convenience.

The vehicles roared down the streets, speeding past cars that were still out before the curfew took effect. Marten pulled the radio handset while they drove, paying scant attention to Antonio and Christopher. It wasn't until they entered Compton that he spoke to them.

"How'd you guys hear one those Humvees is here?" he asked.

"I have ears all over this part of the city," Antonio replied.

Marten glanced back to meet Antonio's gaze, scrutinizing him again. Antonio had an impenetrable poker face.

"Two blocks away, sir," said the driver.

Marten turned away and grabbed his radio to give orders.

They raced past the fenced-off houses, many of them in disrepair. Civilians out on the sidewalk yelled at the convoy as it drove by, and someone threw a beer can that hit the side of the truck.

"Assholes," Marten grumbled.

"Here we go," said the driver.

The trucks came to a stop, and Marten looked to the back seat. "Stay here."

AMP soldiers filed out onto the road, shouldering their weapons and fanning out in combat intervals.

Two men sitting on the porch of the house reached for weapons. Neither succeeded.

Night-vision goggles in place, the AMP team stormed the building. Muzzle flashes behind windows lit up the house, like pulsating lights, and return fire cracked.

One gangster broke a window and dived onto the lawn, only to be shot in the back as he sprinted for the fence between the house and the street.

He crumpled just shy of the fence.

On the other side sat the formerly tan Humvee, now painted in matte black, that the Moretti men had parked there an hour earlier. Two of Marten's soldiers found it a moment later while clearing the property.

Down on the street, Antonio saw the Escalade with his men sitting inside. It pulled away, heading to the warehouse, where he would meet them shortly.

First, though, Antonio had a deal to finish.

Marten gave orders, and his men set up a perimeter as the advance team finished clearing the house. The soldiers in the Humvee turrets aimed their machine guns at approaching civilians, who threw trash and shouted profanities. One woman threw a rock that dinged off the Humvee where Antonio sat.

"The shit is about to break loose," Christopher said.

Marten must have known it, and raised two fingers in the air. One of his men fired up the Humvee in the garage and backed it out.

"Let's move out!" he shouted.

He opened the door to the command vehicle and got back inside, wearing a sly smile. The silver mustache curled around his lips as he turned to the back seat.

"Yes," he said, "I think we can do business, Antonio Moretti. I think we can do a *lot* of business together."

Antonio held back his smile. In one night, he had gotten rid of some of his biggest competition and made a deal with a man who would help the Morettis sell all the product he could get his hands on.

6

Dom left the house at sunrise. A week had passed since the attack on the Palo Verde nuclear plant in Arizona. So far, reports of victims with acute radiation poisoning tallied in the tens of thousands, and that number would continue to grow as the wind spread the airborne isotopes east.

He pulled the bill of his Dodgers cap farther down over his face and smiled when he saw Moose waiting for him on the corner. They set off for the Downey Police Department headquarters.

"Man, I'm *starving*," Moose said. "We finally finished off the rest of our reserves, so I guess it's all rations from here on out."

"Same here. I'm going with my mom and sister this afternoon to try and get some FEMA handouts."

Moose put his hand on his stomach as it growled loud enough that Dom could hear it.

"Whoa," Moose said. "God, what I would do for a Big Mac, baby."

The McDonald's across the street was boarded up,

along with every other food joint in the area. Down the street, boards covered the broken windows of Trader Joe's, making the storefront look like a smile of wooden teeth.

Pedestrians slogged like zombies down the sidewalks. The occasional car sped by, but there were more cyclists now that gasoline had skyrocketed in price and, in many cases, was not even available.

Everyone looked hungry, tired, and in need of a bath and a change of clothes.

He wasn't sure what his family was going to do, but he knew he had to do something, whether it was joining the police or perhaps even enlisting in AMP. His dad was out there, getting exposed to radiation, and Dom was sick of sitting on his ass at home with his shotgun, watching for robbers.

"How's the family?" Moose asked. "Talked to your dad lately?"

"Mom and sis seem okay, but my dad was moved from Atlanta to somewhere east of Phoenix."

Moose stared. "Phoenix? As in the radioactive hot zone?"

"He said he's fine, and he has one of those CBRN suits to protect him from contamination, but I'm still pretty worried."

"I'm sorry, man."

"Thanks, but my old man knows what he's doing."

"Indeed, he does," Moose said. "But I don't know about them AMP guys. That's why I decided on joining the police and not the new Corps."

"I've heard a lot of bad shit, but I don't think it's former National Guardsmen that are responsible. In most cases, it's mercenaries, and some former soldiers discharged from other branches who were never vetted properly."

"They do take pretty much anyone that's not a convicted felon," Moose said. "That's another reason not to join."

A bus full of people passed. The draft of air rustled Dom's sweatshirt with the logo of his MMA training gym, Saints' Row.

"We might not have a choice," Dom said over the rumble of the bus.

"What do you mean?"

"Last time my mom talked to my dad, which was about a week ago, he said the administration is talking about conscripting any able bodies between the ages of eighteen and thirty-five."

Ah, hell no!" Moose said, shaking his head.

They continued their walk in fretful silence. It was the first time Dom had left his neighborhood in several days, but his mom had assured him she and Monica would be okay for a few hours.

The grim sight of boarded-up shops, half-stripped cars, and military presence served as a distraction from worrying about his mom and sis. In less than a year, the city had transformed dramatically, and not for the better. Troops in the black and green uniforms of AMP stood at every major intersection, their faces covered with black masks, automatic weapons cradled.

When they finally arrived at Downey High School, Moose stopped in midstride.

"Holy shit," he murmured.

Chain-link fences topped with razor wire had been

raised around the perimeter of the school, which now served as AMP barracks and base of operations.

The parking lot, once filled with the cars of high schoolers, was now full of military vehicles. Dom had already seen the fences surrounding the football field, but seeing the people caged inside startled and saddened him. Herded into separate pens and forced to drink from community troughs, they weren't being treated much better than livestock.

"Don't think we'll be playing soccer there again anytime soon," Moose said, looking at the hundreds of people detained inside the makeshift jail.

Some of them no doubt belonged there, but Dom knew that many were in for offenses as trivial as graffiti or littering. Seeing their alma mater turned into a military base and prison was hard to get his head around.

The Downey Police HQ was only half a block away. A warm breeze fluttered the clothing of passersby. People walked with their heads down, hoping not to attract any attention. The riots hadn't hit this area of town, but robberies were commonplace, and people didn't like to leave their houses even during the day.

Moose walked around the next corner and halted.

"That's great," he said. "Just freaking great."

The line snaking away from a tarp awning set up outside the police department was almost a hundred people long and didn't appear to be moving at all. Dom and Moose stood in the queue for almost three hours, drenched in sweat, waiting to talk to the two recruiters sitting in the shade.

The sound of diesel engines broke through the afternoon. Several six-wheeler military troop carriers pulled down the street, their canvas-covered beds full of AMP soldiers. Most of them looked not much older than Dom and Moose.

Gauging by their tired faces, they must be coming back from a patrol. One of the guys, however, still had some pep. He stood up in the back of the truck and pulled down his mask, shouting, "Screw the pigs! Join AMP! Better pay and better food!"

Moose chuckled. "Look at this dumb shit. Basically, the poster boy for AMP."

Another soldier in the back of the truck yanked the kid back down to his seat, but the damage was already done. Hearing the talk of better food and pay, several civilians peeled off from the police recruitment line and headed across the street to the high school. The recruiting center was on the other side, past the football field.

Moose hurried forward to close the gap, but Dom didn't move. His eyes were on the flatbed trucks disgorging soldiers into a parking lot behind the gates.

"Hey, Dom, I didn't see you back there," said a familiar woman's voice.

He turned toward the front of the line and saw his friend Camilla Santiago. She had cut her almost waist-length hair to just above her shoulders.

"Oh, hey, Cam." Dom smiled and walked over. He wasn't all that surprised to see her here. She had always been a bit of a firecracker.

"It's a sign of the end times!" Moose said. "You cut your hair!"

She struck a pose and batted her long lashes. "What do you think?"

"Looks good from here," Dom said.

"A bit shorter and you could pass as a guy," Moose said.

She frowned, then gestured toward the guy beside her.

"You know my brother, right?" she said.

The young man was half a foot taller and a few years older than she, but Dom couldn't recall his name.

"How's it going, Dom?" he said.

"'Sup, Joaquín?" Moose said, saving Dom from an awkward moment.

"Good to see you, bro," Dom said. "So, you and Cam are joining the PD?"

Camilla gave a noncommittal smile as she pulled the neck of her sweat-stained T-shirt to fan air under it.

"I've always wanted to be a marine," said Joaquín. "But with AMP taking over, I don't think that's happening."

"From the sounds of it, the marines are done," Camilla said. "Looks like the American Military Patriots is the future of the American armed forces."

Dom furrowed his brow—something his mom was always telling him not to do. "Who said that?" he asked.

Camilla's freckled cheeks flared as she apparently realized she had touched on a sensitive subject. "The news … and—"

"The marines are far from over. My dad is currently at a refugee camp outside Palo Verde, helping survivors, and there are marines all over the country looking for the terrorists responsible."

"Sorry, I just meant—"

The entire recruitment queue turned as more military vehicles drove up the street. Not trucks this time, but two M1 Abrams tanks.

They drove slowly down the center of the street to avoid clipping any cars parked near the shoulders. Both tanks had their turrets open. The gunners were looking the crowd over but kept the barrels of their M240s pointed up, away from the civilians.

Dom felt a surge of pride when he didn't see the black raven's head of the AMP insignia on the side of either tank. These men were marines.

"Speak of the Devil Dogs," he said. "Here they come."

"Sweet, but what the hell are they doing at an AMP base?" Camilla asked, stepping up beside him to watch.

A convoy of sand-colored marine Humvees rolled around the corner, following the tanks. They stopped in the street, and men jumped out, moving quickly.

Moose grabbed Dom and pulled him back.

"We best get out of here," he said. "Something's off."

Joaquín looked over at Dom. "Your dad say anything was going down in LA?"

Dom shook his head.

Four marines ran over to the crowd. One of them, a man about Ronaldo's age, told everyone to leave.

"What's going on?" Dom asked.

The hardened fighter focused on him for a split second, then dismissed him with a wave. "Go home, kid."

"Not until you tell us what's going on," Dom said. "My dad's a marine, and I want to know what's happening."

The guy looked back at him. "Then he would tell you to follow orders. Now, get out of here before shit gets bad."

The police officers outside retreated into their building, and the marine jogged back to his platoon.

There was no doubt in Dom's mind now.

A second civil war was coming. He could feel it as clearly as his thumping heart.

* * *

The city was melting down, but that didn't stop the rich kids from going to Alamitos Beach. Some of them were rich enough that their parents had hired security to accompany them.

Entitled little pricks, Vinny thought as he scanned the beach.

For a Saturday, the place wasn't as busy as usual, but there were plenty of kids out, and even some families trying to get a brief mental escape from the depressing reality that dogged them every day.

Vinny walked on the path looking out over the ocean. The breeze in his hair felt good. He only wished he were here to enjoy the weather, the water, and the American babes.

But today he was here to do something that had him conflicted.

Stopping on the path, he pulled out his phone and brought up the social media apps he used to follow Carly Sarcone. A new picture popped onto her feed, and he scanned the beach, trying to match the background in the image.

So far, nothing looked familiar.

He tucked his phone away and continued walking back to the bench where the other men were camped out.

Yellowtail was smoking a cigarette, his yellow button-down shirt open and the gold chain sparkling in the sun over his hairy chest. Doberman sat with his earbuds in, mouthing the words to whatever he was listening to.

The young wannabe Moretti soldier was just shy of his eighteenth birthday, a milestone Vinny had passed six months ago. But his friend sure didn't act like an adult. Half the time, Doberman was more interested in his electronics than the conversation going on around him.

Forget the millennials, Vinny mused. *It's Generation Y that's really in trouble.* Then again, if America didn't get its act together, all the generations were screwed.

"Looks like tensions are ramped up today," Yellowtail said as another convoy of military vehicles rolled down the road behind the beach.

Doberman took his earbuds out. "What's that all about?"

"I don't know," Vinny said, "but maybe we should get back to the warehouse."

Yellowtail shook his head. "Shut up, pussies. We're not going anywhere until we find Carly."

"What does Don Antonio want with this girl, anyway?" Vinny asked. He thought he knew the answer, but he wanted to hear it from the mouth of a made man.

Yellowtail glanced over and shrugged. "Does it matter? He says do something, you do it. Jump off a bridge, you jump. Drink a gallon of rat poison, you start chugging."

"Why the hell would he tell me to do either of those things?" Vinny asked.

"He wouldn't, dumb ass … although I remember a guy that was forced to drink rat poison back in Naples after one of the captains caught him fucking his wife." Yellowtail took another drag. "That was after they shot his balls off, of course."

"Jesus, who did that to him?" Doberman asked.

Yellowtail looked to Vinny. "Your old man."

"Yeah, right."

Vinny narrowed his gaze, but Yellowtail turned away, leaving the question to linger. Had his dad really done that? He shook the thought away, not wanting to ask, since his gut told him it was true.

It was a good reminder not to get sideways with a made man. As one of the youngest up-and-coming soldiers in the family, Vinny already knew better than to cross anyone with a button. In the world of La Cosa Nostra, betrayal was the worst thing.

Rats got treated like rats.

"I'm gonna keep lookin'," Vinny said. "Doberman, maybe you want to make yourself useful and come with."

Doberman got off the bench and stretched his tattooed arms, yawning. "All right, bro."

Yellowtail relaxed on the bench, enjoying his cigarette and the sights.

Storm clouds rolled across the horizon, but they were too far away for the city to see any rain. A little reprieve from the blazing sun would have been nice, though.

Vinny took off his sweat-rimmed track jacket as he walked.

The whine of sirens drowned out the music blaring from speakers across the beach, and a convoy of squad cars sped down the street.

"Man, this is worse than Naples ever was," Doberman said.

Vinny shrugged. He remembered some bad times in the slums. Seeing the military and the cops out and about wasn't unusual there. Hell, in Rome, you had cops, soldiers, or the Royal Guard at every major street corner, especially around the historical landmarks and financial districts.

Now America was getting a taste of his former life—the life his family had fled. He couldn't deny that things were spiraling out of control.

Doberman seemed to be thinking the same thing. "I'm worried LA's going to get hit by those terrorists," he said. "I don't get how the government still doesn't know who's doing the shit."

"I think they're hiding something," Vinny said. "But honestly, I'm worried about a war more than I am terrorist attacks."

"True enough, man. If this country splits up like that, it'll kill millions. Maybe ..." Doberman got really still.

"What, dude?"

Doberman pulled out his phone and grinned. "I think that's the girl."

Vinny followed his gaze toward a group of high-school-age kids sitting on blankets in the sand. There were six girls and one boy.

Perfect, Vinny thought.

"Come on," he said. "And I'll do the talking." His heart beat like a tom-tom as he crossed the bike path to the sand.

Doberman stuffed his headphones in his pocket and hurried to catch up. "Don't you think we should tell Yellowtail?" he called out.

"Nope."

Vinny wanted to do this on his own, to prove

himself, despite knowing how wrong it was. Besides, there was no way his uncle would kill the girl; he knew that. Kids and women were off limits. The only exception was for prostitution. The mob was easing into the sex trade, just as it had done with drugs.

He hesitated when he saw the dark-haired girl sitting on the blanket, laughing with her friends. What if his uncle did plan to sell her off? Her life would be over. She wouldn't be much different from the customers they sold drugs to, many of whom ended up junkies.

A soldier didn't question orders. And that was what he wanted more than anything: to earn his button—to become a made man in the Moretti family.

He pushed aside the feelings of guilt and put on his best smile.

"Well, look at this beautiful group," Vinny said as he walked up.

The girls turned, eyeing him suspiciously.

Doberman raised a hand and grinned like a nerd.

"I hear this is where the Italians hang out," Vinny said. "Is that right?"

The girls all looked at each other in turn, and the boy, a dark-haired kid as skinny as a beanpole, smiled.

"Well, who are these two hunks?" he said.

The girls giggled.

Vinny ignored the gay kid and looked at the girls in turn, avoiding Carly's gaze. He knew how the game worked.

"So, is this or isn't this where the Italians hang out?" he asked again.

"Only one Italian here," Carly said. "You're lookin' at her."

"Hey, I'm half," said a girl wearing a yellow bikini.

A girl with braids laughed. "You have blue eyes and blond hair, Jennifer."

Jennifer shrugged. "I'm still half."

"Italian blood is Italian blood," Doberman said.

"He's right, and us Italians got to stick together," Vinny said. "There aren't many of us in this city."

"Are you from Italy?" Jennifer asked. "You have an accent."

"Born and raised in Roma," Vinny lied.

Doberman smiled. "We came here to be movie stars, like everybody else in this town."

The girls all laughed, and the boy stood and put his hands on his hips.

"I don't know about you two," he said, looking at the sky and striking a pose, "but I'm going to be a star."

Doberman muttered something under his breath, but Vinny grinned and said, "To be honest, the star of this group is you." He set his dark eyes on Carly.

Her cheeks flushed, and the other girls giggled some more.

"What's your name, gorgeous?" Vinny asked.

Carly gave him another suspicious look, her cheeks still pink.

"What's *your* name?" she asked, cocking a brow.

"Vinny, and this is my boy Doberman," Vinny said. "But don't worry, he doesn't usually bite."

Doberman gave another hangdog grin. He didn't have to pretend to be a nerd.

"Mind if we sit?" Vinny asked. "I got something that might help take our minds off the shit happening out there."

The girls whispered to themselves while Carly studied Vinny. She seemed smarter than the others, more suspicious, which made him nervous.

"You can sit," she finally said.

Vinny and Doberman both took a seat on the blankets.

"Well?" Jennifer flipped her braids back and leaned in. "What you got for us?"

Doberman pulled out a small bag of coke.

"Best stuff in Long Beach," he said.

"Ooh, just what I need!" Jennifer said.

For the next hour, they did a few lines and hung out in the scorching sun, talking and relaxing. Vinny chatted with Carly a bit but didn't come on too strong. Just enough to get her curious. He could tell by the way she was looking at him now that she was interested.

All he needed was the right time to suggest they get out of here.

It came an hour later, with the wail of more sirens.

"Who wants to take this party somewhere else?" Vinny asked. "We got a safe place in Long Beach and some more blow."

Carly looked at him again, but the scrutinizing gaze was gone. She was relaxed, and her sheepish smile told him she was all his now.

Normally, Vinny would have gotten that little rush of adrenaline that teenage boys felt when they knew they were going to get some action, but his gut was a lump of anxiety and guilt.

"Sure, Vinny, why not?" Carly said with a trusting smile.

7

The wind was a real son of a bitch, stirring up dust around the refugee camp. Ronaldo had endured a grueling twelve-hour shift walking the fences.

There wasn't much out there but sand, cactus, and the strange green-barked paloverde trees. The open terrain was located nearly a hundred miles east of Phoenix, and their job was to protect the refugees and aid workers—from whom or what, he had no idea.

His unit continued to wear their CBRN suits despite the low risk of radiation poisoning this far out. The real threat was in the dead zone. It would be some time before the crews could completely stop the release of radioactive materials from the destroyed reactors, because the containment vessels were compromised.

The bombs had been designed and placed to take out all three reactors. It was a catastrophe that would set the United States back decades.

Ronaldo walked back to the mound of sandbags, raising a hand to the rest of the Desert Snakes, who stood guard inside the fort. Bettis had caught up with them after being held back to lead prayer meetings with some refugees looking for a little light in a dark world.

After finding the sick people in the church, Ronaldo and the team were on edge. Even Bettis let a few curses fly about the atrocity. No one seemed to know who had locked the civilians in there or why, but Ronaldo had his own theories, based on what the woman had told him about the soldiers.

"'Sup, Salvatore?" Tooth said.

"Same shit, different hellhole," Ronaldo replied.

"This isn't hell," Bettis said. "Hell is much worse, brother."

"If you say so," Tooth said.

Marks nodded and held up a hand at an approaching pickup truck. There was plenty of traffic, even at seven in the evening.

Tooth checked the driver and then waved him through as several other marines opened the gate behind them. The vehicle drove into the camp, taking a right down a road that curved around the maze of medical tents. Boxes of medical supplies filled the bed of the vehicle.

Ronaldo wiped the grit off his visor and moved into the enclosed sandbag post.

"I'd kill for a cold beer and a burger right about now," Tooth said.

"I'd settle for some water," Marks said. "And some air conditioning would be really fucking nice."

Ronaldo didn't want to think about all the things he wanted, only the things he needed. And only one thing came to mind: getting home to his family.

"Your shift's up, boys," said a voice from outside.

Tooth hopped over the mound of sandbags. "'Bout time!"

The next shift of marines had shown up to relieve the four of them, and Ronaldo grabbed his gear.

Marks, Tooth, Bettis, and Ronaldo made their way through the maze of white tents, pausing to let four medical personnel carry a stretcher with a man squirming on it. He coughed up blood over the edge and groaned as they hauled him to another tent.

Ronaldo said a short prayer and saw Bettis bow his head. The guy was going to need all the help he could get. Most of the people in this zone of tents were dying slow deaths. The only thing that could be done for them was to ease their pain with drugs.

He thought of the woman in the church and stopped to look at the numbering on the tents.

"What's up?" Marks asked.

"I want to stop by and see that lady I carried out of the church," Ronaldo said. "Go on ahead. I'll meet you guys back at the barracks."

Tooth continued trudging along, and Marks gave a nod and followed. Bettis lingered and asked if he could join Ronaldo.

"Sure, brother," Ronaldo said.

With their M4 carbines slung over their CBRN suits, the two marines set off. It didn't take long to find the tent Ronaldo remembered. There was no clearing barrel outside, but Bettis and Ronaldo dropped their magazines and each checked that the other's weapon was empty.

Inside, several medical staff in protective suits attended the sick. A doc wearing black-rimmed glasses looked up from a patient.

"Can I help you, soldiers?"

"Marines," Ronaldo said.

"Pardon me?"

"Ah, never mind," Ronaldo muttered. "We're here to find someone."

The doctor straightened and walked over, his gaze flitting to their guns.

"These people are already terrified of weapons after what happened at that church," he said.

"They're clear," Bettis said, holding his weapon so the doctor could see through the ejection port.

"Thanks," the doctor said. "What are you here for?"

"To see a woman I carried out of the church," Ronaldo said. "About fifty, dark hair with some gray. She had a rosary."

"Oh, Cindy."

"I never caught her name," Ronaldo said.

"Well, if it is Cindy, then you'd better hurry." The doctor pointed to a bed at the end of the tent, where a nurse was changing a woman's bedding.

"I'm going to check on some other people," Bettis said.

Ronaldo steeled himself as he made his way down the aisle, eyes ahead to afford the patients some privacy. Coughing, moaning, and sobbing filled the enclosed space. But these weren't soldiers or marines. They were innocent people, caught in the cross fire of a war that still didn't make sense. Shadowy forces had the country tearing itself apart from within.

Fucking coward terrorists, he thought.

When he got to Cindy's bed, she was lying on her side, curled up in a fetal position. The nurse finished changing the bed, holding in her gloved hands a balled-up sheet covered in blood and feces.

Ronaldo moved out of the way to let her pass. When she was gone, he bent down next to Cindy. Her eyes were open, staring at nothing.

"Cindy, my name is Ronaldo Salvatore," he said. "I got you out of that church. Thought I'd come see how you're doing."

Her eyes slowly tracked over to meet his. A whisper came between raspy breaths.

"What is it?" he asked.

She tried to speak but broke into a coughing fit. Ronaldo moved back slightly as flecks of blood hit his suit. She reached out toward him, but when he went to take her hand, she lowered her fingers toward the floor.

Ronaldo bent down and picked up the rosary. He put it in her hand and then wrapped his hand around hers. He knelt there by her side for several minutes until her raspy breathing slowed. No stranger to death, he knew the process.

He held her hand, met her eyes, and repeated the rosary while she moved her lips and whispered. Within twenty minutes, her hand fell limp in his.

He closed his eyes, said a final prayer, and reached down to close her eyelids. The same doctor from before walked over with Bettis.

"She's gone," Ronaldo said.

The doctor slowly shook his head, and Bettis got down on his knees to pray. When they had finished, they grabbed their weapons and stepped back into the heat just as a mechanical chopping sounded in the distance and grew louder.

Lights crossed the darkening horizon where an Osprey helicopter came hurtling through the sky. It landed somewhere on the western edge of the camp.

Ronaldo lost himself in his thoughts on the way back to their tent. His mind was on his mother, who reminded him of Cindy. She had died a decade ago from a heart attack—a crushing event that he still hadn't recovered from. He had never known his dad, who left home when he was just a boy.

A gunshot pulled him from his trance.

Bettis froze, and both men unslung their rifles, palming magazines in as they took off running toward shouts in the distance.

Ronaldo shouldered his rifle, keeping his muzzle pointed at the ground as he scanned for hostiles in the maze of tents. Bettis took point and stopped just before they reached the motor pool. Humvees, MRAPs, vans, and covered trucks, with army, Marine Corps, and AMP markings, filled the space.

On the other side was the tent where his platoon was holed up. Bettis and Ronaldo watched for movement in the motor pool. Seeing none, they ran to the first line of vehicles for cover.

More shouting guided them to the last row, where civilian cars and vans were lined up. Rounding a van, they got a view of the altercation.

A group of AMP soldiers faced off with a smaller cluster of marines. Ronaldo waited, listening to the men shouting at one another. He couldn't hear everything, but he got the gist of it.

An AMP soldier had buttstroked a marine with his rifle outside the front entrance to one of the tents.

Before the other marines could respond, the AMP pogue fired a round into the air.

Ronaldo prepared to move, then hesitated. This wasn't a random fight. It was a standoff between a group of marines and an even bigger group of AMP soldiers.

"Put down your weapons!" one of the AMP soldiers shouted. The dozen-strong group closed in around the outnumbered marines. Ronaldo could now see that it was Tooth and three others, who also had their rifles up and ready.

Ronaldo didn't see Marks or half the other guys from his platoon.

"Who's the cowboy?" shouted a voice.

Lieutenant Castle came barging out of a tent wearing nothing but a pair of camo pants and his boots, half his face still covered in shaving cream.

"What in the unholy fuck is going on?" he shouted at the AMP soldiers. Then he saw the downed marine and ran over to help. Bullets ripped into the dirt between him and the fallen man, nearly hitting Castle's boot.

Resisting the urge to fire back, Ronaldo kept his position behind the front passenger wheel well of the van. Bettis moved to another vehicle two rows up. Both did what they were trained to do in situations like this: aimed at the head of the highest-ranking adversary, a colonel leading the group of AMP soldiers.

"Drop it, marine," said a voice nearby.

Ronaldo searched for the source and found it too late. He cursed under his breath but kept his aim on the colonel as an AMP soldier approached him from behind the van. Another soldier had a gun on Bettis's back. The AMP pogue behind Ronaldo prodded him to put his weapon down, but he just shook his head and held his aim steady.

The colonel was a man named Doyle Cronin, whom Ronaldo had seen only in passing. He pointed an M9 pistol at Lieutenant Castle.

"You better get those guns out of my face!" the LT screamed.

"We have orders, and the authority, to take your weapons, *Lieutenant*," said Cronin. "The Marine Corps has been disbanded and replaced by the American Military Patriots. You're all relieved of duty."

Castle laughed, then grew serious when Cronin remained stone-faced.

"You got to be fucking kidding me," Castle said.

"Orders from Vice President Elliot," Cronin said.

"President Coleman would never authorize that," Castle said.

This time, Cronin was the one to laugh. "So you haven't heard the news."

Castle stood staring.

"President Coleman was assassinated a few hours ago by a death squad," Cronin said. "Jarheads, all of 'em."

That can't be, Ronaldo thought, keeping his M4 trained on the AMP colonel's head.

"The marines and army have attacked several AMP outposts in states that have declared their sovereignty," Cronin said.

"What's he talking about, LT?" Tooth asked.

"I have no clue," Castle said.

"It's true," Lance Corporal Timmy said. The marine stepped out of another tent, rifle up. "I just heard the news. President Coleman was killed."

"Marines in California and Illinois have surrounded multiple AMP FOBs," Cronin said.

Ronaldo flinched as a gun barrel pressed against the back of his helmet.

"Drop it, man," said the guy behind him. "I don't want to blow your brains out."

"Maybe I just drop Colonel Badass over there," Ronaldo said. "Just try me, motherfucker."

"Please, just lower your weapon," the AMP soldier entreated.

Ronaldo sensed weakness, but that weakness also posed danger if the guy got too jumpy.

"Want me to cap him?" Ronaldo said. "'Cause I'll happily blow that shiny dome right off him. Just try me. I'm the best shot in my platoon. I once shot a dick hair off an insurgent's nut sack. Might have taken one of his balls with it, though, come to think of it."

After a brief pause, the pressure from the gun barrel on his helmet eased. He blinked away the sweat streaming down his brow and tried to govern down his racing heart.

"You're outnumbered, Castle," said Cronin. "Better to lay down your arms. You've got thirty seconds to decide."

Castle's response was to spit on the ground, and Ronaldo prepared for the imminent shit storm. If it came down to it, he would have no problem blowing the asshole colonel's head off.

"You don't all have to pay for what a few marines did at that church," Cronin said. "Those who aren't responsible will have an opportunity to join the ranks of AMP."

Ronaldo narrowed his gaze.

"Church?" Castle said.

"We know it was a group of Devil Dogs that locked those people in there," Cronin said. "And those responsible will pay for it with their lives. The rest of you, well, it's your choice. Fifteen seconds."

Tooth roved his rifle to Cronin. "LT, what the hell is this guy talking about?" he asked.

"He's a lying sack of shit," Castle said. "Nice try, Colonel. We know it was AMP, and I'm willing to guess it was also AMP that killed Coleman when he refused to order the bombing of American cities that Elliot considered rebellious. This is all Elliot. Has been all along, and you're ass-deep in it."

Ronaldo swallowed hard as the realization set in. The atrocities across the country—maybe even the terrorist attacks too—all orchestrated by shadowy forces led by a four-star general who wanted …

A reset. Marks was right.

Now AMP was framing the marines so they could take control as the new face of America's armed forces. President Coleman was out of the way, and Elliot could do whatever the fuck he wanted.

But why ruin what was left of the country?

A crunch and the sound of a body slumping to the ground came from behind Ronaldo, but he kept his gun pointed at Cronin.

"That you, Marks?" he asked.

"You know it, brother," Marks replied. He had sneaked up on the AMP soldier and taken him down. It helped even the odds a bit, but it didn't help Bettis, who still had a gun muzzle at his back.

"How you wanna do this?" Marks asked, crouching down beside Ronaldo.

"Remember that time in Kandahar?" Ronaldo whispered.

"Like yesterday," Marks replied. "But there weren't civilians there. Zones here are all fucked with cross fire, and the moment we start shooting, it changes everything."

Marks was right. As soon as they started firing, there was no coming back from it. The country they had sworn an oath to defend would slide toward a civil war, between AMP and the remaining branches of the military.

"You take down the guy on Bettis first; you're the better shot," Marks ordered. "I'll cause the distraction. On three, okay?"

Ronaldo nodded again and swallowed. He had the AMP soldier behind Bettis in his sights.

Marks counted quietly, and on three, he yelled, "Hey, Colonel Buttfuck!"

A squeeze of the trigger took out the AMP soldier who had Bettis. Ronaldo quickly moved his sight picture back to the scene by the tent. Castle had brought up his pistol and shot the Colonel in the face, but this time the distraction didn't work the way it had in Afghanistan.

A bullet punched into Castle's gut, and he sagged to the ground.

Another marine hit the ground, shot multiple times. Marks and Ronaldo picked their targets carefully, taking down half the AMP soldiers before any of them could figure out where the shots were coming from.

When the remaining AMP soldiers darted for cover, Tooth and the other marines ran them down, squeezing off shots that dropped them to the oily pavement of the motor pool.

In less than a minute, it was over.

Two marines lay on the concrete, and a dozen AMP soldiers were bleeding out. Ronaldo hurried over, disarming the injured men before crouching beside Castle. He lay on his back, looking up with blue eyes that matched the clear sky.

Ronaldo put a hand on his gut and pressed down on the wound. "You're going to be okay, sir."

Castle clenched his jaw and looked at Marks, who joined them.

"Sir, hold on," Marks said. "We'll get you right. Just don't move."

Castle coughed, and his face twisted in a mask of confusion, then horror. His gaze met Ronaldo's. He reached up and grabbed Ronaldo hard on his biceps

"I can't feel my legs, Salvatore," he said. "I can't feel anything at all."

-8-

The president of the United States was dead, killed by marines sworn to protect him. While American soldiers across the country geared up for war, Antonio and his men did too.

Most of the AMP soldiers had already been at war for the past few weeks, in a brutal struggle to eradicate the gangs under the umbrella of the Norteño Mafia.

Antonio hadn't exactly *started* the war, but he had helped escalate it by throwing fuel on the fire. Now he was getting rich off it, selling his product to AMP soldiers across the city.

He could have been celebrating tonight, but before he could enjoy the fruits of his labors and look to the future, he had one last bit of his past to deal with.

The Moretti warehouse in Compton bustled with the precombat sounds Antonio remembered from his days in wartime. Magazines clicking into carbines, straps and boot laces tightening, whispered prayers, and a stereo playing in the background. The rap music was different from the rock they used to listen to, but in a way, it seemed more suited to the violence about to unfold.

Tonight, he welcomed the sounds.

He grabbed one of the M4A1 carbines from a crate and raised it at the ceiling, checking the scope.

A fine weapon.

All around him, his most trusted soldiers, Christopher, Yellowtail, Raff, Lino, Carmine, and Frankie, prepared for their next mission.

For the older Italian men, this wasn't a new experience. But it was for Vinny, who would soon get his cherry popped. Christopher had finally given his son his first kill order.

"This is an honor," Antonio told his nephew.

A curtain of hair hung down over one of Vinny's eyes as he cinched down his Kevlar vest. He brushed it back and nodded at Antonio.

"I'm good to go, Don Antonio," he said.

Christopher looked at his watch and then went over to the radio.

"That presidential address is coming on in a few minutes," he said.

The men huddled up to listen.

"Here we go," Christopher said. He turned up the dial. The gravelly voice of the new president of the United States filled the room.

"*Good evening, my fellow Americans,*" President Elliot said. "*Tonight, it pains me deeply to address you about the state of our country. I must report that our great nation has suffered a terrible blow at the hands of those sworn to protect us. President Nicholas Coleman was gunned down by a group of marines at Camp Lejeune, North Carolina, where he was visiting troops. This coup was meant to divide us further, but I assure you, it will not."*

Christopher, chewing on a toothpick to fight the urge for a cigar, glanced over at Antonio.

"President Coleman was more than a great leader; he was a friend. And I promise to bring all those responsible to justice. Now we know that the source of the domestic terrorist attacks is a sector of our own military hell-bent on destroying the very fabric of our republic. Sadly, they have done an effective job in crushing our already devastated economy and poisoning our farmland and several of our cities with radiation."

Antonio wasn't sure what to make of the news. He had never considered that the attacks might be coming from the military, but why kill President Coleman?

Elliot continued. *"I have charged the American Military Patriots to hunt down all rebel soldiers. Any states harboring them will be considered enemies of the republic, and I will not hesitate in ordering devastating attacks to bring them to heel. If you are a civilian in an area under rebel control, I highly recommend you leave the area. There will be no mercy on the enemies of the United States."*

The newly sworn-in president paused again, clearly for dramatic effect.

"I know that many of you are afraid. I know that many of you are hurting. And I promise you that as your leader, by the power vested in me, I will bring our divided country together when this is all over. But first, I must rid our country of those who wish to destroy it. God bless the United States of America."

Christopher turned off the radio, and all the men looked to Antonio. He was a bit concerned by the president's warning to civilians in areas controlled by rebels or non-AMP loyalists, but he was more concerned about what the fighting would do to his operation.

He had made almost three hundred thousand dollars from his deal with the AMP soldiers at Los Alamitos, and their dealing spots were bringing in thousands each day. The demand for cocaine and opioids was so great that he was having a hard time keeping up.

"This doesn't change anything for us tonight," Antonio said.

The Moretti soldiers, dressed in AMP uniforms, piled into the remaining Humvee they had stolen from the first AMP ambush. The rest got into the Escalade and pulled out of the garage, into the blazing afternoon.

Civilians were already heeding the call of the new president. People loaded their cars with belongings and spent the rest of their cash on gasoline to get out of the city.

While the people ran, Antonio prepared for his next move. Cars clogged the road on the drive through Compton. Civilians were losing their minds, some even coming up to cars and pounding on the windows for help.

Antonio unholstered his new Beretta M9, but most of the people screaming on the streets kept a respectable distance from the Humvee.

Even better, he didn't see a single cop or soldier in the area. They all were busy trying to direct traffic and deal with the standoff between those loyal to the new president and those standing with Governor Jim McGehee of California.

Smoke drifted away from the eastern horizon,

where a standoff between marines and a base of AMP soldiers stationed at Downey High School had ended in bloodshed.

Before they left Compton, Yellowtail pulled over to one of the Morettis' new dealing spots, an apartment complex. The parking lot, usually clogged with vehicles, was down to barely a third full. A mass exodus was under way from the City of Angels.

Antonio could see that his brother was on edge. Christopher's son also seemed unusually quiet, and Antonio was interested to see how he reacted when he discovered what they had used him to do.

The Humvee and the Escalade pulled up to one of the back stairwells. Two Moretti soldiers brought a young girl outside.

"Is that … Carly?" Vinny looked down as the realization set in.

"We're not going to hurt her," Antonio said as the two men put her into the back of the Escalade. "Don't worry. She is a means to an end."

Vinny nodded at that.

With their package secured, Antonio directed Yellowtail to the next location. They took several back roads, avoiding the interstate, but it didn't matter which path they took. Every road in and out of the city was congested with cars that had wrecked or run out of gas.

Just ahead, a pickup had T-boned a car, blocking both lanes. Several men tried to push the car out of the way, but a fight broke out.

"Pull onto the curb," Antonio said.

Yellowtail drove up onto the sidewalk, and the

Escalade followed. Pedestrians jumped out of the way, some of them screaming, others throwing rocks and bottles.

The drive to Los Cerritos took another two hours, and by the time they reached the neighborhood, anarchy reigned. Hundreds of thousands of people were leaving, some of them even on foot or bicycle.

But not everyone was participating in the mass exodus.

As Antonio expected, the man he sought had fortified his estate. Dozens of armed guards patrolled the sidewalks, and the people who had stayed were safely protected behind roadblocks.

Another reason Antonio had decided to use the Humvee despite the risk. If Marten saw him in this, he was going to have some explaining to do, but the dirty AMP colonel had bigger problems on his hands. The Marine Corps was knocking at AMP's door, and Antonio was starting to worry that his new allies could lose the fight.

Here and now, Antonio reminded himself.

They pulled up to the first of the roadblocks, where two men in black fatigues stood guard, holding AR-15s. They both looked well trained and tough—these were not some cheap rent-a-cops.

"What do you want?" one of them asked.

"Let us through," Yellowtail said.

"This area is a priv—"

Yellowtail pulled out his pistol. "I wasn't asking."

The man looked at his partner, who hesitated and then shrugged.

It seemed these men weren't being paid enough to put their lives on the line. Enzo's mistake.

"Go on through," said the guard standing by the driver's door.

Yellowtail pulled through the opening in the gates.

The Humvee continued to the end of the block, but the Escalade stopped halfway, out of view. Yellowtail parked outside the Sarcone villa, nestled at the end of a cul-de-sac.

Antonio pulled the slide back on the M9, decocked the hammer, and holstered the weapon. Then he grabbed his M4.

Four armed men stood in the driveway of the Sarcone house, guarding the six-figure vehicles parked outside the open garage.

"Vinny, you stay here," Christopher said.

Antonio got out of the truck with his brother.

The armed guards walked down the driveway, weapons angled at the ground—clearly not stupid enough to point them at soldiers.

"We're here on behalf of the American Military Patriots, to see Enzo Sarcone," Antonio said.

The four men seemed unsure what to do, and all exchanged glances.

"Tell him to come outside. We just want to talk with him."

A window opened on the second floor of the mansion, and a head poked out.

"What the fuck you want?" a man yelled.

The voice was rough, like that of a smoker, and while Antonio couldn't see his face, he knew that it was Enzo.

"To talk to you," Christopher said.

"Do you know where my daughter is?" he shouted. After a pause, he said, "Then I got nothing to say to you."

Enzo yelled at his guards, "Get 'em the fuck out of here!"

The armed men walked forward, and Antonio sighed. If the old bastard wouldn't come out willingly, he must bring out something to motivate him.

Turning, he motioned for the Escalade.

Frankie drove it down the street and parked behind the Humvee.

Carmine stepped out with the girl, and Lino emerged in the turret of the Humvee, pointing the M249 at the driveway.

More of Sarcone's men emerged from the back-yard, carrying pistols and rifles.

Antonio counted nine of them, but he wasn't worried.

"We have your daughter!" he yelled. "Why don't you come down and take a ride with us."

Enzo returned to the window.

"Carly?" he said.

Carmine ripped the tape off her mouth.

"Dad!" she shouted.

The frightened girl cried out and tried vainly to pull out of Carmine's grip.

Vinny got out of the truck and looked at his dad.

"Get back in the Humvee, Vin," Christopher said.

Carly looked at Vinny, and her eyes widened.

Antonio thought he saw him mouth the word *sorry.*

Vinny was young and inexperienced. It would take time for him to become strong, which was part of the reason he was here. To become a man.

"You piece of shit!" Carly shouted, thrashing again

in Carmine's grip. This time, she managed to get free and ran at Vinny.

Christopher intercepted her easily.

"Let her go!" Enzo shouted from the window.

It didn't take long for the don to walk out of the open garage. An entourage of four more men joined him, along with his gorgeous wife, Lena.

Wearing a three-piece suit, Enzo hurried down the driveway, his balding hair slicked back above his forehead. He looked somehow less Italian than Christopher and Antonio with their sharp noses and chiseled jaws.

"Carly, it's going to be okay," Enzo said. He looked at the Moretti men in turn, still taking them for AMP soldiers.

"What is this?" Enzo said as he approached. "Why did you take my daughter?"

Antonio pushed up his helmet so his old enemy could see his face. In an instant, Enzo's smooth features scrunched into a network of deep lines.

"Antonio ..." he stuttered. He looked over at Christopher and then backed away.

"Let her go," Lena said. "Please, our daughter did nothing."

"What are you doing?" Enzo said.

"Ending one empire and starting another," Antonio replied calmly. He gave a nod, and Lino went to work with the M249. The crack of the big gun was almost deafening. Ejected brass bounced off the top of the Humvee as the rounds blew through body armor and flesh.

Every death filled Antonio with the pleasure that revenge brought to a man who had waited many years for it. He brought up his rifle and fired at the other men before they could raise their weapons.

Christopher shouted as he fired, avenging his wife with each trigger pull.

One of the Sarcone men managed to shoot back, hitting the top of the Humvee, but Antonio took the guy down with a 5.56-millimeter round to the neck.

The gunfire died down almost as abruptly as it began. This was the land of Hollywood, but real violence wasn't like the movies. It was much more chaotic, messier. Narrow trickles of blood ran from the dead guards down the inclined driveway, to the gutter.

Sobs replaced the sound of gunfire. Lena cried in her husband's arms. Enzo reached out toward his daughter, who was again being held by Carmine. The entire family was unscathed, just as Antonio had ordered.

La Cosa Nostra's rules were clear: never kill women or children of another family. A rule his enemies had broken in Naples.

Antonio still followed the code, but that didn't mean he couldn't bend the rules a little and use women as bait. He lowered his rifle and pointed at the Humvee.

"Get in, Enzo," he said. "It's time to take a ride."

Lena wailed, and Carly pleaded for them to let her go.

Antonio nodded at Carmine, and the girl darted over to her father, who wrapped her in his arms. They embraced for several seconds, but Antonio ended their fleeting last moment together with a jerk of his chin.

"Let's go," Christopher said, his jaw tight with rage.

"No!" Carly shouted.

Carmine moved over, his rifle shouldered.

"Why?" the girl wailed. "Why are you doing this to my father?"

Antonio looked to Enzo and said, "Would you like to tell your daughter?"

A few moments of silence passed, broken by Christopher spitting on the ground. "This piece of shit must not remember the day that my wife was gunned down in a house of God."

"I remember," Enzo said, raising his chin. "And I truly am sorry for your loss that day."

"Your apologies are as empty as your soul," Christopher said. He went over with Carmine and yanked him away from his family.

Lena and Carly screamed as Enzo walked with them, his head down.

At least the son of a bitch had enough self-respect not to beg for his life.

"Take them away," Antonio said.

Frankie moved the two women back to the house, out of sight, while Enzo stood there, trying to keep his composure.

"One man descends to hell, while a boy ascends to manhood," Antonio said in Italian.

"For your mom," Christopher said to Vinny. He watched Enzo while his son raised his SR9 pistol to the man's forehead. There was only a beat of hesitation before Vinny pulled the trigger.

The bullet penetrated the skull and destroyed the brain of one of the masterminds behind the ambush that nearly erased the Moretti name.

"Hunt the other men down," Antonio said. "They

can swear loyalty to the Moretti family banner, or join their old boss."

* * *

Hearing the low rumble, Dom ran outside, praying it was just thunder. But the sky had not a wisp of cloud.

His worst fear was coming true.

"Mom! Monica!" he shouted, running back inside.

They had their car packed up and ready to go, but there was no way they were going to get out of the city before the jets came. They had to take cover inside the house.

He ran to the front yard, where Monica and Elena stood outside the sedan packed full of suitcases.

"Dom," Elena said. "Do you—"

"Get inside!" he yelled, waving from the doorway.

Elena backed up as several black dots emerged on the horizon.

This can't be happening, Dom thought. But it was. He had known all along that it was a possibility, and instead of leaving when they had the chance, he had stood in line at the Downey Police Department Headquarters. They had offered him a job, and he was due for his first day of training in a few hours.

But Downey wouldn't even need a police force if President Elliot decided to wipe Los Angeles County off the map.

Dom herded his mom and sister back inside and then led them to the bathroom for shelter. It wouldn't protect them from much, but with no basement, it was the safest place to hunker down.

"Get in the tub," he said to Monica.

She climbed in, and with his mother's help, he hauled the mattress from the twin bed into the bathroom and put it over Monica.

"No, I don't want ..." she said.

"It's okay, baby," Elena said. "Everything's going to be okay."

Dom heard the uncertainty in her voice and saw the fear in her eyes. He felt the same stabbing fear of not being able to protect them. "Get down and stay down," he said.

Elena reached out for him as he left the bathroom. "Where are you going?"

"I'll be right back."

Dom ran down the hallway and grabbed his shotgun, then the bug-out bag he had stuffed full of rations, a water purification system, a medical kit, space blankets, ammunition, and batteries for his flashlight and hand-crank radio.

He stopped to look out the window just as the squadron of twelve F-16s screamed over the eastern edge of the city. Their first pass was a dry run—perhaps a warning, or a flyover to check ground troop movements.

Or maybe, just maybe, they were here to help.

Dom stayed there a moment, praying that was the case.

Then he saw more black dots to the north.

Ten of them.

The F-16s curved to intercept the incoming fighters.

Dom's gut clenched at the sight and the roar of what appeared to be F-35s. They were almost twice as loud as the older F-16s.

He was right: the first squadron wasn't here to drop its payload on the rebels. It was here to protect them from the AMP pilots.

Missiles curved away from the fighters as the battle for Los Angeles began.

"Dom!" Elena shouted. "What's happening?"

"Just stay put, Mom!"

A low emergency siren sounded in the distance. It rose into a wail. Ignoring it, he opened the door and walked outside. At this point, it didn't matter much whether he stayed in the fragile house, or just stood in the driveway. If a bomb fell, they were all screwed, and he had to see this.

Missiles in the first salvo found targets, blowing two F-16s to pieces over the city and maiming an F-35. The pilot dipped low enough to rattle windows as he fought for altitude.

Another explosion rang out, and Dom walked out farther into the front yard, rotating as he watched the battle in the heavens. The F-35s quickly took control of the airspace, taking out three F-16s and losing only one of their own.

An injured F-16 came screaming overhead, smoke trailing as it banked hard to the right to get on the tail of an F-35. Just as it moved into position, another F-35 came from the west and launched a Sidewinder into the F-16's cockpit.

A massive fireball burst over the city, raining down shrapnel into the yard.

Dom slowly backed toward the house, eyes locked on the sky.

Six F-16s remained against eight of AMP's F-35s.

Another F-16 went down in a meteor of flames.

Dom tripped on the bottom porch step, falling on his ass. He sat there, watching the dogfight. Somewhere in the distance, he heard the familiar voice of his mom shouting, but he couldn't pull himself away from the mesmerizing sight.

Two more F-16s met fiery ends in almost the same instant, leaving only three to take on the eight F-35s. And still the pilots didn't cut and run. They launched another salvo of missiles, blowing apart two F-35s and giving the rebel pilots a flicker of hope.

The six F-35s regrouped to hunt the two F-16s, which peeled off in different directions. The AMP pilots gave chase, three on each rebel fighter.

Two of the AMP fighters flew over Downey, so low that the draft knocked Dom back on the porch steps. He shielded his face and turned as the fighters climbed and each launched a Sidewinder at the F-16.

A brilliant blast lit up the skyline, leaving a single rebel pilot to protect Los Angeles from the AMP pilots.

Dom pushed himself to his feet as a chunk of F-16 came crashing back to earth, landing on a house a few blocks over. Flames billowed into the air.

Over the wail of sirens came the sound of a heavy vehicle screeching around the corner. He bolted back into the house and grabbed the shotgun, and got back outside as a Humvee roared down their street.

Dom brought up the shotgun, aimed it at the windshield, and looked for any military insignia on the side.

If these were AMP soldiers, would he have the guts to protect his family?

He had only a second to contemplate the question.

The Humvee screeched to a stop outside the house, giving Dom his first look at the AMP logo on the driver's door. He fired a warning shot, the recoil jerking him backward slightly. The buckshot spread out, bouncing off the armored hood.

Dom pumped the barrel, chambering another shell, and yelled a verbal warning, but his voice was no match for the screaming F-35s.

A man got out of the passenger seat, hands in the air.

Closing one eye, Dom aimed at the man's helmet. He blinked away a bead of sweat and focused on a familiar sunburned face.

"Dad," he whispered, lowering the shotgun.

"Dom!" Ronaldo shouted. "Where are your mother and sister?"

He came running up the driveway as Sergeant Marks opened the driver's-side door.

"Come on!" he shouted. "We have to get out of here!"

There was no time to hug his dad or ask questions.

The last F-16 exploded in the sky, and the F-35s moved in with free rein to strike their targets.

-9-

Six Moretti soldiers huddled in the basement beneath the Compton warehouse where they packaged their drugs for distribution to the dealers. The five stainless steel tables were clean now, with only the scales, trays, and pill-counting spatulas remaining as evidence of their purpose.

Between the high-volume enterprise with the AMP colonel, and the death of Enzo Sarcone, the Moretti family had much to celebrate. But the wine and vodka the men were passing around in the glow of a battery-powered lantern was more to ease their nerves under the AMP jets' bombardment than to celebrate any victories.

The deep *whump* of the bombs and the *pom-pom-pom* of the antiaircraft rattled the bones of the makeshift bunker and the men inside it.

Seated on an ammunition crate with his jacket for a cushion, Vinny looked around him. Carmine sat on a torn leather couch, his normally slicked-back hair hanging loosely over his eyes. Frankie stood with his back to the wall, tattooed arms folded across his chest, his scarred face staring at the floor. Yellowtail sat backward on a chair, and Christopher leaned against the wall next to Vinny. Doberman was messing with the radio on a cutting table.

The attack had started shortly after the mission to kill Enzo, and the team had rushed back to the warehouse—all but Antonio, who had taken the Escalade to Anaheim with Lino, to stay with Marco and Lucia.

Vinny put his head in his hands, trying to block out the distant and not-so-distant sounds of war.

"It's normal to feel like that after you kill someone," Yellowtail said. "You did good, kid."

"Not a kid," Christopher said, raising the bottle of vodka. He took a drink and handed it to Vinny. "You're a man now."

Vinny took a slug, welcoming the burn. He wasn't feeling all that bad about killing Enzo, but he couldn't tell the other men the truth.

He felt worse about tricking Carly at the beach. She had trusted him, and he had kidnapped her for the sake of killing her father.

If that was what it took to be a made man, then maybe he wasn't right for this way of life—assuming that their way of life survived actual war on the streets outside.

The walls of their hideout rumbled from a bomb impact. A fighter jet screamed overhead, and Vinny put his hands over his ears.

"Jesus Christ," Frankie said, looking at the fine dust floating down from the ceiling. "We're sitting ducks down here."

"I should have gone with Antonio to Anaheim," Christopher said. He brushed dust off his black uniform, which still had flecks of Enzo Sarcone's blood on one lapel.

"No," Yellowtail replied. "He gave you specific orders—and good ones too. If something happens to him, you're in charge of the family."

Christopher seemed to consider the words and looked over at Vinny.

The bombardment continued, and more dust sifted down from the ceiling. Doberman had finally gotten the radio to work, and static crackled through the room. The men gathered around to listen to a female reporter. She spoke fast, her voice quaking with fear.

"Battles between AMP soldiers and rebels are occurring throughout the country," she said. *"We're getting reports of attacks on civilians in major metropolises including Chicago, New York, Los Angeles, and—"*

Static crackled from the speakers, and Doberman cursed. "I can't get a clear signal."

"Civilians?" Christopher said. He looked at the stairway leading out of the basement, clearly even more concerned about his brother and the other Moretti men who were out there in various locations.

Another bomb detonated, shaking the ground.

Vinny looked down at his shaking hands. He stuffed them in his pockets, not wanting the other men to see him this way.

Times like these made him miss his mom. He had heard that was what soldiers in foxholes often thought of, and while this wasn't exactly a foxhole, it had the same effect.

The metal tables rattled from another impact. Yellowtail pulled out his gold cross and kissed it. Frankie and Carmine bowed their heads.

Los Angeles was officially rebel territory, and if the reports about attacks on civilians were true, no one was safe, even in a basement.

Christopher walked over to the stairs, his head tilted slightly.

Banging sounded in the brief respite between explosions.

"You hear that?" he asked.

Vinny stood up to listen.

The clanking of the garage door sounded above them.

Someone was upstairs.

Christopher grabbed his M4, and Vinny pulled out the SR9 from the concealed holster behind his back. While the other man loaded their weapons, the father and son tiptoed up the stairs.

Two bombs exploded back to back.

Christopher continued up the dark stairwell, determined to protect their warehouse. He angled the gun at the door overhead.

"Stay behind me," he whispered back to Vinny.

Vinny aimed his gun for the second time that night, prepared to kill again for the Moretti banner.

The clanking stopped, and voices sounded, then footsteps. The door at the top of the stairs swung open, and Vinny moved his finger to the trigger.

Christopher held up a hand a second later and lowered his rifle barrel from the ash-dusted figure standing in the doorway.

"Antonio," Christopher said.

The leader of the Moretti family slowly walked down the first two steps. His black AMP uniform was ripped, and blood ran down his ash-streaked face.

"What the hell happened?" Christopher said, moving aside for his brother. Lino followed him onto the stairs and closed the door behind them.

The men all gathered around Antonio in the basement, none of them saying a word as their tired, injured leader stood there. His normally stoic features had twisted into a mask of disorientation, as if he were really drunk.

"We wrecked the Escalade and had to turn back on foot," Lino said.

"I couldn't make it to Anaheim," Antonio said, shaking his head. "I couldn't …"

"I'm sure your family is okay," Christopher said.

"They will be," Lino assured Antonio. He held his right arm, dripping blood through his fingers onto the floor. "We got hold of Lucia on the phone," he said. "They're in the basement of the apartment building with the other residents."

Antonio gingerly touched the gash on his head, and pulled away a finger slick with blood.

"We got a medical kit anywhere?" Yellowtail asked.

"I'm fine," Antonio snapped.

"Me too," Lino said.

Antonio reached for the bottle of wine, then shook his head and motioned to Yellowtail for the vodka.

Another blast rattled the room as Antonio took a swig from the bottle.

"Easy there," Christopher said. "It's not the end of the world yet."

"No, but maybe not so far off," Antonio said, taking another pull. "AMP is in control of the skies, and those pilots are raining hell down on the city."

"We heard they're hitting civilian targets," Frankie said.

"No fucking shit," Antonio said, glaring.

The men avoided their leader's gaze, including Vinny, who looked down at his bloodstained sneakers.

"I'm not sure whether to root for AMP or the rebels at this point," Antonio said. "AMP could very well end up killing us while winning the fight for Los Angeles. But if they lose, we lose our biggest business partner."

Vinny didn't know which sounded better: being blown to dust by a bomb, or starving with the rest of the city after the attack was over. Either way, the future of the Moretti family was in grave doubt, and he wasn't sure Don Antonio could protect them this time.

* * *

Ronaldo slept a few hours, until a nightmare jerked him awake. Elena, sitting in a chair by his bed, reached over and gently touched his arm.

"It's okay, you're with your family," she said.

My family …

For a while, Ronaldo had thought he might not see them again. After the ambush that nearly killed Lieutenant Castle, the Desert Snakes had no choice but to flee the refugee camp. Now, with AMP in control, they were outlaws.

He sat up in bed and nearly broke down at his wife's gentle touch. A glance over at Monica brought a smile. She slept peacefully on a cot, holding her stuffed elephant, oblivious to the fighting aboveground.

Los Angeles was a war zone, and a quick scan of the grubby basement reminded Ronaldo just how far they were from safety.

Trapped inside the city, they had decided to flee to an office building owned by Zed Marks's family. East of Los Angeles in City of Industry, it was away from most of the fighting, and the building seemed secure enough. But as soon as they had a window to escape, Ronaldo was getting his family out of the city.

"What time is it?" he asked.

Elena brought up her watch and looked at the pale-green radium dial. "Just after 4:00 a.m."

"How come you're not sleeping?" he asked.

"I just can't."

Marks stepped into the basement doorway wearing civilian clothes, holding his M4.

"Everything okay?" Ronaldo asked.

"Better get dressed," Marks said. "I think you should see what's happening."

"Stay with Monica," Ronaldo said to his wife as he threw on his shirt and tied his boots. He grabbed his rifle, then checked that Elena had her pistol.

"I'll be right back," he said.

Ronaldo followed Marks up the stairs to an open atrium of the five-story building. Then he crossed over to another door, which led to a stairwell. With Marks in the lead, they climbed to the roof, where his son waited just inside the low parapet.

In the distance, green tracer rounds lit up the night

like a flurry of shooting stars. Flames flickered on the upper floors of several high-rises.

The jets were gone, but the fighting on the ground had only just begun. Distant explosions and the chatter of automatic weapons echoed through the night. Months of starvation and desperation had turned ordinary civilians into combatants, adding fuel to an already raging fire.

It was like Baghdad all over again. And not just here. Scenes like this played out in every major city and many smaller ones as well. On top of that, the city's hundred thousand gang members were out in force, terrorizing, looting, murdering.

"We should be out there, fighting with our brothers," Marks said.

He looked over, but Ronaldo didn't respond. They both hated leaving after the ambush, but they had been vastly outnumbered.

Now Ronaldo had his family to think about, and until he got them somewhere safe, his duty was to them. Only then would he get back in this fight.

"Dad, I don't understand how this happened," Dom said.

"We were betrayed," Ronaldo replied solemnly. "By a man who's gone crazy as a meth head."

"Elliot's insane, all right," said Marks. "But not in that way. He's the dangerous kind of crazy—the kind that's also a genius. Unfortunately for our country, he's one of the best military tacticians anywhere."

"Maybe so," Ronaldo said, "but if the truth gets out, AMP will fall apart. If people knew they were responsible for Palo Verde and San Fran ..." The smoky air made him want to spit. "Right now Elliot has made the Corps look like an enemy of the state. He's probably going to say we were responsible for those attacks too."

Marks spat on the tarred roof. "Our only chance is if the navy joins the fight. If they do, we might be able to take out that traitorous pile of shit Elliot."

"You good for a bit?" Marks asked. "I could really use a few hours' shut-eye."

"Yeah, I'll take watch." Ronaldo looked at his son. "You go down with your mom and get some rest."

Marks left, but Dom hesitated. He was not one to disobey orders, but Ronaldo could see he didn't want to go.

"Okay, stay a little while," Ronaldo said.

Dom smiled.

They sat down in office chairs nearby. Odd as it felt to be watching a battle in Los Angeles, Ronaldo was just glad to be sitting here with his boy.

"I missed you, buddy," he said.

Dom looked over. "I missed you too."

Ronaldo still didn't know quite what had happened while he was gone, but Elena had said something about a robbery across the street. He decided to wait for Dom to bring it up, rather than put him on the spot. Positive reinforcement was key, especially now, with the world melting down around them.

"You did a good job protecting your mom and sister while I was gone. I'm proud of you."

Dom shook his head. "I should have gotten them out of the city when I could."

"No, *I* should have."

A fireball mushroomed in the distance. Two

seconds later came the boom. It was the third gas station they had seen go up tonight.

Ronaldo lowered his hand as the plume shrank into a raging fire.

"What do we do?" Dom asked.

Ronaldo wasn't sure. He wanted to get his family out of here, but he was a wanted man, and AMP soldiers were everywhere.

"Dad?"

"Thinking," Ronaldo snapped. Dom eased back, and Ronaldo gave his son a rueful nod. "I'm sorry, I just don't know yet."

They sat watching for several minutes before Dom spoke. "You still haven't told me what happened at that refugee camp."

Ronaldo gave a resigned sigh. "AMP ambushed us after President Coleman was killed. Marks and I and a few other marines won the fight, but we lost some good men. We decided to head back to LA—most of us, anyway."

He paused, remembering what Castle had told him after they got him stabilized in one of the medical tents. He repeated the words to Dom.

"LT told me to come back here and take care of you guys."

He left out the second part. *Do it before AMP finds you and kills you.*

Ronaldo sighed. "I booked it out of there with Marks, Tooth, and Bettis in a stolen AMP truck."

"Where are Tooth and Bettis now?"

"They went to join another unit here, to fight AMP, but they all understood my decision to come get you guys out."

"Did the marines really kill President Coleman?"

"Hell no," Ronaldo said. "Elliot planned this all along. When states started rebelling, he must have ordered the dirty-bomb attack in San Fran, and the hit on the Palo Verde nuclear plant."

"But why the fuck would he do that, Dad? And who would carry out those orders?"

"History is full of evil men following evil orders, son." He looked at Dom, not sure how else to explain it. "A reset," he added, recalling Marks's words. "Elliot wants a new America, I guess—one working for *him*."

Dom nodded as if he understood, but Ronaldo wasn't sure he did. Hell, he himself had only the barest sense of what was happening.

"The thing about war is it sometimes doesn't make sense," Ronaldo added. "If you look at past wars, they started over a series of things that each made sense in the moment but escalated out of control. Eventually, it's just what happens."

They looked out over the chaos. Smoke from hundreds of fires across the city choked the skyline, blocking out all the stars.

"Not quite the camping trip I was hoping for," Ronaldo said, recalling his promise to his boy.

Dom chuckled nervously. "If we leave the city, we might be camping for a while."

"True enough."

A shout came from the open service door on the roof, cutting Ronaldo off. He got up from his chair and hurried over to find Elena standing in the doorway with Monica. Marks was in the stairwell behind them.

"What's wrong?" Ronaldo asked.

"There are men outside," she said.

"Where?"

She pointed to the edge of the building, and Ronaldo hurried over to have a look. An AMP Humvee had parked on the abandoned street below.

Marks joined him, crouching behind the low wall at the roof's edge.

A man in a hoodie pointed up at the building, and four AMP soldiers wearing face masks and cradling rifles were looking up at the windows.

Ronaldo stepped back. "I count four plus a driver."

Marks cursed. "Plus the asshole who just sold us out."

"Who knows we're here?"

"I don't know, man," Marks said, "but it's not a coincidence."

"There's only five of them," Dom said, "and you guys are marines."

Ronaldo and Marks looked back at him. He stood by the doorway, holding the shotgun Ronaldo had given him before leaving for Atlanta.

For the first time, Ronaldo saw his son as a man.

Banging sounded below, followed by a crash that echoed through the open atrium.

"They're in," Ronaldo said.

"Sergeant Marks and Sergeant Salvatore," a deep voice shouted, "we know you're in here! Put down your weapons and come out with your hands up! You're wanted for treason."

"How do they know my name?" Ronaldo whispered. He looked to Marks. "What do you want to do?"

Marks didn't reply right away, and Dom chimed in.

"We can take 'em. We have to. If we don't, they'll kill you, like you said."

"Kid's right," Marks said. "We're considered traitors now, and we both know the punishment."

Ronaldo nodded. "Dominic, watch your sister and mom."

"Wait," Elena said.

He expected her to tell him not to go, but she held out her hand and said, "You have my gun."

"Everything's going to be okay," he said, handing her the pistol.

He looked at his family for a second. This time, he was up against other American soldiers acting under orders. But the world had suffered too long at the hands of men who didn't stand up to unlawful orders, and Ronaldo was done with it. He turned and left with Marks, into the stairwell.

Halfway down, a loud click sounded, and the few lights they had on in the building blinked off.

"*Shit*, there goes the generator," Marks whispered.

The stairwell was almost pitch black, and if the AMP soldiers had night-vision goggles …

Letting his eyes adjust, Ronaldo listened for footfalls. Then he cautiously made his way down to the landing.

They exited on the third floor and moved through an open area of desks and cubicles, guided by the dim light from the windows.

Marks flashed a hand signal, and they parted, moving to different sections in the maze of cubicles.

By the time Ronaldo got into position, the AMP soldiers were heading upstairs. He could hear multiple footfalls in the hallway.

Wedged behind a cubicle, he had a clear view of the entire office, and the glow of distant fires provided enough light for a clear field of fire. He brought up his rifle and aimed it at the entrance to the room, where a single AMP soldier entered.

As he suspected, the man had on "four eyes"—night-vision goggles. Keeping low, the soldier panned across the room and moved down an aisle before the second man entered. But where were the other two?

Ronaldo waited, heart thumping.

Footfalls echoed in the stairwell. They had split up. *Shit.*

He took the shot without waiting for Marks's signal from across the room. A three-round burst caught the lead AMP soldier in the helmet and neck, dropping him.

Marks took down the second guy with a burst from the side, and Ronaldo hurried over to make sure the downed soldiers were dead.

One was still moving, and Marks double-tapped him, the muzzle flash lighting up the staff sergeant's weathered features.

There was regret in his eyes. Ronaldo felt it too.

Regardless of the circumstances, killing another American—and a soldier, to boot—was not easy, especially knowing that these men were not much older than Dom.

The two marines didn't linger but took off up the stairwell to intercept the other two AMP soldiers.

When they got to the stairwell, a gunshot rang out, followed by shouting and then two booms from a shotgun. But it wasn't coming from the third floor.

Ronaldo felt his heart lodge in his throat. He pounded up the stairs and through the open service door to find the other two AMP soldiers lying on the rooftop. Standing by a rusted mechanical unit was Dom, his shotgun still trained on the downed men.

Elena and Monica hunkered down behind the air handler, safe and sound.

"Help me," one of the AMP soldiers moaned. He squirmed, gripping his leg, blood gushing between his fingers and pooling around his thighs.

Ronaldo kicked his rifle away and bent down beside him. Pushing up the night-vision optics, he yanked off the face mask, revealing yet another youthful face. The young man coughed, flecking Ronaldo's shirt with blood.

"How did you know where we are?" Ronaldo asked.

The soldier choked again and looked Ronaldo in the eyes before the light left his gaze.

Dom walked over, lowering his shotgun. Then he darted over to another air unit and vomited.

Ronaldo walked over to Elena and Monica, giving his son a moment to compose himself. He had also thrown up after killing his first enemy soldier.

"You okay?" Ronaldo asked.

Dom wiped his mouth off and managed a nod.

"It'll pass," he told him. "Until it does, you're going to second-guess yourself. Don't. You did the right thing."

"You did what you had to do," Marks said. "You protected your family."

"How many did you guys get?" Dom asked.

"We had two downstairs. These two make … Shit, that civilian who told them we were up here could be on the horn selling us out again. AMP could have another team here in minutes. We need to clear out. Fast."

For a tense moment, they all stood in silence. Ronaldo saw their progress in his mind, rushing downstairs, getting to their stolen AMP truck, and pulling away just as more AMP troops surrounded them. He and his family would die, killed by men he once would have called brothers.

He shook off the negative thoughts, listening to the distant chatter of gunfire, the wail of sirens, and sporadic explosions. It sounded like the end of the world.

Over the apocalyptic noises came the rumble of something that made Ronaldo stiffen. He looked toward the sky, holding his breath.

"Get inside!" he yelled.

He got everyone through the door, then looked over his shoulder as several cruise missiles arced across the horizon, moving south, where they detonated in a brilliant fireball.

Ronaldo knew at once what they had hit. The Los Alamitos Joint Forces Training Base, AMP headquarters in southern California, was now a smoking crater. Even if the civilian rat had called in more AMP reinforcements, it wouldn't matter now. He almost shouted in exultation as he clapped Marks on his bloodstained shoulder.

"The navy picked a side, brother! They're with the Devil Dogs!"

10

At seven in the morning, Antonio stumbled out of the warehouse, his stomach in knots and his head pounding from the gash he received in the car accident.

Raising a hand to his eyes, he looked at the brilliant sunrise, feeling lucky to be alive. The past ten hours were some of the worst in his life, rivaling nights in Afghanistan, when he wasn't sure he would see the dawn.

But Don Antonio Moretti had survived the night just as he had then, and so had his men.

Their new business, however, was shattered.

He took in a breath that reeked of burning rubber.

According to the radio reports, while AMP had won the battle for the skies, they were losing on the ground, which meant that his entire deal with Lieutenant Marten was in jeopardy.

He took another step outside, thinking of his family. They were okay two hours ago, when he last got a text from Lucia, right before the service went dead. Raff and several of his other trusted men were there, but that didn't help Antonio feel much better.

Now that the bombardment appeared to be over, he needed to get back to them.

He scanned the skyline for fighter jets.

Smoke columns tilted away from the downtown skyline, where AMP missiles and bombs had wreaked havoc. A cloud of black drifted away from AMP targets the navy had pounded.

Rain drizzled on the smoldering fires and the corpses that were once his customers.

"Son of a goddamn bitch," he grumbled.

Pulling up a bandanna over his face, Antonio walked away from the warehouse to the sidewalk, the cold rain hitting his exposed neck.

Christopher and Vinny remained standing in the open doorway.

"Is it over?" Vinny asked.

"I don't think so," Christopher said.

The constant gunfire had ceased, and they hadn't heard an explosion for over three hours, but Antonio kept his senses attuned to danger. His other soldiers were holed up at another property close by and with his family back in Anaheim. Everyone had strict orders: be prepared for a fight to protect the weapons, cash, and vehicles.

So far, they had lucked out and avoided any sort of bloodshed. But Antonio knew it was coming.

The rats would soon venture out of the sewers, searching for resources.

He scanned the smoky sky for any sign of AMP aircraft. Yesterday, he had watched the dogfight over downtown that kicked off the battle, and last night he had heard the Navy cruise missiles that pounded the Los Alamitos Base.

It felt odd being a spectator to war.

You're not a spectator, he remembered. He was part of the fight for the city, and he had made a deal with the wrong side. Chances were good that Lieutenant Marten and the other dirty AMP soldiers were crispy critters.

"Better get inside," Christopher said. He ushered Vinny back, but Antonio stayed on the sidewalk. To his right, four men were walking up the middle of the street. They wore baggy clothes, face masks, and firearms of various sizes.

Looters, and not just of the garden variety. These guys were gangbangers, even more dangerous than the random lowlifes.

Antonio walked back to the side door of the warehouse and grabbed an M4. Lino, Yellowtail, Frankie, and Carmine stood inside wearing body armor and holding their rifles. Inside, they had close to half a million dollars in the safe, from their recent payment from AMP, not to mention their vehicles and weapons.

The rest of the men were guarding their other valuables in a locked garage, but with cell towers down, someone would have to physically go and get them if they needed reinforcements.

"We might have trouble coming," Antonio said.

He closed the door and walked over to a window to watch the men still coming up the street. They would be no match for his soldiers here, but he didn't want to engage in a firefight if he didn't have to. They had only twenty thousand rounds of ammunition, and it needed to last.

Tires screeched, and a pickup truck careened

around the corner. It slowed behind the four men as they continued their march—or hunt, Antonio realized.

Gripping his M4, he prepared to defend what was his.

But the fight never came.

The four men and the vehicle continued past the warehouse. Antonio relaxed and retreated to his office with Lino, Christopher, and Vinny. When he got to his desk, he slumped in the chair, exhausted from staying up all night. The adrenaline had long since worn off, and he felt a crash coming on.

Picking up his coffee mug, he downed the rest of the cold espresso.

Lino carried the battery-operated radio to the card table and started flipping through the stations. Vinny took a seat too.

"Unconfirmed reports are coming in that President Elliot has been charged with treason by General Macke of the United States Army. Macke claims that President Elliot is responsible for orchestrating the coup against the late President Coleman. Again, these are unconfirmed reports. What we do know is that the navy has joined the army and the marines in the fight against AMP."

"So, basically, both sides are blaming each other," Christopher said.

Antonio set the coffee mug down and cracked his neck from side to side. The news wasn't a surprise. That was how war always seemed to work: each side accusing the other of atrocities, assassinations, and bloodshed.

"Who knows what really happened," Antonio said.

Lino continued to the next station.

"All residents within a two-mile radius of Los Alamitos Training Base are being told to evacuate as quickly as possible ..."

Antonio went over to the radio. "Turn that up."

"We're still not sure exactly how much radioactive material was at the training base, but authorities aren't taking any chances ..."

Lino felt the bandage on his head and looked over at Antonio, eyes wide. The forty-year-old warrior didn't normally show fear, but even warriors got nervous.

Antonio felt his nerves tighten too. He didn't fear the soldiers, the cops, the other crime organizations, or even the gangbangers. But he did fear radiation.

"How far away is that from Anaheim?" Antonio asked.

Christopher shook his head, unsure.

"Well, get out a fucking map," Antonio said.

Lino retrieved one from the Mercedes in the garage and brought it back to the office, where he draped it over the card table. For the next few minutes, they pored over the 112 cities in Los Angeles and Orange Counties. It appeared that Compton was safe, but Anaheim was right on the border.

"Looks like the Sarcone castle is toast," Vinny said. "If they'd bombed the base a couple of days earlier, they coulda saved us some trouble."

Antonio clenched his jaw, resisting the urge to curse a blue streak. He had tried to keep it together for his men, even with this new development threatening his plans.

But knowing that his family was in harm's way sent him over the edge. His men could protect them from bullets but not from radiation.

"I should have walked there last night!" he yelled, slamming a fist down on the table.

"You never would have made it," Christopher said. "Don't worry, brother, we'll get them out of there."

A voice shouted down the hallway. "Those thugs are coming back!" It was Carmine, and he darted back the way he had come, rifle in hand.

Antonio grabbed his weapon and hurried into the warehouse after the others. Sure enough, the truck had parked outside, and six men were standing in the circular drive.

"Open your garage!" one of the men shouted.

He was big, at least six-three, and wearing a tank top that showed off thick biceps and pecs. But he wasn't the leader—Antonio could see that right away. That guy sat in the passenger seat of the truck.

"Frankie, get over to the other warehouse," Antonio said, "and take a truck to Anaheim. Bring my family and the men watching them here."

"You got it, Don Antonio," Frankie said.

The shouting outside continued.

"Open up, or we'll shoot out your windows!"

"Like hell you will," Antonio said. He walked over and grabbed the door handle before anyone could stop him, prepared to show them all exactly what a leader looked like.

"What the hell are you *doing*?" Christopher blurted in Italian.

Leading by example, Antonio thought. If his men were going to follow him into battle, they needed to see he was fearless.

"Why don't we just light these fuckers up, Don Antonio?" Lino asked.

"'Cause I don't want a bloodbath outside. Nor do I want to attract attention to this place. Now, stay here and watch my back."

Stepping outside, he took in a breath of the steamy air. The rain had stopped, but sirens continued to wail. He glanced over his shoulder to see his men shouldering their rifles from behind several windows in the warehouse.

Be smart and be calm, Antonio thought as he walked into the circle driveway.

Six bangers stood along the edge of the concrete. Only two held guns, but of course they were all carrying.

What bothered him most was the guy with the Uzi. He was thin and his movements jerky, which told Antonio he was a junkie or a meth head—not exactly the guy you wanted holding an automatic weapon.

"I said open your garage," said the linebacker.

"And why would I do that?" Antonio said. He stood as tall as he could. "This is private property, and I'm fully prepared to defend it."

The big guy looked at him and then broke out laughing. The other men also chuckled, but then quieted as the leader got out of the truck.

"Where the fuck you from, old man?" said the giant.

"He ain't from 'round here," said the leader. He stepped into view. Dark-skinned, tall and slender, with a salt-and-pepper beard. Unlike his men, he didn't wear a mask—just sunglasses.

"Why haven't I seen you before?" he asked. "I know most everyone worth knowing in this part of

Compton, so that means either you're new or you ain't worth knowing."

A shadow moved over next to Antonio. He could tell by the shape that it was his brother.

"What's the problem here, brother?" Christopher growled.

"I'm *not* your brother. You can call me Mouse." He took off his glasses and squinted at Antonio. "Who do I have the great pleasure of meeting on this fine morning in the hood?"

"Antonio Moretti."

"Ah, so you're a guinea," said Mouse. "I haven't dealt with many of your people, but the ones I've met have heads almost as big as their noses."

Antonio took a calming breath. He wanted to defuse the situation without having to expend any bullets or draw undue attention, but he also wanted to blow this dude's face off.

"I know you got shit in that warehouse," said Mouse. He waved a Glock at the door. "Especially since y'all ready to defend it."

"You aren't listening," Antonio said. "I'm asking nice for you to get off my property."

Mouse frowned and motioned to the big guy, who flexed his pecs and lats and walked over. Christopher stepped up to intervene, drawing the lunk's attention while Antonio pulled out his Beretta M9 and smashed the guy in the temple.

The thug crumpled like a bag of ice, and before any of the other men could aim their weapons, Antonio put a round in the chest of the sketchy guy with the Uzi. Then he aimed the gun at Mouse's head.

"You think you're hard," Antonio said. "But you don't really know what hard is."

Another gunshot cracked, and Mouse took a round between the eyes. He staggered backward and then crumpled to the dirt.

"Shit, shit!" one of his men yelled before he, too, went down from a round to the head. The rest of the bangers took off running as loyal Moretti soldiers moved out into the driveway with their M4s up and ready.

Antonio held up a hand to keep them from firing. Then he called out after the escaping gangbangers.

"Don't fuck with the Morettis, you rat fucks!"

Christopher bent down next to the injured man on the ground. He lay in a fetal position, moaning.

"Don't shoot me," he mumbled.

"What do you want me to do with this prick?" Christopher asked.

Antonio shrugged. "The Morettis are hiring if he wants a job, but he's gonna have to get some new clothes."

The last of the gangbangers rounded the corner and vanished. Antonio lowered his gun and walked over to look at Mouse. The garbage gangster had never dealt with real mafiosi. Soon, the other gang leaders of this city would start hearing stories of the Moretti family.

It was time to bring some class to organized crime in Los Angeles.

* * *

The air-raid sirens gave Dom the chills, but this time the warning wasn't of incoming fighter jets. The fighting in the city had ended almost as quickly as it started, with the navy joining what President Elliot was calling "the rebels."

California had seceded from the union, and Illinois, New York, and Colorado were following close behind.

The United States was crumbling, and it wasn't alone. South America, Europe, and most of Asia had all fallen into anarchy with the global economic collapse. Fighting raged in all corners of the globe.

The apocalypse, it seemed, had finally arrived.

In Los Angeles, the end came with a macabre soundtrack of jet engines, aerial bombs, emergency sirens, air-raid Klaxons, and gunshots.

Dom sat in the back of a Ford Explorer, wedged against the passenger door beside his sister, trying to reassure himself that everything was going to be okay, even though he knew better.

"Come *on*," Marks said, pushing down on the horn.

"There's nowhere to go," Ronaldo said. "Everyone is trying to get out."

Marks looked anxiously in the rearview mirror and then the side mirror. Ronaldo was doing the same thing.

They were wanted men, and Dom was, too, after what happened on the rooftop last night. It was hard to believe that just months ago he was thinking about colleges, taking exams, and preparing for his sixth match in the Octagon. Now he was a refugee trying to escape a postapocalyptic Los Angeles.

He thought of Moose and Camilla, wondering where they were and whether they were safe. God, he missed his friends. He hadn't even had the chance to say goodbye.

Fleeing vehicles crawled ahead, snaking around

cars that had stalled out or run their gas tanks dry. Throngs of people walked along the sidewalks and through front yards, heading out.

Dom watched the chaos, pistol in hand. Several aid workers wearing hazmat suits directed foot and car traffic, but they weren't helping much.

"Dad, are we going to get sick?" Monica asked.

"No, sweetie," Ronaldo replied. "We're going to be just fine."

Dom could tell by the subtle tone in his voice that their dad wasn't telling the whole truth, but part of that was because of the conversation Dom had overheard this morning when he was pretending to sleep in the back seat.

"This could be worse than Phoenix," Marks had whispered. "Anyone within that two-mile radius is going to be cooked from the inside."

"What the hell was AMP doing with radioactive materials?" Ronaldo had said.

Then Elena had stirred awake, interrupting the conversation. Since then, they had been sitting inside the Explorer for the past four hours and had moved only a few miles.

But at least the fighting between the military and AMP had died down. The naval bombardment had done the job, eradicating most of the AMP soldiers in a single stroke.

Dom wasn't afraid of those soldiers at this point. He was afraid of the people who didn't care about the radiation. People who had spent the past month living on the streets, and those living on the streets before the collapse.

Junkies. Meth heads. Wackos.

Dom drew in a deep breath and locked eyes with his dad.

"You good?" Ronaldo asked.

"I'm good."

"You sure?" he said.

"I'll be okay."

Elena reached over Monica and put a hand on Dom's shoulder. "You saved us," she said. "I know this is hard, but don't forget that."

Dom nodded. Killing the two AMP soldiers had left him feeling a deep guilt even though he was protecting his mom and sister. He had known that this moment would come, but now it kept replaying in his mind. Maybe there was another way it could have gone down. The hardest part was thinking of the young soldier he had shot in the thigh. He suffered for several minutes before finally bleeding out.

A fight had broken out in a park to their left, distracting Dom. He turned to watch as four men kicked and stomped a man on the ground. The residents walking on the sidewalk passed right on by as if it were nothing.

"Jesus Christ," Dom whispered. Judging by the scene unfolding all around him, he was going to be faced with violence again. It was just a question of *when*.

He sighed and nudged Monica. "You okay, sis?"

She glanced back at him and nodded. Most girls her age would have screamed and cried their eyes out last night, but she had just shed a few tears and asked her dad for a gun. She was a tough kid, and smart.

They would get through this, as a family.

Dom looked back up at his dad and relaxed a degree, knowing he was going to stay with them.

Traffic inched forward, and a break suddenly allowed an opening. The cars ahead all sped forward, and Marks turned the engine back on.

"Here we go," he said, pushing down on the pedal and giving the engine precious fuel.

They crossed a boulevard lined with palm trees, the fronds rustling in the morning breeze. Smoke drifted across the horizon, fed by dark plumes coming from a location down the block.

Minutes later, Dom saw what was causing it.

The charred building and concrete islands out front were the remains of a gas station—maybe the very one they had seen go up last night.

A half-dozen burned-out cars sat in the parking lot. In one of them sat a blackened corpse, its wrinkled surface the texture of a charred marshmallow.

"There," Marks said, pointing.

Dom followed his finger toward a group of soldiers standing at a roadblock at an intersection to their right. For a second, his heart thumped, but then he saw that the men weren't soldiers.

"Never thought I'd be this happy to see Devil Dogs standing post!" Marks shouted. He pounded the wheel, smiling for the first time all day.

Ronaldo cracked a grin and looked back at Elena, who stared at him with that look—the one that almost always got her what she wanted.

In this moment, it was a silent plea for him to part ways with his best friend.

Marks pulled into the right lane, prompting a driver to lie down on his horn.

"Yeah, yeah, I know, asshole," Marks said. Then he pulled over to the right side of the road and cut into a parking lot. The view gave Dom a better look at the marines holding security at the side street, not allowing any cars into the area. They all wore CBRN suits.

Marks parked the Explorer and heaved a sigh.

"Sure I can't change your mind?" Ronaldo said.

The staff sergeant shook his head. "I've got to find Bettis and Tooth and get the Desert Snakes back in this fight."

"I understand," Ronaldo said. "I wish I was coming with—"

"You got to take care of your family, brother."

Marks kept the engine running and the doors locked. Having a working vehicle made them a target, and Dom again scanned for hostiles as the two old friends said goodbye.

Most of the faces Dom saw were people just like his family: people fleeing the city and trying to get to safety. But he knew there were bad people out there, like those beating the guy in the park, and the ones who had robbed his neighbors.

"Be safe, brother," Marks said. He reached over and shook Ronaldo's hand.

"You too, Zed."

The two men embraced, and Marks twisted around to the back seat.

"Dom, you're a man now. Take good care of your pops and your mom and sister."

Dom shook Marks's hand firmly, the way his father

had taught him when he was a kid. Marks then turned to Elena, exchanged a nod with her, and waved at Monica.

"I'll see you again soon," Marks said. "Be safe out there. I love you all very much."

"We love you too, Zed," Elena said. "Please be careful."

After a brief pause, Marks got out of the Explorer, grabbed his gear from the back, and trotted over to the checkpoint.

"You're TC, Dom," Ronaldo said.

Dom paused, a confused look on his face.

"Take shotgun," Ronaldo explained as he climbed over the console and got behind the wheel.

Dom almost unlocked his door to get out, but as soon as his hand touched the latch, he remembered what his dad had said about security. With a struggle, he clambered into the passenger seat and belted in as Marks joined the other marines outside.

Ronaldo watched, and Dom could tell that he wanted to go with Marks, to fight the AMP soldiers and the gangbangers, but right now his duty was to his family.

"It's going to be okay, you guys," Ronaldo said, putting the Explorer in gear.

"Where are we going, Dad?" Monica asked.

"To Aunt Lydia's in Santa Fe," Elena replied.

Ronaldo exchanged a glance with his wife—just the barest flash of uncertainty, but Dom easily picked up on it. He didn't like the idea of going through Arizona to get to Santa Fe, no matter which way the wind was blowing.

"I'm taking us somewhere safe," Ronaldo said. "I promise."

Monica seemed to relax at his soothing voice, but Dom felt another cold twinge of anxiety. They pulled out onto the street after a driver in a pickup truck waved them ahead.

"There are still some good people," Elena said. "Don't lose sight of that."

The small gesture of goodwill was overshadowed by another fight, in an intersection where a car had stalled. A man was getting his family out of the vehicle when pedestrians started banging on the windows of his car and yelling profanities. Someone knocked him to the ground and kicked him.

"Dad, we should do something," Dom said.

Ronaldo kept his focus on the road, and Dom turned to watch as the car was surrounded. He wanted to believe his dad that everything would be okay, and he wanted to believe his mom about there being good people left in the world, but the sight of the family in need, who could just as easily have been his, told him something else.

11

Wind whipped through the exposed levels of the high-rise parking garage, rippling the black track jacket that Vinny had zipped to his chin. A violent gust came up, knocking his bandanna out of position.

He pulled it back up over his nose, but the thin cotton did nothing to keep out the smoke still drifting across downtown Los Angeles. Plumes rose from a hole in the Staples Center, and Dodger Stadium no longer had an outfield.

The financial district had taken the most damage, the granite cladding of the skyscrapers pocked from high-caliber rounds and missile impacts. The Bank of America Financial Center was no longer standing after AMP bombs turned it into a mound of rubble, rebar, and glass.

The sirens of emergency vehicles wailed through the city.

Dazed and shell-shocked civilians emerged from their loft apartments to view the destruction. Others, finally realizing that it was time to get the hell out of the city, were carrying their belongings as they set off on foot or bicycle.

The fighting between rebel forces and AMP had moved away from downtown, leaving the police and other law-enforcement agencies to restore what order they could.

From what Vinny could see, they weren't making much of a dent.

Christopher snorted at the view. "What a mess."

Vinny knew that his father had seen far worse than this, but seeing it in the American city known for movies and glamour seemed especially shocking.

"Forget the view; we're late," Yellowtail said.

A barrage of gunshots sounded in the distance, and no one even flinched. The sound was common as skirmishes continued between AMP and the rebels, and police and the gangs.

Vinny didn't see any sign of fighting in the empty parking garage.

"Keep sharp," Christopher said to the men guarding their vehicles.

"Don't worry," Vito said in his thick Italian accent as he plucked shells from the bandolier across his wide body and loaded them into his shotgun.

The other nine Moretti soldiers were mostly hired muscle; only one was even Italian. They fanned out to hold security and protect the quarter million in cash, and two bags of gold jewelry in the trunks.

Vinny still couldn't believe that his uncle was doubling down and buying a massive shipment of drugs from their Colombian contact, especially now that their AMP customers were either dead or on the run.

But he trusted that Don Antonio knew what he was doing. He also respected the boss now more than ever after seeing him risk his skin to get to Anaheim, and then confront the gangsters back at the warehouse.

Someday I'll be like that, Vinny thought. *Like my uncle and my dad.*

Christopher opened a door to a concrete stairwell and went inside. Normally, Antonio would have been with them for a meeting of this size, but he was back at the warehouse, resting up with Marco and Lucia.

When this was over, Vinny would join them and they would finally get a chance to celebrate the death of Enzo Sarcone, even if the rest of their plan was starting to go awry.

Vinny heard panting behind him and stopped to see Yellowtail hunched on the landing below, hands on his knees.

"Wait … up," he said between gasps.

"How is someone so strong so out of shape?" Christopher said.

Yellowtail shot him a glare but knew better than to talk back to the underboss. Vinny saw a chance to get a shot in.

"You need to do more cardio," he said. "And you got those peg legs."

Yellowtail was too winded to mount a comeback.

They continued up to the twenty-first floor to look for their Colombian contact, who Christopher referred to simply as "Chuy."

Vinny had never met the drug runner before, and he was excited to finally get a chance to do something else, something bigger, and to prove himself yet again.

It was time to shake the guilt for helping kidnap Carly Sarcone. Her dad had betrayed the Moretti family and may as well have fired the gun that killed Vinny's mom.

Enzo Sarcone was weasel shit and deserved to die.

"Why do they want to meet here?" Yellowtail asked as they continued up the stairs. "I mean, we're in the middle of a fucking war zone."

"The entire city is a war zone," Christopher said. He stopped at the next landing and brushed off his suit.

Vinny did the same thing. Dust and grime from the general destruction had coated them on the way up the stairs.

"Let me do the talking," Christopher said. "We're not just meeting with our friend Chuy; we're meeting with his jefe."

"His boss?" Vinny asked.

Christopher nodded.

"Well, shit, you coulda told me earlier," Yellowtail said. "I would have worn a suit."

"Do you even *own* a suit?" Christopher said.

Yellowtail grinned. "Nah. Hard to find one that fits me."

Christopher shook his head and opened the door to the top level of the parking ramp, letting in a draft of smoky air.

Four men were already waiting outside. All were dressed in sharp suits except for one, a skinny man with a beard and thick eyebrows. The hood of his black sweatshirt whipped in the wind behind his bald head.

Vinny figured that was Chuy and found the boss next. He was the only well-dressed man not holding a submachine gun. The handsome Colombian had a perfectly trimmed beard, black hair parted on the side, and a sharp nose.

"Chrissy, good to see you," said the hooded guy. He walked over, and they exchanged formalities with a kiss to each cheek.

Christopher looked over to the leader, who walked forward.

"Christopher."

The jefe shook his hand. "Javier González," he said in a thick Spanish accent.

Javier fixed Vinny with a piercing gaze that quickly moved to Yellowtail and then back to Christopher.

"I don't want to waste any time," Javier said. "We're here tonight to talk about the future between our two families."

"We have very much appreciated the business we've done together over the past decade in Naples, and now here," Christopher said.

"As have we," Javier said. "My brother likes the Moretti family and regrets not being able to join us tonight."

A sharp grin broke across Javier's bearded face as he looked out over the city. "Due to these unfortunate circumstances, he decided to stay in Colombia, and tomorrow I will be leaving to return home, which I should have done weeks ago."

He pointed at an expensive apartment high-rise a few blocks away, and the smoldering penthouse.

"My condo didn't fare well during the attack."

Now Vinny understood why they had met here. It was close to the boss's stomping grounds.

"We had considered leaving the states too,"

Christopher said, "but Don Antonio—who also regrets not being able to make it—decided Los Angeles is the future for our organization."

Javier turned back to the view of devastation, his brows raised. "There is little future here, *mi amigo.*"

"We believe there is." Christopher remained stone-faced. "In fact, we believe there is opportunity. That's why we have a quarter million in cash, plus a gift to give you tonight, in exchange for more product and a guarantee that it will keep coming."

Javier had a contemplative look in his eyes. The man was clearly intrigued.

"The country is at war, and you want to *buy more*?" he asked. "You might just be loco, my friend."

"That's correct," Christopher said.

Javier shrugged. "I suppose it does not matter what happens to the product after we sell it to you, but I'm afraid our price must go up due to security concerns."

He gestured out toward the city. "You understand that this is a risk to our business, yes?"

"Yes."

"Our price goes up twenty percent for future shipments," Javier said, studying Christopher like a poker player watching an opponent for a tell.

Christopher paused a moment to think before securing the new deal with a shake.

"Good luck to you, *mis amigos*," Javier said.

"Be safe on your journey home," Christopher said.

Javier nodded politely at Vinny and Yellowtail before turning away. He jerked his chin at Chuy, who took his place.

"We'll do the exchange on the fourth floor, okay?" he said.

"Sure," Christopher said.

They took the stairwell back down to the vehicles. The constant aural backdrop of emergency sirens screamed outside as they made their way back down to the level where the Moretti soldiers guarded the vehicles.

This time, Yellowtail led the way, having a much easier time going down than on the way up. When he got to the door, he opened it and staggered back, his body jerking twice before he crashed to the concrete.

Christopher grabbed Vinny by the back of his jacket and yanked him back. It took Vinny a second to realize what was happening, and in that time two more bullets hit Yellowtail in the leg and arm.

A gunshot cracked behind Vinny, making his ear ring. Bullets from his father's gun hit the concrete wall by the door before the shooter could come inside and finish Yellowtail off.

Christopher moved down the stairs, firing again and again. "Vinny!" he yelled.

Vinny snapped out of his trance, pulled his Ruger SR9 out, and moved down the stairs.

"Stay back!" Christopher shouted. He moved to the wall, looked at Yellowtail, then turned and fired off several shots into the parking garage while Vinny moved down despite his father's orders.

Yellowtail was sprawled on his back on the stairs. Blood flowed from a hole in his right leg, and more leaked from his right biceps, A third bullet had grazed his right trapezius, which he gripped with his left hand, groaning in pain.

The cross hanging from his neck was pressed into his chest, just over his heart, with a 9mm bullet lodged in the middle. Flecks of gold leaf had come off around the bullet, showing that the cross was really made of steel.

The cheap, gaudy necklace, the cause for endless ribbing from his fellow soldiers, had saved him for now, but looking at the wounds, Vinny wasn't sure he would make it. Bright arterial blood now spurted from the hole in his right leg.

Vinny pushed down on it, trying to stop the flow while his father fought whoever had ambushed them in the stairwell.

Was it one of their own?

If not, then what had happened to their men?

"Vin," Yellowtail said.

"Don't talk, and don't move, man," Vinny replied.

Gunshots cracked from the garage, and tires screeched. Vinny glanced up as Christopher retreated into the stairwell.

"Get him up," he said. "We gotta move."

"We need to stop this bleeding," Vinny said.

"No time," Christopher said. "Do it in the car."

Vinny bent down and grabbed Yellowtail under the good arm. The man was heavier than he looked. He let out a moan as they pulled him up. Together, Vinny and his father carried him across the open garage toward their two vehicles. It was then that Vinny saw the trunks, both wide open.

Crumpled bodies of Moretti soldiers lay on the concrete, with blood pooling around them. Vinny counted only nine corpses, and none of them was Vito.

A car rounded the corner at the end of the garage,

and he saw the back bumper of a purple Cadillac that he instantly recognized.

Lil-fucking-Snipes.

The boom of a shotgun echoed through the garage, and a loud voice with a sharp Italian accent rang out.

"*Fuck you!*"

Christopher and Vinny helped load Yellowtail into the back of one of the cars, and Vinny jumped in the back. He pulled off his track jacket and ripped his T-shirt to make a tourniquet.

"God *damn* it," Yellowtail muttered, trying to look at his wounds.

"Stop moving," Vinny said.

Christopher finished checking the other men and then jumped in the front seat.

"Are they all gone?" Vinny asked.

"Not all of 'em. Either one got away or one betrayed us."

Christopher peeled away from the scene of carnage, leaving the dead Moretti soldiers in the garage. He squealed around the turn, pulling down a ramp to the next level.

Vinny looked back down at Yellowtail, who gripped his hand tighter.

"Lil Snipes," he grumbled. "That piece o' snake shit."

They tore down the parking lot, wheels screeching.

Another boom of a shotgun sounded.

Yellowtail gripped Vinny's hand harder as they rounded another corner and raced down the ramp to the next level.

"Hang on, bro," he said. "Just—"

Christopher slammed the brakes, knocking Vinny

into the back of the front passenger seat. Yellowtail nearly fell onto the floor.

A burly man ran down the ramp, panting.

"Vito," Christopher said out the window.

"*go!*" Vito yelled back. "*Stop those fuckin' pricks!*"

The race down the parking levels continued. At the bottom, gunshots and the screech of tires echoed through the garage. Then came a crash of metal and glass.

Vinny looked up and saw a car that had been T-boned on the first level and slammed up against a wall by a pickup truck. Two other vehicles were smoking, and a group of men were walking toward them, rifles shouldered.

"Stay with Yellowtail," Christopher said. He put the car in park and grabbed his rifle.

Sirens sounded in the distance, closer than before. The battle may have attracted the attention of the police. Vinny moved back into position. He had already put a tourniquet around Yellowtail's arm and leg, but there wasn't anything he could do to stop the bleeding from his trapezius except to press down.

Yellowtail winced in pain as Vinny clamped his hand over the wound.

Across the garage, men in black fatigues surrounded the two shot-up vehicles and the T-boned purple Cadillac. Lil Snipes was still strapped in the front seat, his head slumped to the side.

Seeing the gangbanger filled Vinny with rage. It wasn't Javier and the González family who had ambushed his men after all—it was the little slime-bag Blood whom Vinny had once considered a friend.

Limbs dripping blood hung out of the open

windows of the other cars, the doors littered with holes, the windows shattered. The scent of gasoline drifted through the garage.

One of the doors creaked open, and a man wearing a red bandanna slumped out. He crawled across the floor, using his elbows, mumbling to himself.

A guy with a bandage on his face approached and emptied a magazine into the man's body.

"Get our shit!" the shooter yelled.

Vinny recognized that voice. It was his uncle.

Don Antonio flashed hand signals and turned toward Vinny. The Moretti reinforcements hurried over to the cars to retrieve their stolen money. All but Raff, who ran over with a pistol in his hand.

"We need a doc!" Vinny said.

When he looked down, Yellowtail had closed his eyes.

Vinny checked his chest. It wasn't moving.

"Let me," said Raff. He set the pistol down and switched positions with Vinny to start mouth-to-mouth.

Vinny staggered away from the car, his hands slick with blood.

"Let's go, everyone!" Christopher shouted.

Vito finally got his considerable bulk down the ramps. Drenched in sweat, he ran with his shotgun past Vinny, but Vinny remained where he was, in shock. The ambush had rattled him, and he found himself momentarily frozen.

"*VIN!*" Christopher yelled.

The shout snapped Vinny out of his daze. He jumped into the four-door pickup with his father and Vito, and they backed away from the purple Cadillac.

Gas leaked out of a hole in the back, forming a puddle on the ground near the deflated rear tire.

Lil Snipes tilted his head toward them. One eyeball bulged grotesquely from the socket.

"Smoke that rat fuck!" Vito yelled.

Antonio walked away from the Cadillac. "Let him suffer," he said.

Lil Snipes turned his working eye at Vinny just as Antonio lit a match and tossed it onto the puddle of spilled gasoline. One final barbaric afterthought to show what happened when you messed with the Morettis.

* * *

A golden sunrise crested the mountains and spread over the line of vehicles creeping north on Highway 395. Ronaldo and his family were in one of them, part of the seemingly infinite caravan trying to reach Oregon.

The spectacular view of craggy mountain peaks rising from the desert sage was one that Ronaldo had seen many times in his life. When he first moved the family to Los Angeles, they had cherished their weekend drives on this highway, heading north, away from the city. But they had never come this far before, and the war raging across the country made the nostalgic sights hard to enjoy.

In a way, it reminded him of how he felt when deployed to Afghanistan, where the terrain was often gorgeous but deceiving. Hidden threats lurked on the open roads just as they had in the mountains.

Ronaldo looked away from the Sierras in the west

and out the passenger window to the east. For the hundredth time, he thought of the row that had turned deadly in the camp outside Phoenix. He wasn't sure where his brothers ended up, or what had happened to Lieutenant Castle, but he had a feeling Marks would find Tooth and Bettis back in Los Angeles.

With a sigh, he focused back on getting his family to safety. Dom was napping in the front passenger seat, and Monica was asleep in the back. But his wife was wide awake and avoiding his glances in the rearview mirror.

She was mad and rightfully so. He had changed the plan of going to her sister's house—the radiation from Palo Verde in Arizona had caused panic and congested the highways. It had been a bad plan from the start, but it got even worse when they set off eastbound and couldn't move much faster than the pedestrians walking on the side of the road. So Ronaldo had turned around and headed north, following the line of least resistance.

After hearing Elliot's radio address, he knew that nowhere in California was safe. The traitor had declared it a rebel state.

Killing President Coleman and framing the Corps for it, ordering the attacks on San Fran and Palo Verde—how could someone be so evil? And how could anyone follow those orders?

Shaking his head, he remembered what he had told Dom on the rooftop back in LA, about history being full of evil men following evil orders.

Ronaldo looked north, toward Oregon, where the seemingly infinite stretch of cars was headed. People like him, trying to get their families out of rebel-controlled territory.

A glance at the fuel gauge made him gulp. They were down to a third of a tank—just enough to get over the state line, assuming that traffic continued at the same pace.

The strategic error of first heading east had cost them over half the gasoline reserves they had stored in the back of the SUV. It was almost all gone now, the last precious gallons already out of the cans and in the tank.

But they were almost there—almost to a safe zone.

The road bent west, and he squinted into the sunset, trying to get a better view. Traffic was slowing again, down to ten miles an hour.

"Son of a bitch," he whispered.

Dom stirred, opened one eye, then shot up, ramrod straight. "What? What's wrong?" he asked.

"Nothing, buddy. We're almost to Oregon."

Dom rubbed his eyes, then grabbed his AR-15.

The instinctive response told Ronaldo his son understood that the world they had lived in was gone. The rules of civilized conduct had changed the moment the Second Civil War started.

"What is that?" Dom said.

Ronaldo pushed down on the brakes as the cars in front of him came to a stop. A FEMA truck had pulled off on the shoulder, cutting through a line of refugees trudging north.

The people on the shoulder next to Dom looked over at the Explorer, their eyes pleading for help. Food. Water. Transportation. These people would gratefully accept anything they could get.

Ronaldo had to look away. He couldn't afford to give anything, and even if he could, stopping would make them a target. He had to think of his family's safety or they would end up on the side of the road as well.

Gunfire shocked him back to hypervigilance.

"Are those gunshots?" Elena said.

Monica looked up.

"Stay down," Ronaldo said.

His wife met his gaze in the rearview mirror for the first time this morning, but it wasn't the rueful gaze he was hoping for. Once again she had a look of terror.

Screaming and shouting broke out along the sides of the road as refugees ran for cover. A woman on the right shoulder, not far from their bumper, fell, and the fleeing crowd trampled her.

"Oh my god," Elena said, putting her hand over her mouth.

Dom went to open the door, but Ronaldo reached over to stop him when he saw the gunmen down the road. Another flurry of shots went off, one of them hitting the windshield.

"Down!" Ronaldo yelled. Keeping low, he looked left to see around the car ahead of him. The oncoming lane looked clear.

Ronaldo pulled out left, then jerked away from a van that seemed to come out of nowhere, nearly clipping him. He kept his cool and drove onto the shoulder, his eyes on the fence and the tall dry grass on the left side of the road. More gunshots sounded.

With nowhere to go except on the grass, Ronaldo decided to take his chances. He drove off the road, knocking down a section of barbed-wire fence. Several other vehicles followed his lead into the open pastureland.

Elena sat up to see what was happening, but Ronaldo

yelled for her to stay down. The SUV handled well, but it was no Humvee, and he drove cautiously while looking for an opportunity to pull back onto the highway.

"It's a robbery," Dom said.

Ronaldo kept his eyes on the grass, looking for rocks or anything else that could blow a tire or break an axle. A moment's lapse in focus could leave him and his family stranded just like the rest of these people.

The pop of gunshots continued, and he darted a glance to the road just as he passed the FEMA truck. He couldn't see much in that fleeting instant, but that bare glimpse made his heart sink.

Several aid workers were on their knees on the side of the road, and the back of the truck was open. Two men wearing black masks stood guard with guns while their accomplices ransacked the back of the truck. More gunmen were going through other vehicles.

Bodies lay on the ground—people who had fought back and paid the price.

Ronaldo caught motion in the side mirror. A blue van full of passengers had blown a tire. It skidded over the field, kicking up a trail of dirt as it came to an abrupt stop.

The other three vehicles moved around it and continued after the Explorer.

"They shot them!" Dom cried. "They fucking *shot* them!"

Ronaldo turned the Explorer toward the shoulder of the highway, jouncing up and down over prairie dog mounds. As he pulled back around the scene of violence, he sneaked another glance and saw that the raiders had executed two of the FEMA workers.

"My God," Ronaldo whispered.

He lay down on the horn as he pulled back onto the highway, forcing his way through the gaps in cars, back to the right lane. A guy driving a Ford F-150 didn't want to let him in, but Ronaldo was in no mood for niceties.

He squeezed past, losing the left mirror on the truck's brush guard. The old guy behind the wheel shouted out the window.

Ronaldo ignored him and pulled into the right lane of traffic, which was now clear. The other vehicles had all moved ahead and were almost out of sight.

With only open road ahead, he pushed the pedal down slowly, careful not to waste gas. The scene of violence grew distant in the rearview mirror, and his heart slowed to a normal rate.

He watched for a moment to make sure they didn't have a tail, before realizing that his wife was also looking in the mirror. But like earlier this morning, she was looking at him, and this time, tears fell from her eyes.

-12-

They neared the state line at dusk. A fiery sunset bled through sky the color of an old bruise. Dom, at the wheel, wondered whether to wake his napping father.

He decided to let him sleep a few more precious minutes. The fuel warning light had just clicked on, but they still had enough to get them across.

He hoped.

"Are we there?" Elena asked.

"Almost," Dom said quietly. "New Pine Creek is about a mile ahead."

The small town sat across the line from Goose Lake, California, which they were currently passing. Dom looked across the highway, past the refugees walking on the shoulder and in the ditches.

On the other side, the vast lake glistened in the last rays of sun.

Monica moved forward from the back seat to look, waking their father. He sat up, yawned, and gestured for her to get back.

"Seat belt, kiddo," he said. "Dom, watch the road."

After a sip of water, Ronaldo grabbed the rifle and leaned to the right for a better view out the cracked windshield. The round had punched through the back seat just a few inches above where his mom and sister had dived for cover. If they hadn't ducked, one of them would likely be dead. But they weren't, and the Salvatore family was almost to safety.

Dom smiled cautiously at the sight of the border. If the rumors were true, the entire state of Oregon was a safe zone, neutral in the war between President Elliot and the rebels. He wasn't sure where his family would go, but anywhere the bombs weren't falling sounded good to him.

"Stay sharp and watch for AMP soldiers," Ronaldo said. He pulled his sleeve over the marine tattoo on his forearm and turned to the back seat. "Remember what our story is?"

Monica nodded. "You're a schoolteacher from Downey High, and Mom is a homemaker."

"What do I teach?" Ronaldo asked.

That got him an eye roll. "Dad, I'm not stupid," Monica said. "In fact, I'm the top in my class."

"I know, sweetie, but it's very important we have the same story if we run into any AMP soldiers," he said. "If they find out I'm a marine …"

"What will happen if they do?" Monica asked.

"Nothing," he said. "We just can't let them find out."

Brake lights came on as traffic ahead slowed.

As the horizon swallowed the sun, the line of cars came to a complete stop. Exhausted refugees on both sides of the highway plodded on, their belongings slung over their shoulders.

Most of these people had likely been traveling for days after fleeing the cities that were attacked: Los Angeles, San Diego, and San Francisco. Many Americans were heading for the borders of Mexico and Canada, hoping for asylum.

Dom thought of his friends still in Los Angeles, especially Moose and Camilla, who were both cops now, fighting against the gangs. Would he ever see them again? With all the violence, chances of them all surviving were slim.

"How long's the gas light been on?" Ronaldo asked.

The urgency in his voice pulled Dom out of his momentary fugue.

"Just came on."

"Do we have enough?" Elena asked.

Monica scooted up to look.

"Sit back, guys," Ronaldo said. "We're going to be fine."

"It doesn't sound like we're going to be fine if we're basically running on fumes," Elena said.

"You heard Dom; it just came on. That's *not* running on fumes. All we have to do is get to the border, and then we can barter for more gas."

"And if we can't find anyone to trade or sell any?" Elena asked.

"Then we walk. This is a safe zone; we will be okay. I promise."

Elena folded her arms across her chest, clearly unconvinced. Seeing his parents fight wasn't unusual, but the tension between them had grown over the past few days.

The car ahead of the Explorer inched forward as the line started moving again.

"See?" Ronaldo said. "We're going to be just fine."

Dom drove into the small town, past old houses and businesses. The crossing was a few blocks in, and he finally got a glimpse of the fence blocking off the border.

"Is that barbed wire?" he asked.

"Go slower," Ronaldo said.

"What?"

"Just do as I say," he snapped.

Dom eased his foot off the accelerator. A moment later, he saw what had his father spooked. A group of armed men stood in front of the gate, checking vehicles and refugees. Dom could tell by their uniforms they weren't police or state troopers.

Then he saw the raven's-head AMP flag behind them, fluttering in the breeze. They weren't marines or army, either ...

AMP soldiers cradling rifles checked the cars ahead, and more stood guard behind a berm of sandbags. The entire roadway had been blocked off with a wall of cars, fencing, and shipping containers.

Behind the barricade, a high stack of concrete blocks separated the refugees from the Oregon side of the border.

Dom spotted another group of AMP soldiers, some of them with German shepherds, patrolling along the edges of the barrier.

"Shit," Ronaldo said quietly.

As they moved slowly forward, Dom saw AMP soldiers on top of the shipping containers, where they had mounted spotlights. The beams clicked on as the last bit of sun dipped below the hills across the lake. Soldiers manning the lights raked them over the road, hitting the refugees on both sides, and the cars waiting to gain entry at the single gate.

A few cars ahead, two soldiers grabbed a man and wrestled him to the ground.

"What's happening?" Elena asked.

Ronaldo put a finger to his lips. He was trying to hear what was going on, but to Dom it was obvious. The state of Oregon was no longer neutral territory, and AMP was in control of the border.

"What should I do?" he asked.

Ronaldo kept staring. "I … don't know. Let me think."

"Those soldiers are everywhere," Dom said.

"I can see that," Ronaldo said. He let out a sigh and cursed under his breath. "You guys go without me. I'll find a way to get through on another crossing."

"*What?* No way," Elena said, pulling against her seat belt. "And if Oregon is now AMP territory, then what?"

"I need you to listen to me," Ronaldo said, glaring at Elena. "I need you to be the strong, smart, protective woman I married and take our kids across the border without me while I find another way in."

"Ronaldo," she said.

"You got the gun?"

"Yeah, but so what? We need you, Ronaldo, and I think we should stay together."

"Mom's right, Dad," Dom said. "Plus, even if we could get somewhere safe in Oregon, how would we find you? And what if you get caught?"

"I don't want you to go, Dad," Monica said.

"If they catch you, they'll kill you," Dom said. "We already know they're looking for you."

Ronaldo seemed to consider the pleas from his family, but the look on his face told Dom he was leaning toward splitting up. They all knew what AMP would do if they captured him, and Dom wouldn't let that happen.

The spotlight hit the car in front of them, and another two soldiers made their way over to check the vehicle.

Before his dad could stop him, Dom put the car back into gear, turned the steering wheel, and pulled into the left lane.

The two AMP soldiers yelled and held up their hands.

"See ya, assholes," Dom said. He pushed down on the pedal, screeching away. "Hold on, everyone!"

"Dom, what are you—" Ronaldo shouted, but Dom cut him off.

"Getting us the hell out of here!"

A gunshot cracked through the night, and Dom checked the rearview mirror to see soldiers aiming rifles at the Explorer.

"Down!" he yelled.

Both Monica and Elena cried out as the back window shattered, glass raining down on the empty gasoline cans.

The southbound lane, heading into California, was wide open. The lights of cars heading north to Oregon glowed like a thirty-mile strand of Christmas lights.

Ronaldo turned with his rifle, but Dom didn't see a Humvee or any other vehicle in pursuit. His mom sat up, pistol in hand, ready to fight.

"Keep your head down," Dom said.

"I'm sick of staying down," she said. "I'll …"

Monica looked up as her mom's words trailed off.

Dom kept his foot on the pedal, heart pounding. They were all at their breaking point, but seeing his mom show strength now helped reassure him they could make it through anything.

"I don't think we're being followed," Ronaldo said. He kept staring out the back window.

Dom drove for twenty minutes at ninety miles an hour, every mile putting them deeper in rebel-controlled territory.

Dom could see smoke on the skyline again. He wasn't sure what city, but it was a reminder they were heading toward the fighting and not away from it.

The engine rattled, then sputtered. They made it another mile before the Explorer coasted to a stop, out of gas.

The refugees walking on the side of the road looked at them, and this time Dom didn't look away. Unless he could barter some gas from someone heading toward the border, his family would soon be joining these desperate people.

* * *

A week and a half after the fighting erupted, over a third of LA's population had fled the violence. Antonio heard that the same was true for other cities in California.

In that time, the Moretti family had taken a beating, losing its main customers after navy cruise missiles destroyed the AMP base at Los Alamitos, and nearly losing their remaining capital in a parking-garage ambush by the Bloods.

But Antonio had known better than to send such a small group of men to so important a meeting. What the gangbangers didn't understand was that *he* had ambushed *them*, not the other way around.

It had cost him almost ten men and nearly taken Yellowtail, but Antonio's younger cousin had proved very hard to kill.

The Moretti family was stronger than ever now that Vito and other relatives had joined them from hiding spots all across the world. Soon, they would be as strong as they once were in Naples.

Moreover, killing Lil Snipes and his posse had netted him street cred that was already riding high after he shot Mouse in the face. Now every gang in the city knew who the Morettis were, and knew better than to fuck with them. Even more importantly, he had proved himself to be the fearless boss who would lead the Morettis into the new age of America.

Everything he had done so far was for their future. Now, having added men to his ranks, weapons to his armory, drugs to his operation, and a new deal with the González family, his plan to expand and rebuild the Moretti empire was coming together.

He would find new customers too, but before that, he had one last thing to do: bring new blood into the Moretti family and reward those who had helped him get this far.

"We're ready for you, Don Antonio," said a voice.

Christopher stood in the doorway of the office, looking sharp in a slick black suit and with a fresh haircut, short around the sides and spiked at the top.

Antonio, also in a dark suit, stood and made sure

the cuffs were straight. Then he walked over to the *Raging Bull* poster and ripped it off the wall. Wadding it up, he tossed it into a can with the bandage he had already removed from his face.

"Why'd you do that?" Christopher asked.

"'Cause I have something better to replace it with," he said. "And I no longer need the reminder about what I have to lose."

Christopher stepped aside as Antonio walked into the hallway. Candlelight flickered from the warehouse at the end of the passage.

Six men, decked out in their finest, stood in the center of the warehouse, eyes on Antonio. They all had their hands crossed over their belts, except for Yellow-tail, who stood with the support of crutches.

He was a lucky man, and he owed part of that luck to his gold-plated cross, which had stopped a bullet meant for his heart.

Behind them, fifty more men sat in chairs, and these were only the most important members of the family. Hundreds more had been added to their growing ranks.

In the center of the room stood a round cher-rywood table. On its polished surface lay a sword, a pistol, and a stack of postcard-size pictures of their family's patron saint, Francis of Assisi.

Candles lit the room, and not just because the grid was down in Compton. It was tradition for the induc-tion ceremony.

Antonio walked toward his most trusted confi-dants. He stopped in front of Vinny first, noting the proud gaze before continuing down the line, scrutiniz-ing them one by one.

Yellowtail. Carmine. Frankie. Lino. Raff.

"You all have sent many Moretti enemies to hell," Antonio said, walking away with his hands clasped behind his back. "You all have proved yourselves in battle."

He turned to look at the men sitting in the chairs. Several were former Sarcone associates who had since sworn loyalty to the Moretti family.

Those that hadn't were on the run or already dead.

"The six men standing before me made the trip from Naples to Los Angeles six years ago, after we spent many years on the run," Antonio continued. "They did so with a great sense of trust in me that I will not forget. Your loyalty since then is also something I won't forget."

He unclasped his hands and raised his right arm, pointing at the boarded-up windows. "While the United States has fallen into chaos and a war rages around us, you have continued to trust me and fight with me."

Antonio moved to the table in the center of the room.

"And soon, you all will see the rewards for that loyalty," he said. "Tonight, however, we are here to give six more of you the honor of aiding in our war."

Christopher walked over and lit a candle. The glow spread over the weapons and the stack of St. Francis pictures. Raff, Frankie, Carmine, Yellowtail, and Lino—already made men—stepped over and joined Christopher, but Vinny remained where he stood, looking confused.

Antonio stopped beside him.

"You've proved yourself to be a man, Vin," Antonio said quietly, "but you still have more to do before you take the oath of silence. Your time will come, but not yet."

Vinny started to open his lips, but he knew better than to reply.

Antonio took the pictures and stepped over to the seated men, then gestured for the six he had decided to make—mostly his cousins and other family who had come over from Italy.

They all stood and joined the men standing in front of the table.

Tradition typically allowed only one or two inductees at a time, but some things had changed since he came to America, and he had decided to do a ceremony for everyone.

Time, for the Moretti family, was of the essence.

The one rule he wasn't bending, however, was *who* he would make. Only true Italian blood could be made.

Over the years, the rules had changed from full-Italian blood to half-Italian blood, but that was as far as he would bend it, even in desperate times like these. Men like Sergeant Rush would never be eligible to join the family. But that didn't mean they couldn't fight.

"Tonight, six men will take the oath of omertà and become members of the Moretti family," Antonio announced. "I had the honor and privilege of taking this oath many years ago with my brother, Christopher, when the Moretti family was run by our uncle, Don Giuseppe."

Antonio made the sign of the cross and looked at the ceiling, thinking of his deceased uncle and his father. Tonight, he honored them and remembered their legacy.

Antonio grabbed the short sword off the table and walked over to the men. Vito, in a suit that was too small, was first in line.

"I'm proud to be with you, Don Antonio," he said. "Don Giuseppe would be very proud of you if he could see you now."

Antonio nodded back at his cousin and handed the sword to his brother. "Hold out your trigger finger."

The Moretti inductees held up their hands, and Christopher pricked their fingers one by one. When he finished, he set the sword back on the table and grabbed a candle. He walked down the line, lighting each picture.

While the pictures burned in the hands of the inductees, Antonio told the men to repeat after him. "As this card burns, may my soul burn in hell if I betray the oath of omertà," he said.

The men repeated the words, the blood-stained pictures burning in their hands as they kept their gaze on their don.

With the oath complete, Antonio gave a rare smile. Pride warmed his veins.

"Welcome to the Moretti family," he said.

There was no clapping or applause, just a palpable silence.

Normally, celebration would follow, but these weren't normal times. Antonio again scrutinized his men, his mind focused on what would come next.

Antonio would give all his orders through his brother. Christopher would serve as the underboss and help with day-to-day operations in growing their business. Carmine would serve as a captain and oversee the new drug operation, including the distribution.

Vito, Lino, Yellowtail, and Frankie would work with Sergeant Rush to eliminate rivals and find new sources of revenue. Raff would be in charge of protecting the women and children, and Vinny and Doberman would continue to help with shipments.

Los Angeles was looking more and more like Naples every day, though the enemies here weren't Italian. They were gangs: Crips, Bloods, Norteño Mafia, and countless others. And now they all knew who the Morettis were.

He motioned for the men still sitting to rise from their chairs. They weren't made Moretti soldiers, but they were still Moretti associates, soldiers in all but name, and they would be the muscle in the war against enemies of the family.

For the first time in his adult life, Antonio had a small army of his own. Enough brave, competent men that he could make a real difference if he deployed them properly. It was time to send them out there and start taking over territory, starting with finding them a nice mansion somewhere in the hills, which Antonio had promised Lucia.

The ash from the pictures of the patron saint curled away and drifted to the floor as Antonio walked away from his men, putting distance between his army and himself.

"The gangs that once ruled Los Angeles are dying," he said confidently, "but the Moretti family has never been stronger in this country. Tonight, before you leave, you will receive new orders that will help get us to our proper place at the top of the food chain."

-13-

There was nowhere to go—nowhere safe, anyway. Not in California.

Almost a week after leaving Los Angeles, Ronaldo's family was out of food and almost out of water. They had lucked into a ride in the back of a rebel army truck that was in between moving supplies and troops from outposts up and down the state.

But eventually, the goodwill ran out. Even the army had to set limits on what it could do for refugees. And so Ronaldo and his family were again walking along the shoulder of Highway 395.

Soon they would turn west toward Mount Baldy, on their way back to where they had started—Los Angeles. It was the only place Ronaldo could think to go. That was where his brothers were, and if he could get back to them, maybe, just maybe, they could find shelter and safety—assuming that Marks, Bettis, and Tooth were even still alive.

The growl of diesel engines pulled him from his thoughts. Ten fuel tankers rumbled down the highway, turning thousands of heads along both sides of the road. With the army no longer giving people rides, the flow of refugees had gone from a steady stream to a flood.

"They must be headed to LA," Dom said.

Ronaldo spotted the army Humvees and two armored M-ATVs following close behind. One of the Humvees sped up to get ahead of the convoy.

Raising his sunglasses for a better look at the soldiers manning the turrets, he wanted to throw a salute up at the beautiful sight. All the old jokes and competition with the other branches seemed stupid in hindsight. To Ronaldo, seeing the army out here was like seeing the Virgin Mary in the flesh. Add in the marines, and it would be the second freaking coming.

Curbing the urge to flag them down, he kept his hands to his sides.

Aside from his family, no one in this group of trekkers knew who he was, and the last thing he needed was for anyone to find out he was a marine.

Some of these people, maybe even half of them, believed that the marines were responsible for everything going to shit, and that made him a target.

It makes your family a target too.

He put his sunglasses back down and looked over at Dom, Elena, and Monica.

An elderly woman stumbled ahead, and a man just as old reached over to steady her. He glanced back at Ronaldo but didn't ask for help. Most people knew there was no help to give.

The filthy, starving, thirsty people were unpredictable, and he couldn't trust a damn one of them. That was why he kept Monica and Elena near the far-right side of the road, where the asphalt gave way to cracked earth. It was also why he and Dom carried their backpacks against their chests and why they had put some of the jewelry in their socks.

Elena could hold her own, especially with her pistol. Even without it, she would claw out eyes and bite off ears if it meant saving her kids, but she was still a target, and so was Monica. Women, and especially children, were marks for the predators out here, and predators there were—men who had little to fear from the law.

The only law on this road was the eight hollow-point rounds loaded in the Sig Sauer 1911 Nightmare holstered between Ronaldo's belly and his backpack. He also had a Glock holstered at his side, under his shirttail. Dom carried a pistol, but they had bartered the shotgun and the M4 for extra water and some freeze-dried meals.

Ronaldo was regretting that decision, especially right now. The service rifle would have come in handy, but as long as he had one gun and ammo, he could put up a hell of a fight.

Gusting wind beat against them, carrying the bouquet of perspiration and piss as the throng slogged ahead. Sporadic shouting and coughing filled the late afternoon as fights broke out between exhausted people.

Ronaldo focused his mind as he had learned to do when dog tired in combat zones. This was bad, but nothing he hadn't been through before.

A memory from after the fall of Baghdad, when refugees were escaping the violence, surfaced in his mind. He had watched from the relative safety of his Humvee on the highway out of the city as thousands upon thousands of civilians made the long trek through the desert.

But he had never thought he would see this in America, let alone be part of it.

He couldn't let the dread and darkness seep in. He had to keep strong for his family.

A dust devil forced him to pull his bandanna up over his mouth. The stinging vortex whipped over the road, swirling under a scorching sun. He mopped the gritty sweat from his brow with his sleeve.

"Daddy, I'm thirsty," Monica said.

Dom pulled the water bottle out of the backpack on his chest. Just as he went to give their last bit of water to his little sister, a middle-aged man with a comb-over blowing like a loose shingle in the wind snatched the bottle.

"Hey!" Dom shouted.

Ronaldo grabbed the guy by the back of his shirt as he brought the bottle to his lips and sucked some down.

Dom grabbed the bottle back, and Ronaldo spun the man around and punched him in the nose. He fell to the ground and scooted on his back, clutching his nose with one hand and holding the other up to ward off any further blows.

"I'm sorry! I'm sorry!" he shouted.

Ronaldo started to hit the man again but hesitated. He could feel the gaze of dozens of people curious to see what he would do with the thief.

"Get the hell out of here," Dom said, kicking the guy in the backside as he stood up.

He let the man take off running into the crowd, which pushed on as if nothing had happened.

The thief got off lucky. Earlier in the day, they had seen a man get shot in the stomach for stealing a granola bar.

Dom handed the bottle to Monica, and she wiped off the rim before taking a drink.

"Gross," she said. After she finished, she handed it to Elena, who also took a drink. Dom shook his head when it was his turn, and Ronaldo decided to save the rest.

A quick shake told him they were down to half a liter. They would die of dehydration if they couldn't get more.

"We need more water," he said to Dom.

Dom nodded. "I'll go up ahead and see if I can barter for any. What do you want me to trade?"

Ronaldo looked at Elena. The last of their cash had gone for gas on the way out of the city. They were down to her most expensive gold and diamond jewelry, his silver watch, and the thousand dollars in silver coins he kept in his bug-out bag. They also had their pistols and ammunition, which were almost as valuable, but those weren't for trade.

Yet.

Aside from these things, they had a small supply of food—mostly just the shit-tasting energy bars Dom had hoarded before the collapse, to fuel his body while training. They tasted like cardboard, but they were far more nutritious than the candy bars that others had to make do with. Most of these people hadn't eaten in days.

A low rumble began, and Ronaldo froze as it grew in pitch and volume. He knew that screaming roar.

"What?" Elena asked.

"Listen," he replied, scanning the sky.

Another memory surfaced in his mind: of fleeing civilians torched in a bombing raid. The roar of
the fighter jets brought back the images of blackened
bodies. Two F-35s appeared from over the barren peaks
of the Tehachapi range, headed right for the highway.

"Run!" Ronaldo yelled, grabbing Monica and
scooping her up.

Dom yanked on Elena's shirt. "Mom, let's go!" he
shouted.

They ran into the ditch and set off across the field
while the other civilians stared after them as if they
were crazy.

"RUN!" Ronaldo screamed. Although the F-35s
were made for the marines, AMP had ended up with
them before the start of the war, and he wasn't taking
any chances.

This was war, and in most modern wars, more civilians than soldiers died.

Ronaldo and his family had made it a few hundred feet from the freeway when the jets fired their first
salvo of missiles. There was no time to find cover, and
no cover to be found.

He dropped and shielded Monica with his body.
Dom did the same with his mother, covering her body
with his own on the ground.

"Stay down!" Ronaldo shouted.

The explosions shook the air and the ground beneath
them. Ronaldo kept his body pressed against Monica's,
trying to hear above the fighter jets and the ordnance they
were unleashing on the civilians. She squirmed under his
body, and he thought he heard her cry out, but he couldn't
hear much over the missile blasts.

"Hold on," he said. "Just hold on, Mon."

To his surprise, no tsunami of fire came to turn him and his family into skeletons of ash.

In fact, he didn't feel anything at all aside from the dirt and the child's body beneath him.

Ronaldo loosened his grip on Monica and looked to the west. The fighters were coming back for a second run. A cloud of smoke rose in the distance, maybe ten miles away.

It struck him then that the target was the convoy of army vehicles and the gasoline tankers they were protecting. The civilians were just collateral damage—insignificant to the AMP command, and potential hostiles.

Ronaldo slowly rose to his feet. As a marine, he was a hostile in the enemy's eyes, and his presence had put his family and all these people at risk.

One of the AMP fighters peeled away, heading back the way it had come. The other pilot performed a 360-degree turn.

"Oh, shit," he whispered.

Crouching back down, he watched in horror as the fighter jet lined up with the strip of asphalt. In seconds, it was lowering toward the refugees several miles down the road.

Something fell from a wing, and again Ronaldo threw his body over Monica.

The terrifying sound that followed was a chorus of human screams, eclipsed by an explosion that Ronaldo felt immediately. The air warmed to a scorching level, stinging his back.

The fighter jet roared overhead, and he forced himself up, grabbing Monica.

"Come on!" he yelled. At least, that was what he tried to say, but the ringing in his ears overwhelmed all else.

Dom pushed himself up, blood dripping down his face.

"Let's go!" Ronaldo shouted. He picked Monica up and herded his family across the dry open ground, away from the road, away from the fighter jet. They had to get more distance before it returned.

"Don't look back," he said in Monica's ear.

She either didn't hear him or couldn't resist a backward glance. Ronaldo twisted to look at the same moment.

The scene of devastation stretched along the road, where a bomb had blown out a massive hunk of highway and killed hundreds of people. Smoldering bodies, some of them still moving, were sprawled in a wide arc around the edge of the crater.

The sight was worse than what he remembered from Iraq. Blackened pieces of humans lay strewn about, seeping blood into the cracked earth. The blustery wind carried the scent of burned hair and flesh.

Ronaldo forced his gaze away, blinking at the sting of sweat in his eyes. As he ran and looked for the fighter jets, he realized it wasn't just sweat. Tears flowed down his face.

He was no stranger to atrocities, but this was the most tragic thing he had ever witnessed, and for the first time in as long as he could remember, he sobbed like a child while holding his own child.

How could those pilots kill so many innocent people? Their own fellow Americans!

The F-35s screamed across the horizon—cowards

leaving without ever seeing the aftermath of their callous inhumanity. The rumble gave way to a scream, and it took him a moment to realize it was his own voice, cursing the mass murderers at the top of his lungs.

There was no coming back from this.

The country he had fought for, bled for, and seen his brothers die for was gone.

* * *

The fighting continued in Los Angeles. The rebel forces had taken control of every AMP base in central LA and pushed the AMP soldiers east into Anaheim. At the Capitol Building in Sacramento, Governor McGehee had officially declared sovereignty. California was no longer part of the United States of America.

Oregon had tried to do the same thing, but AMP had easily taken over the rebel forces there and was now preparing to move south.

Antonio sat at the dinner table with his wife and son, listening to the radio while they ate spaghetti in red sauce from the expansive pantry of their new house. Raff, shotgun in hand, stood by a window, looking out over the property, despite Lucia's several attempts to get him to sit and eat with them.

The mansion in Bel Air had belonged to a Sarcone captain they killed when he refused to swear allegiance to the Moretti banner. This wasn't the compound Antonio dreamed of, but it was a start.

The most satisfying part of everything he had achieved wasn't the cars, houses, or riches—it was the fact that Enzo and his men were dead.

Antonio took a bite of spaghetti, savoring it and his success. But other problems had arisen.

He drowned out the news, thinking instead about what Christopher had told him an hour ago: that they were having a hard time moving the product from their Colombian friends. With AMP gone, Antonio had to find new customers.

The problem wasn't lower demand—drugs would always be a hot commodity, and people could pay with jewelry and other bartered items. The problem was how to move the product safely. The streets were more dangerous than ever, and while the police were barely a concern, the threat from rival distributors and even average citizens had never been higher.

He needed more foot soldiers if he wanted to compete in a postapocalyptic Los Angeles.

"What do you think?" Lucia asked.

Antonio took another bite of spaghetti. "*Delizioso*," he said. "I've missed your cooking."

"You sure you don't want some, Raff?" Lucia asked.

"Yeah, come sit with us," Marco pleaded.

Raff hesitated until Antonio spoke up. "Have a seat, old friend," he said.

Raff, who wasn't much older than Antonio, walked over and sat down while Lucia made him a plate.

"Thank you," he said.

Candlelight flickered over the granite countertops in the chef's kitchen as they ate. The grid was still down in most of the city, but they had a backup generator to power a few essentials in the house, including the stove and fridge. The small luxury had really helped bring his wife out of her melancholy funk.

Lucia enjoyed a glass of pinot noir from the wine cellar. As much as Antonio wanted to try the aged bottle, he had opted not to drink tonight, not even a single glass. He had business to attend to after dinner and needed to be sharp.

"When do I get to hang out with my friends again?" Marco asked.

"Soon, my love," Lucia replied.

"I miss the guys," Marco mumbled. "We were going to have a big-ass party for my birthday. Now I'm being held hostage in this place."

Antonio watched his son pick at the noodles.

"Eat," he said.

Marco glanced up, a strand of brown hair falling over his dark eyes. He brushed it back and shook his head. "I'm not hungry."

"I don't care if you're hungry," Antonio replied. "I said eat."

Marco dropped his fork and crossed his arms over his chest. "How come Vinny gets to do all the cool shit but I have to sit in this prison?"

Ah, so it was jealousy that had him acting like a little *asino*.

"Because you're not a man yet," he said. "When you're a man, you can take a bigger role in this family. Until then, you do as I say. And mind your language at the table."

Marco scowled and looked down at his plate but still didn't obey the order. That seemed to make Raff nervous, and he fidgeted in his chair.

"Do you know how many people are starving out there tonight?" Lucia said, pointing toward a glass window with a view of the hills. "Do you know how many people would kill for what you have in front of you?"

Marco finally started eating.

The conversation gave Antonio an idea ... No. An epiphany.

For the next fifteen minutes, they ate and listened to a radio report from a news station in Sacramento while Antonio considered his new idea for their product.

"Governor McGehee has declared the border of California completely sealed off as secession plans are finalized," said the calm female reporter. *"All AMP soldiers have been ordered to lay down their weapons and surrender."*

Antonio finished his dinner and took the plate over to the sink. Then he walked over to his wife and kissed her on the cheek.

"Thank you for a wonderful dinner," he said.

She nodded and took another sip of wine, watching Marco across the table.

"I'll be home in a few hours," Antonio said. "There's something I need to check out."

Raff nodded at him, but they didn't exchange any words. The man knew his role was to stay here with Lucia and Marco.

Antonio left the kitchen and walked to his study on the second floor. The dead Sarcone captain had good taste, Antonio would give him that.

He had always wanted an office like this, with built-in bookshelves. The rich mahogany desk and a Persian rug pulled it all together. The large glass display case of ancient weapons was his favorite part, but he didn't linger to look at the knives and swords mounted inside.

Instead, he opened a gun safe and grabbed his

Glock and two extra magazines. Then he walked down the staircase to the first floor. Marble tiles, crystal chandeliers, and statues tucked in the corners of the entryway were just some of the rich furnishings here. It was a huge upgrade from the house they had abandoned in Anaheim.

And this was just the start—a place to hang his hat while his empire grew. Soon, he would have a compound to run his operations from.

He walked out to the circular driveway. In the center was a dry stone fountain rimmed by dying green hedges that hadn't been watered for months. The garage held a Ferrari and a BMW M8, but Antonio hadn't driven either car. Both would be targets the moment they drove off the guarded property.

"Don Antonio," said one of several soldiers standing sentry.

He nodded back as he made his way out toward his ride.

Six more Moretti men, commanded by Sergeant Rush, stood outside an Escalade. Rush had traded his camo fatigues for a suit and no longer wore a helmet. With all locally based AMP soldiers on the run or dead, he had officially become a Moretti associate. He even sported the slicked-back hairstyle that so many of the Moretti men wore.

The old Mercedes Christopher drove was parked in front of the Escalade. He leaned against the other side of the car, facing the street and smoking a cigar. Lino and Vinny stood beside him, also enjoying newly acquired cigarettes from a raid a few days ago.

Yellowtail, still on crutches, braced his injured

body against the Mercedes. He was the second-toughest bastard Antonio had ever met, with his brother Christopher holding the title.

It must be a Moretti thing.

Clouds of smoke rose toward the orange sky as the men exhaled. Antonio hated that smell and the way it clung like moss to his clothing, the way it got in his hair. But most of all, it reminded him of his time in the Italian army, and the things he had done as a soldier—the horrible things he did in war.

For some reason, war seemed to follow him everywhere he went. He couldn't escape bloodshed.

"Mount up," Antonio said.

Christopher turned away from the street view.

"Where we headed?" Yellowtail asked. "It's gonna be curfew soon."

"We're not going far, but I want an escort," Antonio said.

Christopher snapped his fingers at Rush, who in turn gestured for his team to get inside the Escalade.

Lino opened the door of the old Mercedes warhorse that Christopher would never give up, but Antonio looked back at the garage and the M8 sitting inside. He had always heard that a Mercedes drove itself, but a BMW—now, *there* was a driving experience.

"On second thought, let's take out the M8," he said. "Back it up, but I'll drive."

Christopher and Lino exchanged a glance.

"Did you hear what I said?" Antonio asked.

Christopher ran over to the garage and backed out the BMW. The turbocharged V-8 engine grumbled down the drive, attracting attention from the house.

"Dad, I want to go!"

Back on the front stoop, Marco stood with his hands in his pockets. Lucia walked out holding her second glass of wine. Normally, Antonio would have told his son to get back inside, but seeing how ungrateful he had been at dinner, maybe what he needed was a good shock.

"Hurry up, then," Antonio said.

Marco hesitated, as if unsure whether his dad was kidding.

"Move it."

Marco bounded down the stairs and bolted across the parking lot. He got in the back seat, and Lino slid in beside him while Christopher took shotgun.

"Don't worry," Antonio said to Lucia as she walked over. "We won't be gone long, and we aren't going far."

"Okay, I love you," she replied.

"Love you too, *amore*."

Two guards opened the gate, and Antonio drove away from the estate. The Escalade followed them out onto the empty street, and they set off down the windy back roads of the Santa Monica foothills.

He gunned the engine down an open stretch, feeling the power of the machine. He needed a few moments of thrill, but he remained vigilant, scanning the road for vehicles or threats.

The fragrance of jasmine drifted through the slightly open windows, filling the car with the scent of money that the millionaires who had lived here smelled every day.

Soon he would smell more smoke from the fires burning in Los Angeles—fires that the already strained fire department couldn't put out.

The view of downtown crested the horizon. The skyscrapers bore fresh scars from missiles and gunfire. Hollywood, hub of the world's entertainment industry, had changed drastically. Entire neighborhoods had burned to their foundations, leaving hundreds of thousands homeless.

Christopher looked over. "You really like to keep me in suspense, don't you?"

"Yeah, Dad, where are we going?" Marco asked.

"You'll see in about a minute."

Antonio took the next corner and turned off on the scenic overlook that provided a great view of UCLA.

"Here we are," Antonio said. He got out of the car and motioned for Marco to follow him to the railing. The boy hurried over, excited to be out of the house.

Antonio wasn't an emotional man, nor was he very affectionate, but tonight he put one arm around his son's shoulders and pointed at the yellow fields of the Bel-Air Country Club, UCLA's Pauley Pavilion, the VA grounds, and several other locations taken over by a sea of tents.

"You see this, Marco?"

"Are those tents?"

Antonio nodded. "Refugee camps like those are popping up all over the city."

Christopher walked over, his muscular arms across his chest.

"That's how a lot of Americans are living right now," Antonio said.

Marco clenched his jaw and narrowed his brow but didn't say a word.

"The people down there are lucky if they go to bed with food in their belly tonight," Antonio said.

Marco continued to stare in silence. He wasn't quite twelve, but he was old enough to understand. He just needed to see things firsthand, which was precisely why Antonio had brought his son here.

"If you go east, you'll see camps full of people dying from radiation poisoning," he said. "Do you know what that is?"

Marco hesitated. "I think so."

Antonio turned at the sound of an engine. A car sped toward the scenic turnoff. Rush and several of his men took up position, rifles at the ready, and Antonio moved with Marco out of view.

The vehicle passed on by without slowing.

"Time to go home," Antonio said. "I'll meet you in the car, Marco."

Marco walked over and got into the back while Christopher stepped over to talk to Antonio.

"So, why are we here?" he asked.

Antonio jerked his chin at the refugee camps.

"You're looking at our new selling ground," he said. "I want you to find us a way inside those fences. Pay off the guards, the cops; do whatever you have to do—I want access to *every* camp in the city to start moving our product."

-14-

The pain paralyzed Dom. He lay in his sleeping bag half awake, half in the grips of a nightmare. Every nerve fiber seemed to scream from the heat.

Wake up, he thought. This was just a dream. A night terror.

Right?

The view of the highway seemed so *real*, as real as the apricot sky and the two black dots cutting through it.

Dom looked down at the flames climbing up his body, then saw the little boy stumbling away from the human debris field. He seemed real too, and so did the stump where his arm had been.

The child raised the charred drumstick at Dom and then fell to the dirt.

Again he heard the shriek of jet engines coming fast and low. The AMP pilots were coming in for another run.

"Dad, we have to help him!" Dom shouted. "We have to go help him!"

"Run!" Ronaldo yelled back. "Keep running and don't stop!"

Dom tried to run, but his legs melted away like butter. He watched as his family was consumed by a wall of fire.

"Dom!"

The voice finally jerked him out of the nightmare. He patted his chest as he sucked air, and he felt his sweat-drenched shirt but no fire. An infinite expanse of black velvet strewn with diamonds greeted him as he sat up.

"It's okay," Ronaldo said, putting a hand on Dom's shoulder. "But you need to get up."

"What's going on?"

"You were having a nightmare," Ronaldo said. "You were screaming."

Dom was still having a hard time hearing after the attack on the highway. His right ear likely had a ruptured eardrum, which explained the bleeding. The ringing hadn't stopped since the attack, but the mild burns on his exposed skin didn't hurt as bad as before, thanks to the ointment his mom had brought along.

Medicine was one thing they hadn't run out of. But it didn't do any good if you were out of water and food.

"Dom, you okay?" Ronaldo asked.

He nodded and looked at his sister and mom. They were awake and quietly packing their belongings in the moonlight.

The camp where they had spent the night was tucked under a rock overhang in a remote area on Mount Baldy. Away from refugees, away from violence.

That was supposed to be the plan, but something was definitely going on.

Dom waited a second for his brain to catch up, recalling the nightmare as he blinked.

Not a nightmare, he thought.

Nightmares weren't real, and what had happened on the highway was all too real. The boy with a missing arm was real. So were the thousands of people they had to abandon back there.

The scene would be forever seared in his memory.

"Is your gun loaded?" Ronaldo asked.

Dom nodded. "Of course."

"Good. Stay here with your mom and sister. I'll be back in a few minutes."

"What?" Dom said. "Where are you going?"

"To check things out. I think I heard voices, and I'm worried it's someone who heard you scream. I'll be right back, but be ready to move."

Dom rolled up his sleeping bag and stuffed his gear inside his backpack. Then he grabbed his pistol and moved over to his sister and mom. They crouched under the overhang, shadowed from the moon.

"Did you hear anything?" Dom asked.

Elena shook her head.

"Mom, I'm scared," Monica said. She nuzzled her head against their mom's chest.

"Everything will be fine," Dom said.

All he could do was try to reassure his kid sister that everything would be okay. The same thing he had been doing since they had to abandon their car at the Oregon border. She had been strong up to that point, but seeing the violence and the desperation of the refugees had broken her down. It had beaten them all down. The attack by the fighter jets had shattered what strength she had left.

Dom was hanging on by a thread, and he could tell that his father and mother were too, especially Elena. Fear and exhaustion had worn them all down.

But Dom didn't have the luxury of giving in to it right now. His father was patrolling because he had screamed in his sleep.

You couldn't help that, Dom thought. But guilt set in anyway. He had to keep strong and calm, especially right now, while he was responsible for his mom and sister. It would be his fault if anyone dangerous found his family.

He checked the left side of the overhang, where he was sleeping only minutes ago. The slope descended a couple of hundred feet—far too steep for anyone to sneak up from that direction, especially in darkness.

Seeing that it was clear, he hunched down and walked past his mom and sister to the other side of the overhang, his tennis shoes crushing a bed of dry pine needles. He flinched, expecting a crunching sound, but he still couldn't hear much of anything—his own noise or anyone else's—and this put him at a serious disadvantage.

His dad had gone down the hill to check the ravine below. That still left the approach from above the overhang. It wasn't a great position to defend, but they had picked it because it concealed all four of them from above and below.

Glancing over his shoulder, he held up a fist for Elena and Monica to stay put. Then he moved around the side to check the forest cresting the hill.

The moonlight faded as a cloud passed overhead, and he waited three or four minutes before it emerged. A carpet of white streamed through the canopy above him.

He aimed his pistol, straining to see human movement.

On the journey back to Los Angeles, his father had taught him how to look for hostiles in a situation just like this. "*Create a two-dimensional canvas and divide the terrain horizontally into thirds*," Ronaldo had said.

Dom scanned the canvas from left to right, right to left.

Limbs moved in the breeze, leaves rustling, oak branches beckoning like ghostly fingers. Shadows moved between the bases as he moved his gun from tree to tree.

Then came a muffled cry.

Dom turned, but too late. A blow to the head knocked him to the ground. His damaged hearing had allowed someone to blindside him. But he was used to taking plenty of abuse during his MMA fights, and he pushed himself back up.

The next blow knocked him facedown. He tasted dirt and blood.

Get up, Dom. You gotta get up!

A boot pushed down on his neck, and he felt cold metal touch the base of his skull—a rifle muzzle.

Pushed against the ground, one eye closed, he had only a side view of Monica and his mom. Two men had them cornered, and a third was rifling through their belongings.

Dom thought about yelling, but his first scream had already attracted the attention of these men. Any more would likely just get him killed.

He said, "Take whatever you want. Just leave us alone."

"Oh, we're taking whatever we want, all right," said the guy going through their bags. He pulled out a smaller bag and shook it. Something small, probably lipstick or a compact, fell out.

"Where's your jewelry?" he said, tossing the bag down onto the dry leaf litter. "I know you got it somewhere. It in your bra?" The man grabbed his mom's shirt and yanked.

"Don't touch me!" she shouted, pawing at the guy.

Dom fought to get up, but every time he squirmed, the boot pressed harder on his neck.

"Stop fidgeting, boy, or I'll put a—"

Dom suddenly felt the weight lift off his back, and the gun barrel move away from his head. He turned to see a burly man wearing what looked like a dark neckerchief or bib below his chin. It dripped onto the pine needles, and Dom could see that the "bib" was actually blood pouring from the man's throat.

In the glow of moonlight, Dom saw his father gently lower the dead man to the ground.

By the time the other three guys knew what was happening, Ronaldo had shot one of them in the chest. The guy who had grabbed Elena went down with a shot to the abdomen.

Elena and Monica tried to move away, but the third guy grabbed Monica and put a knife to her neck.

Ronaldo strode forward, his pistol aimed at the man.

"Drop the knife and I won't kill you," he said calmly, almost mechanically.

"Go fuck yourself," the guy said. "You drop *your* gun or I stick this little bitch."

Dom picked up the rifle and aimed it at the guy gripping his stomach—the guy who had ripped his mother's shirt. His wails were loud enough to penetrate the ringing in Dom's ears.

"I'm going to count to three," Ronaldo said. "Drop the knife and let my daughter go, or you're going to die."

The man glanced at the rifle Dom held.

"Let my sister go," Dom said.

"Back up," the guy murmured.

"Please," Elena begged, holding up her hands. "Please don't hurt my baby."

"You don't have to die," Ronaldo said. "Just let the girl go, and you get to walk out of here."

The man finally came to his senses and let go of Monica. She ran over to Elena, and Ronaldo put two bullets in his chest. The man staggered, his lungs crackling with fluid before he slumped to the dirt.

Monica screamed in horror, and Elena pulled her close to block her view. While she shielded her daughter, Elena watched with apparent grim satisfaction as the man died.

"Let's go," Ronaldo said. "There are more of them out here hunting."

A few minutes later, the family had their gear packed, and Ronaldo had Dom take them around the overhang. Dom knew why.

The guy his father had shot in the gut was still alive—barely, but they couldn't leave him behind if there was a chance he could get back up. Not to mention that he had touched Elena in a way that Ronaldo would never forgive.

Dom held guard and tried to listen, but the ringing

in his ears was too loud. So he scanned the hills for movement.

When his father returned, his shirt was spattered with blood, and his features were void of emotion. His hero dad had done what he was trained to do—and saved them all. Now Dom better understood why Ronaldo had stayed with them rather than go to fight with Marks, Tooth, and Bettis.

"Sometimes, you have to use evil to fight evil," he said, sheathing the blade on his belt. He put a hand on Dom's cheek and said, "Don't forget that, son."

Still in partial shock, Dom set off with his family. They hiked through the early morning hours, moving quietly through the forest.

At dawn, traversing one of the foothills, they got their first view of the rebel-controlled City of Angels. Smoke drifted away from hundreds of fires across the vast metropolis. The strobes of emergency vehicles flashed from every direction as fire and ambulance crews raced around the dying city.

Humvees and armored half-tracks blocked off intersections at military checkpoints. Dom even spotted several tanks moving slowly in the distance. But more than anything, he noticed the long, dense column of ants moving down the interstate below them—tens of thousands of refugees inching along, heading back into the city.

"Welcome home," Ronaldo said.

* * *

The breeze smelled like trash, which didn't help Vinny's mood any. He was still angry about not being made with the other men, but bitching about it would only delay the process further.

The sour stink of rotting garbage with a potent tinge of ammonia was rank, all right, but at the same time nostalgic of the slums in Naples.

As a kid, he would cut through the alleyways to get to school on time. Seeing the junkies living under tarps had always motivated him to study hard, not screw around, and above all, to not mess with the hard drugs.

Los Angeles, with all its junkies, homeless people, and now refugees, was looking more like the slums of Naples by the day. It felt especially weird to drive through Bel Air smelling piss, sewage, and trash. The affluent community had turned into a refugee camp.

Thousands of heavy-duty tents stood on the yellow grass of the Bel-Air Country Club. Hundreds more were set up inside the basketball arena. A sprawling tent city stretched across the campus and into the surrounding areas.

Vinny studied the perimeter as Doberman drove around the barbed-wire enclosures. Across Los Angeles, Moretti soldiers were heading to other camps, to case them and figure out how best to move their business inside.

In an hour, when the sun went down, the soldiers would move in and lay claim to the territory. The very future of the Moretti family depended on these camps.

"This is going to be harder than my uncle thinks," Vinny groaned.

"No shit," said Doberman. He took a right down the next road, driving past the Los Angeles National Military Cemetery. Vinny couldn't help wondering whether the city would start burying the civilian dead in this sacred place, now that every other cemetery in the city was running out of space.

Doberman accelerated to catch up with the twenty-year-old gray Cadillac ahead of them.

"Fuckin' Frankie's got that lead foot," Doberman muttered. "Not a great idea with all the cops out here."

"I don't think the cops are worried about speeders these days."

"Well, he's burning gas," Doberman said. "And he's an asshole."

They drove around the perimeter of the camp once more before the Cadillac pulled off into a parking lot. Several ransacked vehicles were propped up on cinder blocks, their windows broken and tires stolen.

The last bit of sunlight vanished on the horizon, and industrial lights powered by generators clicked on at the UCLA stadium. Several other lights came to life across the camp.

"Go time," Doberman said.

They got out as Frankie and Carmine finished pulling their bags from the Cadillac. Carmine wore a camel-colored coat, torn jeans, and a Dodgers baseball cap. Frankie was dressed in filthy civilian garb that would help the old-school gangster blend in with the masses.

"Plans've changed," Frankie said. "We'll park here and head in on foot."

"I make Captain, and I end up looking like a fucking bum," Carmine groaned.

"Is it safe to leave our vehicles?" Doberman asked. "Someone's at least gonna try and siphon the gas."

"That's why we came with only enough gas to get here and home," Frankie replied.

"You dumb-ass kids got a lot to learn," Carmine said with the wag of his head. "Don't forget, we come from a time when empires were built without cell phones."

Yeah, and people still got around on donkeys, Vinny wanted to say, but he bit his tongue. Talking back would only piss off the older guys. It didn't matter that Christopher was his dad. If he showed a lack of respect, they could slap him around, or worse.

"Let's go, numb nuts," Carmine said to Doberman. He glanced at Vinny.

"Don't look at Vin," Carmine said. "Get going." He pushed Doberman toward the street, and they set off across the parking lot on the west side of the campus.

"Tonight, we're going inside to see how things work," Frankie said. "If anyone asks, Carmine and I are your uncles, and we're all from San Fran."

Carmine chuckled and glanced at Doberman. "No way in hell I'd be related to this birdbrain."

"A bird's smarter than a slug," Doberman said under his breath.

Carmine stopped on the sidewalk at the edge of the parking lot, tilting his head. "What'd you say, you little shit fuck?"

"Come on, guys, let's just get this shit over with so we can get home at a decent time," Vinny said, stepping between them. He looked at Carmine's saggy, scarred features. "Slug" was a pretty good description.

"Vin's right," Frankie said. "Let's do it. I want to get home before the sun comes up."

Doberman walked away, and Carmine spat on the ground, narrowly missing the younger man's pants. Together, the group crossed the street, toward a line of refugees.

A week earlier, when the fighting still raged throughout the city, the line had been thousands long. It was shorter now, though still long, and it slogged forward, inch by inch.

Vinny saw people from other cities, and Angelinos who had lost their homes in the bombardments and the fires that followed. Even the rich had abandoned their mansions for clean water and food now that most of them had used up their supplies. The camps were supposed to be safe zones, areas off limits to AMP bombs or Navy missiles.

Several sheriff's deputies, wearing brown fatigues and bulletproof vests and armed with automatic rifles, worked the gated entrance ahead. Cops and a group of rebel soldiers were also standing guard, talking to one another as the deputies processed refugees.

Vinny pulled the bandanna up around his face when they got into line. The people here smelled even worse than the streets. Most of them were filthy from traveling long distances, but some wore designer clothes and carried designer bags full of their belongings, which suggested they were Bel Air locals.

As the line crawled forward, Vinny tuned out the sobbing and the smells. This was the reality in America now, and it wasn't going to change anytime soon.

An hour later, they made it to the front of the line.

A burly deputy motioned Carmine forward.

"How many of you?" the man asked.

"Four total," Doberman said. He stepped up in front of Carmine to talk to the deputy, whose name tag said he was Nate Press.

"These are my uncles, and this is my cousin. Most of our family was killed in San Francisco, and we came here to stay with my aunt, who …"

The deputy scrutinized Doberman.

"She was killed when Los Alamitos got hit, so here we are for now," Doberman said.

"Sorry to hear that," Deputy Press said ruefully. "You got ID?"

They handed over their California driver's licenses, all with aliases. The deputy looked at each and handed them back.

"Any of you served in the military?" he asked.

"No sir," Doberman said.

Carmine, Frankie, and Vinny shook their heads.

"Is this all of your belongings?" Press asked.

"Yes sir."

"Any weapons?"

"No sir," Doberman said.

"You guys been on foot for how long?"

"Weeks," Doberman said.

Press gave them all a quick glance, checking their sneakers, which looked the part.

"All right, we have space for you in zone four." He pointed. "Just outside the stadium. If you're looking for work, the LAPD and our office have a stand for information. Once you're processed, you'll be able to come and go as you please. Use the north exit."

"Thank you, Deputy," Doberman said.

"Four more coming in!" Press shouted. He reached

into a box and pulled out yellow plastic bracelets. "Put these on."

The gate opened, and Vinny followed the three Moretti soldiers through metal detectors. Two more deputies watched the men as they passed through the final checkpoint.

"You do that again, and I'll snap your neck," Carmine said.

"Dude, your English is shit," Doberman replied. "No way in hell that guy was going to believe your story."

Frankie raised a hand. "Both of you shut the fuck up already. Do you not realize we just got in without even having our bags checked?"

Carmine shrugged. "So?"

"That means getting product in is going to be easy as hookers."

"Yeah, but we still got *those* to deal with," Doberman said. He pointed his chin at one of the recruiting centers the deputy had mentioned. A line a dozen long stood outside a UCLA building with the Los Angeles Police Department logo.

Officers came and went through the front doors. A California flag hung on a pole outside, beside another pole that now had only a chain. This was rebel territory.

"Let's go," Frankie said, walking around the campus buildings and into the heart of the camp.

The place bustled like a beehive. A half-dozen FEMA trailers were parked side by side, and tents of all colors and shapes had popped up in the open areas.

The only unoccupied spaces were around designated fire zones, where flames rose from fifty-five-gallon metal drums. People stood around in circles, warming their hands in the chilly evening air. Vinny spotted the mansions on nearby hillsides, the glaring juxtaposition hard to miss. Lines waited outside hundreds of portable toilets that he could smell from across a huge lawn.

"Let's split up and meet back at the north exit in two hours," Carmine said. "Vin, you're with me. Doberman, you go with Frankie."

Carmine tilted his head, and Vinny followed him deeper into the camp, toward a cluster of white tents being set up under generator-fed lights. The people doing the work all had the same uniform. They were foreign aid workers.

Vinny was surprised to see white UN tents going up. Europe was in dire straits too, like most of the world, but these men and women had come to America to help a country that had so often rendered aid all over the globe.

He felt a pang of shame for the reason he was here. It certainly wasn't to help these people.

Carmine pulled out a notepad as they made their way through the maze of tents and buildings. Vinny didn't need to ask what the old gangster was doing. There was a reason his uncle had selected Carmine to be captain. He was old-school smart and was a loyal soldier that never questioned an order to pull the trigger.

Keeping in the shadows, Carmine noted the locations of guard posts, and where and how often a patrol of soldiers passed. Vinny stood under a palm tree, watching and learning.

"I started as a scout almost forty years ago," Carmine said in a low voice. "Just a runt kid, barely a hundred pounds. They posted me on the corners. My job was to look out for cops and rivals."

He put the notepad away. Vinny walked side by side with him into an open area of matted grass, where people warmed their hands around fire barrels.

"Once I proved myself, I started working at a dealer spot," Carmine said. "This was back before all the hybrid shit we're selling. I ended up taking over that spot and making your uncle millions of euros."

They finally stopped at the north edge of the camp, where an armada of tanker trucks waited, guarded by a dozen soldiers. Hundreds of people with buckets waited in line for fresh water.

With the power out in most of Los Angeles, the city's biggest problem was the shortage of clean drinking water. Vinny and Carmine stood watching the lines for several minutes before Vinny realized that the older gangster wasn't watching the people standing in line, but rather those *outside* the portable toilets.

A pair of Latino men wearing long sleeves to cover their gang ink, and watch caps over their buzzed heads were slipping packets to people in the shadows.

"Latin Kings?" Vinny whispered.

"Or MS-Thirteen, or a clique with the Norteños. Who knows? I can't see their tats from here, but you realize what this means, right, kid?"

Vinny nodded. The Moretti family wasn't the only crime organization looking to prey on these camps.

They had competition here.

The two Latino gangbangers walked away and headed into another zone of the camp, outside the stadium. Vinny and Carmine followed at a distance.

The next area was zone 4, just outside the UCLA basketball stadium. Hundreds of tents were erected around the perimeter. The two men approached a green multifamily tent, where a third banger stood guard. Tattoos showed on his neck and face.

He lifted up the flaps, and the two dealers slipped underneath and into the tent.

Vinny and Carmine moved behind a cluster of portable toilets to watch.

"Stay here," Carmine said after a few minutes. He walked into zone 4 and disappeared from view.

The industrial floods provided plenty of light in the camp, and Vinny used the opportunity to scan the faces while he waited.

Some people sat in chairs outside their tents, talking quietly or sipping from steaming mugs. It wasn't all that cold, but most of these people were used to their perfectly regulated HVAC systems. Sleeping in a tent had to be a tough transition.

Carmine appeared again, this time outside the large tent the two gangbangers had gone into. Vinny waved at him when he saw two police officers walking toward the entrance, hands on their holsters.

"Oh, shit," Vinny muttered.

The sentry standing guard acknowledged the cops with a jerk of his chin and opened the tent flaps, letting them inside.

Carmine motioned for Vinny, and they walked behind another tent, where they could watch while remaining in the shadows, out of sight. The cops went out of the tent shortly after.

They hadn't gone there to arrest the men, Vinny realized—they had gone there to make a deal.

Vinny followed the two cops as they melted back into the tent city. It was his turn to do some investigation. He walked casually up along their right flank, trying to discreetly read their name tags and memorize their faces.

Both men were young, about his age. One had sharp Sicilian features. The other guy was short and dark-skinned, with an athletic build.

Shouts broke out in the distance, and the cops rushed toward the fight, but Vinny was able to spot the name on the black officer's tag before he vanished into a crowd. *Clarke.*

Vinny and Carmine ended their chase, heading in the opposite direction to finish casing the camp. The recon was sobering—this wasn't going to be as easy as he had thought.

Not only did they have competition, they had dirty cops already in bed with that competition.

Vinny went down a sidewalk, cutting through zone 3, and pulled up short. A girl sitting on a chair outside a yellow tent glared at him in the moonlight.

"Oh, shit," Vinny said, backing away. As the girl shot to her feet and pointed at him, he bolted for cover, not stopping until he was a good distance away.

He stood behind a tent, heart pounding for several seconds before Carmine found him.

"What the fuck are you doing?"

"I saw Carly," Vinny panted.

Carmine looked over his shoulder. "Who the fuck's that, one of your girlfriends?"

"No," Vinny said. "She's Enzo Sarcone's daughter."

-15-

A week had passed since Ronaldo and his family returned to their home in Downey, and Ronaldo was up before the sun. The house been ransacked, of course, along with almost every other dwelling in the neighborhood. Only a few of their neighbors had stayed through the chaos.

"*We're alive; that's all that matters*," Ronaldo had said. It took him a while to convince his wife that they were safer here than in one of the camps, where most residents who hadn't fled the city were now living.

Elena was taking it better than he had expected, and the kids didn't seem to mind much. They were just glad to be home and off the roads.

For the past few days, they had worked together to clean things up. Ronaldo had fixed the door, and Dom had boarded up the broken windows. But the boards didn't keep out the shouts, gunshots, and sirens—the sounds of a city gone mad.

Ronaldo sat in the darkness of the living room on their eighth day home. At five in the morning, he turned on a battery-operated lantern and walked into the bathroom, where his uniform hung on a towel hook.

For a moment, he just stared at it, remembering all the places in the world he had worn it, and the brothers who had fought by his side. Marks, Bettis, and Tooth were out there, and he was going to find them.

But first, he had to report to his new duty station at Downey High School, where, in a few hours, he would receive his first orders. He would also learn whether his new CO had any luck tracking down the Desert Snakes.

Ronaldo quickly got dressed and brought his boots out to the living room, where he sat on the couch and laced them up.

A voice from the dark hallway made him flinch.

"You weren't going to say goodbye?"

He let out a sigh as Elena stepped into the kitchen. The moonlight illuminated her features, and even in her nightgown, with frizzled hair, she was as beautiful as when they first married. All their arguments were forgotten, and his resentment seemed to vanish in that moment.

"I didn't want to wake you," he whispered. "Dom is going to watch over you guys while I'm gone. I'm about to wake him up."

She walked over to the front door and stood between Ronaldo and the exit.

"You promised me we'd be safe if we came back here," she said.

"And we are safe, especially now that Governor McGehee has declared sovereignty. We'll make it through this; we just have to be patient. I promise. You just have to trust me."

"I do trust ..." Elena shook her head. "I just can't believe this is happening. It's all one big nightmare. Maybe we should go to a refugee camp. At least, they have security."

"No way," Ronaldo said. "We're safer here. Trust me."

He finished tying his boots and then walked over to her.

She stared at him for a moment, then gave a half smile and rested her head on his chest. He wrapped his arms around her.

"I'm not going to let anything happen to you guys," he whispered in her ear. "But I have to put food on the table. The only way to do that is to go back to work, doing what I do best, and the Marine Corps is the only way I can get us more than those god-awful rations."

"I hope you can find Marks."

"Me too, but knowing Zed, he's just fine out there." He kissed Elena on the forehead. "I'll be back tonight."

Dom walked into the kitchen, rubbing the sleep from his eyes.

"Good, you're awake," Ronaldo said.

Dom yawned. "Kind of ..."

"Better wake up, because—" A scream cut Ronaldo off. He bolted through the kitchen and into the hallway, not stopping until he got to Monica's room.

She was sitting straight up, gasping for air, staring in the dark.

"Sweetie, it's okay," Ronaldo said. He sat down beside her and pulled her close. "You were just having a nightmare."

She sobbed against his chest.

Elena lit a candle, bringing it over to the bed.

"She's okay," Ronaldo said. "Everything is okay."

Dom moved into the hallway to stand guard with one of the AR-15s they had taken off the raiders on Mount Baldy.

"I keep seeing those burned people," Monica whimpered. "They keep trying to touch me … to burn me too."

"It's okay, baby," Elena soothed. "No one's going to hurt you. I'll never let anyone hurt you."

She looked over at Ronaldo, and again he felt the guilt wash over him. He wanted to be here for his family, but they needed to eat. He couldn't protect them if he couldn't feed them.

"Go back to sleep," Ronaldo said.

"Where are you going?" Monica said.

"I've got to go to work."

"I'll stay here by your side until you fall back to sleep," Elena said.

Monica relaxed and laid her head back on the pillow, eyes still on Ronaldo.

"Please be careful, Dad," she said.

"I will," Ronaldo said, kissing her on the head.

When he got to the front door, he spoke in a low voice to Dom. "Make sure they get some fresh air in the backyard today, okay?"

"Okay, will do, but there's something I have to ask you."

"Yeah?"

"I really want to join the police department," Dom said. "My friends Camilla and Moose have both joined. I'll work nights so you can watch Mom and Monica while I'm there. The extra paycheck or rations or what-ever they're paying will help keep us all fed."

"When will you sleep?"

"I don't know."

"Just hold off one more day, okay?" Ronaldo said, trying to hold back his frustration. "We'll talk about this when I get home."

"Okay, Dad. Be safe."

Ronaldo grabbed the mountain bike he had bor-rowed from a neighbor and set off to Downey High School in the darkness. Dog tired, he would kill for a hot coffee. But when he saw the Marine Corps flag flying from a pole at the school, he snapped awake.

The marines at the gate shined a light on him, and he stopped to show his ID. Then he peddled into the parking lot outside the gymnasium. A tarp rippled over the gaping hole where an Abrams tank had blown out the wall.

He ditched his bike and walked to the entrance, where two sentries watched a patrol of army soldiers making their way back from the night shift.

Even in the low light, Ronaldo could see that sev-eral of the men had been injured. One pressed gauze to his head where something had struck him under the rim of his helmet. Another guy limped with his arm around a buddy.

Ronaldo followed the men inside and made his way to the classroom, where his new commanding officer, Lieutenant Blaze, had set up the Tactical Ops Center.

"Good morning, sir," Ronaldo said, coming to attention in front of Blaze's desk. The lieutenant ac-knowledged the greeting with a nod and went back to looking at the papers in front of him. Ronaldo relaxed and went to stand by the windows when the platoon sergeant, a guy named Tom King, walked in holding a bloody field dressing on his shoulder. He stopped and snorted blood out of his nose into a wastebasket.

"Damn, what happened to you, King?" asked Blaze.

King winced as he touched the dressing. "Everyone out there wants to kill us, LT."

"You good to go for this morning's mission?" Blaze asked. "If not, we can have Salvatore here fill in for you."

King looked at Ronaldo and then shook his head. "I'm good to go, sir."

Ronaldo grabbed a chair at the front of the classroom where his son had learned algebra and geometry.

The room began to fill with mostly marines and a few army rangers and army infantry sprinkled throughout—men who, like Ronaldo, had been separated from their units in the chaos of the fighting.

None of that mattered anymore.

They all were here to fight together.

When they all were seated, Blaze walked over to a city map that hung over the blackboard. He was a big man with a clean-shaven head and a deep voice.

"All right, listen up, everyone," he said. "We've still got several pockets of AMP soldiers hunkering down in multiple locations. The largest group is here in Anaheim. Command wants us to take this real estate back this morning."

"Why don't we just drop a bomb on their asses?" asked one of the Army Rangers.

"Because one atrocity doesn't justify another—and they have hostages," replied Blaze. "Governor

McGehee has given us strict orders: hunt down AMP soldiers and clear the cities while avoiding civilian casualties at all costs."

"Even the civilians that are trying to kill us, sir?" piped up a soldier who looked young enough to be just out of basic.

"The gangbangers aren't civilians in my eyes," King added. "We deal with them like we deal with AMP. But you protect noncombatants, such as these hostages, like your own family. Got it?"

"Yes, Sergeant."

"Speaking of gangsters," Blaze went on, "I'm dispatching Team Hammerhead to this area controlled by the Crips. A group of those animals stole a cache of weapons, and I want 'em back." He tapped the map with an unlit cigarette. "The rest of us are heading to Anaheim."

Blaze let King explain the situation in more detail. The remaining AMP forces had retreated to an elementary school and had posted several snipers in houses surrounding the campus.

"I'm not sure how many hostages or how many hostiles we're dealing with," Blaze added, "but two platoons are already there engaging the AMP forces on the perimeter of the school. They are dug in pretty good. This time, we're bringing in the armor. Got two Abramses on the way."

A chorus of hearty *oo-rah*s went up from several of the marines, and Ronaldo felt the urge to chime in. It was good to be back in the Corps again. He kept quiet, though, not wanting to get pegged as too moto.

Blaze turned to Sergeant King, who moved to

stand at the front of the room and scan the assorted soldiers: airborne Rangers, army infantry, and marines. "Gear up, men; it's time to finish taking back this city."

The room started to empty as the anxious soldiers and marines prepared for action. Blaze called out to Ronaldo before he could leave.

"Sergeant Salvatore, your buddy you asked about—Sergeant Marks."

Ronaldo froze. "Yeah?"

"Intel's spotty with all the jamming we got going on, but I got word he may be with a squad that moved in to take that school in Anaheim. They got ambushed. I'm not sure if he is alive or not. I was going to send you with Team Hammerhead, but if you want in on this mission—"

"I'm in, sir." He spoke before he could think of his family. He had promised Elena he would be careful, and now he was volunteering for a battle.

But Marks was out there and might be hurt. He couldn't leave him.

Blaze nodded. "We leave in ten minutes. Get with the armorer."

"Yes, sir. Thank you, sir."

Ronaldo bolted out of the room and took off down the hall to the makeshift arms room. He kept checking his watch as he waited for the armorer to issue him a weapon, magazines, and ammunition. He got an old-school M16A1 and almost took off without signing the arms receipt.

Then he raced through the school, not stopping until he was at the parking lot, where a dozen Humvees were being loaded up. He put on a helmet and body armor, then grabbed a headset. The ritual tap of magazines on helmets and the snap of them clicking into place carried across the parking lot.

The convoy rolled out as the sun rose over the San Gabriel range.

Ronaldo checked his comms. When he was good to go, he took the turret in his Humvee, happy to be up in the open. He wasn't here to make new friends; all he cared about was surviving the mission and finding his brothers.

Marks was still alive. He could feel it.

The drive east to Anaheim made Ronaldo wonder. Fingers of smoke rose away from the fighting zones. There were no choppers or fighter jets in the airspace around the city.

The navy controlled the airspace over California right now, and the fighting was mostly on the ground. But it was only a matter of time before the madman who had caused the Second Civil War would again strike civilian targets.

This wasn't going to end until President Elliot was dead or the Marine Corps and allied forces surrendered. *And Devil Dogs don't surrender.*

Ronaldo charged the M249 machine gun mounted atop the Humvee and aimed the muzzle east, adrenaline soaking his nerve fibers.

He closed his eyes for a split second, putting his family out of his mind as he always did when going into combat.

The convoy raced down the Santa Ana Freeway through light traffic—mostly law enforcement and civilians who had decided to flee the city before the day got going.

Scars from the AMP air attack were everywhere: bridges blown in half, debris pushed to the side of the road, orange cones surrounding deep gouges in the asphalt.

Framing the interstate, businesses, and residential areas were charred stretches of landscape from fires that had raged unchecked in a city without water pressure. Ronaldo spotted several city trucks with mounted plows pushing the remains of cars off the roads.

Thirty minutes later, they entered Anaheim. Ronaldo took in a breath of smoky air. Rebel forces from across the city moved into position to help push out the final AMP resistance. If not for the hostages, the fight would already be over.

The crack of gunfire sounded in the distance as the convoy pulled off the freeway and headed into the residential area surrounding the elementary school. Ronaldo jammed the butt of the M249 against his shoulder and looked for targets.

The convoy turned down a street of mansions pocked by high-caliber rounds. One of the houses smoldered from a fire that had spread to the adjacent garage.

A blackened car smoked in the middle of the road, where the battle had left a small team of marines pinned down behind vehicles without a safe exit route. Bodies lay crumpled in the street, and spent shell casings rested in the pools of blood.

Ronaldo swallowed, wondering whether one of the fallen marines was Marks.

The convoy slowed and was preparing to stop when a whistling noise broke the calm. A streak slammed into the Humvee ahead of Ronaldo—a direct hit from an AT-4 antitank rocket to the hood.

The explosion blew out the front, and the truck bounced up from the street to crash back down in a smoldering heap.

Shrapnel dinged off the turret's armor, and smoke filled Ronaldo's lungs. He bent down for cover as more shrapnel whizzed through the air.

When he popped back up, the passenger door of the destroyed Humvee flung open, and the flaming body of a marine spun wildly, screaming for several seconds before crashing to the asphalt.

"Move it, marines!" Blaze shouted over the comms.

Ronaldo blinked away the shock, habit taking over. He scanned for targets and saw the silhouettes of two AMP soldiers on a rooftop.

Don't miss, he thought, aiming as one of them lifted a rocket tube.

Ronaldo fired first, hitting his target in the chest with a burst. The tube fell back onto the roof, and the second man spun away from a second burst.

"Rooftop clear!" Ronaldo shouted.

Marines fanned out of the vehicles, and he squeezed off bursts of suppressive fire as they moved across the street to cover their exit. A muzzle flash alerted him to another AMP soldier in a second-story window.

Ronaldo lined up the barrel and fired at window where he had seen the muzzle flash, riddling the frames high and low with rounds. But it was too late for the Army Ranger dragging a marine to safety on the road. A sniper hit him in the helmet and then in the chest. The marine got hit next and went limp in the street.

Ronaldo held his fire, watching for the sniper. A muzzle flash winked from another window in the same building, and the ding of a bullet against the turret's shield forced him down as the second sniper began firing on him.

Inching back up, Ronaldo fired at the window until the frame and wall were riddled. The sniper had to be dead—a mouse couldn't have survived in that fusillade.

Ronaldo abandoned the turret, slid down into the Humvee, and joined the dozens of marines and soldiers running for cover. They found it behind a brick wall framing a driveway.

"We clear this street, and then we move in!" Blaze shouted. He stood and then fell to his knees, his face erased by another sniper.

Warm blood sprayed Ronaldo's cheek. He blinked away the stars and looked around the corner of the wall at the shot-up window frame, where the sniper he had thought he killed was still shouldering a rifle.

Two marines pulled Blaze away, not realizing that part of his head was missing. The rest of the team stood and opened fire on the window. A body slumped out, the rifle that had killed Blaze falling to the ground.

"LT's dead," one of the marines said, looking up from his mangled corpse.

The men behind the wall ducked down, trying to figure out who was in charge. One of them looked at Ronaldo—the young man who had asked all the questions during Blaze's briefing. He met Ronaldo's eyes and said, "You're in charge now, Sergeant. What do we do?"

In less than five minutes, Ronaldo had risen to

ranking NCO of the platoon. He wiped the blood from his face and tamped down the fear.

"Eyes up, everyone," he ordered. "We move forward in overwatch teams. Find the rest of the snipers!"

The ten marines divided into fire teams, with half of them moving out under a corporal's command. Ronaldo took point with the other half and signaled for the men to advance into the houses. They had to get to cover and knock out the AMP snipers before they could advance to the school.

With his fire team stacked behind him, Ronaldo bolted for a garage. He breached the side door with a kick, cleared his near corner, and ran the wall while his team filed in behind him. They had entered a three-car garage with a BMW still inside.

His four marines followed him into the kitchen, stacking, breaching, and clearing as they moved. They confirmed that the first floor was empty, and moved up a staircase to the second floor, where they split up to search the other rooms.

Coming out of a bedroom, Ronaldo met his other team leader's eyes and motioned that the room was clear. The corporal returned the sign. They had one room left to search.

Ronaldo signaled his team to follow him into the last bedroom. Once they confirmed it clear, they pulled the shades back to look for the snipers. They were on the north side of the house, with a clear view of the school.

Hundreds of soldiers and marines from supporting platoons were moving into position on the east side, having cleared the exterior AMP soldiers from the houses.

"Got the last sniper," came a voice over the comms.

"Copy that," Ronaldo said. "We're good to go. Get to the highest floor and set up shop."

Ronaldo grabbed a pair of binos from one of his men and zoomed in on the elementary school. Four AMP soldiers led a group of civilians to the edge of the flat rooftop.

"They aren't going to surrender," said the marine next to Ronaldo.

"Jesus Christ," Ronaldo whispered.

He had to force himself to keep eyes on the scene.

These were all Americans—the AMP soldiers, the civilians. How could it have come to this?

"They won't do it," Ronaldo whispered. "They won't execute hostages."

The whoosh of rotors broke through the sounds of war, and two Black Hawks cut across the skyline. They moved toward the rooftop, the gunners bringing their M240s to bear on the AMP troops.

Watching the birds circle, Ronaldo glimpsed a soldier inside the troop hold with a bullhorn.

"They're going to negotiate," Ronaldo said. He closed his eyes and said a prayer—the only thing he knew to do in this moment.

When he opened them and brought the binos back up, the AMP soldiers lowered their weapons and raised their hands, and the yellow AMP flag came down.

Ronaldo let out a sigh of relief.

"Let's go!" he said.

The platoon finished clearing the houses and met back on the street. Wounded soldiers and marines lay in the grass, corpsmen tending to their injuries.

Ronaldo cradled his rifle, realizing he hadn't even fired a shot from it. He walked over to the dead and saw the burned body of Sergeant King, and the ruined face of Lieutenant Blaze.

Two more marines dead. And for what?

Ronaldo lowered his head, seeing the blood spatter on his uniform. He fell into a trance until a familiar voice called out.

"Salvatore! Ronaldo, is that you?"

He turned toward a group of marines walking up the street. Their fatigues were covered in ash and speckled with blood.

"*Bettis?*" Ronaldo shouted. He slung his rifle and ran toward his friend.

He wasn't alone. The other two Desert Snakes walked beside him.

Marks stopped, lowering his cradled rifle.

A wave of emotion gripped Ronaldo. His vision blurred, though he didn't know whether the tears were of joy, or sorrow.

"The surviving members of AMP are on the run," Christopher said.

The fight for Los Angeles was over for now, and Antonio had lost his biggest customer. He stood in the office of his new house in Bel Air, hands cupped behind his back as he looked out the window at the lush foot-hills. The million-dollar view, and the fact that Enzo Sarcone was a rotting corpse, helped him relax.

"There's something else, Don Antonio," Christopher said.

Antonio's brother looked uncharacteristically nervous.

"One of our soldiers is missing. John Recelli didn't show up last night, and his girlfriend said he never came home. We suspect he was kidnapped."

Antonio had known that it was just a matter of time before this happened. One enemy was erased, but a new, more dangerous one had taken its place.

"This is why I waited to make my move," he said. "The gangs know who we are now. This is their first play: take one of our men and torture information out of him."

Christopher said, "You think someone's testing us?"

"I would bet our new market on it."

"What do we do?"

"We wait, and we keep preparing," Antonio said. He changed the subject to other business. "Is the warehouse ready?"

"Yes."

"Good. Get the men ready. I want to see it."

"I don't know if that's a good idea, what with this new security risk—"

Antonio snorted. "We have the men to protect me. Don't worry, brother."

"I'll get the trucks ready."

Christopher shut the door, and Antonio sat down at his desk. Losing AMP had thrown a wrench into his long-term plans for expanding the business, but moving into the refugee camps had made up for the short-term hit.

The growing Moretti army had already laid claim to the new territories and was distributing product as fast as Christopher could buy it from the González family.

Within a week of making the move, his men were distributing drugs in every refugee camp in Los Angeles. Taking cash, jewelry, and whatever valuables people were willing to part with for a temporary respite from their bleak existence.

But they had competition in the camps—competition that had already secured deals with the police.

And now the Moretti organization had attracted even more attention.

Chances were, John Recelli was suffering in some basement, being "interrogated" in all sorts of inventive ways for information on the Italians.

Antonio slammed his hand down on his desk. This new enemy wasn't intimidated by the street cred he had earned over the past few months. He would have to be more emphatic in demonstrating that the Morettis were not to be fucked with.

He went downstairs to an early dinner with Lucia and Marco. Yellowtail, who was living with them while he recovered from his injuries, limped into the kitchen. Raff was at his normal spot standing near the glass door, watching the lawn with his shotgun. The man had done a superb job of caring for Antonio's family, and Antonio was eternally grateful.

"Raff, are you hungry?" Lucia asked.

"No, ma'am, I'll eat later. Thank you."

"How about you, Zachary, or do I need to ask?"

Yellowtail grinned, and she got up to make him a plate of spaghetti.

"Thank you," he said, wincing as he reached out for the plate. His tank top exposed scars from his old wounds and the bandages still covering the new ones.

Marco glanced over as he ate. "Did the bullets hurt?" he asked.

"Nah, are you kidding? It felt great," Yellowtail said, chuckling. He shoved a forkful of pasta into his mouth, chewed, and swallowed. "It hurt like hell, kid, but then I didn't feel much at all. They say if you don't feel pain, that's when you're in real trouble."

"Oh," Marco said.

Yellowtail shrugged. "But it was worth it, you know?"

Marco hesitated, unsure how to reply.

"'Cause chicks dig scars, my man," Yellowtail added.

Lucia frowned. "Not true."

"It isn't?" Antonio asked.

She shot him an embarrassed look.

After they finished, Antonio returned to his bedroom, where Lucia helped him dress in a new black Armani suit. She smiled as she tucked a red silk square into his pocket.

"If I didn't know better, I might be a little jealous seeing you go out of the house dressed like this," she said.

"You know my eyes are only for you."

Lucia nuzzled against his five o'clock shadow, breathing in his scent. The blood warmed in his veins as it traveled downward, but he pulled away and kissed her on the cheek.

"I have to go, my love."

"Oh?" She pulled back her blouse, exposing her breasts for a glimpse of what awaited him when he returned home.

"Your men can't wait?"

He cracked the cocky grin of a high-schooler on prom night.

They made love in the same bed where his enemy had fucked his whores just a month ago. He didn't bother trying to be quiet. Their room was halfway across the house, and Marco would never hear the headboard thumping against the wall, or his mother's moans.

Antonio finished and rolled off, wanting a smoke.

She let out a sigh of pleasure. "You haven't fucked me like that for a long time."

He slipped his suit pants back on as she lay catching

her breath. By the time he was dressed, she had recovered, and helped him straighten his collar.

"Come home early and I might give you round two," she said.

Antonio kissed her hard, then hurried downstairs. Raff was standing near the front entrance, looking out a window.

"Don Antonio, your vehicle is ready," he said.

As Raff opened the door, Antonio saw their three new black Suburbans, stolen from an abandoned compound, sitting in the front drive. His men wore suits and held automatic rifles.

"Be careful," Raff said. "I'll keep an eye on things around here."

"I know." Antonio patted him on the arm. "Thank you, my friend. When this is all over, I want you to find a wife. You deserve to be happy."

Raff gave a smile so sad, Antonio knew that he would never experience the love of a woman again after losing his fiancée to cancer many years ago. His heart belonged to God now, and the family.

"Don Antonio," Frankie said. He opened the back door to the second SUV, and Antonio slid into the back seat. Lino took shotgun with Christopher behind the wheel. The other two vehicles boxed them in as they set out on the dangerous roads at dusk.

Antonio couldn't help but wonder what rich asshole had once ridden in this black chariot. Some B-list star, perhaps, or maybe an athlete who played for the Dodgers or the Lakers.

Most of the stars had fled the city by now, leaving some of their riches unguarded. Looters had already taken all the easy pickings, but Antonio had a small team dedicated to finding what was left, and the Suburbans were a recent score.

"Who's got an update on the camps?" Antonio asked.

"We're just starting to move product," Frankie replied. "The other gangs are in the camps too, and they realized the same thing: the most valuable currency now is people."

"I didn't give some of the gangs enough credit," Antonio said, looking into the distance, "but don't worry. The Crips, Bloods, and small cliques won't survive long. Our main competition is the Norteño Mafia. That's why we need to find out who their leadership is. We end them, and their organization crumbles."

"Yellowtail and I are working on it," Lino said.

"We're still trying to find the crooked cops," Frankie said, "but it seems they've already made deals with the other gangs."

"Leave that to me," Antonio said.

He gazed out the passenger window, but not for threats—his men could do that while he visualized the next step of his plan. It required a powerful ally in the LAPD.

Pazienza, Antonio. Pazienza …

The drive to East Los Angeles was broken up by multiple checkpoints. Most of the cops were rookies who hadn't even made it through an academy. Above the face masks, Antonio spotted youthful eyes looking into the Suburban at each stop. The city had resorted to hiring high-school kids. And that was what had given him the idea.

The police presence thinned out as they drove farther east. When they got within a mile of the Citadel Outlets, not a cop was in sight. Or anyone else, for that matter. Just a year ago, the parking lot surrounding the mall would have been jam-packed with vehicles, but a bomb from an AMP fighter jet had left a house-size pit in the asphalt.

Christopher drove around the crater and into an industrial area on the other side of the shopping mall. Half of a fighter jet's delta wing stuck like a fin out the side of a hotel.

The fighting had been intense here, leaving most of the area uninhabitable. And that was precisely why Antonio had selected this to replace the warehouse in Compton. It was also the grid for his newest search, for a place to build the compound he had dreamed of since leaving Naples. Bel Air was nice, but the foothills were exposed and difficult to guard. Also, his men were too spread out, and with cell towers still down, it would be hard to call in his army on short notice.

What he needed was something easily defensible, where his family and soldiers could live. A place like the Commerce Hotel and Casino.

He eyed the abandoned resort in the distance. It had exterior damage, though nothing major from what he could see. But that didn't mean it would be an easy buy.

"Lino, I want you to do some research on the Commerce. See if it's for sale."

"You got it, Don Antonio."

Once the Second Civil War ended, there would be endless opportunities to take advantage of: real estate, gambling, prostitution, human trafficking.

Organized crime was the new American dream, and Antonio had a variety of businesses in mind to diversify the portfolio.

Christopher drove into another industrial area, where companies had once stored their goods. Semi trailers sat idle in rows, their back doors wide open, the contents long since pilfered.

"We're here," he said.

A group of Moretti soldiers stood guard outside a building tucked behind several warehouses. One of them waved Christopher into an alley.

Antonio got out in the shadows of the narrow passageway. He pulled at his cuffs, eyeing several lookouts positioned on the rooftops.

Security was coming together, but they still had work to do.

The front doors to the building were guarded by two Moretti guards wearing face masks and holding M4 carbines. They stiffened as Antonio approached, like soldiers in the presence of a general.

Christopher opened the doors, and Antonio stepped into his new distribution warehouse for the first time.

"Sure beats what we had in Compton," Christopher said.

"Indeed, brother."

The other soldiers fanned out through an open room furnished with metal tables. Masked workers were busy preparing the various products from the González family's latest shipment. The most popular item was a hybrid opiate.

Vito raised a gloved hand at Antonio. The big soldier was mixing cocaine with caffeine in a blender to "bulk up" the batch. He was the best in the business at this, having learned from the masters in Bolivia.

A second floor of offices surrounded the open

ground floor. More guards patrolled on the platform walkway, watching the workers.

"Our security is operating around the clock to keep this place a secret," Lino said. "But we'll eventually need police protection."

"Leave that to me," Antonio said. He walked up a stairwell to a second-floor office with a glass wall overlooking the first floor.

Carmine was leaning over his desk when Antonio opened the door. He looked up, cocaine powder in his mustache.

"Don Antonio," he said, standing up and brushing the powder off his nose. "I didn't know you were …"

Antonio shook his head at the sorry sight. "What the fuck did I tell you about this shit?"

Christopher walked into the room and stood in front of the door, arms crossed over the front of his pin-striped suit.

"Sorry, Don Antonio," Carmine said. "I was just testing—"

"I didn't make you captain to test this shit," Antonio snapped back. "If I see you doing it again, you'll wish for the luxury of those refugee camps, because you will no longer be working for me."

Carmine raised his scarred chin, clearly enraged but not stupid enough to argue.

"You got something you want to say?" Antonio said. He moved behind the desk, stopping just inches from Carmine's droopy face.

"No, Don Antonio. I don't."

Antonio snorted. "We don't use the product, Carmine. Or *test* the product. Vito knows what he's doing—he doesn't need you running quality control. Don't forget that, old friend."

"I won't, Don Antonio."

Antonio held his gaze for a moment and then turned, tilting his head for Christopher to follow. Now that he had seen his warehouse, he was ready for the main purpose of this trip.

The soldiers returned to the Suburbans and drove back toward Bel Air, not stopping until they got to the refugee camp, where they pulled into a parking lot. Christopher pulled up next to a pickup truck, and Vinny and Doberman got out of it. Dressed in grubby civilian garb, ball caps, and ratty sneakers, they looked like refugees.

Frankie and Lino got out of the Suburban Antonio and Christopher were in, and gestured for Vinny to get into the back seat with Antonio. The doors shut behind Vinny, and the other soldiers turned their backs, standing guard outside.

"Don Antonio," Vinny said.

Christopher turned from the front seat.

"What's this about?" Vinny asked.

"We have a new mission for you," Antonio said.

He could see the trepidation in his young nephew's face as he awaited the new orders.

Antonio looked at his brother for any last-minute objections. Christopher nodded.

"What do you need me to do?" Vinny asked.

"We need a mole," Christopher said.

"A mole?" Vinny said, looking at his dad and uncle in turn.

"We need you to join the LAPD."

* * *

Sitting down to dinner, Dom smiled for the first time in days, and not because of the tasty meal being served. His ears no longer rang, and he was looking forward to talking with their guests.

Joining his family tonight were three of his father's marine friends: Marks, Bettis, and Tooth. He was thrilled to be sitting with the warriors he so respected.

But the marines weren't cracking jokes and bantering as they had in past gatherings. They were too exhausted and banged up from weeks of fighting against AMP.

Dom was brimming with questions, but with Monica and Elena in the kitchen, he decided to hold back. He would hear the stories soon enough.

"I hope this is good," Elena said, though it always was.

She set a bowl of mashed potatoes in the center of the table, then returned to the kitchen and came back with roast beef, green beans, and macaroni.

"Smells great, Mrs. Salvatore," Tooth said politely.

Bettis smiled as he loaded his plate. "Thank you for having us. I can't remember the last time I had a home-cooked meal."

"I've missed your cooking, Elena," Marks said.

Candles placed around the dining room cast an eerie glow over the plentiful food and the rifles leaning in the corner.

Ronaldo, sitting at the head of the table, steepled his hands together. "Close the book, kiddo," he said to Monica, who had an open novel next to her plate.

"Are these MREs again?" she moaned as Dom scooped mashed potatoes onto her plate.

"Nope, these are the real deal," her mother said. "Go ahead, I promise you'll like it."

"Let's pray first," Ronaldo said.

Dom looked at his father. He wasn't used to praying before a meal.

"Bettis, will you do the honors?" Ronaldo asked.

"Of course." Bettis folded his hands together and bowed his head. "Thank you, Lord, for bringing us all together tonight and for the food that is about to nourish our tired bodies. But most of all, thank you for watching over us during these dark times."

"Amen," Tooth said.

Bettis touched his forehead and crossed his chest, and Dom followed his lead.

"All right, let's eat," Elena said.

Monica took a bite, chewed, and said, "Not bad, Mom."

"Very good," Tooth said.

Dom savored every bite. It was his first meal in weeks that didn't involve government rations or energy bars.

"So ..." Elena said. "Are you guys going to tell us what's going on?"

Marks looked to Ronaldo, who nodded back.

"AMP is on the run in California," said Marks. "But they're winning the fight in other states. You guys saw how easily they beat the Oregon rebels. Our CO is saying to prepare for an invasion soon."

"That's why we're still here and haven't been deployed elsewhere, is my guess," Bettis added.

Elena lowered her fork. "Invasion?" she said quietly.

"Don't worry," Ronaldo said. "It won't come to

that. I truly believe this will all be over soon. As soon as Elliot is dead, there will be peace, and we can start to mend."

Ronaldo must have noticed how crackpot his words sounded. There would be no mending anytime soon. America was on its last legs, and Los Angeles was hanging on by a string of gristle.

That was why Dom wanted to do his part. Why he *had* to do his part.

As they were finishing dinner, a knock came on the door. Ronaldo shot up from his chair and grabbed his rifle. The other marines did the same while Dom shepherded Monica and Elena into the kitchen.

Ronaldo cautiously made his way to the boarded-up window and looked through a crack between the plywood sheets. "I can't see who it is."

Tooth moved to the living room for a better view. "Looks like a cop," he said. "There's a squad car in the driveway."

Dom stepped away from his mom and sister. "It's probably just Moose."

"I didn't know he was coming," Ronaldo said.

"Me either," Dom replied.

Ronaldo opened the door to find his son's best friend standing on the porch, looking surprised at all the firepower that met him.

"Whoa there, Mr. Salvatore," Moose said, raising a hand.

Ronaldo slapped Moose on the shoulder. "Good to see you, bud."

"You too, sir."

"Not 'sir.' I work for my pay."

The other men grinned at the standard reply by a noncom addressed as an officer.

"Andre, how are you?" Elena asked as Moose stepped inside the house.

"Good evening, Mrs. Salvatore," he said. "Sorry to interrupt. I came to pick up Dom and take him to the station. It's his first night ..."

Moose looked to Dom and shut his mouth.

"Moose is going to show me the ropes before my training starts," Dom announced.

"*Training?*" Elena looked at Ronaldo, who remained silent.

"Don't worry, Mom. I'll be careful, and this is the only way I can help put food on the table. There aren't any other jobs, and I'll make a good cop."

"*Great* cop," Moose said.

"I can't believe this," Elena said. "You're both just boys, and with such bright futures. Andre, you—"

"My dreams of playing pro ball or acting are over, Mrs. Salvatore," Moose said. "I've accepted that, and I've joined the force like my brother because it's the only option."

"We're not boys, Mom," Dom said. "We're men."

"Yes, you are," Ronaldo said. He looked at Elena. "The world has changed, and it's not going to be the same for a while. Maybe never."

"I'll go grab my stuff," Dom said before his mother could protest again.

"Can I come?" Monica asked.

"*No,*" Elena and Ronaldo chorused.

Monica lowered her head, pouting as she turned to the hallway with her book in hand.

Seeing his sister like this tugged at Dom's heart. "Hey, sis," he called out.

She turned in the hall outside her bedroom door.

"Maybe when I get my own squad car, I'll take you to the Griffith Observatory, okay?"

Her dimpled face lit up. "Really?"

"Yeah."

She nodded eagerly and ran over to give Dom a hug. He said goodbye to his parents and the marines.

"Be safe out there," Bettis said.

"Don't worry, I got his back," Moose said. "And thanks. You guys did a hell of a job against AMP. The LAPD is really grateful. All of us are."

"Doing our duty, son," Marks replied.

Dom followed Moose out to a squad car that had seen some rough duty.

"Damn, she—"

"Runs *just* fine, baby," Moose said, patting the hood.

"Are those bullet holes?"

Moose ran a hand over the punctured body metal. "Got hit in a drive-by a few days ago." He patted his vest. "Lucky I had this on."

Dom opened the creaky passenger door, which had also caught several rounds. Brown stains discolored the black seat. A computer with a cracked screen glowed as Moose started the engine.

The car rattled to life, and the dash-mounted radio chirped.

"Be right back," Moose said. He popped the trunk and returned holding a Kevlar vest. "Put this on."

Dom took off his hooded sweater and pulled the

Glock from the back of his jeans. "You okay with me bringing this?"

"Dude, I wouldn't *want* you riding with me without a piece," Moose said.

A spiderweb of cracks obstructed the view out the windshield on the passenger side, but Dom could see the house's boarded-up windows as Moose pulled into the street. He couldn't see his mom, but he had a feeling she was watching.

She still hadn't quite accepted that the old world was gone and that this was the new one. But Dom and Moose knew that their old dreams were dead.

Dom looked ahead. This was his future now.

"You ready for this, baby?" Moose said, a note of excitement in his voice.

Dom shared the excitement, and not just because he was getting out of the house. He was ready to fight—something he knew he was good at.

"Good to see your pop's doing well," Moose said. "And his buddies too."

"They're all lucky to be alive."

"I heard it was bad, man."

Dom sighed. "A lot of good men died in Anaheim."

"We've been hit hard too. Lot of cops are dying on the streets, as you probably know. Camilla almost ended up a statistic yesterday."

"What!" Dom said, looking over at him.

"A group of Bloods attacked her car, killing her partner, and then broke the passenger window and pulled her out. They were going to rape her, but backup showed just in the nick of time."

"Jesus," Dom said. "Is she okay?"

"Yeah, she's already back to work. Got a few bruises, but it's the inner wounds that are going to be the worst."

Dom shook his head. Just six months ago, he was talking with her about colleges and what they wanted to do after. He had dreamed of being a professional MMA fighter but knew he didn't have the talent to make it pay, and had decided to pursue a degree in business.

She wanted to be a teacher. And Moose could have gone into acting or played pro soccer. Now they were fighting for survival as beat cops.

It didn't seem to be bothering Moose, though. He grinned as he accelerated past pedestrians, people on bicycles, and a pickup loaded with junk.

"The fight for the city might be over for now between the rebels and AMP, but it's just beginning for the LAPD," Moose said. "I'm glad you're with me, man. Maybe I can convince the LT to assign you as my new partner."

Dom looked away from the road. "What happened to your old one?"

"He got killed on his third ..." He shook his head sadly. "Killed on his third day on the beat. Was our age, man. Kid named Skip."

"Wow," Dom said, not knowing what else to say. He felt the wind seeping in where the bullets had punched through the door and into Skip's flesh.

Reaching down, Dom tightened his vest.

The dashboard radio crackled, and the dispatcher's voice filled the car.

"Two forty-five, assault with a deadly weapon. Multiple suspects, officers request backup. Any available unit."

"Unit eleven-sixteen responding," Moose said. "Eight minutes out."

He replaced the radio hand piece. "And the evening begins," he said with a sigh.

The sirens blared as he turned on the strobe and sped through a four-way stop. The light cross traffic waited as the squad car roared through.

Moose turned onto Highway 605, heading northeast toward City of Industry and Mount Baldy. Fences and walls surrounded the houses in the affluent neighborhood off the interstate. Many were abandoned or taken over by squatters.

"The gangs have abandoned their old stomping grounds and moved into this area," Moose said.

Dozens of squad cars were parked on a residential street. Several more were stacked in an intersection. Moose unbuckled the strap on his pistol.

"Shit. Looks like we're late to the party," Moose said. He parked and looked over at Dom. "Stay close to me, bro."

Dom got out of the car, trying to grasp that this was the world they lived in now, where his best friend talked nonchalantly about violence, and people killed for a granola bar.

This scene they arrived on looked more like a gang shootout. Multiple bodies lay sprawled in the street. Another hung halfway out of a bullet-riddled car.

"We got a live one!" shouted a cop.

He opened the back door of a black SUV and backed away with his shotgun angled into the back seat. Moose drew his pistol and motioned for Dom to get back.

The officers swarmed the vehicle and quickly had

the suspect cuffed facedown on the asphalt. He didn't look like a gangbanger—a burly guy with an expensive suit, pointy shoes, and slicked-back hair that looked perfect even after he'd been tossed around. A dark stain on his suit told Dom he'd been injured in the shootout.

"All clear," said another officer.

One of the wounded guy's dead comrades still sat in the front seat, head slumped against the window. The other two vehicles were beater pickups that had slammed into the SUV in the intersection, in what appeared to be an ambush.

Several bodies were in view. By their clothes, shaved heads, and tats, Dom put them with the Norteño Mafia.

"All right, let's bounce, man," Moose said. "They got this covered."

"Who are those guys?"

"MS-Thirteen or some shit, but I don't know about the guy with the fancy shoes. He was cussing a blue streak in Italian when we found him. At least, I think it was Italian."

Dom watched the paramedics put the guy on a stretcher and into the back of an ambulance. He was lucky to receive treatment. In his limited experience, the emergency crews usually arrived long after the victim had bled out.

Back in the squad car, Moose said, "Got a few minutes to burn. Wanna see the future of Los Angeles? It's not far."

They took the interstate northeast, continuing toward Mount Baldy.

"Power's off, water is tainted, and refugees are

coming in from all directions," Moose said. "But the mayor and city council have a plan, I'm told."

They drove past City of Industry until the horizon lit up with the glow of floodlights. The chug and clatter of diesel engines grew louder, and as the squad car crested the next hill, Dom could see the source of the lights and noise. Dozens of industrial vehicles were busy working into the night.

"What are they doing?" Dom asked, unable to see much through the cracked windshield.

Moose pulled off atop the hill overlooking eastern LA County. They got out and walked to the side of the hill for a better view.

"Are they …?"

"Building a big-ass wall, man."

Dom frowned, puzzled. "But a third of the metro area is on the other side."

"Yup." Moose folded his muscular arms over his chest. "City is preparing evacuation orders and telling residents to move to the refugee camps inside the new city limits. The barrier's only gonna be twenty-five miles long—from the mountains above San Dimas down to Chino—but that'll force most foot and vehicle traffic to take the more heavily watched routes into the city. And we'll be watching."

In the distance, a crane lowered a shipping container onto a stack while clanking bulldozers pushed auto bodies to form a wall of metal.

"We're going to help save what's left of Los Angeles," Moose said. He slapped Dom on the shoulder. "I'm glad to have you with me, brother. You're going to make a hell of a cop."

-17-

Christopher parked the Suburban a block away from the LA Memorial Coliseum. The USC Trojans flag was gone, replaced by the Los Angeles Police Department logo.

"This is crazy," Vinny muttered. "You really agree with Don Antonio about these orders?"

Christopher stroked his graying goatee. It wasn't a yes or a no, and Vinny could see that his dad was too conflicted to answer one way or the other.

"It'll pay off in the end," Christopher said. "Trust your uncle. He's the leader of this family and he hasn't led us astray yet. This is the path to your button."

Vinny breathed in deeply. "All right. I'll do what it takes."

"There's something else," Christopher said, grabbing him by the arm. "One of our convoys got ambushed last night. Vito survived, but the cops grabbed him. We want to know where they're holding him."

"How the hell am I supposed to find *that* out?"

"Just figure it out, Vin; you're a smart … young

man." Christopher slapped him on the cheek. "Now, go. Do your duty."

Vinny got out of the SUV and walked toward the stadium with his hands in his hoodie pockets. Generator-powered lights filled the empty stands with a white glow, illuminating the haggard faces of five hundred people who had answered the recruiting call.

At eight in the evening, he joined the recruits in the chilly evening air on the grass inside the coliseum, listening to some asshole LAPD captain with a megaphone against his porn 'stache blather on about what duty and sacrifice meant.

Yeah, dude, I know. That's why I'm here listening to this shit.

Around him, men and women of all races and ages stood listening intently, thrilled at the prospect of a paycheck even if it meant putting themselves in harm's way. Cops in uniform and staff members sat at tables around the edges of the field, where they would start conducting interviews in a few minutes.

Little did the officers know that a Moretti scout was here in their presence. He doubted they even knew who the family was—yet. The only Italian crime syndicate these officers would have heard of in Los Angeles was the now-extinct Sarcone family. Unless Vito was talking, and Vinny doubted that was the case. He was a fat fuck, but not a fat *rat* fuck.

"The City of Los Angeles needs men and women to defend its borders during the war and to deal with the rampant violence and crime from criminal gangs inside our borders," the captain said. "Make no mistake, this is a dangerous job, but we need you now more than ever."

Vinny had heard there was another recruiting effort, by the rebels, going on across town today. Before Christopher dropped him off, they had seen the line outside. Thousands were waiting to sign up.

It was either join the police or join the military. The only others hiring were the gangs.

Vinny still couldn't quite believe he was here. He just had to keep in mind his father's words. *Trust your uncle.*

He did trust his uncle and his dad too, but their plan worried him. If it failed, he could end up in jail with Vito, or worse. But if he succeeded, he would be a made man, finally. No longer just an errand boy.

Vinny stiffened with pride. He would do what it took to earn his button.

After the introduction by the captain, the recruits were all herded to the tables set up around the field, for initial interviews. Most of the people manning the tables were older men and women who had probably come out of retirement to make a much-needed buck.

Minutes turned into an hour, and an hour became two. By the time Vinny got to the front of a line, it was nearing ten o'clock. His feet ached, and he was starving, not to mention thirsty.

The older cop sitting at the table hardly looked up from his notebook as Vinny approached. He reached out lazily and said, "ID."

Vinny handed his over.

The officer's gray brows scrunched, and he glanced up. Dark, suspicious eyes studied Vinny, the old investigator catching the scent.

"Nathan Sarcone, huh?"

"Yes sir," Vinny replied.

"As in the Sarcone crime family?" The cop shifted uneasily in his plastic chair.

Vinny let him wait a moment before nodding. "Yes, sir. Enzo Sarcone was my uncle."

"Was?"

"He was killed by the American Military Patriots, sir."

The cop slowly got up, his joints creaking, or maybe that was the chair. He held the ID and looked at Vinny. "Stay here a minute." He moved away from the table, then paused. "Don't move, okay?"

Vinny shrugged. "I'm not going anywhere."

He stuck his hands in his pockets and tried to calm his kicking heart. The ID was real, and while he looked a lot like Nathan Sarcone, he was twenty pounds lighter. If anyone asked, Vinny could always point out that everyone in the country had lost a few pounds.

Trust your uncle.

Don Antonio was betting the cops would never know the difference—not now that the real Nathan Sarcone lay buried in a rubble heap near Los Alamitos. Before anyone ever found him, Vinny's job would be complete.

But what if the cops saw through his story? What if they knew he was lying?

To take his mind off such troubling questions, Vinny scanned the faces in the line to his right. He watched a woman with short white hair and a baseball cap, who had finally made it to the front of a table. She stiffened, trying to hide her crooked back.

The officer shook his head as soon as he laid eyes on her.

"Ma'am, you're too old," he said. "I'm sorry."

"No," the woman pleaded. "I can work. I can fight."

The cop shook his head again, annoyed. Then he raised a hand and motioned the next person forward.

A woman half the age of the one in the ball cap stepped up, giving the cop a seductive grin. Vinny had seen a lot of that lately. People used whatever resources they had to survive. It was human nature.

The older woman wasn't having it. She bumped the younger girl out of the way and put her palms on the table. "I can work as a dispatcher, or at crime scenes. I have a background in—"

The officer stood, his annoyance turning to anger. "Ma'am, please, you need to leave," he said. "I can't help you. Report to a refugee camp. They might have something for you."

"I just stood here for three hours!" she snapped.

"Not my problem, ma'am. Now, please make way for the next person in line." He gestured again for the younger girl, but the woman doubled down.

"Listen, asshole, I know there is something I can do for the LAPD, and I'm not leaving until you at least give me the chance of an interview."

The recruiter frowned, then waved at a uniformed officer, who hurried over with his hand on his baton, prepared to escort the woman away the hard way or the easy way.

She looked over at Vinny as she chose the latter option. Eyes glazed with tears, she let her back relax into its normal bent posture. He wondered how long it had been since her last meal.

Vinny swallowed the vestige of empathy he felt. Moretti soldiers didn't have time for such emotions.

His dad had taught him that, and if he wanted to be made, he had to act like a made man.

"Nathan Sarcone," said a deep voice.

Vinny pivoted back to the table, pulling his hands from his pocket.

Another cop in uniform now stood in the older guy's place. The big black man with linebacker shoulders and a square face directed kind eyes at Vinny. Not the eyes he expected in a cop who looked like a Special Forces operator.

"I'm ... Nathan Sarcone," Vinny said, catching himself.

"This way," the big officer said.

Every face in the lines seemed to focus on Vinny as he walked between the two metal tables and followed the officer into the bowels of the stadium. They entered a hallway where the USC Trojans had once streamed onto the field. Vinny took in as much as he could while the cop led him past a locker room and into a block of offices.

Lanterns lit the way, but the farther they walked, the darker it got. Anxiety made Vinny jumpy. He suddenly felt like a prisoner being led into a dungeon.

"Where are we going?" he asked.

"You want a job?" the linebacker said, looking over his shoulder at him.

Vinny nodded.

"Then keep walking."

They finally stopped outside an office. The cop knocked on the door.

"It's open," said a voice.

"Go on in," the cop said, opening the door.

Vinny stepped into a room thick with smoke. There

was a single desk with a wooden chair in front of it. Behind the desk sat the captain who had spoken to the crowd earlier. He slid a pack of smokes across his desk.

Vinny took one and thanked him.

"As you know, I'm Captain Brian Stone," the man said. "You can call me 'Captain' or 'sir.'" He reached across the desk with a lighter and lit Vinny's cigarette, then nodded at the big cop still standing in the doorway.

The door clicked shut.

Vinny took a drag while the captain watched.

"Not many of those left in this city," Stone said. He stubbed out the butt of his cigarette and sat back in his leather chair.

"So tell me, Nathan, why do you want to join the LAPD?"

"Easy," Vinny replied.

Stone waited for Vinny to take another drag and exhale. The smoke rose toward the ceiling, and Vinny took a seat in the chair and leaned forward to flick his ash in the glass bowl.

"Revenge," he said.

The captain's white handlebar mustache curled slightly.

"My great-uncle was killed by AMP, but now that they are defeated in Los Angeles, I want to go after the rival gangs that hunted and killed the rest of my family like we were dogs." Vinny knew what the next question would be. "I survived by hiding, and waiting," he said. "Now's my time."

The captain still looked at Vinny as if he was a suspect.

"And why should I trust you?" he asked.

Vinny shrugged. "Because I'm not my great-uncle and I'm probably the only guy left in this city who knows more about the gangs than your officers do. I know because my job for Uncle Enzo was to keep tallies on his enemies. They called me 'the auditor.'"

Stone folded his hands together and arched one brow. The guy reminded Vinny of some old-school cattleman.

"I've been jumping from camp to camp since my family was murdered," Vinny said, "and I've taken my skills with me."

"How so?"

"I've been watching. Waiting. Planning. In the Bel Air camps, for example, the Sureños and Norteño Mafia are dealing drugs to refugees."

Captain Stone nodded once, and Vinny felt the truth of his story like a fire in his chest. It was always easier to fool people when you had the facts on your side. Stone motioned for him to continue, and he did.

"At the camp in Santa Monica, three more groups are doing the same thing. You got the Bloods operating in the Compton camp and around there. The Russians, led by Nevksy, have infiltrated the camps in Santa Ana, Irvine, and Long Beach ..."

Vinny continued rattling off dozens of gangs that had risen from the ashes. He had baited the hook and cast the line into the water. Now he had to wait and see whether his real uncle was right about all this and whether Stone would bite.

If Don Antonio was correct, then Vinny would be on a fast track into the upper tiers of the LAPD, but if his uncle was wrong, the guy who had brought him here would be leading him away in handcuffs.

He was nearly finished when Stone put up a hand and said, "Normally you'd make a good CI." Stone stood behind his desk. "But I think you might come in handier working in a different role. First, though, you're going to answer some more questions."

* * *

Dom got home in the predawn as Ronaldo was leaving for his patrol. Seeing his son wearing a police vest snapped him awake.

"How'd it go?" Ronaldo asked.

Dom shut the door, careful about the noise. "About what you'd expect," he said, taking off his vest. "Started off with a drive-by gang shooting, and then Moose took me to see the wall we're building." He frowned. "Did you know they're basically cutting off everyone east of Industry?"

"Yes," Ronaldo said, "but let's talk about it tonight when I get home."

"I'm going back out with Moose tonight and meeting with his CO," Dom said. "Moose thinks they'll approve me for on-the-job training based on grades, character, and MMA history."

It didn't surprise Ronaldo. The police were looking for fighters, and there was little time to sit in classrooms and read manuals while the city bled.

"Son," he said, "we haven't even had a chance to talk about this yet, and I want to know more before you make any—"

"Is everything okay?"

Elena stood in the hallway, in her nightgown.

Dom went over to give his mom a hug. Monica shuffled in, yawning.

"You sure you're not too tired to watch them?" Ronaldo asked Dom.

"We'll be fine for a few hours," Elena said. "He can catch a few—"

"*No.* I want Dom on guard until sunup."

"I'm fine, Mom," said Dom, trying to mask his fatigue. "Wide awake, actually."

"Let me see if I have a little coffee left." Elena walked into the kitchen.

"I want to talk to you before you leave tonight, okay?" he said.

Dom nodded.

"Your word?"

"Yes, Dad."

Ronaldo headed out on the mountain bike. He hated leaving his family like this, but he couldn't miss the patrol.

By the time he got to Downey High, the teams of soldiers and marines had their new orders from Marks, who had received a battlefield promotion to gunnery sergeant.

"You're late, Sergeant Salvatore," Marks said.

"Sorry, Gunny. I was trying to talk to Dom."

"How'd his first night go?" Tooth asked. He lit a hand-rolled cigarette.

"Didn't get much out of him. He said something about a drive-by, and he saw the border wall going up."

"That's probably where we'll be assigned next," Bettis said.

"So back to square one with babysitting refugees, like Atlanta?" Tooth grumped. "I want to get in the *action*, man. Head north and take Oregon back from AMP."

"You just might get your chance for some action today," Marks said. "We're on mop-up duty."

The marines walked across the lot, toward the vehicles parked along the fence around the football field. A dozen AMP prisoners were confined there. They lay in the dirt, curled up in their black uniforms. But they weren't all sleeping.

"Brother, can I have a smoke, please?" one of the men said.

Tooth looked at Ronaldo. "You believe this dumb 'tard?" he muttered.

He started off toward the fences.

"Tooth," Marks called after him.

The younger marine didn't listen. He bent down at the fence and took another drag, savoring it. Then he blew the smoke in the man's face. "There you go, *brother*."

"Kid never learns," Bettis said, shaking his head.

Walking past, Ronaldo made eye contact with the AMP soldier. The guy was middle-aged, probably Marks's age. Ronaldo wondered briefly about his background, whether he had kids, a wife.

Whether he had killed marines.

Ronaldo spat in the dirt. These bastards had killed many of his brothers. It was still hard to believe that this had happened in America, where the military had sworn an oath to uphold and defend the Constitution.

Ronaldo got into the back seat of the Humvee with Bettis. Tooth took the wheel, and Marks rode shotgun.

"All teams are headed to locations where reports indicate AMP soldiers may be hiding," Marks said.

"We're on our own?" Ronaldo asked. "Who wrote this bullshit OPORD?"

"Not me," Marks said. "I wanted us all together, but we're one of the only platoons in this area. If you thought Helmand was rough, think again. We're stuck with a single fire team doing the work a platoon would normally handle."

"So, where are we going and what are we doing?" Bettis asked.

"Movement to contact," Marks replied. "We're headed back to Anaheim."

Tooth grinned wide, as if to show off his fangs. "Moppin' up AMP—great way to start my day."

The other teams pulled out of the parking lot in their vehicles, off on their own missions. "Good to have you back on the Desert Snakes," Bettis said to Ronaldo.

"It's great to be back, brother. Guess I'm lucky Marks here got that promotion."

"Still had to convince the colonel," said Marks. "But I mentioned you were probably the very first marine to shoot an AMP soldier."

"So now *I* started all this?" Ronaldo asked. "Thanks for nothing, Gunny."

The image of that AMP gunner in the Black Hawk, slaughtering civilians, would be forever etched onto his brain. Ronaldo didn't feel a shred of regret for shooting the murdering scumbag.

The sun peeked over the rolling hills. The raging wildfires had turned the eastern sky the color of an infected wound. The Santa Ana winds were finishing what AMP had begun. Palm trees swayed in the smoky breeze, and ash drifted down onto the straggling line of refugees along the shoulder.

They wore bandannas or rags across their faces, but Ronaldo knew they would be coughing up black gunk for days. Even inside the air-filtered Humvee, he tasted soot with every breath.

The sight of newcomers flooding into eastern Los Angeles County prompted another memory of Atlanta. But unlike the migrants on the road weeks ago, these poor wretches were on their last legs—paler, thinner. Desperate.

Ronaldo sighed, but not as discreetly as he had intended.

"You good?" Marks asked.

"Yeah, Gunny."

"Well, *I'm* not," Tooth said. "This shit is fucked up. It's like a shit volcano that just keeps growing. And eventually, the volcano is gonna blow, bro, and the shit is gonna fly into the sky, covering us all in more shit when it comes back down."

Bettis shook his head. "What are you even talking about?"

Tooth took one hand off the wheel to make a sweeping operatic gesture. "Dude, *everything* is turning to shit."

"Yeah, I get it. I just don't understand your way of explaining the situation."

Tooth shrugged. "Sorry I don't talk like Shakespeare or the pope."

"You don't need to talk like the pope, dude," Bettis replied. "Just throw in a little English."

Ronaldo cracked a half grin at the exchange, but as soon as they pulled off the highway, he snapped into combat mode.

"Get ready," Marks said.

Each man charged his weapon as Tooth drove into a lawless zone of abandoned apartment blocks, the shells of stores, and boarded-up fast-food joints.

Cars sat on cinder blocks, stripped down to the chassis. The ash-laden wind blew trash through shattered windows. And permeating everything was the stench of raw sewage.

Ronaldo was inured to the smell by now, but with the lack of potable water, this was a textbook recipe for cholera. He had seen it in Iraq, and as in war, the children were always the most vulnerable. The danger of disease was now almost as big a threat as flying bullets.

He knocked on his helmet twice for good luck as they arrived at their target: a four-story apartment building surrounded by trees and fences. The area looked abandoned by all but a few homeless people, pushing everything they owned along the sidewalk.

"Intel said several AMP soldiers are hiding on the top floor," Marks said.

"*Several?*" Ronaldo asked. It wasn't like Marks to be vague with critical mission details.

"That's all I have, guys. Like I said, Helmand was Club Med compared to this bullshit."

Tooth parked them behind a building across the street and killed the engine. The men got out, rifles shouldered.

"Eyes up," Marks said. "On me."

They set out moving fast and low in two-man teams, hugging the side of the building. At the corner, they ran across to a parking lot of more stripped cars. Marks stopped to scan the top windows of the building before flashing hand signals.

Ronaldo and Tooth took point, moving toward the back of the building through a gap in the chain-link fence.

A feral cat darted away from the stairway and vanished into the brush. The exit door was broken off its hinges.

Ronaldo slipped into the dark hallway beside an open stairwell door. Tooth came in tight behind him, sweeping for contacts. The place reeked of piss, but nothing moved.

The door to each apartment was either open or missing. Ronaldo moved forward, sweeping the first doorway with his muzzle. Bettis and Marks were posted at the stairwell. On Marks's signal, Ronaldo moved up the shadowy stairwell with Tooth behind him.

Careful not to kick any debris, they cleared each landing and hallway before moving up to the next level. Bettis and Marks held rear guard, crouching at the top of the stairwell.

The top floor was only two apartments, one on either side of the hallway. The fire team breached both doors simultaneously, and Tooth moved inside first. Ronaldo was right on his six, checking the near corner and running his wall.

In the trash-strewn living room were two filthy mattresses. Ronaldo cleared the back bedrooms and bathroom.

"Clear," he said.

Across the hallway, Marks and Bettis were stacked by the door, rifles up.

Ronaldo and Tooth watched their exit route while Marks led the breach-and-clear of the second apartment. He and Bettis came back a few seconds later.

"Looks like they already jumped ship," Marks said.

"Damn, I was hoping to put my foot up some asses today," Tooth said.

"Want to double-check the other floors?" Ronaldo asked. "Just in case?"

Marks nodded. "Yeah, we better be sure."

They moved back to the third floor. It was still empty,

with no new signs of activity. The second was no different. Finally, they reached the ground floor, where Ronaldo discovered an old guy in a back bedroom. He was wearing a pair of torn sweatpants and sleeping on a bare mattress.

"Show me your hands!" Ronaldo said.

The guy bolted up, raising hands covered in fingerless gloves. He opened a mouth of few teeth.

"Whoa, don't shoot!" he shouted.

Ronaldo walked into the room and gasped at the eye-watering reek of a body unwashed for months. Stepping over a syringe and a bent spoon on the floor, he scanned the room.

The other marines walked in behind him, and Tooth raised his sleeve to his nose.

"How long you been staying here?" Ronaldo asked.

The junkie shivered but managed to keep his hands in the air. "Few weeks, maybe. I … I don't know, man. I lost track of time."

"Did you see any AMP soldiers at any point?"

The old man nodded.

"Where did they go?"

"How the fuck am I supposed to know?" He lowered one hand to scratch an open sore on his chest, and Ronaldo let him. The only threat this guy posed was his smell.

"When did they leave?" Marks asked.

"Middle of the night. I only know because they told me to get out if I knew what was best."

Ronaldo exchanged a glance with Marks.

"They say why?" Tooth asked.

The guy pointed at the pack of smokes in Tooth's breast pocket.

"I don't give information away for free."

Tooth laughed. "I'll give you a cig if you tell us everything you know."

"Two."

"Half a cig."

The junkie frowned. "Fine, one."

Tooth held out a smoke, then pulled it back from the man's reach. "First, tell us what you know."

"I heard them talking about an attack," said the old man. "Beyond that, not much else."

Marks and Ronaldo shared a look. "Could be legit," Marks said.

"Or bullshit," Bettis said.

The junkie reached out again, and Tooth finally gave him the cigarette.

"Thank you," he said, bringing it to his lips. "Been a long time."

They left him there and headed back to the FOB. As soon as they arrived, Marks decided to relay the intel in person rather than risk letting the AMP pukes listen in on their frequencies. Once they got back to the FOB, he jumped out of the truck and left Ronaldo with Bettis and Tooth.

"You think that junkie was telling the truth?" Bettis asked.

"One thing I've learned is 'never trust a junkie,'" Tooth said.

They passed around a canteen and another cigarette as they waited. One by one, the other teams returned, some of them with AMP soldiers in handcuffs.

Half an hour later, Marks came back with their new orders. He was halfway across the parking lot when the ground shook.

"Shit, it's an earthquake," Ronaldo said.

The smoking cigarette fell out of Tooth's mouth, and he brought his hand up to shield his eyes as a light brighter than the sun ballooned up in the distance to the south.

"That ain't no quake, brother," Tooth said.

The flash died away, leaving a cloud like a tall, spindly cauliflower.

Ronaldo stepped back and squinted at the massive and growing mushroom cloud in the south. Marines and soldiers in the parking lot watched in stunned silence.

"Oh, dear God," Bettis said. "Where is that?"

"San Diego," Ronaldo replied, feeling sick. "No, wait, I think that'd be about—"

"Camp Pendleton," Marks said. "North end of San Diego County."

"That can't be," said Bettis.

"Why?" Ronaldo said. "The governor's probably in a bunker there. Using a nuke was a sure way to kill him and get rid of a lot of marines."

"Feckin' gobshites!" snarled Tooth in an unfeigned Irish lilt. "That's why the AMP soldiers took off in the middle of the night. They knew it was coming."

"There is no invasion," Marks said. "Elliot wants to wipe the Marine Corps off the map."

The words made Ronaldo's heart pound harder. He pushed past Marks, who grabbed him by the arm.

"Salvatore, where are you going?"

"We have to get people to shelter," Ronaldo said. "The wind's still Santa Ana. My family and everyone else in Los Angeles are right in the path of that fallout. It'll start floating down in five hours, max!"

-18-

Over the wail of distant air-raid sirens came a whine from the future heir of the Moretti empire.

"I don't wanna leave!" Marco yelled.

Antonio's glare silenced the boy. Lucia came down the mansion's grand stairway, holding a bag of jewelry and other valuables. Wearing a fur coat, three jewel-studded gold necklaces, and diamond earrings, she looked like a queen. And soon enough, she would have her castle.

Antonio took the bag from her and helped her down the last two stairs.

"Please hurry," Raff said in a calm voice, taking Marco by the hand and ushering the family outside. Two Suburbans waited in the driveway, where armed men in suits awaited Rush's orders.

Antonio felt a pang of sadness at the sight of his wife and son being hurried to the vehicles. It wasn't the first time they had fled their home, but this time it wasn't because their enemies had found them.

He looked at the mushroom cloud rising in the

southeast. The nuclear blast had advanced the schedule for his next move. They weren't going far, but the journey would be risky.

From his days in the Alpini, he understood enough about nukes to know that if they didn't get out of the area soon, the fallout could kill them.

He had protected his wife and son from the ambush in Naples, and he had protected them here from rivals and AMP attacks since the war started. But he couldn't shield them from the radioactive fallout that a lunatic president and the prevailing winds would bring to Los Angeles only hours from now. And when that happened, all bets for survival would be off.

Things were unraveling around Antonio, with another group of his men ambushed and Vito, his master cocaine cutter, in jail somewhere. He still didn't know which particular bunch of rat fucks was targeting his family, but the threats were coming from all sides.

"Don Antonio, we're almost ready," said Rush. The former AMP sergeant pulled a walkie-talkie from the belt under his suit jacket.

"We need to get moving *now*," Antonio said.

Marco looked at him with frightened eyes.

"It's okay," Raff said. He helped Marco and Lucia into the vehicle while Antonio did a head count. Lino ran over, and they both realized that Yellowtail was still inside the house.

"God damn it," Antonio said. He ran back up the drive and loped up the front steps, stopping when the oak door swung open. Yellowtail limped outside, juggling a bag in one hand while trying to work his crutches.

Antonio took the bag and helped his much younger cousin over to the SUVs.

"Most of the other men and their families are already on their way to the safe house," Lino said. He opened the driver's door and got behind the wheel of the Suburban.

Antonio and Raff helped Yellowtail into the back. He winced as he put his crutches down.

With his family secure, Antonio walked around to take shotgun.

"Sir, we're ready to move," Rush said. He handed Antonio an M4 and shut the door, then jumped into another vehicle.

"Let's go," Antonio said, patting the dashboard twice.

The Suburbans followed two BMWs and a black Mercedes, all packed with his security detail. Antonio looked in the rearview mirror as they pulled out of the driveway. He would miss the mansion, but he had known that it was only temporary.

"Buckle up, everyone," Lino said.

Antonio looked to the back seat. His son was trying not to look scared, but his wide eyes said otherwise.

Yellowtail kissed his cross as he stared out the window. He insisted on wearing it still, even though it was bent and some of the gold plating was shot off.

Everyone with a car and any gas was leaving this part of the city. While some people had opted to shelter in place, enough were leaving town to choke every road. People without autos rode bicycles, adding to the congestion.

Lino followed the other Suburban and the cars around several stalled vehicles. Horns honked, and pedestrians shouted as the convoy raced by. A biker hit a curb to avoid a car and went over the handlebars.

"Why aren't we taking the interstate?" Antonio asked.

"Rush says it's too dangerous," Lino replied. "Surface streets will be quicker."

Antonio didn't like it, but he had chosen his men well and he trusted them. Their job was to keep him safe, and they had done a damn good job so far.

They pulled onto a four-lane street, joining the eastbound exodus.

"Dad, are we going to die?" Marco asked.

The fear in his voice bothered Antonio, not because he felt bad for him, but because his son wasn't brave. He promised himself that when this was over, if they survived the fallout and the war, he would spend time teaching his son to be a man, just as Christopher had taught Vinny.

"Not today, we're not," Antonio said.

"Then why are we leaving the house?" Marco asked. "I really liked it there."

"It's not safe anymore," Raff said.

Marco bit his lower lip and looked to his mother.

"Everything's going to be fine," Lucia said in her most soothing voice.

She was always the one to enable him, always the one to coddle him, and it wasn't what the boy needed. The world they lived in ate the weak and picked its teeth with their bones.

Antonio had to toughen his son up if he was to have any prayer of surviving what was coming.

"Oh *damn*, look at that," Yellowtail said. He

pointed to a field with hundreds of different-colored tents, and not a soul in sight.

The cops were doing a good job evacuating people and getting them into buildings. Antonio normally hated police, but he had to respect those who had stayed on the job in the face of such danger.

The Suburban ahead of them swerved to avoid a woman trying to cross the street, but that put it on a collision course with a man on foot. He jumped out of the way just in time.

"Stupid assholes," Lino muttered.

"Take it easy," Antonio said. "We have time."

"Chrissy's got a lead foot," Lino said.

The convoy gunned through the traffic at fifty miles an hour as more vehicles pulled onto the road. Lino glanced in the rearview mirror. When he did it a second time, Antonio said, "What?"

"I think we might have a tail," Lino muttered.

Antonio discreetly checked the side mirror as a red car muscled around another vehicle to get behind the Suburban. Both the driver and the passenger wore tank tops and sunglasses. Tattoos covered their arms, necks, and bald heads.

They didn't appear to have any luggage in the back, or anything strapped to the top. These guys weren't trying to escape the city.

The sons of bitches had waited until he left the house to strike. His gut tightened as he calmly said, "Floor it, Lino."

The Suburban in front of them pulled into the left lane, but when Lino tried to follow, the car ahead of it cut him off.

"*Figlio di gran puttana*," Lino growled.

The rest of the Moretti convoy moved into denser traffic ahead.

Antonio turned to the back seat, not wanting to scare his son and wife but seeing no way around it.

"Lucia, Marco, I want you guys to get down on the floor, okay?"

"What!" Lucia gasped.

Marco blinked rapidly. "Why, Dad?"

"Just do as I say." Antonio nodded at Yellowtail, who pulled a pistol from his waistband and racked the slide. Raff did the same thing, then helped Lucia and Marco onto the floor.

"Give me the radio," Antonio said.

Lino pulled out his walkie-talkie and handed it to Antonio.

Before he could call Christopher, the red car behind them picked up speed.

"Everyone stay down!" Lino shouted.

He jerked the wheel to the right, blocking the red car from coming up on the shoulder. Metal screeched, and sparks flew along the guardrail.

The driver eased off and then punched it, pulling into the left lane to flank them.

"Yellowtail, take them out!" Antonio shouted.

Yellowtail pointed the pistol out the window, at the tires. But the driver braked again, and both shots missed.

The passenger raised an Uzi and returned fire, shattering the Suburban's back window.

Lino slammed on the brakes as a tan pickup skidded sideways and stopped in front of them. The driver opened fire with a handgun, his bullets spider-webbing the glass and hitting the back seats.

Rounds blew through Antonio's headrest. Raff shielded Marco and Lucia with his body while they screamed in terror.

"Get us out of here!" Antonio shouted at Lino.

Another flurry of shots slammed into the back of the Suburban. Antonio prayed they would not hit flesh.

"GO!" he shouted.

Putting the SUV in reverse, Lino backed away from the two vehicles that had stopped on the road.

Three men jumped out of the pickup, firing assault rifles.

Antonio could see his wife and son on the back floor now, under Raff, who had cubical shards of safety glass all over his back and head.

"FUCK YOU!" Yellowtail screamed. He sat up and fired at the man with the Uzi, hitting him twice in the chest. The guy crumpled on the street.

"GO, GO, GO!" Antonio yelled. He raised his rifle to fire just as a different car slammed into the side of the SUV. His seat belt dug into his chest as the airbag exploded in his face. Smoke and powder filled the vehicle as they skidded to a stop.

Antonio felt warm blood running from his nose and heard the distant moans and cries from his family. He got a blurred image of Lino slumped against the door, blood streaking from his forehead. The walkie-talkie on the floor crackled next to the M4 Antonio had dropped in the crash.

As men surrounded their vehicle, he stretched to

grab the gun, but his fingertips hit the grip, pushing it out of reach.

He twisted slightly to see Lucia and Marco moving on the back floor. Yellowtail was there with them now, shielding their bodies with his own. Raff was either dead or unconscious after being tossed against the door.

Bullets pounded the back door.

"Stay down," Antonio managed to say. He unbuckled his seat belt and reached again for his rifle, coughing from the smoke.

Through the haze, he saw a man approaching the driver's door. A rifle butt smashed through the glass, and a hand opened the door. The assailant grabbed Lino's limp body, holding a toothed blade under his chin.

Antonio finally grabbed the gun just as his door opened. A hand seized him by his suit jacket. A second hand wrested the gun away from him, and an arm wrapped around his neck, tightening until he couldn't breathe.

Two more men grabbed Yellowtail from the back seat, pulling him off Marco and Lucia.

Antonio tried to yell, but the muscular arm cut off his air.

"Antonio Moretti," said a deep Spanish-accented voice, "you are one *stupid* hombre."

He watched in horror as his wife and then his son were yanked from the vehicle.

"You made a mistake trying to come into my territory," the man said. "Your man told me all about you rat guineas."

Something thumped on the dashboard and rolled to the floor. Antonio looked down to see a severed head. The lips and eyes were stitched shut, but he recognized the gray-streaked hair of John Recelli, their missing soldier.

The arm around his neck loosened, and Antonio twisted to see a man about his own age with tan skin, a mustache, and a cowboy hat. The barrel of a silver .357 Magnum hit Antonio between his eyes.

"Too bad no one told you Esteban Vega is the new king of Los Angeles," he said, cracking a handsome smile. "Remember that name; it's the last you will ever hear. But before I kill you, I'm going to make you watch your family and your men die."

Antonio looked over at Lino, who had just regained consciousness. The man holding him captive laughed as he began to saw at Lino's neck with the serrated blade. But Lino fought back, and the knife's teeth found his chin instead of his jugular vein.

"You slippery fuck—!" The shriek of tires cut the Vega soldier off. He vanished in a blur of metal as one of the Moretti BMWs roared up alongside the Suburban, sandwiching him against the door and snapping it off.

Lino slumped over onto the center console, his eyes locked on Antonio.

Antonio seized on the distraction and threw an elbow, catching Esteban Vega in the ribs. Gunfire rang out from multiple directions, and rounds pinged off the Suburban.

Reaching behind him, Antonio pulled out his pistol. The road was clogged with vehicles and civilians huddling behind them as stray rounds pinged off metal and whined through the air.

He looked for Esteban in the chaos and spotted him running for a pickup with two of his men. Raising the pistol, Antonio aimed it at the self-proclaimed king of LA.

"You're going to have to do better than that to kill me, you cocksucker!" Antonio yelled. He fired several shots, taking out one of the guards, but Esteban ducked behind the pickup, and his other soldier turned to fire at Antonio, forcing him to take cover.

Screams and gunfire rang out as Moretti soldiers jumped out of their vehicles and fired on the remaining Vega soldiers.

Antonio hurried over to his wife and son, huddled on the other side of the Suburban.

"We're okay!" she shouted.

Yellowtail had limped over to the driver's side and was reaching in to grab Lino.

"Get them out of here!" Antonio yelled to his men.

Rush and Christopher put Lucia and Marco in the BMW that had saved them during the attack. The grill guard was bent and bloody where it had slammed into the man who tried to kill Lino.

"Don Antonio, we've got to move!" Rush yelled.

"I'll meet you there!"

Rush ducked into the BMW and sped away with the Moretti queen and crown prince safely inside.

"Watch our back," Antonio said to Christopher, who shouldered a rifle while Antonio went around to the driver's door of the Suburban.

Yellowtail had his hand pressed against Lino's chin and the flap of flesh hanging off it. Lino stared at Antonio.

"Hold on, brother," Antonio said. He then went to the back to check on Raff. There was a pulse, but he had hit his head hard.

They pulled him out gently and laid him on the back seat of the remaining Suburban, then did the same with Lino.

Police sirens blared over the air-raid Klaxons as they drove away from the wrecked vehicles and dead Vega soldiers.

Antonio took over for Yellowtail, pressing his hand against Lino's gash. The Vega soldier had sliced into his neck but missed the artery and jugular. If the BMW had hit the man a half second later, Lino would have already bled out.

As they raced away, he struggled to keep his eyes open, blinking and focusing on his boss. Raff was breathing, but his lungs rattled.

Speaking in Italian, Antonio told his old friend that everything would be okay, that they would fight many more battles together.

Antonio looked up to Christopher in the front seat.

"Where the *fuck* were you earlier? Vega almost killed my family!"

"I'm sorry," Christopher replied. "We got cut off. I turned around as fast as I—"

"Shit," Yellowtail said, pulling a bloody hand away from his side. "I think I got hit again."

"How bad?" Antonio asked.

Yellowtail pulled up his shirt. Blood trickled out, and he put a hand down against his love handle. "Going to have another scar, but I don't think it hit anything vital—just through the fat."

"We're almost there," Christopher said.

Lino squirmed on the seat, kicking the door. His lips opened, but Antonio shushed him, saying, *"Non parlare, Lino. Non parlare."*

Christopher weaved in and out of traffic, clipping a car with the right mirror. On an open stretch of road, he floored it, hitting what felt to Antonio like a hundred miles an hour.

Ten minutes later, he finally saw the Commerce Hotel in the distance.

"There it is," Christopher said. He pulled out his walkie-talkie to say they were coming in.

The Suburban squealed into the parking lot a minute later and pulled up to the front drive, where a dozen Moretti soldiers were already waiting. Two had medical training.

"Sir, I need you to move," one of them said to Antonio.

Suit and hands covered in blood, Antonio staggered away, watching as they carried away two of his most trusted men.

"Dad!"

The voice pulled Antonio's eyes to the lobby, where Lucia and Marco stood behind more Moretti guards. He made his way toward them, wiping his bloody hands on his pant legs. Lucia threw her arms around his neck, her body trembling against his.

"It's okay," he whispered. "We're safe now."

Marco grabbed his sleeve. "Are you okay, Dad?" he asked.

"I'm fine," Antonio said. He kissed his wife on the forehead, smearing blood in her wild hair.

"What about Raff?" Marco asked. He watched wide-eyed as Raff and Lino were carried into the lobby.

"He's strong," Antonio said. "God willing, he will be okay."

Marco looked around at the floor filled with slot machines and card tables.

"What is this place?" he asked.

Antonio put a hand on his shoulder and said, "This is our new home, son."

* * *

Two hours after the attack on Camp Pendleton, Dom sat huddled with Monica and their mother in the Downey High School auditorium. The gymnasium and most of the classrooms were already full of families, and more were still shuffling in with their meager belongings.

"How long do we have to stay here?" Monica asked, closing her book and setting it on her lap.

"I don't know," Dom said. "It depends."

"On what?"

Monica glanced over at their mother, but Elena was staring off into space, lost in her thoughts.

"Mom?" Dom said, reaching out to her, "You okay?"

Elena snapped out of whatever she was thinking about. "Yes, it's just … my college roommate and her family live—lived—in Mission San Luis Rey, just south of Pendleton."

"They might have made it out …" He didn't sound convincing, and his mom wiped a tear away. They both knew that her friend's chances of surviving were slim to none. Even if they had been shielded from the blast, the intense heat would have vaporized them.

The doors to the auditorium swung open, and Ronaldo walked in, still in his fatigues and carrying his rifle. He motioned to Dom.

"Mon, why don't you tell Mom about that sci-fi book you got there?" Dom said.

Elena took a seat, and Dom moved down the aisle of chairs, past several other families who were sitting and talking quietly.

He met his father in the hall as more people came in through the building's side entrance.

"Hurry up," said one of several marines standing guard.

Three of the men worked to seal off the entrance with tarps, wet sheets, and anything else they could find to keep out any radioactive fallout now that nearly everyone was inside.

"I need to talk to you," Ronaldo said quietly. They walked halfway across the room until they got to the administrative offices. Tooth and Bettis were inside with Marks and six other marines, listening to a radio.

"What's up, Dad?" Dom said.

Ronaldo stopped outside the door and checked for anyone listening.

"This wasn't just Camp Pendleton," he said.

Dom held a breath in his chest, waiting for his worst fears to be confirmed.

"Sacramento, Chicago, Denver, New York, and Seattle were all hit. Elliot, that son of …" Ronaldo closed his eyes and took a deep breath. "The deranged bastard went after the biggest population centers, and some of the capitals, of almost every state under rebel control, including several marine bases."

Dom felt his face warming and realized he still hadn't taken a breath.

Ronaldo said, "The only good news, if you can call it that, is the bombs were some of the new low-yield nukes that the government just rolled off the assembly line a year before the war. Smaller even than the fifteen-kiloton one we used on Hiroshima."

"So that means we're safe here?"

"Not exactly," Ronaldo said. He let out a low sigh, and his lip curled—something he did when he was nervous and angry. "The fallout from Pendleton is still going to sow death across the state for hundreds of miles. That's why we're sealing off everything we can to keep it out of the school. I just want you to know we're going to be here a while, and I'm counting on you to help your mom and sister however you can, okay?"

"Of course, Dad. You can count on me."

"I know." Ronaldo put a hand on Dom's shoulder and leaned in closer. "Even when this is over, it's going to get worse before it gets better. You saw what it's like out there."

"Yeah."

"Then you know what we face when we make it out of here. The fight for survival is just starting." Ronaldo looked back to the office. "Wait here a minute."

Dom had hoped the war was almost over and that things would get better soon, so he could focus on being a police officer. But things had just gotten a whole lot worse, and right now his family needed him more than ever.

The office door opened, and Ronaldo led the other marines out into the hallway.

"We need your help, Dom," he said.

The marines returned to the entrances, where the tarps were going up. People stood on chairs, putting duct tape over the vents.

"Won't that cut off our air supply?" Dom asked.

"We got a team outside setting up a filtration system that we normally use in tents," Ronaldo replied. "The same kind we had in the shelters in Phoenix. Don't worry, okay? I just need you to go to the gym and help move supplies."

"Okay, dad, no problem."

Minutes later, Dom was toting cases of MREs and bottled water into a classroom. The windows were already secure with plastic wrapping and duct tape along the frames.

Two young enlisted army soldiers carried a stack of boxes inside, talking as they walked.

"No way in hell this is going to feed all these people," one grumbled. "We shouldn't have moved most of our supplies to the other location."

"I was just thinking the same thing," said the other guy. "I'm all for sharing with the locals, but …" The man set his box down, his words trailing off when he saw Dom standing there.

The soldiers remained silent as they walked out of the room, leaving him by the window. Bathed in sweat and anxious from the conversation, he turned to look outside at the streets.

A squad car had pulled up and let out a family. Four more mouths to feed.

The officer drove away, and Dom thought of Moose, out there doing his duty. Knowing his best friend, he was probably still driving around trying to get people to go indoors, and here Dom was, already safe and secure.

I should be out there too.

And if it weren't for his father, he probably would have been. Ronaldo had demanded he come to the school with his family, and Dom had followed the order. Now he was stuck here.

He stepped away from the window but froze when he saw a Humvee drive into the parking lot. Tires squealed and shouting followed as the driver broke through the front gate and turned onto the street.

Two marines ran out onto the grass, waving and yelling. The two men hurried back inside, and Dom saw that one of them was Gunny Marks.

He thought of the two army soldiers and their conversation about supplies. Was it possible they had really jumped ship in a Humvee?

A hand touched Dom's shoulder, and he flinched.

"Sorry," Monica said, seeing she had startled him.

"What are you doing here?"

She shrugged. "I came to find you. Do you need help?"

"No, I'm good. You should really go back and stay with Mom."

"She's crying, and I don't know what to do to help."

Dom sighed and wiped the sweat from his forehead. "Okay, I'll go talk to her, but I need to find Dad first and talk to him."

He started away, but Monica walked up to the window.

"What?" he said, turning.

"Is it snowing?"

Through the translucent wrap covering the windows, he could see pale gray flakes drifting down from the sky. He carefully removed a strip of tape and pulled the plastic back just a crack.

"What is that?" Monica asked.

Dom studied the snowlike flakes. They weren't just radioactive material. They were all that remained of people vaporized in the Camp Pendleton nuclear holocaust.

People like his mother's college friend and his father's fellow marines.

Dom didn't have the heart to tell his sister the truth about the flakes floating down.

"Just ash from the fires," he lied. "Why don't you get back to your book, sis? Everything's going to be okay."

-19-

By the sixth day of holing up at Downey High School, the meager supplies of water and food were almost gone. Ronaldo paced in the hallway outside the auditorium, furious at the soldiers who had abandoned them.

They had taken MREs, water, and, most importantly, the CBRN suits, leaving the Desert Snakes and a small team of marines stranded inside. The colonel had bugged out with his HQ staff as soon as reports of the nuclear attack came in. So with no officers here, Marks had rank. He was doing his best to hold things together, but Ronaldo was getting more anxious by the hour.

The air filtration system was working, and the school had been sealed off, but without food and water, things would go downhill fast.

He stopped briefly to check his wristwatch. Five after midnight.

For the first time today, the facility was quiet, aside from the sporadic coughing or sobbing coming from the nearby classrooms that the military had turned into barracks. Over five hundred people were safely sheltering in place at the school now, and with dwindling supplies, tensions were rising.

Ronaldo continued pacing.

He was exhausted, but he couldn't let himself sleep. There were too many things to worry about for his fatigued brain to shut off.

Instead, he did what he always did when he felt anxious: he went to work.

For the next hour, he patrolled the hallways to make sure none of the civvies were trying to break into the supply room. Two guards held sentry inside just in case someone tried to break a window from the outside.

Another two marines stood post outside the doors. They were sitting down, but Ronaldo didn't hassle them over it. Everyone was at the end of their rope.

He gave them a nod and returned to where his team had camped out along a row of lockers. They had survived this long, but Ronaldo knew he had to make something happen if they were going to hold out much longer.

If you don't, who will?

Marks stood leaning his back against the wall, a hand on his forehead, eyes closed. Was he really sleeping standing up?

Of course he is. Sleeping anywhere, under any conditions, was one of the first things a marine learned how to do.

"Gunny," Ronaldo said quietly.

Marks pulled his hand away and opened his eyes. "Yeah." He blinked. "What's up, Salvatore?"

"I think it's time we made a run for the supplies at the safe house."

Marks's eyes narrowed. "You *crazy*? The safe house is almost three miles away, and we don't even know if it's been contaminated or raided or—"

"The only people who know about it are right here, so I doubt it's been raided." Ronaldo looked around to make sure no one was listening. "It could be another week before we get the all clear, and we'll be out of water in two days. When that happens, we're going to be in big fucking trouble."

"Yeah, I know, man." He ran a hand over his short-cropped hair and looked down the hallway, where Tooth and Bettis were leaning against their rucksacks, fast asleep.

"I wouldn't ask you to come, but I got no one else," Ronaldo said. "It's a big risk, especially without any protective gear."

Marks cursed under his breath. "I still can't believe those assholes."

"Nothing we can do about them now," Ronaldo replied. "But we have to do something before we run out of supplies. We won't be exposed long." He checked over his shoulder again. "I won't even tell anyone we're leaving."

"And what happens if we get attacked out there?" Marks stepped closer to Ronaldo and kept his voice low. "You thought of that?"

"That's why we got these." He hefted his M4. "I won't let anyone get within a hundred feet of us."

"You really have lost your damn mind, haven't you?"

Ronaldo scratched his chin. "The entire world has lost its damn mind."

Footsteps echoed down the hallway, and both men

turned as a man helped his wife into the bathroom, carrying a fresh bucket. As soon as they opened the door, Ronaldo caught a whiff.

They had done everything they could to keep things somewhat civilized over the past few days, but without running water, they were down to living like an underdeveloped nation.

"I guess I could use some fresh air," Marks said.

"I don't know about *fresh* …"

"You know what I mean."

The annoyance in Marks's tone was better than resignation, and Ronaldo patted his friend on the shoulder.

"I knew I could count on you, Gunny. Or should I call you *sir*, since you're the acting commander?"

Marks laughed. "Now you *are* going to piss me off."

Ronaldo forced a smile as he led them to the supply closet. The route went past the auditorium, and he decided against looking inside, in case Dom was awake. His son would insist on coming with them. So he ducked under the windows and rounded the next corner in a hurry.

"Wait up," said a voice.

Ronaldo and Marks stopped in the next hallway. The heavy footfalls sounded like military boots.

Bettis and Tooth came around the corner.

"Where you two going?" Tooth asked.

"To get supplies," Ronaldo replied.

Bettis and Tooth exchanged a glance.

"You're going outside?" Bettis asked.

"That's the idea, yeah."

Bettis shook his head, paused, and said, "Not without us, you aren't."

That got a glare from Tooth. "What do you mean, *us*?"

Ronaldo continued walking. He didn't have time to argue with either of them. Two pairs of boots followed, and a few seconds later, he heard a snort and the rap of more footsteps, in double time.

"Wait up, fellas," Tooth called out. "The Desert Snakes stay together."

Ronaldo didn't stop until he got to the janitor's closet. He unlocked the door and began the search for the next-best thing to a CBRN suit.

"What are you looking for?" Bettis asked.

Ronaldo grinned when he found a box of black garbage bags. He kept digging through the supplies and found latex gloves and a half-used roll of duct tape.

"Ah, hell no," Tooth said. "I'm a marine, not a garbage man."

Ronaldo held up the box. "It beats your insides melting and losing all your teeth."

"These teeth jokes get pretty fucking old, you know that? Do I tease you about that mole the size of Pluto on your chin?"

"Nope."

"Or about that curly black pube growing out of it?"

Ronaldo chuckled and pushed the box out. "Just put these on if you're coming."

They dressed in the small closet, and a few minutes later they walked down a dark hallway.

"Okay," Ronaldo said, "we run to the M-ATV, drive to the safe house, then come straight back with as much food and water as we can get in the back. We come in, go straight to the clean room, and wash off, okay?"

Three nods.

"All right, let's go," Ronaldo said.

As soon as they opened the door, the Desert Snakes bolted for the armored vehicle through the layer of ash covering the asphalt. The truck fired right up, and they tore out of the lot.

Marks flicked on a mounted beam that augmented the headlights in cutting through the lingering haze, but it seemed nothing could penetrate the inky black of the skyline. The dense smoke created a bowl of blackness, blocking out the moon and stars.

"Must be forest fires feeding the smoke," Ronaldo said.

"Another thing we'll have to worry about when it's finally safe to come outside," Marks said.

From the looks of it, that wouldn't be anytime soon.

The men fell into silence on the eerie drive through abandoned streets. Cars covered in the radioactive ash sat idle, like vehicles parked on a street during Christmas.

They spotted the first body three blocks from the school, lying on a sidewalk, curled up in the fetal position and covered in ash.

"Is he—" Tooth began to say.

Marks cut him off. "Dead. Nothing we can do for him. Let's just focus on what we came out here for. We're almost there."

The last mile of the drive took them through more abandoned neighborhoods and a park. Tent flaps moved slowly in the breeze, exposing more bodies. People who had ignored the warning to get indoors or had nowhere else to go were already dead from acute radiation poisoning, which meant they had likely gotten horrifically high doses—twenty thousand millisieverts or more.

Bettis crossed his chest.

"Looks like fairly fresh tracks," Marks said.

A tire trail curved from a connecting street and headed east—the same direction they were going.

"Keep your eyes peeled," Ronaldo said.

The safe house was tucked behind several abandoned businesses two blocks away. The Snakes' former commander had decided to store some of their supplies there just in case the high school was attacked.

Ronaldo just hoped the assholes who abandoned their post hadn't come here first to raid the supplies. He didn't see any military vehicles or tire tracks outside the warehouse doors.

Marks shut off the headlights as they approached. He backed the M-ATV up to the main garage door. "Tooth, Bettis, you hold security while we load shit up."

"Of course I've got sentry," Tooth grumbled. Bettis simply nodded and grunted, "*Oo-rah.*"

Ronaldo froze when he saw footprints in the ash outside the window. He pointed them out, and the team got cautiously out of the M-ATV.

Marks flashed a hand signal to Tooth, who shouldered his rifle and set out on patrol with Bettis. Ronaldo and Marks walked to the main garage door of the warehouse.

Using a bolt cutter, Marks cut off the lock. Then he and Ronaldo moved over to the side door and kicked it in. They flicked on their tactical lights and entered the small warehouse, their beams crisscrossing through the inky darkness and capturing crates of supplies.

"Hell yes, they did leave everything," Ronaldo whispered. Even better, no one was home, giving them free rein to take whatever they needed.

Marks pulled open the bay door and opened the back of the M-ATV.

"Get as much loaded as you can," Marks ordered, calling Bettis and Tooth back in. "Quick, guys."

The marines worked fast and efficiently, creating an assembly line to the get the boxes into the back. MREs, dried food from FEMA, boxes of bottled water, and several drums of fresh water.

When they were halfway done, a voice sounded.

Not a voice, really—more of a scratchy or raspy breathing sound.

"Guys," Tooth said, "I think someone's coming."

Ronaldo unslung his rifle and flicked his light back on, peering through the falling ash. He pointed the beam down the street to the source of the noise, a woman crawling over the dust-covered sidewalk.

"Shit," he said, lowering his rifle.

"Hold up," Marks said, raising his fist. "Could be a trap."

Not a trap, Ronaldo thought. The woman had acute radiation poisoning; that much was obvious.

"Help … me," the woman croaked.

"I'm going over there," Ronaldo said.

Marks lowered his hand. "Nothing you can do for her, man. But knock yourself out. I'll finish loading this up. We leave in five."

Ronaldo trotted over to the woman and crouched beside her.

"Ma'am," he said, reaching out with a latex glove.

She tried to lift her head. When she finally saw him, she let out a screech.

"Get back!" she yelled.

It occurred to him how he must look in the dark, wearing garbage bags, like some alien creature in a space suit.

"It's okay," he said. "I'm not going to hurt you."

As he reached out to her, she grabbed his arm and pulled, shredding the bag he had taped over his arm.

He yanked free of her grip and fell on his butt. Cursing his stupidity. Now he, too, was exposed to the radiation.

"Don't touch me!" she screeched.

"Chill out, lady," Ronaldo said.

She pushed herself up to her knees. Vomit had dried to her shirt, and her exposed skin was smeared with ash. Going down on all fours, she scrambled away like a wild animal before collapsing to her stomach and moaning.

"Salvatore, we got to move!" Marks said from the truck.

"One minute." Ronaldo replied. He waved Bettis over.

She raised a hand to shield her face from the glow of his flashlight.

"Who are you?" she said. "Where am I?"

Tooth and Marks walked over.

"Dude, we got to go," Tooth said.

"We can't just leave her here," Ronaldo said. "She needs help."

"She needs a priest," Bettis said. He handed his rifle to Tooth and bent down beside her.

"I'm a chaplain, ma'am. Would you like me to pray with you?"

She gave a deep, rattling cough and lay back on the sidewalk. "Everything aches," she said. "I just want to sleep."

"We got any extra blankets?" Ronaldo asked.

Tooth brought one over and laid it over the woman as Bettis said a prayer and performed last rites. Leaving her there to die alone was one of the hardest things Ronaldo had ever done, but Marks was right; there was nothing they could do for her.

They got into the M-ATV and drove back to the school, loaded up with enough food and supplies to get the occupants through a few more days.

Marks looked over at Ronaldo, who was taping his sleeve back up.

"What happened?"

"Lady ripped it," he said.

"Shit, man …"

"It's fine. I'll get cleaned off right when I get back."

They drove to the school's cafeteria docking area. Several marines were waiting in the open bay door, and with them stood Dom.

"We rinse off before we do anything else," Ronaldo said. He got out of the vehicle and held up his hand for the marines and Dom to stay back.

"We're contaminated, so stay your distance," he said.

"What did you do, Dad?" Dom asked.

"My job," he said.

"Did you guys hear the news on the radio?" one of the marines said. He almost sounded excited.

"What news?" Marks asked.

Ronaldo's heart skipped. Had another city been hit with a nuke?

Dom smiled for the first time in days.

"President Elliot's dead," he said. "Killed by his own men."

"AMP and the rebels are meeting tomorrow to talk about a treaty," said another marine. "The war is almost over."

* * *

Antonio stood in the suite that would soon be his office, on the top floor of the Commerce Hotel and Casino. He had a commanding view of a suffering, broken city brimming with opportunity.

Three days had passed since Elliot's own generals ended his short, bloody reign, and with the threat of nuclear Armageddon over, the country could start on the slow and painful path to recovery.

And though Antonio had lost more men, he was readier than ever to move ahead with his plans. Lino had lost a lot of blood but was expected to recover, and the Morettis finally knew who their biggest enemy was: Esteban Vega, the wannabe narco king, and his younger brother Miguel.

Antonio stood at the window, enjoying the solitude and watching the first halting recovery efforts in Los Angeles. City trucks with plows were already busy pushing the radioactive ash off the streets, piling it up like drifts of deadly snow.

This was just the first step. Over the next few months, every habitable area of the city would have to be decontaminated. In the meantime, a lot of people would die from poisoning, starvation, dehydration, and waterborne disease.

The bloody fighting was coming to an end for the government, but for the average citizen, the fight to survive was a war all its own.

Not for the Moretti family.

He had invested a lot of resources into preparing for something just like this, and the former hotel was stocked with enough food and water to last them months. The problem would be in defending this place if his enemies found them.

Movement below pulled Antonio closer to the window.

One of his soldiers, in a CBRN suit, walked outside the front entrance. Four others joined him and got into a vehicle. They were heading to check on several Moretti properties, including their drug cutting and packaging facility.

Antonio had decided to limit their next shipment with the González family to just opiates and marijuana. With Vito still behind bars, they would focus on the drugs that would be in high demand for civilians suffering from acute radiation poisoning.

Painkillers would be gold.

A knock on the door turned him from the city view.

"Antonio …"

Lucia walked inside wearing a black dress with a V-shaped gold collar. A necklace of huge pink pearls hung over her cleavage. She gave him a kiss and then looked at the scab on his forehead—one of many wounds he had gotten over the past month.

"That might end up turning into a scar," she said. "I may have to agree with what Yellowtail was saying to Marco about that."

"So, it's true? Chicks really do like scars?"

She chuckled and followed him to his new desk, where she ran her fingers over the inlaid mahogany.

"I like it," she said. "We'll need to get you some new artwork, though—maybe hire our own painter, like a proper king would."

"I have something in mind if I can find someone," he said.

She walked over to the glass cases displaying some of the ancient weapons he had taken from the Sarcone property in Bel Air.

The double-bladed *haladie*, a knife used by the Rajput warrior class in India, was one of his favorites. He also treasured the fourteenth-century Japanese *katana*, but perhaps the most precious was a Spartan *kopis* from the Bronze Age. He picked up the ancient weapon, admiring the curved blade and the gold decoration on the hilt, and tried to imagine the Greek warrior who once held the relic.

"So, tell me," she said. "How long will we stay here?"

"This is our home for the indefinite future," he said, putting the sword back in its place. "In time, it will become a compound with walls and beautiful gardens. You'll see, my love."

She was leaning in to kiss him when another knock on the thick wooden doors interrupted the moment. Christopher opened them both and walked in wearing a suit that matched the silver streaks in his goatee.

"Are you ready for us, Don Antonio?" he asked.

Antonio kissed his wife. She started to leave, but he reached out. It wasn't traditional for a don's wife to sit in on these gatherings, but she was an essential part of the Morettis' future.

"I want you in this meeting," he said.

Frankie and Carmine followed Christopher into the office. Next came Raff, wearing a bandage around his head, and Vinny, who watched him like a hawk to make sure he was okay. Finally, Yellowtail limped in on crutches. The guy had taken a real beating over the past few months.

"Have a seat," Antonio said, gesturing toward the long table near the window. "How's Lino?"

"Hanging on like a warrior," Christopher said. "He'll pull through."

Antonio sat down beside his wife. "Good," he said. "We'll need his leadership in the days to come, which is why I have called you all here this afternoon." He turned on the radio to hear the news that had the entire world listening.

"*AMP and the rebels have finished meeting and have agreed to terms,*" said the announcer. "*An Executive Council has been formed to figure out next steps in creating a new government.*"

"The war is really over," Christopher said.

"Not our war," Antonio said. "And not our peace."

"We have to be strong," Frankie said. "We need to go after Esteban Vega, his *piccolo stronzo* brother Miguel, and his whole damn family for what they did."

"I agree," Carmine said. "It's time to end those pricks."

"I'm all for going after them," Yellowtail said, "but

we don't know much about the operation yet—how many men they have, what areas they control. All we know is that they're narcos and they tried to hit us."

"That's what makes your job so important," Antonio said, looking at Vinny. "You will find out who my enemies are, and feed the right info to the right cops."

"And make friends," Christopher said. "We want to know every crooked cop on the force so we can add them to our payroll."

"I met with Captain Brian Stone before the nuke hit the marine base," Vinny said, "but I'm not sure he trusts me yet, even after all the questions."

"You're not in jail with Vito, so that tells me you'll be fine," Antonio said. "You will provide a service to Stone, gain his trust, and feed him information that will benefit your family."

"I'm at your disposal, Don Antonio," Vinny replied.

"I don't like this at all," Frankie said. A wooden match bobbed up and down between his lips as he spoke. "No offense, Don Antonio, but since when did we become rats?"

Antonio narrowed his eyes at the soldier. Such blatant disrespect, especially in front of Lucia, made his blood boil. He wanted to light the match in Frankie's mouth, but the gratification he felt would be only temporarily.

"Got to agree with Frankie again," Carmine chimed in. "We worked with the cops in Naples, but we never had one of our own *join* them. What if Vinny screws up? What if he leads them back to us?"

Antonio walked over to the window, seething with anger. "As much as Los Angeles is starting to look like

Naples, it is *not* Naples and never will be," he said. "The soldiers and police in the city will stop worrying about finding AMP soldiers and divert all their attention to the gangs, which makes it more dangerous for us. We have to have someone on the inside, and Vinny is right for this job."

Raff, who normally didn't say much, nodded. "I think this will give us a great advantage, Don Antonio. I'm with you."

"Vinny isn't the brightest star in the sky," Yellowtail muttered. Then he grinned and thumbed his chest. "That would be me, of course. But he's better for this job since I've been shot five times."

Some of the men chuckled, and even Lucia smiled, but Carmine and Frankie sulked in disapproval of the plan.

"I've made up my mind, and this is the route we're taking forward. Vinny will join the police. In the meantime, since we obviously can't sell until the streets are cleaned, I want everyone focused on finding Esteban Vega and his brother. Can you handle that?" Antonio said, looking at Carmine and then Frankie.

Both men nodded.

"Good. Then make yourselves useful and get out of my sight." Antonio gestured toward the door, his gaze on the two brooding assassins. "Vin, Christopher, I want you to stay a few more minutes."

Carmine, Frankie, Raff, and Yellowtail left the room, and the doors clicked shut.

"You want to tell him, or should I?" Antonio said to Christopher.

"What?" Vinny asked.

"You can't live here anymore," Christopher said.

"We can't let the cops link you to the family. Once it's safe to go outside, you're going to have find another place. We've already talked to Doberman. He's going with you."

Vinny scratched his dark five o'clock shadow. "Like I said, I'm at your disposal, Don Antonio."

"Now, on to other business," Antonio said. "I don't like how Carmine and Frankie spoke to me. Their disrespect is getting worse."

"They're stuck in the old way of doing things," Lucia said. "That's not how it works here. You have shown that to all of us."

"She's right," Christopher said. "I'm sorry for ever doubting you, brother. You've done a hell of a job getting us to where we are now."

"Maybe you should replace Carmine as captain with one of the younger men, like Lino," Vinny said. He raised a hand. "Just a suggestion, Don Antonio. You're the king and you know best."

Antonio turned back to the window, considering the suggestion from his nephew. Vinny was still young, and he was wrong about one detail.

"Not a king yet," Antonio said.

As, he looked out over the city, Antonio recalled Esteban Vega's words during the highway ambush.

"There can be only one king in the City of Angels," Antonio said. "His name will be Moretti."

-20-

"Los Angeles County residents have been given the all clear to leave their shelters!"

The crowded high school gymnasium filled with applause. Hundreds of displaced people had gathered to hear the news from a battery-powered radio an electrician had rigged up to the school loudspeakers.

Dom let out a sigh of relief and hugged his mom and Monica.

"Everyone, please quiet down!" Gunny Marks shouted over the crowd.

The noise tapered off, and the person with the radio tuned to a different channel. This time, a monotone prerecorded voice from the emergency broadcast alert system listed counties in California and rated their nuclear contamination levels.

The crowd fell silent when Santa Barbara County was listed at the highest levels of radiation exposure. A cough here and there broke the silence, and finally, the monotone voice confirmed what the newscaster had said a few minutes earlier.

Almost two weeks after the nuclear detonation ninety miles away, radiation levels in Los Angeles had diminished to the point that it was safe to go outside.

"Does this mean I get to go back to school?" Monica asked.

"Soon," Elena said. She put an arm around each of her children and gave the first smile Dom had seen in the two weeks they had been holed up here.

Families embraced, cried, and laughed as the crowd dispersed.

"We're going to be okay," Elena said. "Everything is going to be okay now."

"Promise?" Monica asked.

Elena looked to Dom, who nodded. It was good to hear his mom being optimistic and to see her smile. Maybe she would finally come out of her depression and be back to her old self. He saw strength in her to-day—a good sign.

"All right, everyone," Marks said. "You're free to go home now. But don't forget, you still need to wear pro-tective masks to keep the dust out of your lungs. The threat of radiation is low, but it isn't gone. We have cases of N95 dust masks by the exits. Take one, *and only one*, for each member of your family. Supplies are short."

"Thank you!" someone shouted.

A single clap sounded. Then multiple claps. More people joined in, and within a few seconds, most of the crowd was clapping and cheering.

Dom looked for the other heroes who had made sure these people had the supplies to survive while shel-tering in place.

Bettis, Tooth, and Ronaldo stood near the exit

door, shying away from the applause. They had risked their lives because it was their duty.

As the gymnasium emptied, the refugees patted the marines on the shoulder, shook their hands, and thanked them.

Dom, Elena, and Monica were the last out of the room.

"You guys ready to go home?" Ronaldo asked.

"So ready," Monica said. "I need a new book."

"Library doesn't have enough?" Tooth asked.

Monica put a hand on her hip. "The next one on my TBR list is in my room, and I don't read out of order."

"TBR?" Tooth asked.

Monica rolled her eyes. "To be *read.*"

Tooth fussed with his spiked hair and grinned. "Oh, right. I got an extensive one of those."

"Yeah," Bettis deadpanned. "Only yours is more of a TB*C* list—to be *colored.*"

Ronaldo grinned at the gibe. "I have to talk to Marks," he said. "Meet you guys at the exit."

Elena put her hand on Monica's back. "Let's go home, sweetheart."

Dutifully putting on their dust masks, the hundreds of refugees began filing out of the school. Dom was glad to see people honoring the rule of one mask per person. He helped Monica with hers.

"What about you?" she asked.

"I got a bandanna; don't worry." He tied it around the back of his head. "See?"

They moved into the corridor, where the tarps had been pulled away from windows and exit doors. Carrying their bags, Dom walked out the open doors, into the first rays of sunshine he had felt in weeks.

Sirens whooped in the distance, and a dog barked.

While most of the people headed down the sidewalks toward home, the Salvatore family waited for Ronaldo.

He showed up a few minutes later, and from the look on his face, Dom could tell that Marks finally had new orders for the Desert Snakes, and they weren't good.

"What's wrong?" Elena asked.

Ronaldo ran a hand along the salt-and-pepper beard he had grown over the past two weeks.

"Our new CO has ordered us to patrol along the border," he said.

"So you're being deployed?" Elena glared. "Do you know how dangerous it is out there?"

"You have to leave the city, Dad?" Monica asked.

Ronaldo squatted down in front of her. "I have to work on the border they're building. But we won't be gone long, so don't worry, kiddo."

"When?" Elena asked.

"ASAP," Ronaldo said. "We're moving out as soon as we can clear out the high school."

Elena sighed. "I'll see you at home, Ronnie," she said in an annoyed tone. And grabbing Monica's hand, she led her away from the school. Dom stayed put, halfway between his mom and dad, torn again.

Ronaldo said, "Watch after them, okay?"

"Yeah, no problem. Be safe out there, Dad."

Dom ran to catch up with his mom and sister, who were already on the sidewalk and about to cross the street. Two squad cars drove by toward the Downey Police Station. Dom squinted to make out the driver of one of the vehicles.

"Hold here a second," he said.

Elena and Monica waited while he waved the car down. The officer parked and got out wearing a dust mask, gloves, and a hat over her short-cropped brown hair.

"Cam?" Dom said. "Is that you?"

She pulled down her mask and flashed a smile that he had missed more than he realized.

He hurried over to her and gave her a fierce hug.

"What are you doing here?" she asked.

"I sheltered at the high school with my family and the marines," he said. "We just got the all clear, so I'm walking my mom and sis home."

"No, you aren't." Camilla waved at Elena. "Mrs. Salvatore, bring Monica. I'll give you a ride home."

"You don't have to do that," Dom said.

"I insist," Camilla said. "Besides, it's not exactly safe out here right now, and I'm not talking about radiation."

"How do you mean?"

"The bangers and dirtbags came out of their holes not long after the fallout stopped, and have been tearing up the city. Looting, burning down buildings, killing each other over street corners—it's insane."

Dom saw the bruises and cuts still on her face, but he didn't bring up the attack that almost left her dead. She had proved she wasn't tough only on the basketball courts. She was also a hell of a cop.

He gave her another fierce hug. "I missed you, Cam."

She hugged him harder this time. "I wasn't sure I'd see you again."

"Same, but then again, I know it would take a lot to kill you."

She laughed at that as he pulled away.

"How's Moose doing?" he asked.

Camilla bit her lip.

"What?" Dom said. "He's okay, isn't he?"

"He's fine, but his parents aren't." Camilla forced a smile as Elena and Monica approached.

"Hi, Mrs. Salvatore. Good to see you."

"Good to see you too. How are you doing?'

"I'm alive, which is better than some can say." She held up a hand for Monica to slap. "And how are you, kiddo?"

"I'm not a kid," Monica said.

"We better get off the streets," Dom suggested.

"Right." Camilla opened the back door of the squad car.

"Cool," Monica said. "I've never ridden in one of these. "Dom said he's going to take me to the Griffith Observatory when he gets his own police car—right, Dom?

Camilla looked over at him. "Maybe I'll let him drive once he gets his badge," she said.

"Moose said he has me covered, but thanks."

Camilla got back into the car, picked up the radio transmitter, and relayed a message to the dispatcher.

"Moose is on the clock right now too," she said, pulling away from the curb. "After we drop your mom and sis off, we can go meet up with him if you want."

"I've got to watch them until my dad gets back," Dom said. "But once he does, I'm going back out there with Moose."

"Good. We need all the people we can …" Her words trailed off as she pulled onto their street.

"Oh my God," Elena said, cupping her hand over her mouth.

Camilla slowed to a stop, and Dom hopped out of the car.

"Jesus," he whispered.

Half the block was nothing but charred shells of houses. Graffiti covered an unburned garage of the house across the street. "PIGS DIE!"

Dom took several steps toward the blackened studs and foundation that remained of their home. Monica and Elena got out of the squad car.

"My books," Monica wailed.

Dom turned back to their house and held up a hand to keep his sister and mom back. They would be able to salvage nothing from the burned-out pile.

He put his arm around his sister and helped her back into the squad car.

"I'm really sorry," Camilla said ruefully. "I didn't know—haven't been through this neighborhood recently. But I think I know why. What do you notice about all these houses? Think plumbing and electric."

Dom gave her a puzzled look.

"Every one of these quarter-million-dollar houses got torched for a hundred bucks' worth of copper."

"Of course," Dom muttered. "And that copper's already gone up someone's nose or arm by now—damn speed freaks."

Elena held her daughter and let her sob against her shoulder.

"Where do you want me to take you guys?" Camilla whispered.

Elena heard the question. "Back to the school," she replied. "I want to talk to my husband."

"Okay, no problem."

Camilla drove back to Downey High School, passing families who also seemed to be returning.

"They must have lost their houses too," Dom said.

"Wouldn't be surprised," Camilla said. "Fires have destroyed a lot of residential areas. Most people will have to go to the camps until the city figures out something more permanent."

"Aren't the camps contaminated?" Dom asked.

"The city's working on cleaning them up. Bringing in trailers and prefab housing units." She looked over at Dom. "Basically, they're making warehouses. For people."

Dom watched the people on the sidewalk. Some were crying; others trudged ahead with blank stares.

So much pain and suffering, and despite the good news about the war's end, things would get worse for the survivors before they got better.

Back in the Downey High School parking lot, a group of the marines were already loading up their remaining M-ATVs and Humvees. Several newly homeless people had already arrived at the school and were being directed back inside.

"Looks like we get to stay here a bit longer," Dom said. He turned to his little sister. "I'm sure they have some great books in the library that you haven't read yet."

She looked up from Elena's shoulder and wiped away a tear. "I wanted to sleep in my own bed."

"So did I, but we have to make the best of what we have, and be happy we're still alive."

Monica looked down, and Elena thanked Camilla for the ride. They got out of the car, but Dom stayed a moment longer.

"How bad is it out there?" he asked.

"You haven't seen anything yet. Same thing happened to Moose's house, but his parents were still inside ... Never made it out."

"*What?*" Dom said, his voice cracking from shock. He had known the Clarke family for the past five years. They were good people, always doing things for others. And now they were dead, burned alive in their own house by gangbangers or junkies.

"We're being hunted," Camilla said. "Anyone with a badge who doesn't play by the rules."

"What rules?"

"The rules the gangs are making. A lot of the cops on the force are working with them now."

"What do you mean, 'working with them'?"

"They're dirty," she said. "So, you sure you still want to join?"

Dom avoided her gaze to look out the window at his sister and mom in the parking lot, their hair blowing in the wind, eyes swollen from crying.

He would do anything to protect them.

But part of protecting them was to fight against the very sort of animals who had burned down their house and killed Moose's parents.

"Yeah," he said. "I'm not turning back now. The sooner I get a badge, the better."

Camilla cracked a grin of perfect white teeth. "Okay, then. Let's get started."

He rolled down the window and called out after

Elena, who had turned to wait for him. "Tell Dad I'm going out with Cam. I'll be back later tonight."

"Dom, wait," Elena said, raising a hand.

"Go," Dom said to Camilla.

She seemed conflicted as she put the cruiser in reverse.

As she pulled out of the parking lot, he drew his pistol and pulled back the slide to chamber a round. Since the nukes went off, life was never going to be what he had always thought it would be.

He would probably never go to college, never fight in the Octagon again, never work a nine-to-five job and raise a family in a safe world with weekend beach trips and backyard barbecues.

The American dream was gone, stolen by some of the very men who had sworn to defend it.

His destiny was clearer now than ever. He was a fighter like Camilla, and he would focus that strength on saving one of the last American cities from the demons hell-bent on destroying it.

* * *

"Stay where you are!" shouted a guard. "And show me your hands."

Vinny stopped in front of the Los Angeles Police Department headquarters building on First and Main and slowly pulled his hands out of the pockets of his black hoodie.

"Turn around!" the officer yelled.

Vinny slowly turned with his hands in the air until he was again facing the LAPD headquarters. More of a fortress, really. The cops had transformed the building into what looked more like a high-security military base.

He couldn't help but wonder whether this was what his uncle had envisioned for the nine-story Commerce Hotel: a modern-day castle in a sprawling postapocalyptic city.

Razor-wire fences and a main gate separated Vinny from the parking lot. Two guard towers, each manned by a single officer with a scope-mounted automatic rifle, flanked the gates.

One of those rifles was now pointing at his head.

"What's your business here?" the man yelled, his voice muffled by a breathing apparatus.

"Nathan Sarcone, here to see Captain Stone," Vinny called up.

After a brief pause, the guy not aiming a rifle at him signaled down to the sentries on the other side of the gate. The chain-link barrier rolled aside far enough to let him walk through.

Vinny made his way through the gauntlet of checkpoints, receiving two pat-downs. He passed more officers in riot gear patrolling the front steps of the building, and a group standing behind a fort of sandbags.

He didn't stop until he was inside the building, at the front desk. After he explained his business to two more officers, a door buzzed, and a heavyset man with acne scars and a weedy mustache stood looking at him.

"Yeah?" he said in the raspy voice of an inveterate smoker.

"I'm Nathan Sarcone, here to see Captain Brian Stone." Vinny looked at the officer's badge: *Sergeant Billy Best.*

"Nah, you're with me today, kid," Best said. "Come on."

They walked down a hallway that ended in an open room with dozens of desks, all of them occupied. The place was a hive of activity. Officers walked back and forth carrying files or tablets.

They had power here, even air-conditioning. *Probably a generator*, Vinny thought.

Sergeant Best stopped at a small office and opened the door. He blew air from his mouth up into his bristly mustache.

"Well, what are you waiting for?" Best said.

Vinny walked into the room, and the sergeant closed the door, shut the blinds, and faced him.

"All right, punk, I don't give a flying fuck who your uncle was," Best said. "I was three years away from collecting my pension when this war started. Now, instead of looking forward to sitting on a beach, eating lobster rolls and drinking Mexican beers, I have to babysit your sorry crooked ass."

Vinny started to reply, but Best cut him off.

"You're not a cop, and you're not a CI," he said. "Until you tell me everything you know about your uncle's enemies and where they are, you're nothin'."

"How about I *show* you?" Vinny said.

The sergeant moved closer, and Vinny pulled back slightly from the rancid breath. Best gave him a coffee-stained grin from beneath his shaggy mustache.

"You're going to show me, all right," Best said. "And if you fuck anything up or get any of my boys hurt, Captain Stone has given me permission to throw you in jail with the rest of the dirtbags. And with that pretty face, dropping the soap is going to be the least of your worries."

Vinny wanted to ask about Vito, but this wasn't the time. Instead, he gave a crocodile smile. "Looks like I better not fuck up, then. Let's start with the camp at Arcadia Park. Most of the refugees are living in the prefab shelters that got shipped in, right?"

Best scrutinized him for a few seconds.

"The Norteño Mafia controls that area with several of its affiliates, like the Eighteenth Street Gang," Vinny said. "But you should already know that, right?"

"Yeah."

"They're making it harder to spot them, wearing long sleeves to cover their tattoos, but I can pick 'em out like a hooker on a corner."

Best smiled, sort of. "All right, you guinea rat, time to prove your worth."

Vinny clenched his jaw but let the insult roll off him. After all, he was the lady of the evening right now, and he was prepared to take one for the Moretti team.

An hour later, they were riding in an unmarked car, on their way to the refugee camp in Arcadia, not far from the border barriers the city was constructing. So far, everything that Don Antonio had told Vinny to say had worked.

But underneath the relaxed facade, he was sweating bullets.

He didn't like Best or Darwin, the bald Viking-looking dude riding shotgun. A thick beard, the bottom of it braided and beaded, hung from his square jaw, and he had more ink than Doberman.

He looked like the kind of cop who enjoyed

breaking skulls. No doubt, he would get the chance soon enough.

The radio chirped with reports of violence. A mass shooting in East Los Angeles, another shooting at a FEMA ration distribution point, and a riot at Cedars Sinai Hospital.

"Glad I'm not a rookie," Best said. "They got more shit to wade through than a hog farmer."

"I'm surprised the hospitals are even functioning," Darwin said, looking out over the city. "Medical supplies are running low, and the gennies are running on fumes."

"What surprises me is that Mayor Buren hasn't ordered Chief Diamond to let them tap into what's left of our supply."

"If that happened, we wouldn't be able to protect anyone, now, would we?" Darwin said.

Vinny sat in the back seat listening, recalling a conversation between his dad and his uncle about a gang hoarding fuel in an East LA warehouse. They had hijacked three full tanker trucks a few weeks before the nuke and were trying to sell them to the highest bidder.

"I might be able to help there," Vinny said.

Best looked in the rearview. "You a doctor now too?"

"Hah," Vinny chuckled. "No, I mean with the gasoline."

Now both men were looking at him.

"The Sureños jacked some tanker semis a few weeks back. I don't think they've moved anything yet, either."

"Where?" Best asked.

"You want to go to Arcadia, or you want the gas first?" Vinny asked. It didn't matter to him. Either way, he was about to prove himself.

"Tell us where the gas is," Best said.

"Exchange Avenue, next to that big meat company."

The sergeant looked over at his partner and said, "Get a team."

"Sarge, isn't that a dead zone?" Darwin replied.

"For three tankers of gas, I don't much give a shit."

Instead of reaching for the radio, Darwin pulled out one of two walkie-talkies he had up front, and relayed a message in Spanish.

"All right, Nate the Rat," Best said. "Let's see if you're right."

"Better fucking be," Darwin said. "Or he's gonna learn what it's like to fly."

Vinny had heard that one before, but he wasn't worried. He was playing these two goons like a violin.

Two hours later, they were climbing to the top of an abandoned warehouse two blocks away from the meatpacking business. The rooftop gave them an eastern view of the building. Darwin used binoculars to check out the street.

"There's some guards outside," he said. "And something else … Oh, shit. You better see this."

He handed Best the binoculars.

Vinny didn't need the optics to see a human body hanging from a light pole.

"That's the Sureños' calling card," Best said. "Skinned the poor bastard alive."

Vinny had seen their brutality before, but flaying a guy alive and hanging him from a lamppost? That shit didn't go down even in Italy. Not since Mussolini, at least, but at least they had shot the traitorous bastard first, and they let him keep his skin.

This sort of truly barbaric shit was exactly why the Morettis hadn't come after the Sureños yet. They were strong, and Don Antonio wanted Vinny to help thin out the pack.

Screeching tires distracted him from the grisly view.

Several black undercover cars raced toward the Downey Road intersection, turning onto Exchange Avenue. Tan pickups entered down the street, their beds full of men in black fatigues and wearing masks.

"Here we go," Best said. "Better get your head down, kid. Wouldn't want to mess up that nice slick 'do with a bullet."

Vinny crouched and peered over the parapet at the warehouse's loading gates. The guards there were already fanning out to engage the pickups that had slammed into the metal gate at the front.

Gunfire lanced into the vehicles, but it was already too late.

The men in the pickup beds fired, cutting down the minimal security in the open lot.

The black cars followed the pickups, screeching into the cleared area. Dozens of men jumped out, firing at the Sureños, who were now retreating. Several men emerged on the rooftop, firing rifles at the tide of cops. Both snipers went down in a flurry of automatic gunfire, falling over the half wall and smacking into the concrete.

In moments, all the Sureños were dead or on the way, and the LAPD officers were streaming into the facility through multiple entrances.

Vinny squatted behind the cinder-block parapet, impressed. Ten less Sureños the Morettis had to worry about. Antonio would be pleased.

"Let's go," Best said.

They took the fire escape down to the first floor of the building and made their way back to their car, parked in the alley and facing the street. But when they got inside, the sergeant didn't fire up the engine. He just sat and waited.

"What are we doing?" Vinny asked.

Neither man responded.

The sporadic gunshots tapered off, and static crackled over the radio.

Darwin spoke in Spanish again.

"It's done," he said.

"And?" Best asked.

"Kid was right. There were three tankers of gas, plus a whole shitpot full of guns."

Best and Darwin both twisted around to the back seat.

"Told ya," Vinny said. He grinned but then tensed up when he saw men approaching from the end of the alley.

"Bogeys at one o'clock," he said, pointing.

Darwin and Best turned back around to the windshield.

"I'll handle this," Best said. He got out of the car, leaving Darwin with Vinny.

Two Latino men wearing button-down patterned shirts and jeans with silver belt buckles walked toward the vehicles, their weathered features half hidden under expensive cowboy hats.

Six more men accompanied them, all wearing fatigues and face masks and carrying AK-47s angled at the ground.

"Those don't look like cops," Vinny said.

"You're smarter than I thought," Darwin replied.

The two men wearing cowboy hats spoke to Sergeant Best, and one of them handed him a small paper bag. They shook hands and parted ways.

One of the guys looked back at the car and tipped his cowboy hat. Vinny squinted, trying to make out his features. He looked … familiar, maybe.

Best opened the door, wearing a shit-eating grin.

"You did good, kid," he said as he fired up the engine. "The Vegas paid a pretty penny for that find."

He looked in the rearview mirror, meeting Vinny's gaze, but Vinny looked away, unable to keep his poker face as realization stabbed him like a knife to the gut.

Best had never called in LAPD backup. He had called in the Vegas. Instead of hurting their biggest enemy, Vinny had just helped them.

But how the hell was he supposed to know that Best and his crony cops were in bed with the narco king, Esteban Vega?

"Keep this shit coming, and I might tell Captain Stone to get you added to the anti-gang task force," Best said, still smiling. "Hell, might even give you a piece of the action."

-21-

A swath of the Angeles National Forest burned, choking the skyline with dense smoke. Ronaldo said a prayer for the firefighters deployed to keep the flames from reaching the city limits. They certainly weren't going to be getting any air support or water tankers.

Most of those brave firefighter crews were on their own.

Not so different from the Desert Snakes.

Ronaldo's small team trekked with their new platoon across the mud, toward the tracks, to meet the next train of refugees. He was glad to be here to help, but he still wasn't sure why Command wanted them along the border and not in the fight against the gangs. And if Marks knew anything, he wasn't talking.

A mobile Los Angeles County Emergency Operations unit was set up in the parking lot to their right, and standing on a platform in plain sight was Sarah DaBuke, the FEMA incident commander.

For the past decade, she had worked on some of the biggest natural disasters that had led to the crash of the economy, and now she was in Los Angeles, trying to save it from becoming a statistic like the other major metro areas across the country.

So far, she had solidified her glowing reputation by successfully organizing the refugee camps in Los Angeles County and working with the city officials to block off roads to the east.

Ronaldo was impressed with her ability to respond quickly and efficiently to situations like this. But she didn't seem to like the military much.

"What the hell do you think you're doing?" she said to Marks.

Ronaldo hung back but not too far to hear their conversation.

"What do you mean?" Marks asked her.

She gestured toward the twenty-odd armed marines making their way to the train platform.

"We have orders to help here, ma'am," Marks said politely.

"And while I respect that you have your orders, these incoming refugees are sick and scared. I ask that you remain out of sight while we work to get these people assigned to case workers and medical support."

"Sorry, ma'am, no can do. My orders are clear. We're to remain on the platform and help supervise the orderly movement of these refugees."

"Then I kindly ask you to leave your weapons locked in your vehicles."

Marks tilted his head. "You can't be serious."

"I'm dead serious. These people have had their lives torn apart by this civil war. The last thing they need is to get off this train and see men in uniform, holding machine guns."

Tooth stepped up next to Ronaldo. "What the hell is this lady saying?"

"You don't want to know."

Ronaldo turned to the rest of the platoon standing in the soupy field. He had taken on the duty of first squad leader, under Marks as platoon leader. But not knowing most of them was making things dicey, and he did worry that someone might do something stupid.

They certainly looked intimidating in their layered camo, gas masks, and neoprene gloves. Not to mention the weapons they carried.

A horn blared in the distance, and a train engine emerged on the tracks to the east. The FEMA staff and aid workers fanned out across the platforms, wearing breathing masks and goggles against the gusting wind.

"We're not losing the weapons, ma'am, I'm sorry. Doing so would put my men at risk—and your people too, as well as the very refugees we are here to protect." Marks pulled off his gas mask to look her in the eyes. "However, you have my word that we will be professional and empathetic with these people."

Sarah DaBuke folded her arms across her chest. "I'll hold you to that."

She walked away, and Marks slipped his mask back on and gave Ronaldo a nod.

"All right, let's do this," Ronaldo said.

The platoon trudged forward to the tracks. Halfway across the field, a gunshot pierced the early evening, and Ronaldo stopped dead in the slop.

It didn't sound far. More than likely, it came from the

other side of the border barriers. Not surprising, either. Everything on that side had fallen into complete chaos.

This was *exactly* why they needed their weapons.

Chances were good someone was taking potshots at the train and this next batch of terrified refugees the city had accepted.

Welcome to the City of Angels.

The locomotive pulled dozens of shipping containers on flatcars. The colorful train crawled forward. The cargo inside wasn't coal, processed foods, or medical supplies. It was people.

The marines moved out onto the platforms, spreading outward to team up with aid workers for each arriving car.

"Stay frosty, everyone," Marks said over the comm. "And by that, I mean, do *not* raise your weapon unless you are being assaulted by a goddamn flesh-eating zombie elephant."

Tooth made a trumpeting sound, drawing a laugh from several of the men.

"God damn it, Tooth, fix yourself," Marks said.

"Oorah, Gunny," Tooth said.

The train rounded the next corner and began to slow, screeching to a stop. Ronaldo joined a woman wearing a FEMA baseball cap and an American flag bandanna up to her nose.

"I've got this," he said.

The marines down the platform approached the doors, each fitted with a square-foot grate to let in air. Eyes peered through the grates as Ronaldo unlatched the door. He opened it to somber faces, spirits broken, little remaining but the instinct to survive.

They shuffled toward the door, some of them shrinking back from his reach.

Even with the activated-charcoal filtration mask on, he could smell the stench from inside.

"One at a time," he said, stepping up to help people down.

The aid worker got behind him to help guide the people away. Several people jumped out without accepting Ronaldo's hand.

A woman wearing a tattered sweatshirt that exposed part of her breast stepped up. Bruises framed her eyes, so that she reminded him of a raccoon. When he reached up for her, she hesitated in the open doorway, and he saw the fear in her dull green eyes.

"Come on, lady!" shouted the guy behind her.

"It's okay," Ronaldo said calmly. She finally took his hand, and he helped her down. Next came two brown-haired boys wearing nothing but T-shirts and shorts. No shoes or socks, every inch of exposed skin covered in grime.

He grabbed each boy around the waist and lifted them down from the car, setting them down in front of the aid worker.

"Where are your parents?" she asked.

The older of the two shook his head.

"I'm sorry. Go to that truck over there, and you will be assigned a case worker."

The kids walked away, heads down, and Ronaldo turned back with a heavy heart. It continued to break as he helped the survivors out of the car. Each one seemed thinner and filthier than the one before.

When the last person jumped out, he saw the body on the floor inside.

A blanket half-covered the woman, and he could tell right away that she wasn't breathing. He climbed inside to check just in case, stepping over a small mound of feces.

The buckets were filled to the brim with diarrhea, which made sense. Most of these people were from Nevada, New Mexico, and California. They all were sick with mild to severe radiation poisoning, dehydration, or worse.

Cholera was no longer a worry. It was bordering on becoming an epidemic.

When Ronaldo got to the woman, he bent down and took off a glove to check for a pulse just to be sure. Feeling nothing but cold flesh, he pulled the blanket up to cover her corpse.

He put on his glove and moved back to the open door, trying his best to avoid the muck on the floor. A sea of refugees staggered past the open door, each following the feet in front of them, like livestock.

The tattered clothes, protruding ribs, and filthy faces were a grim snapshot of war's human cost.

How had this happened in America?

Then he remembered the madman Elliot.

Burn in hell, asshole. Move over, Hitler, Mussolini, Stalin, Mao.

As Ronaldo jumped back to the platform, static crackled from the comms piece in his ear.

"Snake One to Snake Two, where are you?" said Marks.

Ronaldo looked up the line of cars, counting. "Snake One. I'm at car fourteen, over."

"Report to car forty-one."

"Roger. On my way," Ronaldo replied. He started weaving his way through the crowd, anxious about what he would discover in the train car.

"Sarge!" shouted a voice.

Ronaldo could see Tooth waving across the platform, where he had moved to supervise the line.

"Watch out. Move. Out of the way, please," Ronaldo said as he gently moved people aside.

He worked through the tide of people coming from the cars down the track, finally making it through to Tooth. They jogged along the outer edge of the platform, next to the hundreds of refugees heading toward the aid trucks and workers.

Everything seemed to be going smoothly enough. Organized, efficient, calm. But he had a feeling something had happened down the rail.

"Snake One to Snake Two, where the hell are you?"

"On my way, Snake One."

Ronaldo waved at the people in front of him. "Let's move it, folks!"

Another gunshot cracked in the distance. This time, it was close—this side of the barrier.

"Ah, shit," Ronaldo muttered.

Pushing less gently now through the moving horde, he saw panic in the faces around him, and people began to cry out in alarm.

"Stay calm, everyone," he said. "Please keep moving and stay calm."

The marines' greatest worry was a terrorist attack from some die-hard AMP loyalist, but these people had already been searched before boarding. It was more likely that someone had gotten killed over a candy bar or a canteen of water.

The tide of refugees parted as Ronaldo advanced, and he could see the marines outside a car near the end of train.

Two men were on their knees at the edge of the platform, and a third was sprawled on the ground.

"Shit, shit, *shit*!" Ronaldo growled.

He ran harder now that the path was clear, and Tooth kept pace alongside him. They passed a car with multiple dead bodies, and he could hear aid workers inside puking up whatever they had managed to eat today.

A marine stood guard, watching them vomit.

Ronaldo slowed his pace as he approached car 41. Two medical workers had climbed inside and were working on a rail-thin girl curled up on the floor, holding her equally thin teenage sister. She looked as though she had barely survived the trek.

Then Ronaldo realized that she hadn't. The girl was as white as the ashfall.

He continued over to the group of marines, who had formed a circle around two men on their knees. A third lay in a growing pool of blood.

Ronaldo didn't need to ask what had gone down. But the young marine who had shot the guy would need a hell of a good explanation for executing an unarmed man.

The marine who had pulled the trigger was sobbing.

"This piece of garbage raped her and then her sister, Sarge," the man said. "He got what he had coming!"

"Get him the fuck out of here," Marks said.

Bettis and Tooth grabbed the marine and pulled

him away from the platform while Marks spoke to Ronaldo.

"Got a shitty situation here, Ronnie," Marks said. "First, we found what appear to be two former AMP soldiers in car thirty-five, both of them murdered, their testicles stuffed in their mouths. And now we got this ..."

Footfalls pounded the platform and both marines pivoted to see the incident commander, breathing heavily.

"What on earth is going on here?" Sarah DaBuke asked, trying to catch her breath.

More like what in bloody hell, Ronaldo thought, but he let Marks do the talking.

"Got three guys accused of raping this girl and her dead sister. One of my men decided to play judge, jury, and executioner. Happened before I got here."

DaBuke scanned the scene and then walked over to the boxcar, where she held a sleeve over her mask. She said something to the medical workers attending the surviving girl and then turned back to the two men still on their knees beside their dead compadre.

"Did you do this?" she asked the men. "Did you rape and kill that girl's sister?"

One of them shook his head. The other gave her the black and broken grin of a meth head. His gaze flitted to Ronaldo, who was tempted to put a bullet in his groin and another between those soulless eyes.

"The other guy was laughing when my man shot him in the head," Marks said. "Thought this shit was funny, just like his friend."

Marks used the butt of his rifle to hit the still-grinning guy in the back, knocking him to the ground.

Ronaldo expected DaBuke to protest, but she just looked at Marks with the gaze of a woman who had seen her share of casual violence.

"Do an investigation," she said, "and if they did it, I'm sure you will take the appropriate action." Then she moved back to the car. "Someone, help us get her out of there."

Ronaldo climbed into the car and took off his gas mask to avoid frightening the already terrified young girl. The foul air inside nearly made him gag.

"It's okay," he said. "I'm here to help you."

The girl looked up at him, and for a moment, he was transported back to Mount Baldy, holding Monica in his arms as she cried and cried after the attack in the woods.

"Is it okay if I pick you up?" he asked the girl.

She managed a weak nod.

Ronaldo gently picked her up, disturbed by how light she felt. She sobbed as they left her dead sister in the boxcar.

Ever so carefully, he eased down from the car onto the right-of-way.

He carried her past the dead man, turning to shield her from the view. The guy had deserved far worse than he got.

That night, Bettis and Ronaldo sat by the girl and prayed with her as she succumbed to her injuries and severe dehydration that there was simply no coming back from.

The next day, they buried her in a park, next to her sister.

* * *

Antonio felt played. The entire point of getting Vinny onto the police force was to feed them information, trick them, and get intel on his enemies. Now that he had the intel, he knew that his biggest enemy was on the payroll of the LAPD anti-gang task force. Ironic, and it complicated things. But there was always a fix to a problem like this. Instead of starting off at the bottom of the ladder, he would take the express elevator.

He had the men. He had the weapons. And now he had a special tool that was going to help him deal with the Vegas.

Getting up from his desk, Antonio walked down the eight flights to the casino floor, where his brother was sitting at a blackjack table with Frankie, Raff, and Carmine.

Yellowtail stood behind the table as the dealer.

"Don Antonio," he said.

The other men all turned and stood.

"Enjoying yourselves?" Antonio said.

"Just waiting on you," Christopher said. He took off his suit jacket, folded it, and laid it on the chair. Frankie and Carmine did the same, and Raff stood, nodding his bandaged head.

As they walked to the service floor, Antonio rolled up his sleeves.

Christopher guided them into the kitchens that had once served thousands of tourists and gambling addicts who burned their money in the slots and at the tables.

Antonio wasn't much of a gambling man, not unless he was the house or playing a private game of poker. He never did understand why people pissed their money away at games like blackjack. Since the Morettis' escape from Naples, he understood more than ever how tough it was to be the underdog with the odds stacked against him.

But the game had changed, and over the past few years, he had flipped those odds.

When they got to the industrial-size kitchen, Frankie spat the matchstick out of his mouth and walked over to the freezer door. Christopher put the lantern down on a stainless-steel food-prep table.

They still didn't have the generators working, but they had plenty of batteries for their flashlights and lanterns.

With a loud click, Frankie unlatched the freezer door. He pulled out a flashlight and directed it inside at three naked men tied up by their hands and feet.

One of them, wet with piss and blood, squirmed across the floor. The other two men lay still, their bodies covered in bruises and cuts.

The crawler was the one Antonio had come to visit. His men dragged him across the floor and hoisted him onto a metal chair. Frankie went to shut the door, but Antonio shook his hand.

"Make them watch," he said.

The guy in the chair squirmed again, making little squealing sounds like a baby pig.

Christopher moved the lantern, and the light illuminated the man's weathered skin and jet-black hair. A large, drooping nose, square, bony features, and short stature told Antonio he was of Mesoamerican Indian descent, perhaps Mayan.

Many of the narcos had campesinos on their

payroll, giving them more money in a week to commit horrific crimes than they would make in a year working the land in their home country.

Judging by this guy's wrinkled forehead and callused hands, he was no stranger to working in the fields. His eyes widened as Carmine and Frankie walked behind him to hold him down and untie the bandanna they had used to mute his screams.

Raff watched, his arms folded across his chest. Normally, he wasn't involved in the violence, but after what happened on the road, he had requested to be here.

That was good. The soldier needed to see this.

Carmine pulled off the bandanna, and as the prisoner wriggled in his chair, Antonio bent down and put a finger to his lips as if shushing a baby.

"*Por favor, jefe*," the man groaned. "Please don't kill me."

"That all depends on what you tell me," Antonio said.

"I don't know notheen'," he said. "I swear. I'm just a driver—*un trabajador*."

Antonio shook his head and held out his hand. Carmine handed over the bandanna. The man's gaze flitted back and forth, then locked on Christopher, who held a canister of gasoline.

"Oh, no," the man moaned. "*Por Dios, no.*"

"Cut the shit," Antonio said. "I know you work for Esteban Vega, and I want to know where he's hiding. I also want to know who his contact is in the LAPD."

Antonio knew that it wasn't the sergeant. It had to be someone above him, and Vinny was never going to get access to that information.

That left one option.

Antonio nodded, and Christopher doused the bandanna with gasoline. The Vega soldier squirmed and moaned. Raff lowered his arms, and his lips moved, but he didn't protest.

"Do you like flank steak?" Antonio asked.

"*No, por favor, jefe,*" the prisoner pleaded.

"I wasn't talking to you," Antonio said, his eyes on Raff.

Raff nodded as if to give him permission.

Antonio nodded back and walked over to the long kitchen table, the prisoner's wide eyes following his every move. First, he picked up a long filleting knife. Then he checked out a serrated knife for cutting bread. He held up each blade, turning it from side to side.

He had learned the art of torture while in Afghanistan—not from the Italian military, but from the jihadists they fought. He had lost a brother to the brutal bastards, who hacked the young soldier apart while videotaping the entire thing.

But of all the barbaric acts he had seen, it was the American torture technique of waterboarding that seemed to work best. And Antonio was about to take it to a new level.

"Last chance," Antonio said. "Where are Esteban Vega and his brother Miguel? And who is their contact in the LAPD?"

The man sobbed and put his head against his chest—praying, perhaps, or just unable to watch his fate approach.

Frankie yanked his head back, and Antonio draped the gasoline-soaked bandanna over his weathered features while Carmine helped hold him down.

Then Antonio took the red cannister and poured it over the lumps that made up the Vega prisoner's nose and lips. He fought and fought, twisting and turning, spitting, and snorting out the liquid that made it into his orifices.

After a quarter of the canister was gone, Antonio let up.

"Where the FUCK is Esteban hiding?" he screamed. "And who is his contact?"

The Vega soldier spat and gasped for air. He had managed not to swallow the gasoline, but he could hold his breath only so long.

"I don't know," he said between breaths. "Please … *¡Por Dios!*"

Antonio looked at Carmine and Frankie.

They pulled him back again, and he repeated the process, draining another third of the precious gasoline on the already soaked bandanna, sprinkling it back and forth over his eyes, nose, and lips.

"Looks like it's flank steak tonight, boys!" Christopher shouted.

The guy finally cracked. "Stop," he choked. "No more! I'll talk!"

Antonio stepped back and nodded to his men. They pulled off the bandanna, allowing the guy to catch his breath and spit out the gasoline that had seeped into his mouth. His red eyes blinked at the lantern, trying to see despite the burn.

"Esteban and Miguel split from the Norteño Mafia," he mumbled. "He's starting his own organization, working with some captain in the police."

Antonio smiled. This guy spoke way better English than he had pretended.

"What's his name?" Antonio asked.

"Stone, I think. I don't know …"

Antonio wasn't sure he believed it. Stone was the guy who brought Vinny in, which made sense, but he had figured it was someone higher on the totem pole, maybe even Chief Walt Diamond himself.

"The Vegas did take out the Sureños at the meat plant," Christopher said. "There's definitely a turf war going on."

Antonio considered these revelations. The Norteño Mafia, one of the most powerful criminal organizations, was crumbling, with Esteban Vega rising from the rubble.

"Where are Esteban and his family hiding?" he asked.

The man shook his head again. "I don't know. I swear."

Hard-soled shoes clicked into the room, and Antonio glanced into the shadows behind the table.

"Please, I swear on my daughter," the prisoner begged.

"Okay, I believe you," Antonio said, patting the man on the head the way he might pet a dog. He walked to the table and put the gasoline can down, nodding at the Moretti soldier in the shadows.

The Vega soldier let out a heavy sigh and lowered his head. "Please, let me go. I'll find out where Esteban and his family are and I'll tell you."

Antonio smirked, then walked back to the prisoner and bent down. He didn't trust a word this guy said, not even about having a daughter. The only thing he did believe was that Captain Stone was the contact. It made sense, and how else would the man know his name?

"It's okay," Antonio said.

At the sound of clicking shoes, the red-faced

prisoner twisted, trying to look at the Moretti soldier who came out of the shadows to stand behind his chair.

He walked into the lantern light, wearing an expensive suit and a bandage on his chin and throat.

"Good to see you, Lino," Antonio said.

"And you as well, Don Antonio," Lino replied in a gruff voice.

Raff walked up next to Lino.

The Vega man glanced at them in turn, then looked to Antonio, who handed Lino the bread knife.

"No!" the man cried. "You said you would let me go!"

This time Raff grabbed the squirming soldier, pulling his head back by his hair so he could see Lino's face clearly.

Antonio stepped back and folded his arms across his chest to watch Lino take his revenge. There was only one way to win this war.

The Moretti family had to be more brutal than its enemies.

"Nooooo!" The man's muffled scream turned to a howl that cut short as Lino sawed a smile across his neck with the dull serrated blade.

-22-

It wasn't the funeral the Clarke family deserved, but it was the best they could do with the resources available. Dom and his mother had helped make the arrangements. The closest thing they could find to a priest was Bettis, and the only available burial plot that didn't require driving for miles was at Hollydale Regional Park.

Dom stared at the basketball courts where he had played with Moose and his brother Ray just a couple of months ago. Camilla had been there too and was by his side now.

"Such a shame," she said. "His parents were good people."

"The best," Dom said.

They walked on to the open green space on the other edge of the courts. Fresh mounds of dirt covered dozens of graves, and hibiscus flowers rustled in the smoky breeze.

A small group had already gathered behind a freshly dug grave. Moose helped his grandma walk over to the hole where they would bury her son and daughter-in-law. At ninety-four years old, the woman had outlived both her children.

Bettis clutched a Bible against his uniform, waiting for Ray to show up so they could begin the ceremony.

Not far away, another elderly person had come to the cemetery to bury a loved one. Dom knew that it was the man's wife wrapped in the blanket on the ground only because he had helped dig the hole. His dad, Marks, and Tooth had helped, too, when they'd arrived earlier with Bettis. The guy sat by her corpse now, sobbing, unable to finish the act of putting her body in the ground.

Dom found a spot to stand between Camilla and his sister. She looked up at him, her eyes already tearing up.

"Are you okay?" Dom asked her.

"Yes," Monica choked out.

Dom put his arm around her and pulled her closer. Elena stood beside Ronaldo, their hands intertwined for the first time in as long as Dom could remember.

Sometimes, it took death to remember what was important in life.

Screeching tires shattered the moment. It came from the parking lot near the courts, where a police car jolted to a stop. Ray, in uniform, got out and jogged over, sweat dripping down his dark forehead.

He carried a purple velvet bag containing the remains of his parents, gold strings knotted to keep the ashes from spilling.

They still didn't know which gang had burned their house down with their parents inside. But it wasn't a random accident or a crazed junkie.

The evidence all pointed to the house being

targeted because Moose and Ray were cops. Their parents, like so many other families, had just been collateral damage.

"Please gather around," Bettis said, holding his arms out wide.

Dom exchanged a nod with Ray as he joined the group. Their little squabble on the basketball court was in the past. Today they stood here as brothers—brothers in uniform, including Moose.

The big guy wasn't taking things well. He stood with his chin up and chest out, obviously doing his best to hold back the tears. He helped his grandmother stand as Bettis began the ceremony honoring two people who had played a vital role in their community.

"In their life together, John and Patrice raised two fine men," he said. "Both Raymond and Andre are proudly serving as police officers in these troubling times. They loved their boys more than anything and worked second jobs during another difficult time, when the country was in the throes of the Great Recession."

"My mom always worked two jobs," Ray recalled. "Her whole life—my dad too. Hardest-working people I ever knew."

Dom felt Camilla's soft hand brush against his. He took it and gave it a squeeze.

Bettis held up a picture of John and Patrice. "The Clarkes were a pillar in this community," he said. "Had their lives not been cut short, I have no doubt they would have helped the city in its recovery. They have gone on to the Lord's care. It falls to us to honor their memory and to see that their commitment to justice is not forgotten."

"I'll find justice," Moose said. "One way or another."

Dom wasn't used to seeing his happy-go-lucky friend so enraged.

Bettis opened the Bible. "Let us pray."

Dom said a short prayer for his friend while the group joined hands in front of the burial plot. When they finished, Ray and Moose lowered the velvet bag into the ground.

People approached in ones and twos to pay their final respects. Then Moose and Ray shoveled the dirt gently back into the hole. They embraced before turning to their family and friends.

"Really appreciate you guys coming out," Ray said to the marines. "Corporal Bettis, thank you for the words—beautiful send-off for my folks."

Bettis nodded.

Dom shook Moose's hand, then hugged him hard.

"My parents always said you were the best influence," Moose said. "Much better than Ray here."

They shared a solemn laugh, and Camilla chuckled nervously.

Dom reached out to Ray and said, "I'm going to help find those responsible."

Ray seemed distracted for a moment. After a short pause, he shook Dom's hand and said, "Thanks, bro. Glad you joined up."

"Me too," Camilla said.

The family and friends departed the park-turned-graveyard and got in the van they had carpooled in. Moose helped his grandma in, then Elena and Monica. The marines walked back to their Humvee, ready to head back to the border.

"I'll see you guys later," Camilla said, waving. She got into her squad car to return to work. Dom watched her go, praying she would be safe.

Then he joined Moose and Ray at his squad car. He didn't need to ask what their plan was for the rest of the day. They were going back on the beat for revenge. And Dom was going with them.

"You got any new leads?" Moose asked Ray.

"I know that Captain Stone and the anti-gang task force are starting to believe one gang is responsible for most of the cop killings, but we don't know who."

"Camilla said something like that," Dom said. "How cops that won't work with the gangs are being hunted."

"Cam doesn't know shit, and this ain't her business or yours," Ray shot back.

Dom held up a hand. "Sorry. Just trying to help."

"Yeah, well, ain't nothin' you can do, bro," Ray said. "Leave this to me. I'll find who's responsible."

He turned and walked to his car.

There were no goodbyes, no reminders to take care or watch out for yourself. Just an abrupt end to the conversation.

Moose watched his brother go. "He's just upset," he said. "Don't take it personal, Dom."

"I'm not. I understand."

They got into the car and drove to the station. Dom strapped on his assigned primary weapon, a Glock 19. He still didn't have a badge, but a weapon was part of the on-the-job training he had been approved for.

Already halfway through their shift, they hit the streets.

Dom looked over at this best friend as they set out. "You sure you're okay to go out here today?" he asked Moose.

"I'll be okay when I bury the motherfuckers who killed my parents."

As the afternoon sun warmed the city, the calls started coming fast. While Moose drove, eyes glued to the road, he explained how to rank them by priority.

"Sometimes, you report to a shooting instead of a stabbing," he said. "Depends on your location, but the main idea is to deal with the biggest threat first."

The afternoon went fast as they responded to several assaults, a robbery, a fire, a shooting. At four in the afternoon, a call came in about gunshots in the refugee center at Downey Promenade Mall.

"Great," Moose said. "I never liked the mall even when it was just for shopping, but now it *really* sucks."

He turned on the sirens and pushed the pedal to the floor.

Dom's heart thumped when he saw the shopping center. Since the fallout, most of the refugees in Downey had been moved here, where they laid out their sleeping bags and cots inside the walls.

The tents that had littered the parking lots were gone now, destroyed after the radioactive fallout polluted them. In their place were dozens of FEMA trailers, and new aid trucks that had brought in food from the rails.

"There's our problem," Moose said.

A fence blocked off the semitrailers, but a swarm of people had surrounded the perimeter.

"Got another potential riot on our hands," he said. "Stay close."

Dom felt a flash of anxiety. He wasn't trained for this, and Moose must have sensed his reservations.

"Don't worry, man, I got you," he said. "And this is hella good street experience."

Moose parked by two other police cars that had just arrived. He grabbed his shotgun and acknowledged the other six officers who had responded to the call.

They appeared better prepared, dressed in riot gear and carrying AR-15s. One of them, a patrol sergeant, carried an automatic M4 carbine.

"We've got an officer down somewhere behind that crowd, and another who's been injured," said the sergeant. "First priority is to get them out of that horde."

The horde he spoke of was three hundred angry refugees who had surrounded the fence. Several aid workers were on the roof of a trailer, yelling for people to back up, and somewhere on the ground near the truck was one of two officers assigned to help oversee the food distribution.

"Stay calm," said the patrol sergeant as the group of officers approached.

Moose either didn't hear the order or didn't care. He pumped his shotgun and fired it into the air. That got everyone's attention.

Hundreds of faces turned toward them, stopping the other officers in their tracks, including the patrol sergeant, who shouldered his carbine. But Moose kept walking, and Dom stayed by his side, a hand on his holstered weapon.

"Back the fuck up!" Moose shouted.

Several people shouted back at him—curse words and even some racist bullshit.

This is not the day to piss my man off, Dom thought.

"Mind if I say something?" he asked.

Moose shrugged his linebacker shoulders. "Be my guest."

They stopped a hundred feet from the edge of the crowd, and Dom recalled something his MMA coach had taught him about street altercations.

Fight anger with empathy. If that fails, make sure you are angrier than the other guy.

He also recalled what his father had said in the forest when the men touched Elena.

Sometimes, you have to use evil to fight evil.

Dom used his authoritative police voice. "I watched my friend here bury his parents today, and we *really* don't want this to end with anyone else having to go to a funeral."

He paused a second to let it sink in.

"I know you're all hungry, and I know you're mad. I am too. But we're here to help you, and we need you all to get out of the way so we can get our brother medical help. Then we will hand out meals in an orderly and *fair* fashion. Okay?"

"A pig killed my brother!" someone yelled.

"The fuckers beat my uncle!" another added.

Moose glanced over, shaking his head wearily as if to say, *I told you so.*

"You have every right to be angry," Dom said. "But we aren't the enemy. Fact is, we're being targeted for trying to help you. Being hunted by the gangs. Just help us help you, so we can focus on the real bad guys."

The crowd went quiet aside from a few hushed voices. Desperate, half-crazed eyes were on him. Many here had lost seven-figure portfolios and bank accounts, and they were not happy about their new lifestyle.

A woman finally broke the silence. "Give them a chance!" she shouted.

Moose looked over at Dom again.

"Let 'em through!" someone yelled.

The crowd began to part near the gate in the fences. Moose waved for the cops behind them to stay put, and they did. Even the patrol sergeant reluctantly lowered his rifle. He was young, maybe twenty-five, and seemed to be okay with Dom and Moose handling the situation. Together, the two cops walked through the gap in the crowd.

"I'm sorry about your parents."

A boy no older than ten looked up at Moose as he passed, and Moose nodded back.

The state aid workers and FEMA disaster staff climbed down from the trailer roof to the ground, where an officer was getting treatment from two state workers. A second cop had his gun pointed at the crowd. His hand was shaking.

"Easy," Dom said.

"Back up, everyone," Moose said to the people lingering around the fence.

The crowd continued to move back. When they were clear, a male aid worker unlocked the gate and let the cops inside.

Moose gestured for the patrol sergeant, who ran through the parted crowd with a second officer to help the wounded cop lying by the trailer.

The young officer had taken a bad whack to the head from a brick. The other cop had been hit on the chest and back. He limped over, gripping his side.

"Who did this?" Moose asked.

The cop shook his head. "I don't know, man. I didn't see them coming."

"Two guys threw rocks and bricks," said a guy wearing a black baseball cap with the California seal. "We decided to lock off the gates until backup could get here."

"You got enough meals to feed all these people?" Dom asked.

The man took off his hat and pulled his long hair back as he looked out over the crowd. "I think so," he said. "But the problem is when people fight and try to take more than one ration."

"Can you *subtly* show me who hit the officers?" Dom said. "Don't point. Just describe him and his location."

"Ten people back, to my right, your left. White, six feet, ponytail, thirty to midthirties. Guy to his left has a Dodgers cap."

"Good, job," Dom said. He turned his back and waited while the injured officers were moved away from the scene.

A squad car drove them to a hospital, leaving four cops behind. They remained on the edge of the crowd, patrolling with their rifles angled at the ground.

Dom walked over to Moose and relayed the intel. When Dom glanced back into the crowd, the two guys were squeezing through to get away.

"We've got this, Sarge," Moose said.

The patrol sergeant nodded and cradled his rifle while Dom and Moose moved out into the throng. As soon as they got a few people deep, the two guys took off, pushing and shouting.

The officer on the edge moved to intercept, but the guy with the Dodgers cap body slammed him, knocking him to the ground. The second suspect bent down to wrest his rifle away.

Moose hunched down like a linebacker, lowered his antler 'do, and slammed into the guy just as he picked up the cop's rifle. The blow sent the man airborne. He landed on his back with a thud, losing the rifle and cracking his head on the concrete.

Dom tackled the other guy, pinned him down, and put him in a hammerlock to keep him still. The one thing he didn't have yet were handcuffs, but that didn't matter.

Somehow, the man Moose had slammed got back up. He shouldn't have. A right hook from Moose put him out before he hit the concrete.

"Get off me, pig!" shouted the guy under Dom, who tightened the hammerlock, eliciting a yelp.

Moose finished cuffing his dirtbag and looked over.

"Nice work, bro," he said to Dom. "I told you you'd make a good cop."

* * *

Vinny still didn't know where Vito was being held, but he did know that the cops were losing the fight against the gangs. Four naked bodies, all of them mutilated beyond recognition, hung from a steel I beam on a prewar construction site of what were intended to be million-dollar condos. The project was located on the eastern edge of Central Los Angeles, not far from one of the big refugee zones.

It was a chilly evening, and the air reeked of excrement and smoke. Vinny pulled his breathing apparatus over his nose and followed Sergeant Best and the anti-gang task force crew toward the latest casualties in the gangs' war on the LAPD. They stopped at the edge of a parking lot and stared up at the hanging corpses.

Sergeant Best shook his head. "Poor bastards," he said. "What a way to go."

Darwin spat on the ground. "Fucking animals that did this."

The county medical examiner's team was already busy at the scene, while other officers put up a perimeter of yellow tape to seal off the area.

Vinny didn't need to ask who the four corpses were. Cops, all of them. One was a woman. And he had a feeling it was the Vegas who had killed them.

The grisly murders were yet another sign that the uncorrupt officers of the LAPD were losing the battle for control of the streets. The Norteño Mafia had fractured, and the Vegas had absorbed members of the once allied cliques such as MS-13, the Sureños, the Latin Kings, Florencia 13, and a dozen other gangs.

Vinny had watched the narco family grow faster than the American Military Patriots. He wouldn't admit it to Don Antonio, but Esteban Vega was, in many ways, like the *jefe* of the Moretti family. Both were building powerful crime organizations in the wake of the apocalypse.

But not *all* the cops were losing the battle. Sergeant Best and his guys were thriving, partly due to the intel Vinny was feeding them—intel that included the locations where various Moretti rivals were keeping their weapons, drugs, and cash.

Just enough not to look suspicious.

Not that it really mattered, Vinny thought. Best seemed to care only about the finds. After their last raid, on a warehouse containing a cache of weapons and half a million in cocaine from the Nevsky family, Best had given Vinny a gold Rolex.

"You're a smart little shit, I'll give you that, Nate," Best had said. "Stick with me, kid. We're gonna be rich. I might even get to that beach paradise after all."

Vinny had gone home to his new apartment in Santa Monica that night to find Doberman working on a map of the city. He had checked off the locations of the gangs Antonio was currently attacking using the anti-gang task force as his surrogate soldiers. It was brilliant, and Vinny and Doberman sat talking about the endgame.

"Don Antonio is erasing his enemies one by one, without even losing a man," Doberman had said.

"Yeah, but Vega is out there adding five men to his ranks for every one he loses," Vinny had replied.

He snapped out of the memory when he heard tires crunching over gravel in the distance. Not one but several vehicles.

"He's here," Best said.

"Who's here?" Vinny turned as four squad cars and two black Chevy Tahoes pulled up into the parking lot surrounding the abandoned construction zone.

"The chief," Best said. He looked over to Darwin. "Make sure the guys keep their traps shut."

Darwin walked over to talk to the other guys while the vehicles emptied in the lot. Vinny still hadn't gotten a good look at the man in control of the small army that was the LAPD. Before today, he had only glimpsed Chief Diamond from a distance.

The six-foot black man got out of a Tahoe and was quickly surrounded by cops in riot gear, like a cohort of the Praetorian Guard surrounding the emperor. Everywhere Chief Diamond went, his protection detail followed. It made sense now that the gangs were killing cops daily.

Vinny looked up as two men in a cherry picker lowered the bodies one by one from the steel beam. The scene was straight out of the drug wars in Mexico and Columbia.

The cartels went after anyone who crossed them: cops, soldiers, politicians, lawyers, judges, families, including women and kids. Hell, it didn't matter *who* you were. If you pissed off the cartels, you died, often in the most horrific of ways.

It was happening in Los Angeles now, and just as in South America, some police were complicit.

He didn't know the details, only that Best was working with the Vegas and other gangs to benefit from the chaos. What Vinny couldn't figure out, and what Don Antonio longed to know, was where the corruption stopped. Was it Captain Stone orchestrating the bribes, or was Chief Diamond himself in Vega's pocket?

What Vinny did know was that he had landed himself smack-dab in the middle of both worlds. A gangster and a cop.

Sort of. He didn't have the button of a made man, or the badge of a cop. That was going to change very soon.

"Nate, let's go," Best said.

Vinny walked away from the parking lot and down

a path that led around the crime scene. Diamond and his men led the way, pausing only briefly to see the last of the flayed bodies being lowered to the ground.

When the group of cops got to the top of a hill, Vinny saw that the construction zone wasn't completely abandoned. Cranes, bulldozers, and other heavy equipment sat idle in the dirt, surrounded by evidence of their recent activity. Diamond and his men looked out over the construction site, and Vinny listened to the discussion.

"The Crips are sending us a warning that this is their territory," said one officer.

"And I'll send them one right back," Diamond said in a deep voice. "This real estate is the most important part of the future. We can't let them intimidate us. We have to be strong."

He turned away and walked over to the crime scene with his contingent of bodyguards.

"Why the hell are we here?" Darwin asked.

"My guess is I'm going to get new orders in a few minutes," Best replied. "But honestly, I don't know."

"What did the chief mean about this being the most important part of the future?" Vinny asked.

"Keep this shit quiet, kid," Best said. "You're looking at one of four major federal projects the mayor and chief of police have been negotiating with the new government. The future home of two million people."

"Where do you think all the refugees and displaced folks are going to live?" Darwin asked.

"In a week, the chief, mayor, and everyone who's anyone are going to be here to announce the project," Best said.

Vinny swallowed. In his mind's eye, he pictured the public housing going up in the distance, and like his uncle and father, he saw dollar signs. He had to get this info to Don Antonio.

The next war for the city would no longer be over the camps. Whoever controlled the public housing would be king.

"Hey, Nathan," said a voice.

Best and Darwin turned as a group of Chief Diamond's guard approached. The chief walked in the middle of the group, hand on his holstered pistol.

He was bigger than he looked from a distance, with wide shoulders and a muscular frame. Creases formed on his forehead as his piercing brown eyes narrowed.

"Are you Nathan Sarcone?" Diamond asked.

Vinny nodded. "Yes, sir."

"What's this about?" Best asked.

"The reason I called you here," Diamond replied to the overweight sergeant. "You got a rat in your rafters, Best."

He pulled the pistol from his holster and nodded at several men, who moved out to flank the task force. Vinny did his best to look calm.

"This fucker right here," Diamond said, raising his pistol and pointing it at Vinny.

"I'm no rat, sir," Vinny replied, trying to keep his lips from trembling. "I've been working with Sergeant Best for three weeks now, providing important intel on the gangs."

"You sure have," Diamond said. "But intel that benefits *who*? That's the real question."

Best raised a hand. "This has got to be some sort

of mistake, Chief. This is Nathan Sarcone, nephew of Enzo Sarcone."

"No," Diamond said. "The real Nathan Sarcone was found in a shallow grave this morning." He took a step closer to Vinny. "So, the question is, who the fuck are *you*?"

Vinny opened his mouth, but no words came out. Before he could react, someone kicked him in the back of the knee. He fell to his knees, right in front of Chief Diamond.

The chief looked at the bodies being bagged and loaded into two ambulances. Then he holstered the pistol and returned his gaze to his captive.

Vinny managed to turn slightly and avoid some of the blow as the Chief punched him in the side of the head. He slumped to the ground, stars bursting across his vision.

Maybe he was going to find out where they were keeping Vito, after all—assuming Diamond didn't kill Vinny first.

-23-

After weeks of patrolling the city's newly established eastern border, the Desert Snakes had finally been transferred to the Port of Los Angeles for a new mission.

Ronaldo wanted to believe he was prepared for whatever came next. They had already defended against raiders hunting treasure in abandoned mansions and aided refugees suffering from radiation poisoning. And through it all, his heart had hardened against the violence and suffering, especially after holding the dying girl from the train. The short time he had spent with her during her last hour on earth had reaffirmed what he already believed.

Sometimes, you have to use evil to fight evil.

It was the only way to win against the sorry fucks trying to exploit the apocalypse—men like those who had raped and killed her and her sister. Men like the gangbangers who were hunting cops.

Seeing what humanity was capable of made him wonder whether *anything* could be done to save the country. Hell, he wasn't even sure Los Angeles could be saved.

He had seen terrible things in war zones overseas, though the evil he had seen at home was in many ways worse. But he wouldn't stop fighting, and neither would the other soldiers and cops.

Together, they were putting up a fight against evil forces within the city and without. The border west of Anaheim now stretched from the Angeles National Forest all the way south to Chino Hills State Park.

Every major intersection surrounding the city had checkpoints manned by sheriff's deputies. Other access points were blocked off by junked vehicles and rubble from destroyed buildings.

Ronaldo leaned his back against a shipping container at Terminal Island. Gulls squawked overhead, hoping for a morsel of food or a fish head to snack on.

The entire harbor stank of rotting fish. All along the coast, millions of them were washing up along with dolphins, sea lions, and other marine life—all dead from radiation poisoning.

"How long we got to play babysitter?" Tooth asked. "It fucking smells like a dollar whorehouse out here."

Bettis let out a sigh, and Marks shook his head wearily.

"Tooth, do you ever shut up, man?" Ronaldo asked. "Can't you just do your job for one day without complaining? And how many dollar whorehouses you been in, anyway?"

Tooth futzed with his breathing apparatus. "These new things suck ass."

Ronaldo walked away from the shipping container, cradling his rifle, savoring a moment of peace. Other than Tooth's griping, it was quiet out here, at least. Just the rumble of mechanical equipment as container cranes unloaded the huge cargo ships docked in the harbor, and the occasional shout from a stevedore.

Being by the ocean was calming, and seeing the signs of recovery filled Ronaldo with a dangerous emotion.

Hope.

Power had been restored to key areas of the city, including the port. Gasoline was also coming in by rail and sea. Food and medical supplies were being shipped from countries such as Australia and New Zealand, which hadn't suffered as greatly from the global economic collapse. Even cell phone towers were being fixed. It was a long road to recovery, but things were moving slowly in the right direction.

On the horizon, dozens more vessels sailed to the port, each waiting its turn to unload. Marks joined Ronaldo by the edge of the water to watch the ships. They stood in silence for a few moments, listening to the waves slap fish carcasses against the rocky beach.

"I got something to tell you," Marks finally said.

Ronaldo turned toward his longtime friend, preparing himself for the bad news.

"This stays between us, brother," Marks said.

"What?"

"I heard they're pushing a new base realignment and closure effort, and it includes disbanding most of the Corps. Army too."

If Ronaldo weren't wearing a mask, Marks would have seen his jaw drop. "What the hell are you talking about, Zed?"

"It's part of the agreement. AMP wanted assurances they wouldn't be treated like criminals. Here we go with fucking Reconstruction again. Remember how well that worked last time?"

"Okay, but what's that mean for us?" Ronaldo asked.

"Nothing yet, but it sounds like they're going to ADSEP anyone and everyone who isn't deemed mission critical."

"We're good, then," Ronaldo said.

Marks shook his head. "Wish that were the case, brother. Guys like you and me? We'll be *encouraged* to join the local PD. The military is maintaining only a small peacekeeping force at key points around the country. All the remaining MEUs are being recalled."

Ronaldo laughed. "Okay, now I know you're bullshitting."

But when Marks pulled down his mask, his dark eyes held no glint of humor.

"I wish I was joking, but the government's in shambles," Marks said, his salt-and-pepper beard ruffling in the breeze. "I only know about this because there isn't anybody around here with higher rank right now. It sounds like bullshit, but brass wants to reduce any threat of embers flaring up again. Instead, we'll be working with former AMP soldiers to help restore order."

"No fucking way."

"We did the same thing after the first Civil War, North and South working side by side to heal wounds and rebuild. Sometimes, the hard way is the only way."

Ronaldo took a moment to digest the news before responding. "So, you're telling me we're going from the Marine Corps to the LAPD or Sheriff's Department?"

"Nobody's ordering you, brother. You get to make the call, but there aren't many jobs out there right now."

Marks looked over his shoulder at Bettis and Tooth, who were talking to a couple of dockworkers.

"What are you going to do?" Ronaldo asked, though he could tell that Marks's mind was already made up.

"LAPD. Going to fight the gangs. I'm not good for much else but fighting, and there's still an enemy that wants to tear the country apart."

"Jesus," Ronaldo said. "All this time, I just wanted to retire and spend my time at home with Elena and the kids. But the Corps is my second family."

"I know, brother. I know." He sighed and pulled his mask back up over his mouth and nose. "The announcement will be coming in the next few days, but I wanted you to hear it from me first."

"Thanks," Ronaldo said. "Elena will be happy, that's for sure. But now I need to find a way to pay for a new house, and no way in hell we're going to live in public housing. It's going to be a stomping ground for the gangs."

"I know. And that's another reason the city needs us."

Ronaldo took in a breath of filtered air that still reeked of rotting fish. He kicked a rock into a surf full of scales and white bellies. The shoreline was ripe with death and decomp.

"There's something else too," Marks said. "I heard Lieutenant Castle's been moved from a field hospital in San Diego to LA."

"No shit?" Ronaldo turned from the rocky beach. "Well, that's some good news, at least. Maybe we can go see him soon."

"Yeah, but he's paralyzed from the waist down. Going to be in a wheelchair the rest of his life."

Ronaldo remembered holding the marine while he bled in the dirt outside Phoenix. It was remarkable that the guy had survived at all, but knowing Lieutenant Castle, he would continue to serve his country one way or another.

A horn blared in the distance.

"Here we go," Marks said.

They looked out at a massive red container ship with a big ONE stenciled on the side, slowly sailing toward the harbor.

"Come on," Marks said.

They jogged back to Tooth and Bettis. Both marines stood near a crane, their rifles cradled, watching the tugboats push and pull the monstrous ship to its berth.

"Holy shit, that's a big mother," Tooth said.

One of the longshoremen hanging out below a crane joined the four marines.

"This is it," he said. "The one we've been waiting for, and the reason you boys are here, I reckon."

"Why? What's on that beast?" Tooth asked.

Ronaldo studied the ship. There had to be hundreds of containers on the deck, but there was something else. Massive gray cylinders that looked like some sort of sewer pipes.

"A gift from the emperor of Japan," said the dockworker.

"Gift?" Bettis asked.

"Advanced desalination technology that isn't energy intensive," Marks chimed in. "It's going to solve the biggest problem Los Angeles faces in the recovery."

"You knew about this?" Ronaldo asked.

Marks nodded.

"About this … meaning what, exactly?" Tooth said. "What else are you keeping from us, Gunny?"

While the tugs pushed the container ship closer to its berth, Ronaldo walked away to let Marks share the news with the men. For the first time in his life, he had no idea what he was going to do for a job, or how he was going to feed his family. In his heart, he knew that besides being a husband and a father, he was meant to be one thing: a marine.

* * *

The stage was set, and thousands of people had come out to watch the politicians sell their snake oil that would magically heal the city and the country.

Don Antonio was present, but not for the same reason. Unlike most of these people, he knew that the United States was history. The country would never return to the greatness it had once achieved. Hundreds of thousands of people were dying from radiation poisoning in the nuclear wastelands that the crazed former president had spread across the land. Even more were dying from starvation, dehydration, and communicable disease.

The economy was destroyed, and most of the world had plunged into darkness. The twenty-first century had started off with a technological and medical bang, and the country's population had grown—not because of immigration or a rise in birth rate, but because people were enjoying longer lives.

That was then. The apocalypse had changed all that, and the Moretti family was reaping the benefits of the fallout, literal as well as figurative.

Antonio walked up the narrow rows of the Hollywood Bowl amphitheater with Christopher. For the first time in a month, he had left his family at their new compound at the former Commerce Hotel. Marco and Lucia were in good hands with Raff and the other soldiers.

Antonio hadn't left the safety of his new fortress just to lap up the latest load of horseshit from the politicians and crooked cops. Despite the dangers in leaving his compound, he had business to attend to if he wanted to keep benefiting from the new world.

Tonight they came dressed for the occasion. Antonio and his brother had swapped their suits for less formal attire, to blend in with the locals who had come out to hear Mayor Buren and the rest of the lineup speak.

Yellowtail and Frankie, both wearing track jackets, had joined them. Rush, the former AMP sergeant, was also here, eyeing the crowd like a Secret Service agent.

Antonio had a feeling Esteban and maybe Miguel were in the audience, but he wasn't worried about an attack from the narco king or his cockroach affiliates. The security just to get into the arena was top-notch, and it would be impossible to sneak in a weapon, especially a gun.

Christopher walked to the top of stairs, to the highest seats he could find.

"We're going to get Vinny out, don't worry," Antonio said to his brother. "Same with Vito. Just need time."

"It was a mistake letting Vin join," Christopher said. "I never should have agreed."

Antonio understood his brother's anger, but he needed to have faith. Vinny had played his part and helped them take an upper hand in the turf war for Los

Angeles. As long as he didn't spill to the cops, he would be fine, and so would the family.

The setting sun lit up the arena and the Hollywood sign on Mount Lee. The *Y* had tumbled away, and both *L*s looked crooked. Not even the iconic sign had come out of the war unscathed.

And the violence was far from over. The war over who controlled Los Angeles was still raging, but thanks to Vinny feeding information to the cops, several big players were already out of the game. The Crips and the Bloods were scattered in disarray. The Norteño Mafia had crumbled, leaving behind dozens of cliques that the Vega family had absorbed.

Only a few key players remained who could claim the throne: the Nevsky family of Russians, the Vegas, and the Morettis. And the cops still had no idea how powerful he was.

Several police officers walked onto the stage below, and more lined up inside the confines of the white arches that made up the half shell of the stage.

A few minutes later, a tall bald man with a red tie walked up to the podium and tapped a microphone. Static crackled from the speakers onstage.

Lights flicked on across the lip of the stage, and for a moment Antonio almost forgot why he was here.

"Good evening, everyone," said the man at the podium. "I'm City Councilman Lewis Banker, and I'm pleased to be with you tonight to discuss the future of our beloved city."

The crowd clapped, and Antonio brought his hands together in a mechanical fashion, dutifully playing his part.

The councilman blathered on about recovery efforts and all the other important progressive shit the city was doing. Antonio tuned it out and scanned the crowd, stopping on a group of Latino men wearing cowboy hats and tacky silk button-down shirts. Narcos for sure, but he didn't see Esteban or Miguel in the group.

"And now I'd like to introduce Mayor Matt Buren," said the councilman.

A man in a blue suit strode onstage. His brown hair was slicked to the side, but Antonio couldn't see his features well. He couldn't make out the pin on the guy's lapel, but he doubted it was a US flag.

Mayor Buren shook the councilman's hand and grabbed the microphone off its mount. He walked around the edge of the stage, looking out at the crowd, back and forth—the sweeping gaze of a politician sizing up his public.

"Today I've received outstanding news," he said cheerfully. "As you may know, the federal government has reorganized, disbanding Congress and the executive branch. We now have, in the presidency's place, an Executive Council …"

Antonio zoned out the history lesson and returned his attention to the narcos several rows below him and to the right. There were four—two around his age and two who looked young enough to be bodyguards.

"Here's the good news," Mayor Buren said. "In my negotiations with the new federal Executive Council, I was granted one of the first shipments of energy-efficient desalination technology from Japan. It will help provide clean water to over a million people here in Los Angeles."

The crowd erupted in applause.

Buren held up a hand for the audience to quiet down. "This is only part of an energy-efficient Los Angeles," he continued. "We're also building solar farms, with a project completion goal of two years, to power the entire city. And that's not all …"

The mayor walked to the center of the stage. "You may have seen some active construction zones over the past few weeks. At those four sites, the city will be working with the federal government and several foreign governments including Canada, China, Japan, and others, who have offered to help build public housing that will help end our refugee crisis. These towers will go up in the next six months to a year."

People stood and cheered.

Both Antonio and Christopher rose to their feet with everyone else. Antonio wasn't happy about the Chinese helping, even though it made sense to benefit from their expertise gained while dealing with their own refugee issues. He worried about the projects attracting crime organizations that might see an opportunity with the public housing projects, just as he did.

"We all have lost much over the past few months," Buren said. "It will be a long road to recovery, but with the help of the citizens of Los Angeles, we will rebuild a better city together."

The mayor bowed his head slightly as if in prayer. When he looked up, he let out an audible sigh into the microphone.

"But before we can rebuild, we must address the violence that plagues our city. So many of our brothers, sisters, mothers, fathers, and children have fallen victim to these senseless acts."

Buren turned back to the white arches as another man walked onto the stage. He wore a formal dress police uniform, right down to the white gloves and peaked hat.

"That's why I've asked Chief Diamond to join us tonight and explain his plan to fight the gangs," Buren said. "Please join me in welcoming this brave soldier fighting around the clock to ensure the safety of our families and our city."

The chief shook the mayor's hand and stepped up to the podium.

Antonio watched him as intently as a hawk watching a rabbit. From the intel Vinny had provided, the chief was not in play. Indeed, he was doing everything he could to combat the gangs. It was Captain Stone, not the chief, who was on Esteban Vega's payroll.

"Good evening, everyone. As you know, I'm Chief Diamond. I've served in the LAPD for over twenty years and served as chief for four. When I accepted this duty, I promised the citizens of Los Angeles that I would cut gang violence by half in a year, and I'm happy to say we accomplished that. Then the war happened."

The crowd had all sat down. An eerie silence passed over the amphitheater.

"As the economy deteriorated and fighting broke out across the United States, the gangs again crawled out of their holes and tried to destroy our community," Diamond said, anger breaking through in his tone. "My new promise to you tonight is that we will crush the cockroaches and send them scurrying back to their holes for good."

The crowd clapped, and Antonio felt a sly half smile forming on his face. Diamond was a brave man, to be sure, but a stupid one. If he had any smarts, he would have worked with the gangs rather than try to take out an enemy he couldn't beat.

He had to know that cockroaches were one of the most resilient species on the planet.

Or maybe he doesn't.

"My officers tell me that the gang members outnumber our forces two to one," Diamond said, his voice growing louder and more impassioned. "But we have something they don't have. We have *honor*."

The audience applauded, and many rose again from their seats. A moment later, everyone was standing, even Antonio. He listened intently, curious to see how far Diamond would take his rhetoric before the grand finale.

"As we recruit more officers, I ask you to put the word out in your communities that we will not be intimidated. That we will not surrender. That we will not—"

It came faster than Antonio had anticipated. His half smile turned into a full-fledged grin as the top of Diamond's peaked hat flew into the air, with part of his skull and scalp still inside.

By the time anyone knew what was happening, two more distant rifle shots rang out, the bullets hitting Diamond in the back and shoulder, turning his body as he fell. A fourth, final shot hit him in the elbow.

The audience cried out in horror, and officers flooded the stage, their weapons raised, sweeping for the shooter as they called into their radios to the officers on the hillside.

The LAPD and Sheriff's Department had security up there, and they would no doubt be searching for the assassin. But they wouldn't find him—at least, not the real killer. Carmine had trained as a sniper and was too clever to be discovered. He would escape through the trees, leaving his rifle next to the recently deceased body of one of the Vega soldiers Antonio had held captive in the basement of his new fortress.

Antonio hoped the Vega brothers were somewhere in the arena. Soon, every officer in the city would be hunting for the man who ordered the assassination of a hero cop.

"We just started another war," Christopher said quietly.

Antonio watched the officers below surrounding Diamond's limp body. A team of medics rushed from under the arch and joined the cluster around the fallen chief. Christopher stood and tipped his head at the exit. Time to leave.

Antonio stayed a moment longer, watching the emergency crew work on Diamond. Somehow, despite all odds, he was still technically alive. But no one could survive those wounds, and soon there would be a new chief of police. And this one would be in the pocket of the Moretti family.

-24-

Dom shivered at the sight of his sister sleeping peacefully on the cot inside the former high school history classroom. She had fallen asleep with a book still open in her hands.

He didn't want to leave her, knowing that this could be the last time he would ever see her. But, like their father, he had a duty.

Leaning down, Dom kissed her softly on the forehead, then turned back to his mom. They walked quietly out of the room and into the hallway.

"I'm coming home," Dom said. "Don't worry."

Elena sniffled, trying to hold back her tears. "Dominic," she said as if unsure what else to say. She grabbed him and pulled him tight, whispering, "I've seen your father go to war so many times, and now I have to watch you go too."

"I'll be okay," Dom said. "I know how to fight, and I have to do this. I have to protect you guys."

He held on to her, looking down the hallway, where three citizen soldiers stood sentry with rifles and shotguns. Plenty of people were here to watch his family while he and his father were gone, and most of the fighting was downtown anyway, where his father's unit had been deployed.

"I'll be back as soon as I can," he said. "I love you, Mom."

Two tears rolled down her face, but then they ceased, like a faucet shutting off.

"I love you too," she replied after wiping them away. "Please, *please*, be careful."

He nodded, then hurried down the hallway, stopping only to tell the three guards at the main entrance to do their damn job and to stay at their post no matter what happened.

Half an hour later, he was with Moose and Camilla at the Downey police headquarters, waiting in the chilly predawn in a parking lot with dozens of other officers and volunteers. Soon, they would board the buses that would ship them off to battle.

So far, there were already twenty-one dead cops in Central Los Angeles, nine in Anaheim, four in Long Beach, ten in Santa Monica. A whopping nineteen in Compton.

And that was just last night. It also didn't include civilian casualties.

The gangs had rallied after Chief Diamond's assassination and his vitriolic speech promising to scrape them off the streets like crushed insects. After his death, the LAPD had declared all-out war on the gangs, and the gangbangers had responded by forming small armies, fortifying positions, and taking hostages.

They were parasites and had infested everything:

the camps, the neighborhoods, and without a doubt, the police force itself.

Dom knew in his heart that he had to stop the spread of the disease before it became too late for the city and his family.

He finished putting on his riot gear as the first of the buses rolled into the parking lot. He could see the fear in the other officers' faces. He felt it too.

This wasn't just another day out on the beat with Moose. Today, the LAPD was going to war.

Dom took a seat beside his best friend, and Camilla took the seat across the aisle. She placed her helmet on the seat next to her and checked her assigned AR-15 rifle.

"Piece of crap," she muttered.

Most of the officers were armed with older-model weapons or shotguns. Moose carried a pump-action twelve-gauge. Like Camilla, Dom had been issued an AR-15 and three magazines. Bullets were in short supply, and every single one needed to count.

The bus lurched forward, and the sergeant in charge stood at the front of the aisle. Álvaro Cortez was a short, muscular man with a buzz cut and a square jawline. He and many of the other sergeants in charge had been Army Rangers who signed up with law enforcement after their units disbanded.

Soon, Dom's father would also be out of a job, but for now the marines were helping the LAPD and sheriffs in the fight for Los Angeles.

"San Diego has fallen, and San Fran is teetering," Sergeant Cortez said in a deep voice. "What *we* do today determines whether Los Angeles is next." Cortez grabbed a seat as the driver fired up the engine. "I'll be honest with you," he continued. "We are outnumbered, and some of us probably aren't coming home tonight, but it is our duty to our city and our families to fight, even if it's to the death."

Dom looked out the window at the school in the darkness. Leaving his mom and sister was one of the hardest things he had ever done, not knowing whether he would ever see them again.

He had a new appreciation for all the times his father had left them on deployments. Ronaldo had always been strong for his family, and now Dom would be as well, despite a hard truth. According to recent statistics, a quarter of the officers on this bus would be injured or dead in less than a week. The statistics didn't lie, but he also believed he made his own luck.

Be smart, fight hard, stay alive.

"We're headed to Florence this morning to aid in a battle against F-Thirteen," Cortez said. He lowered his head to the radio on the outside of his vest to listen to a transmission.

"Great," Moose said, loading shells into his shotgun. "F-Thirteen are some of the craziest fuckers out there."

"They're allied with the Vega family," Dom said.

Everyone knew that Esteban Vega had been behind the assassination of Chief Diamond. The chief had declared war, and a minute later, Esteban had fired the first shot.

As the bus moved out, squad cars flanked the convoy on the route to the interstate. Embers flickered on the horizon, indicating the locations of the most intense fighting.

Some of the officers in the bus looked out their windows. Others bowed their heads in prayer.

Camilla continued checking her gear. She met Dom's gaze, and he noticed a hint of fear in her eyes. She always had come off as a badass, and while some of that was an act, she was truly a strong young woman. Seeing her jitters brought out his own.

"You okay?" he asked her.

She shrugged. More of her tough-gal act.

"It's okay to be scared," Dom admitted. "I am. My dad always said anyone not scared before a battle is either insane or stupid."

She nodded. "I'm not scared of dying. I'm scared of letting you guys down."

"Listen up," Cortez announced. "We're headed to a strip mall off Florence and Roseberry. Scouts report that the remaining F-Thirteen members have retreated and taken hostages there at the northern end. We don't have numbers of friendlies, just that they exist. Our platoon will infil from the south end of the mall. It should be a clear approach, but don't get complacent. Eyes up and weapons ready as we move. This is a raid, people. We want to rescue as many hostages as we can, but priority is neutralizing the enemy. Because we're running on fucking fumes here, we don't have any flash-bangs to hand out, or CS. So suck it up and get ready."

The hush of conversations echoed through the dark bus. Most of the cops didn't even understand what the hell Cortez was saying, but Dom had grown up around marines and understood perfectly. This was a raid, and things weren't going to be pretty.

Moose nudged Dom.

He glanced over at this friend. "Yeah?"

"I don't know what's going to happen today, but I want you to know you've been more of a brother to me than Ray, and …" Moose shook his antlered Afro. "I just really appreciate all you've done for me over the years."

"I love you, bro, and I've always got your back."

"And I got yours."

"You two wanna get a room?" Camilla asked.

Moose all but smiled. "I'm ready to break some bones."

"That's what I'm talking 'bout," Camilla said, reaching over with a fist. She winked at Dom.

The convoy pulled off the interstate and sped toward the glow of fires. As soon as they hit the outskirts of Florence, the gunfire started.

Cortez hunched down as a round hit the windshield, splintering the glass in a web that blocked the view out the right side.

"Everyone down!" he yelled. "Prepare to dismount!"

An officer screamed out as a round punched through the metal body of the bus and hit him in the gut.

"Get us out of here!" Cortez yelled at the driver.

Moose got down on his knees and moved over to the wounded officer, who had slumped into the aisle. He put his hand on the guy's stomach to apply pressure. Another cop bent down to help.

Dom slid over in the seat, away from the windows and toward the aisle, nearly bumping into Camilla, who was leaning out of her seat. The fleet moved down another street, the bus swerving erratically to make the turn.

"Get ready!" Cortez shouted. "This is it. Judgment Day. Send 'em where they belong!"

Squad cars raced past on the right side of the road

and pulled off with several ambulances prepared to care for the wounded.

Hissing like a monstrous snake, the bus doors opened to the night.

Gunfire lanced through the windshield, hitting the driver.

"DISMOUNT! MOVE IT!" Cortez yelled.

Moose helped the injured man up as the bus quickly emptied. The first officers out were immediately struck by a wave of gunfire. By the time Dom got out, two cops were on the pavement, one of them crying out in pain.

"Mama!" he wailed. "I can't feel my legs!"

The other cop was already dead, his body sprawled at an unnatural angle. Dom bent down to help the screaming officer, but muzzle bursts flashed across the rooftop of the building across the road, forcing him back. He darted to the cover of an ambulance, where Camilla had taken cover.

"Sweet Jesus," Camilla said. "It's a fucking war zone."

Dom crouched and reached out to the injured cop, who was crawling toward them.

"Come on!" Dom shouted. He recognized the eighteen-year-old volunteer who had joined up not long after Dom.

"Cam, cover me!" Dom said.

She raised her rifle and gave a nod.

"Now!" he yelled.

At the crack of gunfire, Dom bolted for the injured cop. He grabbed him by his body armor and dragged him toward the safety of the ambulance, watching pinpricks of fire flash from the rooftop.

Dom pulled the man around to the back of the emergency vehicle. Moose was there with the cop who had taken a round to the stomach. EMTs were already working on him.

Several snipers continued firing from the rooftop, trying to pick off anyone who hadn't taken cover. Bullets cracked and pinged off the concrete, and one punched through a tire.

Camilla laid down more covering fire, and Dom hunched down to the man he had dragged to safety. He'd been calling for his mother but was quiet now.

Dom went to check for a pulse when he saw two fresh holes in the cop's armor. Blood trickled from both wounds and also below a hole in his helmet.

"Fuck," Dom muttered, letting go of the guy's limp hand as if it were contagious. He cradled his weapon and waited to switch positions with Camilla, ready to avenge the poor officer.

"We got to get out of here and draw their fire away from the ambulances," Moose said. "You guys cover me!"

Dom brought up his rifle and fired, but his finger met resistance. He moved back to cover when he realized he still had the safety on.

Stupid gets you dead, he reminded himself.

Camilla took his place and fired as Moose sprinted across the road toward another strip mall. Rounds punched into the pavement beside Camilla, and Dom grabbed her and pulled her back just in time.

"Let's go!" Moose yelled across the road.

"I'll go first and cover us," Dom said to Camilla. She nodded and patted him on the shoulder. He stepped out to provide covering fire, aiming where he had seen muzzle flashes.

Short bursts. Conserve your ammo.

Camilla didn't hesitate, racing across the road to Moose's position.

Dom fired again and then ran, head down now that the muzzle flashes had ceased. He sprinted as fast as he could and didn't stop until he reached the wall of the building where Moose and Camilla had taken cover.

"You good?" Moose asked.

Dom sucked in air and looked down for wounds. He seemed fine so far—no blood squirting, or pain shooting through him.

The chatter of machine-gun fire broke through the sporadic crack of semiautomatic weapons, snapping him back to reality. This was just the beginning of the fight, the first wave, with plenty more enemies waiting to take him down.

Camilla changed the magazine in her AR-15 and followed Dom and Moose toward a group of cops hunching behind a brick wall and several dumpsters.

One guy was down in the middle of the street, not moving.

More rounds bit into his limp body. Dom flinched at each one. Moose moved through an open side door into a pharmacy. Cortez was there, barking orders at a group of almost twenty officers huddled inside.

"We need to get up on the roof," he said. "First Squad, you're on that."

Another former Ranger gathered his men and moved out.

Cortez turned to the remaining officers. "I need

at least three fire teams with me to flank that building. Let's go, men."

"And women," Camilla corrected.

Cortez looked over at her and nodded.

Dom, Moose, and Camilla fell into line behind the sergeant and a half-dozen cops as they navigated the maze of looted shelves and trash littering the floor.

The radio on Cortez's vest crackled, and he stopped to listen.

"Sounds like we're sending an armored vehicle in from the front," Cortez said. "SWAT will go in to support First Squad on taking the roof from inside. Once the vehicle arrives, we make a run for it. Suppressive fire on the rooftop so SWAT and First Squad can get in there and wipe those motherfuckers out."

Everyone nodded back.

"Top off your weapons before we move," Cortez said. "When we're in position, pick your targets. Watch your ammo. One shot, one kill."

"What about the hostages?" Camilla asked.

"Already dead," Cortez said. "Executed before we even got here."

Camilla stared down at the ground, and Dom patted her on the back.

"They won't die in vain," she said.

The group of cops set off low and fast to the front of the pharmacy, where they crouched within view of the smashed window.

The rumble of a vehicle sounded over the gunfire, and an armored SWAT truck gunned past the pharmacy. The driver began to turn around a corner to the front of the mall.

Dom saw heads pop up on the rooftop, and then a man holding what looked like a large rifle. A streak of flame confirmed it wasn't a rifle, but rather a shoulder-fired rocket. The projectile hit the pavement, exploding into a fireball a few feet in front of the truck.

The driver swerved around the blast.

A second rocket slammed into the front wheel of the truck, blowing it onto its side. It slid across the pavement, shooting a fountain of sparks like a roman candle from under the bumper.

Another rocket streaked away. The projectile hit the belly of the vehicle, the explosion sending shrapnel in all directions. One piece of metal lodged in the wall above Dom, and more streaked into the pharmacy.

"Down!" Cortez yelled.

Dom bent down, spotting an officer in riot gear climbing out of the burning vehicle.

"Run!" Camilla shouted.

The guy looked around, disoriented and coughing.

"Over here!" she yelled.

The officer turned in her direction and started moving toward the pharmacy. Camilla got up to help, but Dom held her back as automatic gunfire cracked out overhead.

The injured officer was caught in the fire, his body riddled with bullets. He collapsed, raised a hand toward Camilla, and went limp.

Camilla choked out a scream. "You bastards!"

Dom had to wrestle her to the floor to keep her from firing and getting herself shot.

An officer behind Dom prayed out loud. "Lord in heaven, have mercy on us."

Another cop sobbed. "This isn't happening," he said. "This—"

"Shut the fuck up and get your heads in the game, or we're going to end up like our brothers on the street," Cortez said.

He spoke into his shoulder mike and confirmed an order with a grunted *oo-rah.*

"FRAGO, people," Cortez said. "We're moving out as soon as SWAT takes out those snipers. They'll suppress so we can move into position. We'll be supporting First Squad inside."

Dom heard Cortez's words, but all he could think about were the men who had already died without ever getting a chance to shoot back. In the glow of the burning truck, he could see the F-13 soldiers on the rooftop, fist-pumping and crowing in victory. To them, this was a game. For Dom, this was his chance.

"MOVE!" Dom yelled.

Cortez held up a hand and shouted after him, but it was too late.

Dom led the way out of the shattered entrance and took off across the parking lot toward the part of the strip mall controlled by F-13. Weaving around overturned cars, he raced toward the wall surrounding the mall.

Gunshots cracked overhead as the gangbangers snapped out of their celebration. But the rounds missed Dom, pinging off cars and pavement. He jumped over a car hood, sliding across the surface, and bolted the final yards to the wall of the enemy building.

Right behind him came Moose, then Camilla. Four more officers joined them, including Cortez.

"You're a crazy son of a bitch, whoever the fuck

you are," said the sergeant. "And if you ever run off like that again and risk getting people killed, I'll shoot you myself. You hear me, Mr. Badass?"

"His name's Dominic," Camilla said.

Cortez stared at her for a second. "I don't care if he's the second coming of Audie fucking Murphy. You don't pull that shit again!" he said, poking Dom in the chest.

Dom didn't mind being lectured. They all were still breathing for now, and that was what mattered.

"What's the plan, Sergeant?" Moose asked.

Cortez shook out of his fury. "This may not be the army, but I still outrank you," he said to Dom. "You follow my orders. Understand?"

Dom nodded. "Yes, Sergeant."

Across the street, police snipers moved out onto the roof of the pharmacy, laying down fire while Cortez talked into his shoulder mic.

Dom used the stolen moment to get his bearings. They were to the right of an underground parking garage, its entrance blocked by multiple vehicles. Several other doors led into the shopping center, but there was no way to tell what was on the other side.

"All right," Cortez said. "We have four more teams at the other side of the building. First Squad is in position. This is go time." He pointed to Dom, Camilla, and Moose in turn. "You three with me." To the other cops, he said, "Y'all are on the left flank."

Cortez nodded at Dom. "You got point, Dominic Badass."

Dom led the way to the right. Camilla and Moose fell in behind him along the wall. The F-13 soldiers on the rooftop continued exchanging gunfire with the officers across the road.

The distraction allowed Dom to move quickly, but he slid to a stop when a banger plummeted over the edge of the building and crunched into the sidewalk. His weapon clattered across the pavement and stopped a few feet away.

Dom moved past the dying man, leaving his jerking broken body to suffer. They didn't have bullets to waste on these assholes.

As he continued, he saw tracer rounds ripping across the skyline. Military units were giving the gangs hell—units like the Desert Snakes. The sight fueled him with courage.

A torrent of gunfire snapped him back to the fight in front of him. The shots were coming from the other side of the building, where the other teams of officers were preparing to raid the front entrances.

Dom steeled himself as he came up to a door. He took a breath, grabbed the handle, and turned it, but it wouldn't budge. Moose aimed the shotgun and waved everyone back.

He pulled the trigger and kicked the door in, pumping a new shell into the chamber as he rushed into the hallway.

"GO, GO!" Cortez yelled. He moved around Dom and Camilla to head in behind Moose.

A muzzle flash lit up the passage as they entered. Cortez took out a gangbanger waiting at the end of the hall. Now Moose was against the wall, firing as fast as he could pump the action on his shotgun.

Return fire riddled the ceiling, and Dom dropped

to the filthy carpet soiled with blood. Smoke burned his lungs and filled his sinuses, but he pushed through, keeping low.

Cortez was the first one into the offices of a former AMP recruiting center. The gangbangers had fortified the large, open bull pen by turning over desks and stacking them.

In the weak light, Dom could see little aside from muzzle flashes. He fired at them, keeping eyes on his zone and trying not to let the screams of his companions distract him.

Cortez went down, and Dom crawled over to find part of the sergeant's face erased by two gunshots. Blood bubbled out of his mouth and the hole where his nose had been.

"Dom!" Camilla shouted.

Moose's shotgun sounded like bombs going off in the enclosed space of the office. Dom crawled over to Camilla and Moose, who stood and fired another blast.

A banger came around the corner holding a machete. He raised it above his head to swing down on Moose, but Dom blindsided him, breaking the banger's jaw with his rifle butt. Then he put a burst in the guy's chest.

Dom turned his rifle on the other hostiles in the room. He counted at least three.

Even numbers, but the F-13 soldiers had Dom and his team pinned down, and now two more bangers slipped into the room from the far hallway.

Dom fired a shot that dropped one of the guys, but return fire forced him right back down. He kept his head low, right next to Camilla.

"We have to get out of here," she said.

Dom nodded.

"Go," Moose said. "I'll cover you."

"No way, man. We go together," Dom said quietly.

The shooting paused, and in the second's lull, Dom heard a thump and roll.

"Grenade!" Moose yelled. He grabbed the dead machete wielder and heaved the body onto the grenade as Dom and Camilla bolted for the door.

Dom dived into the hallway right behind Camilla as the explosion ripped through the office. The corpse seemed to absorb most of the blast, but a piece of shrapnel cut his arm. Another lodged like a red-hot knife in his boot.

Dom knew pain. He could handle pain. He was more worried about Moose.

Smoke drifted through the room, and Dom groped about for his rifle. He found it and brought the barrel up, scanning for hostiles and also for Moose.

Heart thumping, he strained to see in the smoky darkness.

Someone coughed. Then a flurry of gunshots forced Dom to roll over to the wall. He got up on one knee, aimed at a target, and squeezed the trigger.

The enemy's muzzle flash went dark.

"Andre!" Dom shouted. He got up and started back toward the open office area. Camilla grabbed him by the arm, but he yanked free, moving back to find Moose. Four steps later, a second bright flash exploded in the room.

The blast knocked him backward into Camilla.

Broken ceiling panels rained down on them.

Dom breathed in cordite and coughed, his ears

ringing. He tried to get up but fell back to the floor. Blood dripped from his lips.

"Moose," he mumbled.

Through the swirling smoke, he saw a figure moving like a ghost, from the bull pen out into the hallway.

Dom reached for his rifle but couldn't find it and drew his pistol. The phantasm coming through the smoke coalesced into the small frame of an F-13 soldier.

It took three shots to take him down. He slumped in front of Dom's boots but then reached up, a crazed look on his face. He screamed through ragged gray speed-freak teeth.

Dom pulled the trigger twice, blowing off his chin and silencing the bloodcurdling shriek.

"Behind us!" Camilla shouted.

Dom whirled about to see two men moving through the open door outside.

He blinked again, eyes stinging from the smoke, and raised the pistol. Both men wore helmets mounted with night-vision goggles.

These weren't gangbangers. Or cops. They wore fatigues that he had seen almost every day that his dad was home from deployments.

These were marines.

"Salvatore!" Marks shouted. "Hold up!"

Ronaldo sprinted down Roseberry Avenue, ignoring the bullets that zinged by his helmet. An ambulance rushed past him, heading in the opposite direction with injured cops who had joined the fight against F-13.

The Desert Snakes had beelined it to Florence as soon as they heard that cops from Downey were pinned down in the streets and shopping center.

Don't be too late. Please don't be too late.

His earpiece crackled with enraged and confused voices as he dashed to the school buses and police cars parked in the street by a strip mall. Another ambulance did a U-turn and blared off toward the closest hospital.

The radio chatter painted a desperate picture of the medical situation. The lack of doctors, nurses, and medicine had resulted in ad hoc triage. The limited staff were now working only on people they could save, and that didn't include any wounded gangsters.

An explosion boomed from a shopping center

across the street. Several Humvees had parked right outside, but no living marines or soldiers were in sight.

There were only corpses on the sidewalk and road around the building. Some were gangbangers; others …

Ronaldo resisted the urge to shout his son's name. He scanned bodies for his boy, and then the buildings for the sniper who had fired at him earlier. Spotting no one on the rooftops, he glanced over his shoulder to confirm that Marks, Tooth, and Bettis were on his heels.

They had spent most of yesterday at the port, holding back angry mobs of civilians looking for a handout, when the fighting started. Since then, the four marines had aided the police in skirmish after skirmish with the gangs, in what was fast becoming all-out urban warfare.

Then word had come that Dom's unit was pinned down and taking heavy casualties only a few miles from where the Desert Snakes were operating.

A muzzle flash came from a rooftop half a block away. Rounds picked at the pavement behind him. He crouched behind a Humvee and sneaked a look around the bumper.

Shadows moved through a parking lot to his right— men in hoodies and tank tops running to find cover. Ronaldo brought the rifle scope to his night-vision goggles, looking for the sniper. He found the dumbass sticking his bald head up.

"Eat this, shithead," Ronaldo said. He squeezed off a shot and got back up, running as the man sagged out of view. Another sniper got up to take his place, but gunfire from the pharmacy roof took him out before he could fire on Ronaldo.

Thank God, he thought. There *were* still cops up there after all.

One of them yelled down, "Get off the road!"

Tooth caught up to Ronaldo and gave him a *what the fuck?* glare.

They ran to the safety of the shopping center across from the pharmacy. A smoldering armored truck lay on its side, looking like a charred turtle.

"Salvatore, what the hell, man?" Marks growled as he and Bettis ran and joined them at the wall. "You got a death wish?"

Bettis remained silent, but he was pissed too.

They all were dog tired, bruised, and banged up from twenty-four hours of fighting.

"This isn't how we do things," Marks said.

"Sorry, man. My son's here somewhere." Ronaldo started moving around the side of the building. He stopped at the corner, checked for contacts, looked back. "It's clear. We need to get to the front."

The police sniper on the pharmacy roof waved at them and held up two fingers, indicating that two F-13 snipers were still on the roof above them, then one finger for a sniper on an adjacent rooftop.

Ronaldo gave him a thumbs-up and pushed his night-vision optics back into position. Taking point, he took off running with the other three Desert Snakes behind him.

A gunshot cracked. Then two. Two more followed, almost simultaneous.

For an eerie moment, the night was completely quiet. Ronaldo hoped the silence didn't mean the police sniper was dead.

He kept running, using the time the brave cop had bought them to get to Florence Avenue. He took a left and halted at the sight of friendlies.

A group of ten marines and six cops were hunkered down behind a retaining wall outside a restaurant patio.

"Who's in charge here?" Marks asked.

A marine raised his hand. "Staff Sergeant Patel."

"I'm taking over," Marks said.

"And who are you?"

"Gunnery Sergeant Marks."

The marine straightened a bit and said, "Good to have you with us, Gunny."

Ronaldo searched the faces one by one, then turned to his team. "He's not here."

"Who are you looking for?" asked the staff sergeant.

"Dad?" came a voice.

Ronaldo pushed his NVGs up and looked at the blood-streaked faces of two officers who had walked down the outside stairwell leading to the entrance of the restaurant. They stepped out into the moonlight, both wearing body armor that looked a size too big.

When Ronaldo saw Camilla and his son, his heart leaped.

"Dominic," Ronaldo said, running over.

"Where …? How …?" Dom stammered.

Gunfire hit the retaining wall, forcing the men to scatter. Ronaldo moved in front of Dom and Camilla, shielding their bodies with his as he returned fire at the shadowy figures across the road.

One fell, his head bouncing off the concrete like a Ping-Pong ball. The other made it to cover behind a tree.

"Four o'clock!" Tooth shouted.

Staff Sergeant Patel led a team of marines to a car in the street and took up position. They fired over the hood and bumper at the approaching F-13 reinforcements who had flanked from the parking lot.

"Clear!" one of the men shouted. He ducked back down as more rounds came in from gang members still hiding in the lot.

"Get this AO locked down, God damn it!" Marks yelled.

Ronaldo motioned for Dom and Camilla to back away from the sidewalk. He joined them in the stairwell and gave his boy a hug.

Camilla nodded to Ronaldo. She limped down a stair, wincing in pain. "Great to see you, sir."

"Are you guys okay?" he asked.

Dom's lips quivered. "They killed Moose."

The words took the air from Ronaldo's lungs.

"What?"

Dom sniffled, and Ronaldo realized that his son had been crying.

"He saved us," Dom said. "Sacrificed himself to let us escape."

Ronaldo didn't ask what happened, but it didn't matter. All that mattered was that they kill the scum who had done this and get out of here before more of their scumbag friends joined the fray.

Marks moved over, keeping low. "Shit, Dom, good to see you're okay," he said.

Dom managed a nod.

Marks didn't waste any time. "They think there's about six hostiles left inside," he said. "But they have at least four cop hostages, and we're sitting-fucking-ducks right here."

"When are reinforcements arriving?" Tooth asked.

"They're not," said one of the marines. "We're lucky you guys showed up."

"What? You mean we're *it*?"

The marine who spoke was still crouched behind the retaining wall with the others. Most of them were down to their handguns.

Ronaldo didn't want to tell them that the only reason they were here was the radio transmission he had heard earlier. He exchanged a look with Marks. They had come here to save his son, and they would do everything they could to make sure the cop hostages got out alive.

"Reform this perimeter," Marks ordered again. "I want it tight. Combat intervals. Eyes up on that roof. Who's my best sharpshooter here?"

"That would be me," Ronaldo said.

"I meant out of them," Marks said.

The other marines all looked over the wall as a voice in Spanish shouted, "*¡Pinches puercos!*"

"Some asshole just called us fucking pigs," Camilla said, raising her rifle.

The young woman was more of a firecracker than he remembered.

"Stay behind us," Ronaldo said to Camilla. Then he glanced over the retaining wall at the courtyard between the shops and offices in the L-shaped building. Movement among the picnic tables and palm trees caught his eye.

An overweight police officer with his hands in the air staggered out across the concrete.

A gunshot pierced the silence, forcing him to run.

Laughter from one of the storefronts sounded as the F-13 soldiers took potshots.

"Over here!" Tooth yelled, waving.

The officer ran hard, avoiding another two shots. When he was a hundred feet from the retaining wall, a round to the back of the knee sent him crashing to the asphalt, screaming in agony.

"*¡Ven a buscar a su hermano cochino!*" one of the gangsters yelled.

"What did he say?" Ronaldo asked.

Camilla snorted with anger. "He said to come get your …" Her features tightened. "Your filthy brother pig."

"They're baiting us," Marks replied. "They'll shoot the first person that moves out of cover."

Tooth looked back at Marks for orders as the injured officer pleaded for help.

Another gunshot cracked, and a second bullet hit the man in his other leg. He howled in pain. Then he started crawling toward the wall, a hand up.

The next bullet took off a finger or two.

"Fuck this," Tooth said. He moved around the corner and took off to grab the cop.

"Covering fire," Marks said. "But watch your targets—there are hostages."

The marines fired suppressing bursts, but Ronaldo couldn't see any targets. Gunfire cracked behind them, in the opposite direction. They were being flanked again.

Tooth grabbed the guy and pulled him behind the wall, where a corpsman started to work on his injuries.

Marks bent down and said, "Where are they?"

The officer moaned and squirmed in agony. His

eyelids began to close. Marks wiped the smear on his tag to read his name.

"Officer Peter," he said, slapping the guy in the face to get his attention. "You have to tell us where these guys are, so we can save your friends."

Peter mumbled something, then gritted his teeth in pain.

"AMP ..." he said.

"The AMP offices," Dom said. "That's where they killed Moose. They must've all moved back inside from the other stores."

"Show us," Marks said.

Ronaldo hesitated. He had come here to rescue his son, not put him in more danger. But looking at him, he no longer saw a boy who needed protecting.

Dom pointed across the street. "They're in that building, the one with the desks all piled up in front of the windows."

Marks studied the area. He looked at another building. "If we can get to that rooftop, we might give a strike team a chance to get close. Once we start shooting, you guys have to move in fast."

He glanced at the other Desert Snakes. "Salvatore, take the team and go with Dom. Get up there and lay down covering fire. The rest of us will hold position here until it's clear to move up."

Camilla called out as Dom got up and began to limp after the marines.

"Not without me!"

"No, stay here, Cam," he said.

She hesitated, then said, "Fuck that; you're not my CO."

Ronaldo almost smiled, but he was too enraged and too tired to show any positive emotion. Keeping low, he followed his son across the street with Tooth, Bettis, and Camilla.

They stopped at a car and scanned the area. It looked clear. The building Marks wanted them to get to was only fifty feet away.

"I'll take point," Tooth said.

He got up, but Ronaldo grabbed him, then brought up his rifle and zoomed in on the intersection of Albany Street and Saturn Avenue, a block away.

A dozen men walked onto Albany, on a collision course with the marines and cops. All of them were carrying rifles, and one even appeared to have something bigger.

"Snake One, we're about to have company," Ronaldo said into the comms. "Twelve hostiles, carrying small arms mostly. Maybe one rocket launcher."

"Roger," Marks replied. "We'll be ready. Now, get on that roof."

Ronaldo moved around the car and saw Marks across the street. They exchanged a wave, and Ronaldo took point.

Inside, his small team quickly cleared the rooms and found the roof access. Tooth went first, sweeping his rifle back and forth. Two cops lay where they had been shot. Their sniper rifles were beside them.

Ronaldo flashed hand signals.

Tooth, Bettis, and Camilla moved over to the left side of the roof to ambush the incoming posse while Dom followed Ronaldo to the dead cops.

Bending down, he picked up one of their sniper

rifles, a bolt-action Remington 700 in .223 caliber, a round already chambered. He brought the weapon up and followed Dom's finger toward the AMP offices.

Sighting through the scope, Ronaldo could see several guys moving behind a fort of desks. He zoomed in to look for the hostages but didn't spot any.

"Sergeant," Tooth hissed across the roof. He relayed hand signals to tell the story. The gangbangers would be in range in thirty seconds.

Ronaldo looked through the scope, but the gangsters were out of sight.

"Where the hell'd they go …?"

"What's going on?" Dom asked.

A body suddenly flew out the broken window. Another guy, this one shirtless, went out next, pile-driving on his head in the courtyard.

"Execute," Tooth said, keeping his voice low.

Dom ran over to help as they fired on the F-13 reinforcements below. The marines and cops on the street joined the firefight.

Ronaldo lined up his sights on the two men outside the offices. The shirtless guy had gotten back up and reached for a gun in his waistband. Ronaldo squeezed the trigger, knocking the guy back down with a broken spine.

The second guy turned to look in his direction as Ronaldo chambered another round, sighted, and fired, hitting him in the neck.

Pinpricks of light brightened the interior of the offices as the hostages fought their captors. Ronaldo looked for targets but couldn't figure out who was who in the chaos.

The fight on the street below continued, the gunfire punctuated by screams and wails. He kept his focus on the storefront, finger on the trigger, waiting. He eased off when he saw a big man climbing over the desks.

Reaching back inside, the guy helped two more people over the desks blocking the door.

Cops.

He zoomed in on the face of the big guy who had tossed the smaller men like rag dolls.

"*Dom*," Ronaldo said. "Dom, you gotta see this."

Dom ran over, panting. "We got those fuckers," he said.

Instead of replying, Ronaldo handed his son the rifle. "Look at this."

As soon as Dom took the gun, Ronaldo moved over to the roof and looked down at the massacre below. All the bangers were down, but several were still moving, and one was begging for mercy.

"What do we do with those guys?" Camilla asked.

Ronaldo unslung his rifle and aimed at the guy crying for mercy.

"Only one thing to do with these monsters," he said. He fired twice into the two men who were trying to crawl away. "We fight evil with evil."

Bettis and Tooth both looked over at Ronaldo. He couldn't see their eyes beneath their optics, but he knew he would find disapproval there, and he really didn't care. The gangsters were not worthy of mercy. The fewer of them in the city, the better.

"It's Moose!" Dom said, running over. "Cam! Moose is still alive!"

Ronaldo watched the two young officers embrace

as a thin rind of gold fired the eastern horizon. A new day had begun in the City of Angels, but the fighting raged on.

The comms crackled to life with a message from Marks.

"Snake Two, get back down here. I just got a message about Downey High School."

Ronaldo clenched up. "What about the school? Is my family okay?"

Dom looked over at him.

"Return to rendezvous, Snake Two," Marks repeated.

"Tell me what's going on," Ronaldo snapped.

"There's been some sort of attack," Marks replied. "That's all I know."

* * *

"You're going to tell us who you are and who you're working with," said the burly detective, "or I will make sure you never walk again."

Vinny sat handcuffed to a chair in an interrogation room deep beneath police headquarters. He had been in custody for several days now, but the cops had been too busy to spend much time interrogating him. That had changed a few hours ago.

The two cops questioning him were more serious than the others, and they were getting sick of his silence.

The one asking questions wore a button-down shirt and tie. He was young, no more than thirty.

The other detective, the bald one, was in his forties and almost twice as thick. He wore an LAPD polo shirt a size too small, probably to show off his pecs and biceps.

It was funny to Vinny. He wasn't scared of these guys. They weren't Vega soldiers or Crips. They couldn't skin him alive or cut off his balls and stick them in his ass.

All they could do was keep him locked up and ask him questions that he would deflect or answer with a lie.

The big detective bent down close, but Vinny kept his eyes on the mirror, wondering who was on the other side.

"You may think we're just normal cops like the guys that have been asking you questions over the past few days," the man said quietly. "You may think I can't hurt you and put you in a wheelchair."

"You'd be wrong," said the younger guy at the desk.

"You're wasting your time," Vinny replied calmly. "You've got nothing on me, because there's nothing to get. I've done nothing wrong, unless helping Sergeant Best and the anti-gang task force is wrong. And the only way that can be wrong is if you guys are in bed with the criminals."

"That's funny," the big guy said. "And I'm getting tired of this shit."

The cop stood and, before Vinny could brace himself, blindsided him with a punch to his right ear. The sting was just the start of the pain. When his chair toppled over, his left cheek smashed against the floor, and his wrists twisted behind him.

Pain shot up his arms and across his face.

The cop picked him up and righted the chair.

When Vinny blinked away the stars, the guy was squatting in front of him with a shit-eating grin that showed off a chipped front tooth.

"Listen, kid, things don't work the way they used

to," he said. "I can beat you like a piñata until your guts fall out your runt hole if I want."

The young detective stood up and leaned with his palms on the desk. "I've seen him do it before—smells worse than you think. So I'm asking again, who are you and who do you work for?"

Vinny gathered the metallic-tasting saliva in his mouth and spat it in the face of the pig who had hit him.

"My employer—that's who you want?" The cop wiped the bloody spittle off his face, shook his head, and turned to his partner behind the desk. The guy pushed something silver across the surface.

Vinny swallowed blood. "My *employer* is going to carve both your hollow fucking heads into jack-o'-lanterns!" he yelled.

"Is that so?" The bald cop grabbed a pair of pliers off the desk.

"Time to play dentist," the young detective said.

Vinny squirmed as the two men moved closer. They were bluffing. They couldn't do this—things hadn't changed *that* much.

"No," Vinny mumbled through clenched teeth as the smaller cop got behind him and tried to work a letter opener between his jaws. He fought it, but after several minutes of jerking and squirming, the big guy got the pliers into his mouth.

"Hold still or I'll take your tongue too, asshole," he grumbled.

Vinny yowled as he gripped an incisor, levered back and forth, and ripped it out with a pop.

"Tell me who you are and who you work for!" the man with the pliers shouted.

"FUCK YOU!" Vinny yelled back, rage boiling through his veins. Blood dribbled down his chin.

The door cracked open, and a familiar face appeared.

"Captain Stone," said the bald guy, lowering the pliers, like a teenager caught with a joint.

"These motherfuckers are torturing me, sir," Vinny said. "You can't do this, you can't ..."

Stone walked over.

For a second, Vinny expected him to bend down and unlock the cuffs. Instead, Stone punched him in the gut so hard, the chair rocked backward. He braced for another fall, but he couldn't do much to lessen the impact.

Sometime later, Vinny jerked awake to distant shouting. He sat up and brought his hand up to his head, touching what felt like a bandage. His tongue went to the swollen hole in his gums where one of his front teeth had been.

He looked around him at concrete walls and a metal toilet. Memories flooded his mind—the interrogation and the events that had led to it.

Swinging his legs over the edge of the hard slab that was supposed to be a bed, he placed his naked feet on the cold floor and walked to the door.

Outside the small glass window, there was movement in the hallway. Several officers had prisoners in cuffs and were leading them out of their cells.

Soon, two cops in riot gear stopped at his door and opened it.

"Get back!" one of them shouted.

Vinny held his hands up. "What's going on?" he asked.

"Shut the fuck up and do as we say," said the other guard.

"Okay, just chill, man," Vinny said.

That got him a baton in the gut. He doubled over, glaring at the guy who hit him.

"Don't even think about it, asshole," the guard said. "I'll make sure you can never suck a cock in prison again." He slapped the baton into his palm.

"Then you'd be doing me a favor," Vinny said.

The guy raised the baton, but the other guard stopped him. "Come on, we gotta move."

Lowering the baton, he said, "Hands behind your back."

Vinny turned and they cuffed him, and a hand gripped him under the arm and jerked him out into the hallway.

The door at the end clicked open onto a squad room alive with activity. Officers were carrying file folders and gear. It looked as if they were leaving.

"What the hell's going on?" Vinny asked.

His answer was a shove in the back. He was led through the bowels of the Los Angeles Police Department headquarters to an underground parking structure, where an armored car waited.

The other prisoners were already gone.

"Where are you taking me?" Vinny asked.

The guards opened the back doors and pushed him inside.

A moment later, the armored car started up the parking ramp levels, to the street.

Still in his cuffs, Vinny tried to calm himself, but the pain from his injuries escalated his anxiety. He had a bad feeling they were taking him somewhere where they could do worse than yank a few teeth.

His mind raced with the possibilities. Just when he was getting to the really nasty stuff, the sound of gunshots pulled him back to the present.

The truck jolted out onto the street and took a hard left. Through the armored walls, he could hear the distant crack of small-arms fire, including automatic weapons.

It sank in then: the abrupt end to the interrogation, the gunfire outside. LAPD headquarters was under attack. But if that was it, why move the prisoners? Why not just keep them in their cells and duke it out with the gangsters right there at HQ?

The armored car sped up as rounds pinged off the side.

A few minutes later, the driver eased off the accelerator, and the gunshots faded.

Vinny relaxed against the armored bulkhead. If they did get into trouble, the metal would protect him. It was the destination that had him worried. Not being able to see outside made his anxiety worse, but judging by the silence, they had made it through the worst of the fight.

He closed his eyes and thought of his mom—the one thing that always seemed to bring him solace. He could hardly remember her features or her voice, only that it was soothing. And he would never forget what she would say before bed every night.

I love you, my sweet little angel.

He felt like smiling but didn't get the chance. The warm memories were ripped away as the truck turned sharply and then jolted in the opposite direction.

Vinny felt like the piñata the burly detective had threatened to turn him into. His body caromed off both walls as the truck flipped and skidded.

His head hit the floor hard, and red swirled across his vision. On his back, he blinked up at the ceiling of the armored cargo space.

Not the ceiling, he realized. He was on the ceiling, looking up at the floor.

Gunshots sounded outside. Then a muffled scream.

Something hit the back doors with a huge bang, and sparks burst inside. Smoke flooded the cargo space. He coughed and blinked, eyes burning.

The groan of bending metal came next, and before him stood a blurred shape holding a long crowbar. Blinding sunlight filled the space.

"Hold still; I'm unlocking your cuffs," growled a voice Vinny didn't recognize. He blinked at the bright morning sun as he was helped out of the vehicle.

The crushed front of a cab-over semi smoked near the curb. A man jumped down wearing a ski mask and carrying an M4. Voices called out, and gunfire hit the armored vehicle.

Two BMWs jerked to a stop, and multiple figures wearing black fatigues and masks hopped out.

"We got to move!" shouted one of the guys. "The military's coming!"

The man from the semi pulled off his mask, and through the smoke, Vinny made out a square jaw with a salt-and-pepper goatee.

"Dad?" he mumbled, squinting.

Christopher stopped on his way over, pointing the rifle with one hand and blasting an injured cop crawling across the pavement.

"Get in," said the Moretti soldier, helping Vinny around a BMW.

The next person he saw was Vito, sitting in the front passenger seat, his face bruised and bumpy. The man helping Vinny opened the back door and told him to get in. Vinny ducked inside and scooted onto the back seat.

Now it made sense. The attack on the police HQ, the cops moving all the prisoners out of lockup—it was all so they could give the Morettis a way to free Vinny.

"Good morning," said a calm voice. Don Antonio sat relaxed and drinking a coffee. He gave Vinny a quick scan, reached over, and put a hand on his cheek. "You talk to the pigs?"

Vinny tried to speak, but all he could do was shake his head.

"Good boy," Antonio said, slapping his cheek gently. "You earned your button."

-26-

The sun rose over a city gone mad, its rays barely penetrating the lingering cloud of smoke. Shooting had continued into the morning all across the city, but most of it had moved downtown, where police and military units fought pitched battles with the gangs.

It was Judgment Day in the City of Angels.

Chief Diamond's death had rallied the military and police to answer his call to arms, but the gangs weren't going to surrender easily.

While Dom and the Desert Snakes raced toward Downey High School, the Los Angeles Police Department was being hammered from all sides.

The radio in the Humvee buzzed with reports and requests for aid, but Marks was having no luck gleaning more information about the school.

Marks rode shotgun, with Tooth and Bettis flanking Dom in the back seat. Dom's mind raced with worry, not only about his sister and mom, but also about Moose and Camilla. She had stayed with Moose as he was being transported to the nearest medical center.

Ronaldo kept his hands on the wheel, not saying a single word. The roads were mostly empty except for occasional military trucks, emergency vehicles, and cop cars. Almost all of them were going in the opposite direction.

The Humvee was headed east, away from the worst of the fighting, but it was still dangerous out here, and Dom was terrified of what had happened at Downey High School.

For the first half of the ride, the men had changed their magazines, checked their gear, and caught their breath.

Now they all sat quietly, waiting to see what had prompted the call to Marks back at the shopping center.

Moose had survived. How, Dom wasn't sure, but the news filled him with the hope he needed to face whatever awaited them at Downey High School.

Gunfire snapped him out of his thoughts.

"Hold on," Ronaldo said. The first two words he had spoken in a half hour sounded as if a robot had spoken them.

He swerved around two cars billowing acrid black smoke and gunned the engine.

"Holy shit!" Tooth said, bracing himself against the seat.

Bettis whispered to himself, and Dom glanced over to see he was praying.

"Christ!" Tooth said.

The truck blew through the smoke and continued down the street.

Marks checked the side mirror and then let out a sigh of relief. "Must have been a random sniper. Keep frosty, Salvatore."

Ronaldo nodded.

"We're almost to Downey," Marks said. "Everyone, get ready."

They passed through a neighborhood of houses burned to their foundations. Here and there, wisps of smoke still rose from the blackened ruins.

To their right, Dom glimpsed a group of people running across the street, firing weapons at someone he couldn't see. On the left side of the road, more fighting was under way. The battle had spread to every city block, it seemed.

Three squad cars raced past on the opposite side of the road. Tooth turned to watch them fly by.

"Must be going to LAPD headquarters," he said.

"Same with those," Marks said, pointing to the skyline.

Two Black Hawks crossed over the city, vanishing into a tower of smoke.

Dom felt a pat on his knee and looked down to see Bettis's gloved hand. "It's going to be okay, son."

Dom realized that his legs were shaking.

He held them still, and the pain in his foot returned. Good. It would take his mind off his sister and mom.

More gunfire popped across the road, and a bullet pinged into the door.

"Down!" Ronaldo shouted. He pulled to the left and pushed the pedal down on an open space of road.

Another flurry of gunshots came from the other side of the street, peppering the windshield and hood with bullets. A round broke through the spider-webbed windshield and punched into the seat, inches from

Dom's shoulder. The Humvee pulled back to the right, catching more bullets from that side of the road.

"Where are they?" Ronaldo shouted. "I don't got eyes!"

"Keep driving!" Marks yelled back.

Ronaldo stomped the pedal and raced away from the ambush site. Dom poked up to see several guys running out into the road, firing rifles.

"Twelve o'clock!" Marks shouted.

Dom turned back to the broken windshield. Peering between the cracks, he saw an abandoned truck ahead, and two men standing with rifles aimed over the hood.

"Tooth! Turret!" Marks shouted.

Tooth started to move, but Dom beat him up into the armored turret. He grabbed the M249 and aimed at the truck. The two men standing there fired first, their muzzle flashes winking over the hood.

Bullets glanced off the turret's armor, but Dom held strong. He could hear the marines yelling inside the Humvee, until the bark of the M249 drowned them out.

Lining up the barrel, he swept the truck right to left with continuous fire. One of the men spun away; the other fell out of sight.

He swiveled the barrel, looking for more targets as Ronaldo drove around the pickup. Dom turned as they passed, and saw the two men lying in pools of blood.

A tug on his leg pulled him back into the Humvee.

"Nice shooting," Marks said.

Ronaldo kept his eyes on the road, not saying a word. Dom had seen his dad like this only once before, in the forest after killing the raiders who had put their hands on Elena and Monica.

Please be okay, Dom prayed.

He closed his eyes but couldn't concentrate. They were just a few blocks from the high school now.

Flying around the next corner, Ronaldo slammed on the brakes. A body lay in the middle of the street.

"Is that a cop?" Marks asked. He opened the door and moved in front of the truck to check, bending down out of sight.

Ronaldo backed up and moved around the body that Marks was now dragging out of the road. He got back in the Humvee, cursing.

"Dead," Marks confirmed. "Multiple gunshot wounds to the chest."

Ronaldo sped the rest of the way to the high school.

"Lock and load," Marks said.

Dom checked his rifle magazine for the third time. As they pulled into the front lot, he moved from side to side to get a better view through the windshield, but he couldn't see much of anything.

The Humvee jerked to a stop, and all the doors swung open. Dom followed Bettis out and hopped down onto the concrete.

Looking toward the front of the school, he saw bodies.

Dom recognized both men. They were two of the guards he had told to protect his sister and his mom with their lives. It appeared they had kept their promise.

The marines shouldered their rifles and moved toward the entrance in combat intervals, crushing spent brass under their boots. A skirt of glass covered the ground, and bullet holes peppered the walls inside the vestibule they had sealed off from fallout.

Ronaldo took lead, his muzzle sweeping left to right, then forward.

"Clear," he said.

Coming in last, Dom stepped over the glass shards and followed the marines into an empty hallway. They moved in silence, though he wanted to yell out for his sister and mom.

At the first intersection in the corridor, Ronaldo flashed hand signals. Tooth and Bettis went right, and Marks went straight.

"Dom, stay here," Ronaldo whispered.

"What? No way!"

Ronaldo gave him a glare. Then he was gone, running down the left hallway while Dom remained in the center. He turned in all directions, straining to catch any sign of life.

Over thirty people had been here when he left last night, and so far, he hadn't seen or heard a single person.

He didn't wait long.

"Down here!" Tooth yelled.

Dom hobbled down the right passage, wincing from the shrapnel wound in his foot. He didn't stop until he got to the auditorium. Tooth and Bettis were standing inside the open door, motioning for people to come out.

Over a dozen filed out into the hallway, looking around, some of them visibly shaking, others sobbing.

"What happened?" Bettis asked them. "Where is everyone else?"

A man Dom didn't recognize shook his head. "Masked men came in shooting and … took people."

Dom looked around for his mother and sister. "Where's my sister Monica, and my mom, Elena?" he asked. "Has anyone seen them?"

"They took Monica, and your mom went after them," said someone at the back of the group. A man in a wheelchair moved forward. He had a pistol in one hand. It was Samuel and his wife, Lucinda, the neighbors who had lived across the street before their houses were burned down.

"Mr. Kent," Dom said. "Who took my sister?"

"I don't know," Samuel said, shaking his head. "Men in masks, with machine guns. Your mom ran after them with several other people."

He looked ashamed to have been hiding in here, but Dom didn't blame the wheelchair-bound veteran. He had protected these people and done what most people would have done.

Dom stumbled away. His heart pounded so hard, it seemed bent on escaping the confines of his chest. His vision clouded, and he felt light-headed.

"I'm sorry," Samuel called after him. "I'm sorry I couldn't stop them!"

Dom ran down the hall, the pain a distant thought. He had to find his mom, had to find his sister.

Shouting came from another passage, and Dom rounded the corner to see his dad straddling a man on the ground. Marks tried to pull him off, but Ronaldo jerked free and punched the man again.

"You were supposed to protect them!" he shouted.

"Come on!" Marks said. "Get off him; we have to go find Elena!"

Dom hobbled over to see the man his dad was hitting. It was the third guard from last night. An open storage closet door told Dom all he needed to know. The man had hidden from the attackers.

Ronaldo hit him again and yelled, "Chickenshit!"

Marks had to grab Ronaldo by the neck to pull him off the man, who remained on his back, trembling.

"I'm … sorry," said the guard, holding up an arm to protect his battered face.

"Forget him!" Marks yelled. "We have to go. Now!"

Ronaldo hesitated.

"Dad, come on!" Dom said. "We have to go find Mom and Monica!"

Ronaldo turned toward Dom but hardly looked at him as he strode past, moving like a machine toward the exit.

* * *

Fight evil with evil, Ronaldo thought. He should have killed the bastard who hid in a closet while soulless men came in and took his daughter and several other kids.

If not for Marks, he probably would have killed the guard he had trusted to protect his family. But he *would* kill the men responsible. Once he found them, he would kill them and gut them, though not necessarily in that order.

Ronaldo ran outside the school, to the Humvee, with the rest of the Desert Snakes and his son following.

"ELENA!" Ronaldo shouted.

"Everyone, spread out," Marks said. "She couldn't have gotten far."

Bettis and Tooth took off running in different directions, and Marks followed Ronaldo over to the Humvee. Dom piled in with them.

"I'm coming," he said.

This time, Ronaldo didn't argue.

Marks grabbed the radio to report the missing kids and to ask whether any units had heard of kidnappings in the area.

Ronaldo hardly listened to the responses flooding over the channel as he pulled out of the school lot. He searched the street from left to right and decided to go in the direction where they had found the dead cop. Chances were, Monica's captors had gone that way, and Elena couldn't have gotten far.

They came up on the dead cop's squad car. Its windshield was riddled with bullet holes. An officer was still behind the wheel, his head slumped against the door. His partner's body was still lying on the side of the road, where Marks had dragged it out of the way.

Only months ago, Ronaldo would have had trouble imagining the sort of ghoulish animal that kidnapped kids and killed two cops. But now the world was full of these demons.

His heart iced as he drove farther away from the school, eyes flitting back and forth to look for Elena. He checked the rearview mirror and saw Dom brushing something away from his eye.

Ronaldo felt the warm blur of tears. *Don't do that, Salvatore. You will find your family.*

Marks continued talking into the radio while Ronaldo drove. The responses crackled. There were so many reports of violence and atrocities, it was impossible to keep up with them all.

Ronaldo looked down at a light that flashed on the dashboard. They were almost out of diesel fuel.

Cursing, he pounded the steering wheel once, then twice, so hard that his hand hurt.

He took a right on the next street and resisted the urge to burn precious fuel by gunning the engine. Instead, he accelerated slowly, avoiding several wrecked vehicles and swerving to miss a dog that limped across the street.

A woman came out of a house screaming and waving, but Ronaldo didn't even slow.

It wasn't his Elena.

"Where is she?" he mumbled.

Fear stabbed his heart at the thought of his daughter with men who would do her harm. He tried to block out the thoughts of evil, but they kept breaking through.

He pounded the steering wheel again, tears streaming from his eyes.

Marks looked over but didn't speak.

The Humvee was speeding through an intersection when Dom yelled, "Stop!"

Ronaldo slammed on the brakes and looked at the back seat.

"Back that way!" Dom said, pointing.

Reversing the truck, Ronaldo spun the wheel and accelerated down the road Dom had pointed at. Sure enough, a woman was walking down the middle of the street.

She wasn't facing them, but Ronaldo recognized her long dark hair. She staggered along like an exhausted refugee.

He eased off the pedal as he approached. Then he parked the Humvee on the side of the road, killed the engine, and jumped out.

"Elena," he said, trying not to spook her.

She kept walking, mumbling to herself, a pistol in her hand.

"Mom!" Dom called out.

She stopped without turning, the gun shaking in her hand.

Ronaldo moved out in front of her, his hands up. "Sweetheart," he said. "Please give me the gun and get out of the street."

Her eyes flitted from Ronaldo to Dom, who had joined them.

"Mom," he said.

Her lips quivered; the lower one was swollen. Blood trickled down her chin.

"Elena," Ronaldo murmured, his heart breaking at the sight of her bruised features. He reached out to take the gun.

She pushed back at him, screaming, "No! Get away!"

"Mom," Dom said, reaching out gently. "Mom, it's me, Dominic."

She raised the gun and for a moment Ronaldo thought she was going to point it at her head. Out of instinct, he grabbed it and disarmed her before she could hurt herself or one of them.

"NO!" she yelled. "I have to save Monica. I have to protect my baby!"

Ronaldo put the gun away and held up both hands again. "Please, Elena, you need to calm down."

"Mom, it's okay," Dominic said.

She looked at him, and her gaze seemed to soften.

Marks got out of the Humvee and slowly walked over.

"Elena," Ronaldo said. "It's your husband and son. We're not going to hurt you. We love you."

She looked at them in turn again and then dropped to her knees, sobbing with her head against her chest.

"They took Monica," she wailed. "They took my little girl."

Ronaldo crouched down and reached out until she finally collapsed into his arms.

"I promise I'll find Monica and the people who took her," he said. "I promise you on *my life*, I will bring our girl back."

Marks looked as though he wanted to speak.

"What?" Ronaldo said.

"No word about any kidnappings in this area," Marks said. "But the cops have regained control of HQ. Maybe we can get some help looking for Monica."

"Come on, we have to get up," Ronaldo said. He helped Elena to her feet, and he and Dom moved her into the truck.

"We'll find Monica, Mom," Dom said. "Dad and I will bring her home."

-27-

Two days had passed since the battle for Los Angeles ended, and the Moretti family was celebrating tonight. The main floor of the former Commerce Casino was hopping with activity. This section of the city still didn't have power, but Antonio had authorized use of the generators to power the casino floor.

In the glow of chandeliers, hundreds of his soldiers and associates sat around the card tables, betting silver and other currency. Waitresses in short skirts and tops that left little to the imagination served endless drinks to the men while they gambled their paychecks.

It was only ten o'clock, and half of them were drunk.

They had earned it, and plenty of soldiers were outside standing guard. Everyone, down to the teenagers cleaning dishes in the kitchen, had been vetted in the hiring process, but Antonio still swept the space with the skeptical gaze of a predatory animal.

He had certainly earned a break, but the burden of being a leader weighed heavily on him tonight, and there was still business to attend to. When it was finally finished, he would retire to his chambers with his queen. She was up there now with Marco and several other family members, watching movies and eating pizza.

"Don Antonio!" the men shouted. They raised glasses in salute as he made his way to a table of his captains and most trusted soldiers.

Frankie, Carmine, Yellowtail, Raff, Vito, and Christopher sat at a blackjack table, each with a stack of chips and a drink. At first glance, none of them appeared drunk. And it appeared Carmine had avoided the powder. His eyes were clear, and his scarred face wasn't bright red.

That was good.

After Carmine blew off the top of Chief Diamond's head, Antonio had reconsidered a very difficult decision about his old friend who was on thin ice. As long as he stayed clean, that ice would remain firm under his feet and he would stay a captain, in charge of the drug operation. But if Antonio caught him doing blow again, it would be the end for Carmine Barese.

The elevator, up and running now, took them to the top floor. Two associates in suits, each armed with an M4 carbine, stood guard outside Antonio's office. They opened the double doors, letting in all the soldiers of the Moretti family.

Refreshments awaited on the Italian marble wet bar that his men had installed a week ago. Yellowtail went over to make a drink, and Christopher lit one of his new cigars, blowing smoke rings into the air.

Antonio filled his lungs with the pleasant scent as he crossed the room to the war table he had always dreamed of. Lucia had put the word out to the men to look for a ten-piece dining room table while out on their raids. They had returned three days ago with a custom-made Italian table with a chestnut finish and gold trim.

Maps of the city were now spread over its surface, and Antonio leaned over the table to study them again. He already had the four selling zones of the city memorized, but he wanted to give it another glance before his business partners arrived.

A rap came on the door, and Yellowtail opened it to talk to the guard.

"Our friends are coming up," Yellowtail said.

Antonio gestured toward the table, and Christopher, Yellowtail, Carmine, Frankie, and Raff all sat down. He remained standing, eyes on the door.

Another knock sounded.

Christopher blew out a cloud of smoke as a man walked in. None of them were expecting to see Lino standing there.

"Don Antonio," Lino said in a gruff voice. His favorite black suit hung loose on his muscular frame—an indication of more weight loss, on a frame that didn't have much to lose, in the month since the attack that almost left him dead. His shirt collar covered most of the scar on his neck, but his chin would always have a cleft that was not there at birth.

The Moretti soldiers all rose from their seats as he entered the room.

"Good to have you with us, my friend," Antonio said. He walked over and pulled a chair back for Lino—something he had never done before. This got everyone's attention.

"Would you like something to drink?" Antonio asked Lino.

"No, thank you, Don Antonio," he said, his voice cracking. "A clear mind for me this evening."

A third knock sounded, and this time when the door opened, two new men walked in. One wore a blue suit with the flag of California on the lapel. Antonio was right back at the Hollywood Bowl. Mayor Buren wasn't wearing an American flag, then or now. Looking trim and fit in his tailored suit, he seemed quite proud of his perfectly trimmed Vandyke beard.

The police lieutenant accompanying him, by contrast, was pear-shaped and had a real soup strainer covering most of his mouth. His shirttail had come partly untucked under his ill-fitting blazer.

"Welcome," their host said. "I'm Antonio Moretti, and these are my men."

"Thanks for having us," Buren said. "This is Lieutenant Billy Best. He will be filling in for Chief Stone tonight because, unfortunately …"

Best took over when the mayor hesitated.

"Chief Stone was just sworn in and has very important business to attend to," Best said.

"I know that's a lie," Antonio said. "He can't have more important business than this meeting, can he?"

Best and Buren opened their mouths, but neither man replied.

Antonio grinned. "I'm joking." He shook their hands in turn and said, "Something to drink?"

The mayor hesitated, then nodded. "Sure, why not. I'll take bourbon on the rocks."

"Beer for me," Best said.

Yellowtail brought the drinks over, wearing the stone face he usually reserved for enemies. Inviting a cop here—especially the cop Vinny had once worked for—had all the men on edge.

Vito sat with his arms folded over his belly, chewing on a toothpick. Antonio didn't blame his cousin. The guy's face still showed the abuse he had endured behind bars.

Vito and Yellowtail weren't the only ones who didn't like seeing cops in the Moretti stronghold. Frankie and Carmine had opposed his decision to invite the cops here—or to work with them at all, for that matter.

Which was exactly why Antonio had asked his associates to attend the meeting: to show them who was in charge, but also to show them why they needed Mayor Buren and his police henchmen.

Buren took a sip of his whiskey. "Very nice."

"The best," Antonio said. He returned from the wet bar with a glass and raised it.

Buren held up his glass but then lowered it back to the table. "Let's hold up a minute here and get something straight," he said. "This deal we're here to discuss only works if you make me a promise you won't kill cops."

"I'll leave that up to my nephew," Antonio said. He gestured to Yellowtail, who pulled out his phone.

Buren raised an eyebrow, and Best waited to sip his upraised beer. "What's going on?" he asked.

"Relax, gentleman," Antonio said. "All will become clear in a moment."

Yellowtail opened the doors to the office, and Vinny came in. He wore a three-piece suit, and his hair slicked back on one side and cut short on the other.

Best dropped his beer on the floor when he saw his former rat.

"Something wrong with your drink?" Antonio asked.

Vinny moved with his father to the balcony doors, where Christopher pulled back the shades. Then he flipped the light on outside, illuminating a naked man bound to a chair on the patio.

"What the hell is this?" Buren asked.

"Chief Stone?" Best said. He reached for his waistband, but Lino suddenly had a gun out and pointed at his head. "Don't even think about it, pig," he said.

Best let his hand down slowly. "You can't do this," he said. "You'll never get away with it."

"I wouldn't move if I were you," Raff warned. He walked over and lifted the gun from Best's holster.

"One more test, Vin," Antonio said. "You decide. Do you kill Chief Stone, or does he become our partner? The choice is yours."

Raff handed the cop's gun to Vinny, who looked at it as he weighed the decision.

"I say blow his brains out," Carmine said.

Frankie, chewing on a match, nodded. "Pig can't be trusted."

Buren started up from his chair, eyes wide with fear, but Yellowtail grabbed him by the shoulders and pushed him back down. "Relax, Mr. Mayor," he said.

Antonio went outside with Vinny and Christopher. Chief Stone squirmed in the chair, his hands and feet bound. He mumbled into the bandanna gag over his mouth.

Christopher walked around the chair and untied the bandanna.

"Please," Stone gasped through his handlebar mustache. "I'll do whatever you want."

He looked at Vinny. "Kid, I'm sorry, I …"

Vinny pointed the gun at his head. "First off, I'm not a kid."

Stone looked down, and something trickled onto the ground.

"He pissed himself!" Christopher chuckled. "Good thing he's got no pants on."

Antonio wasn't encouraged by the sight. It told him the chief was weak and sniveling. Now he hoped Vinny would blow his brains out. Working with someone so weak was dangerous.

It appeared that Antonio was about to get his wish.

"You let those fuckers torture me," Vinny said, thumbing the hammer back on the .45. The pistol shook in his hand, and he blinked several times, as if trying to suppress the memory. "You let them treat me like I was garbage. Like a *dog*!"

Vinny jammed the barrel against Stone's temple. He clenched his jaw, and his hand stopped shaking. Antonio watched his finger move to the trigger.

"I'm sorry," Stone whimpered. "I didn't …"

Antonio folded his arms across his suit jacket, filled with pride. He had watched his nephew transform from the nervous boy who executed Enzo Sarcone, to a strong leader who was about to execute the chief of the largest police force left in the country.

Vinny had more than earned his button. Seeing him master his rage and emotions proved that now more than ever.

"Open your mouth," Vinny said, pulling the gun

away from Stone's temple. The chief resisted, shaking his head.

"Open your fucking mouth," Vinny said.

Stone shook his head again, and Christopher yanked it back by tugging on his hair.

"Stop this, please!" Buren said from inside the office. "If you kill him, I can't make a deal with you, Antonio."

"*Don* Antonio," Yellowtail said. "And you will do what we tell you to."

Stone closed his eyes and finally opened his mouth, sobbing like a child.

"Spending your final moments on earth like a sniveling baby," Antonio said. "At least, Enzo Sarcone died with dignity."

"You do this, and there's no deal!" Buren shouted.

"Forget him," Antonio said. "We own this city now."

"That's why I can't kill him," Vinny said. He decocked the hammer and stuck the pistol inside his waistband. "I can't work with the cops if they know I executed Chief Stone. But I can do this."

He took a pair of pliers from his coat pocket.

"What are you doing?" Stone asked. His wide eyes followed the pliers as Vinny lowered them toward his mustachioed upper lip.

Stone struggled in Christopher's grip, but Vinny managed to jam the pliers into his mouth and clamp on to a tooth. The chief howled as Vinny pried forward and backward, then yanked it out with a cracking sound.

Stone screamed in agony.

Vinny held up the bloody tooth. "Eye for an eye, as they say. And a tooth for a tooth."

He dropped the pliers onto Stone's naked lap. Christopher let go of his head, and the chief leaned forward, blood drooling from his lips.

"Stone is an asshole," Vinny said, looking over at Antonio. "But he's a corrupt asshole, and now he knows who the king of Los Angeles is going to be. Right, Chief?"

Moaning, Stone managed a nod.

"And you know what will happen if you cross us?" Vinny asked, crouching down in front of Stone.

Stone met his gaze. "I'll never cross you," he said. "I swear on my kids."

"Tell Don Antonio," Vinny said.

Stone's eyes flitted to Antonio. "I swear it, Don Antonio. I'll never cross you."

At first, Antonio was disappointed in his nephew, but then he saw the brilliance behind his decision. He started to smile, but it quickly turned to a sneer.

"I hope you're not as weak as you smell," Antonio grumbled, looking at the piss puddle on the balcony deck. "That's why I selected you for chief and not one of the other two candidates."

"*Selected* me?" Stone mumbled.

"What, you thought you got this job on your own merits?" Antonio said.

Blood drooled from Stone's lips and down his hairy chest. "I …" he said. "I …"

"I paid Mayor Buren a mint in silver to get you that spot," Antonio said. "Isn't that right, Mayor?"

Stone's eyes flitted to the open doorway as he digested the news.

"Get him some clothes," Antonio said. He walked

back inside, leaving his nephew to untie the chief. Christopher followed his brother into the office.

Antonio pulled out the head chair and sat back down. Then he took a drink from his glass. "So, Mayor Buren, about this deal you're here to discuss—tell me why you want to work with us."

Buren quickly regained his composure. Pulling on his cuff links, he said, "I believe the Moretti family brings something to the table that the Vega family didn't."

"Oh?"

"Unlike so many of these dirtbags running loose, you all follow a code of honor," Buren said. "The Vegas are brutal: skinning cops, lopping off heads. We can't have that. We *won't* have that. You demonstrated mercy by keeping Stone alive."

"You have my word," Antonio said. "We don't go after cops as long as they stay out of our way and obey my orders."

Buren seemed to think about it and looked over at Stone as he dressed.

"Chief Diamond was strong but stupid," the mayor said. "He didn't realize that sometimes it's necessary to work with …"

That's right, asshole. Pick your words carefully.

"… to work with an organization such as yours to keep order. He wanted to wipe out all organized crime, but that would have destroyed the city in the process. I believe in a more rational approach—what I call 'organized chaos.'"

"Organized chaos," Antonio said, lifting his glass. "I like that."

Buren held up his drink, and Antonio sealed the promise with the clink of glasses.

Lino took the gun off Best, who let out a sigh of relief.

"You didn't piss yourself too, did you?" Antonio asked. "Get him another beer, Lino."

Lino brought Best a new bottle.

"Now that we have that out of the way, let's gather around and talk about the future of the city," Antonio said. He got up and looked outside, then said in a loud voice, "Hope you're listening, Chief Stone."

Best reluctantly stepped over to look at the maps with Buren.

"As you know," Antonio said, "the city has essentially been divided into four selling zones, or territories, controlled by different crime organizations."

He ran a finger from the eastern edge of downtown to Pasadena's border with the Angeles National Forest, then down to the city's new eastern border at Chino Hills. "We control everything over to the barriers here, but most of our operation will be run at the Four Diamonds public housing blocks."

Then he pointed to Anaheim and Santa Ana, both circled in blue. "The Russians have won the battle for these areas. Sergei Nevsky grows stronger by the day."

Next, Antonio pointed to the areas outlined in red. "Skid Row and parts of downtown are still under the Bloods' control. I'm told Lil Snipes somehow survived his wounds from a few weeks ago." He shrugged. "Now people will know what comes of messing with the Morettis."

He pointed again at the map where the Angel Pyramids were being built in Inglewood, just south of the

Forum. "Everything from west of downtown to the ocean, and south to Long Beach, is Esteban Vega's territory—for now."

Best scratched his mustache. "We're still looking for him, and when we find him, we'll take him into custody. When that happens, zone two is as good as yours."

"Just remember," Antonio said, "Esteban Vega is mine. If my people get him first, he's a dead man. If your people grab him up, I want him handed over. *Alive*. I have special plans for the narco king."

"Understood," Best said.

Antonio looked back to the map and ran his finger around Ascot Hills Park. "The Four Diamonds public housing units are being built by the government here," he said. "When they're finished, they will be our biggest selling grounds. You will receive a fair shake, and you have my word that none of your men will be harmed— nor any police, for that matter, as long as they stay out of our way."

"Just find a way to keep your, um, commerce discreet, okay?" said Buren.

Antonio nodded. He already knew exactly how to move his product.

"You got it," he said.

"You got a deal, then," Buren said, extending his hand.

Antonio reached out, and they shook on it. Then he looked back to the patio door. Vinny led Stone inside. He was back in his uniform now and held a bloody handkerchief to his mouth.

Vinny gave him a shove into the office, and the chief limped over to Mayor Buren and Lieutenant Best.

"I'll be in touch, Antonio," Buren said.

"*Don* Antonio," Christopher said.

"See ya' later," Antonio said, purposely omitting his name and title.

The three men left the room steaming but knowing who their handlers were, thanks in part to Vinny.

Antonio went to his display case of ancient weapons. Selecting a sword, he joined his men under the stars on the outside patio. Christopher and Lino worked quickly to set up a table, lighting candles in preparation for the oath of the omertà.

Vinny waited with his hands folded across the button of his suit jacket, looking out over zone 4 of the city—a massive territory that he had helped Antonio secure for their family by killing Enzo Sarcone and infiltrating the police force.

It was time to reward his nephew for his sacrifices and loyalty.

"Vincent Christopher Moretti," Antonio said, "it is my great privilege to welcome you into the ranks of the Moretti family tonight. You have done more to earn this than any man your age."

Christopher stepped forward, taking the cigar butt out of his mouth and grinding it under his shoe. "Vin, I'm fucking proud of you," he said.

Raff patted Vinny on the back. "You aren't a boy anymore, and I'm proud to serve with you."

"Thank you," Vinny said.

The other soldiers formed a circle around the soon-to-be youngest made man in the family. Antonio handed the sword to his brother.

"Hold out your trigger finger," Christopher said.

Vinny smiled during the poke, his upper lip feeling the gap left by the pulled incisor. Then he dripped the blood on the picture of Saint Francis of Assisi. Christopher brought out a candle and set the picture ablaze in his son's hand.

"Repeat after me," Antonio said. "As this card burns, may my soul burn in hell if I betray the oath of omertà."

Vinny repeated the words, holding Antonio's gaze while the image of the Moretti family's patron saint crinkled in the flames. When it was nothing more than a curl of ash, Antonio put a hand on Vinny's left shoulder, and Christopher put a hand on his right shoulder.

"Welcome to the family," Christopher said.

Antonio looked upon his nephew with pride, hoping that someday his own son would become a brave and smart young man like his cousin.

"Are you ready for your first mission as a made man?" Antonio asked.

Vinny nodded. "I'm at your disposal, Don Antonio."

-28-

"How's it feel to have your button?" Doberman asked.

Vinny looked out over the Santa Monica Pier, considering the question. The moon sparkled on the ocean, and the waves lapped at the receding beach. Not far from here was the spot where they had first approached Carly Sarcone.

The memory of kidnapping her and then shooting her father in the head played in his mind's eye. He flinched from his anxiety-ridden thoughts. The things he had done to earn his button would also earn him a place in hell for eternity.

He shivered in the warm breeze.

"Vin?" Doberman asked.

"It feels good, man," Vinny lied.

Truth was, he felt low and dirty for the hand he had played in a lot of things over the past few months. Not only with Carly, but also some of the things he had done when posing as a police officer.

Was damnation worth the price?

This was what he had always wanted: to be a soldier

in the Moretti family. A gangster. And while he had committed heinous acts, his family's future was brighter now than ever, and he was a part of that. It had to count for something.

Doberman pulled out his cell phone to answer a call, distracting Vinny from the question he seemed unable to stop asking himself.

Get your head on straight, he chided himself.

The Vega family, the Nevsky family, and the other gangs would reorganize. The next fight would be for rule over the four zones, and though the Morettis had the police in their pocket, Esteban Vega was still as dangerous as ever.

Vinny had to be ready for anything.

"*Porca miseria!*" Doberman growled. "These new cell towers suck ass."

Five people came up the boardwalk as Doberman called their contact back. Vinny kept his eye on the men and one woman, all of them wearing hoodies much like his.

In his short time working with the anti-gang task force, he had learned how to look for threats, and these guys weren't one. Just a few young twentysomethings here to hang out on the beach.

Doberman slipped his phone into his jacket pocket, and they made their way back to their tinted black-on-black BMW, parked in a lot near the boardwalk.

The twentysomethings weren't the only ones out for a leisurely stroll tonight. A group of teenagers smoked a joint in the back of a pickup truck. Pulsing rap blasted from other cars, the bass so loud it vibrated the Beemer's trunk.

If Vinny didn't know better, it would have seemed like a normal prewar night at the Santa Monica Pier.

Their next stop was far from the beautiful views of the ocean. Vinny pulled his mask up to help mitigate the sour scent of garbage.

Mission one, he thought as they pulled up to the Santa Monica Waste Collection facility. The meeting spot was next to a row of garbage trucks. Piles of trash, tires, and junk littered the dirt site.

"I don't like this," Doberman said.

"Don Antonio knows where we are, right?"

"Yeah."

"Then we have nothing to worry about."

Vinny got out of the car and approached one of the trucks. A burly man wearing shorts and a tank top sat in the open passenger door. He jumped out, several thick silver chains popping out of his shirt.

"This the guy?" Vinny asked.

"They call him Mexican Mikey," Doberman said quietly. "Guy's a psycho, so better keep any jokes to yourself for this first meeting."

"¿Qué pasa?" the man said as they approached.

A dozen shadows moved away from the piles of junk.

"Shit," Vinny muttered. He didn't like being surprised.

"What's this?" Doberman asked.

Mikey shrugged. "I believe in a thing called insurance, and I don't know you two guineas."

Vinny kept his cool. "I was told this would be one-on-one."

"You brought one of your dogs; you expect me not to bring mine?"

Doberman smiled. "Nah, you're good, man."

"Still don't know what you want with my operation," Mikey said, "so let's cut to the fucking chase."

His men formed a perimeter, some of them holding guns, others carrying bats or crowbars. One even had a chainsaw—probably just for intimidation, but Vinny didn't want to find out.

"We're here to talk logistics," Vinny said.

"Logistics?" Mikey raised a brow. "The fuck you talking 'bout, *ese*?"

"Transportation," Vinny said. "We want your garbage trucks."

Mikey tilted his head and took a step closer. Vinny could smell his rancid breath.

"They aren't for sale, yo," Mikey said. "I was told you guys had a long-term deal for me."

"We don't want to buy them," Vinny said. "We can do that on our own. We want to *rent* them."

"We want to hire you to drive and deliver our product," Doberman said.

Mikey glanced at him, then back to Vinny, realization manifesting in a black, rotting grin.

"Now you're talking, *ese*!" he said.

"Good. We'll start small, do some test runs, and see how things work out," Vinny said. He reached into his track jacket. Several of his men stepped closer, raising their weapons.

"Relax," Vinny said. "It's a down payment. We brought you some silver, and some chips that you can use at our casino."

He held out a bag to Mikey, who snatched it from his hand like a feral child grabbing a scrap of food.

Mikey looked inside and grinned even wider. "Gracias," he said.

"*De nada, amigo*," Vinny said with a forced smile. "I'll have my people contact you when we're ready to start." He reached out, wishing he had a glove on to shake the garbage man's grubby paw.

The meeting concluded as abruptly as it began, and Vinny and Doberman returned to the BMW. Their next stop was across town, near the construction site of the Four Diamonds. With a half hour's drive ahead, they had plenty of time to discuss their arrangement with Mikey. His uncle's idea was ingenious, as long as Mikey and his crew held up their end of the bargain and didn't do anything stupid.

Vinny didn't like the guy, but part of his job was to work with lowlifes.

The full moon climbed in the sky, shedding a carpet of white over the construction site that would become the biggest drug-selling zone in California. Vinny wasn't sure who Antonio would assign to run the area, but his job was to make sure they had enough supply to keep up with the demand, and a safe way to transport it. With step two secured, his job was now to make sure that the police under Chief Stone stayed out of the way.

Doberman parked at the edge of the construction site and killed the engine. "Looks like our contact is late," he said.

Vinny scanned the empty parking lot and spotted a black Audi parked between a bulldozer and a front-end loader.

"No, he's over there," Vinny said. "You wait in the car this time and keep it running."

Doberman turned the engine back on, and Vinny got out. He jogged over to the Audi, slowing as the driver's door opened. A dark-skinned man in a black leather jacket stepped onto the pavement, flashing a smile that reminded Vinny of his own.

"Vinny?" the man asked.

"Yeah."

Vinny stopped and scanned the construction site for threats but saw nothing moving in the moonlight.

"Detective First Grade Ray Clarke."

Vinny studied the cop. "I've seen you before somewhere …"

Ray shrugged one shoulder. "Probably. I've been through it all, man. The war, the fighting, the camps—"

"The camps," Vinny said, cutting him off. "That's where I saw you and another cop, going into a tent. I believe those guys were Sureños you were collecting from."

"Could be, man, I don't remember. Does it matter?"

"Nah," Vinny said. "Long as you realize who you're working for."

Ray licked his lips.

"That would be the Morettis," Vinny reminded him.

"I work for whoever Chief Stone tells me I work for. Guess that's you boys now."

Vinny didn't like this guy much better than Mikey, but when you were dealing with shady assholes, better to keep expectations low.

"Once these buildings are up, I need a guarantee you'll help me keep your buddies in blue from doing anything stupid with our operation," Vinny said.

"You got it, man. Easy-peasy, long as we get paid."

Vinny met his gaze and Ray held it.

"All right, we can do that," Vinny said. They sealed their new partnership with a one-two handshake.

"Yo, I do got a favor I need," Ray said.

Vinny snorted. "I don't think you realize you're the one that's supposed to be doing the favors, not me."

"I do, man, but this is something near and dear to me, and it will go a long way if you can help me out."

"What? Hurry it up, I want to get the hell out of here."

Ray reached into his jacket, and this time Vinny was the one to take a step back.

"Just a picture," Ray said when he saw his reaction. He handed it over to Vinny.

"I'm hoping you can find some info about this girl. She's the sister of one of my cop buddies. Got kidnapped in Downey a few nights ago."

"How old?"

"She just turned twelve."

Vinny studied the picture. The girl did look young, but many of the girls sold into the human-trafficking black hole were young. His gut sank at the possibility that someone in the growing Moretti crew had done this. They were expanding into all sorts of selling operations now, including people.

"I'll see what I can do," he said.

"Thanks, man, I appreciate it."

Vinny watched the crooked cop get back into his car. For a moment, he just stood there, holding the picture. Chances were good that someone in the Moretti family had taken the little girl. Chances were even better that she would end up as a sex slave and live a short, hellish life in some filthy brothel.

It was finally sinking in that he was a made man, a Moretti soldier, and what that really meant. They had a code, but that didn't mean they weren't evil. The terrible things his uncle had done weren't over. He would do whatever it took to claim the crown of the gang capital of the world, in one of the last cities in the United States.

As the Audi drove off, Vinny walked over to the fence surrounding the construction site and hurled his dinner up into a bush. He wiped his mouth and began the slow walk back to the BMW, wondering whether he was really made out for this life after all.

* * *

Dom straightened the collar of his new LAPD uniform and filled his lungs. The relatively fresh air at Dodger Stadium didn't bring back any good memories, nor did it do much to calm his nerves.

He really didn't want to be here today. This moment away from the streets was time he could be searching for his sister. Monica was somewhere out there, and his heart hurt knowing she was in danger.

Almost two weeks had passed since her kidnapping. The battle for the city had ended not long after, with the gangs shattered and on the run. He didn't know where she was or whether the gangs would reorganize, but he did know, now more than ever, that becoming a cop was his destiny. He was born a fighter, and he was damn good at it.

Today, he was surrounded by thousands of other fighters. He sat in the third row of chairs on the yellow grass of Dodger Stadium, with the newest inductees to the Los Angeles Police Department. Warriors like Camilla and Moose, both still recovering from their injuries fighting F-13. They sat in the rows ahead, covered in bandages from the night of hell.

Moose had nearly lost his right eye to a piece of metal that lodged in the bone beneath his eyebrow, and he had undergone two surgeries to remove shrapnel and fix a broken rib.

Today was his first day back in uniform since the battle that nearly cost him his life.

Many of the soon-to-be cops surrounding Dom had injuries from the fighting. Today, these brave men and women sat in their dress blues, waiting to be inducted officially onto the force.

He didn't recognize most of them. They had come from departments all over the county after the reorganization placed them all under the LAPD banner. Now they all would wear the same uniform, with the same logo, and fight together to take the streets back entirely from the gangs.

With everyone together here, there seemed to be a palpable feeling of hope in the air, though Dom couldn't bring himself to feel much of anything but dread. He fidgeted in his seat, anxious to get out of here and back on the beat, looking for Monica.

He stared ahead blankly, trying to manage the dread and the anger that came with it.

The California and US flags whipped in the wind on the flanks of the stage. Behind them, the outfield wall had collapsed, providing a view of the crater in the parking lot—a vivid scar from the Second Civil War.

Beyond that, smoke drifted above the San Gabriel

Mountains. Wildfires were encroaching from all directions, darkening the skyline—yet another threat facing the city.

Dom twisted around to look at the stands. Family members were filling the seats to watch their loved ones, but not his family. His mom was back home, mourning, while his father was out on the border.

Ronaldo had recently decided to join the LA County Sheriff's Department now that the marines had been disbanded along with most of the military. When he wasn't looking for Monica, he was responsible for securing the city's eastern border wall, fighting looters, and vetting refugees, as he was today.

Bettis and Tooth had joined up with Ronaldo, but Marks had decided to take a lieutenant's post in the LAPD, where he too was helping search for Monica.

Dom noticed three people in the stands who could have been his family. The mom and daughter waved at an officer sitting a few rows behind him, and the father sat looking down proudly on his son or daughter.

It wasn't just families in the stands. Snipers were perched throughout the stadium, and armed teams patrolled for threats down the rows and aisles. After what happened at the Hollywood Bowl, security was tighter "than a camel's ass in a sandstorm," as Dom's dad used to say.

He turned back to the stage, where a portrait of Chief Diamond sat on an easel next to the LAPD flag. The hero cop's final words before his assassination had rallied every officer and sheriff's deputy, and even the citizenry, in the fight against the gangs.

But it was the help of former rebel units such as the

Desert Snakes that had made the crucial difference in crushing the organized gangs and sending them scuttling back into their holes, just as the chief had predicted.

The fight wasn't over, though. Far from it. Some of the police officers sitting in the audience, onstage, and in the stadium were, without a doubt, corrupt—men and women who had done business with the gangs and would continue to work with the remnants.

Rumors of new, powerful crime families had circulated throughout the ranks of the department over the past few days, and Dom suspected that they were behind the kidnapping of Monica and the other kids, as well as thousands of other atrocities across the city.

The thought filled him with rage.

Speakers crackled, and music started. The crowd stood as two dozen officers filed over to chairs onstage. All heads turned to Chief Stone, who walked up to the podium. Mayor Buren had selected him over the other contenders for the spot to replace Chief Diamond.

If it were up to Dom, he would have made Marks the chief of police. The marine, aside from being practically family, was about as stand-up as they came.

Stone stepped up to the podium and looked out over the people in the stands. Then he smiled, revealing a missing front tooth, before promptly clamping his lips shut. He gripped the sides of the lectern and, in a deep voice, said, "Today, I am honored to welcome new officers to the LAPD."

The new chief again swept the crowd with his gaze before continuing. "I can still remember when I was sitting at my academy commencement ceremony—something most of you never got to experience. But the experience you have already gained on the streets has given you far more than what I learned in training and inside classrooms. They say the best learning is hands-on. And all of you here got that."

Yeah, those of us that made it.

In his mind's eye, Dom pictured all the cops who had died over the past few months. The people who rushed to the call of duty when their city was imperiled. And the soldiers, marines, and heroic civilians—the magnitude of suffering and death was hard to fathom.

"The faces I'm looking at this morning are those of survivors," Stone said. "You have given everything you had to give, but are still willing to give more, and for that our city thanks you. Today, we celebrate your bravery and look to the future as the citizens of Los Angeles prepare for a brighter tomorrow. Receiving your shield today is the final step to becoming an officer, and it comes with the great and solemn responsibility to protect and serve."

He paused for reflection and then raised a hand over the outfield, pointing at the cranes rising over a construction site in the distance.

"With the disbanding of the army and Marine Corps, in this postwar world, your duty will be to become our soldiers—a different kind of soldier, who will protect the new public housing across the city, the desalination plants, the solar farms, and the traditional farms that will once again produce food for the great state of California.

"You are the future of this, one of the very last metropolitan cities in the United States that are still functioning."

The words sent a chill through Dom.

"I'm keeping this short this morning because our work starts now," Stone said. "Good luck and Godspeed. I will be here with you to fight this fight."

The cops all stood and clapped as Stone walked away and another officer took his place. He called names to come forward and accept their shields. The rows slowly emptied, and by the time Dom got to the front, the armpits of his uniform were dark with sweat.

With every step, his injured foot throbbed from the tight dress shoes and the sweat burning the wound. He gritted his teeth, ready to be out of the stiff, hot wool suit.

When he was next in line for his shield, a voice called out. "Welcome to the force, brother."

Ray Clarke stood in the third row of the officers onstage. Newly promoted to detective first grade, he flashed a perfect white smile, clearly proud of himself. Neither he nor Moose had found their parents' killers yet, but the hunt was still on, and now they had joined the hunt for Monica.

Dom stepped forward, next in line. Chief Stone held out his hand.

"Dominic Salvatore, congratulations," he said.

"Thank you, sir."

They shook hands, and Dom accepted his shield and limped off the stage and down the aisle of empty seats. Behind home plate, the spectators clapped politely.

Dom took in another deep breath, feeling a wave of pride like what he once felt after winning a fight in the Octagon. But the pride faded away.

He didn't deserve to feel anything but the guilt

eating at his guts for not being able to protect Monica, and he wouldn't allow himself to feel pride until he found her.

After the ceremony, Camilla and Moose joined him in the parking lot. That they all were standing here together was nothing less than a miracle, and this wasn't lost on any of them.

In Dom's eyes, Moose was a hero. He had saved both Dom and Camilla in the AMP office. But Moose didn't see himself as anything special.

"Don't worry, Dom," he said. "We're going to find your sister, and we're going to find the bastards who killed my parents. Then, when we do, we're all going on a long vacation."

Camilla blinked. "Ugh, I'm not sure I want to come on a vacation with you two."

Moose laughed, but Dom didn't feel much like it.

"You're stuck with us, Cam, like it or not," Moose said.

They started toward the buses that would ship them back to the LAPD headquarters, when a voice called out across the parking lot. Dom turned to see his father and his mother hurrying away from a parked Humvee.

"I'll catch up with you guys in a bit," Dom said.

"Dominic," Ronaldo called out.

"Dad, Mom, what are you guys doing?" Dom said.

For a moment, his beating heart hoped they had information about Monica. Was it possible? Had she been found?

"Tried to make the tail end of the ceremony," Ronaldo said. "I'm sorry we missed it."

Elena nodded. "I'm sorry," she said, her tone full of resentment.

Dom gave her a hug, hoping that someday she would forgive him and his dad for leaving her and Monica at the school. But he wouldn't blame her if she didn't.

"It's okay; I didn't expect you to come," Dom said.

Elena pulled away, her mascara a mess—evidence she had cried on the way here. She wasn't doing well, and Dom wasn't sure how to help her. She spent most days in their new housing unit, sitting and thinking while he and his father were out working or looking for Monica.

He had already promised he would find her, and so had Ronaldo, but both knew that the chances were growing slimmer by the day.

"Come on," Ronaldo said. "We'll give you a ride to the HQ."

Dom followed his parents back to their vehicle. He glanced over his shoulder at all the newly minted cops boarding buses, their eager faces so full of enthusiasm. How many of them would make it through their first year on the job? And how many of those who survived would still live by the department's motto, "To protect and to serve," when they saw the easy money to be made?

Everyone from the mayor to the news anchors was fond of making blithe pronouncements about how the fight for Los Angeles was over, but Dom didn't share their sunny outlook. He couldn't escape the nagging sense that this was just the lull before an even bigger fight.

It wasn't so much the gangs that had him worried. They would regroup over time and get at least some of their mojo back, but they were old-school and crude in their methods, relying on brute force and terrorism to accomplish their ends. The forces for good had beaten them and would beat them again.

But another, more sinister threat was quietly on the rise. The powerful crime families, the scourge of eastern cities for over a century, had never been a factor in California. The civil war had uprooted the social institutions, creating fertile ground for these mastermind criminals with the vision and the sophistication to infiltrate the government and make the system work for them. These new enemies were coming out of the shadows, and soon they would be at the gates.

And Dominic Salvatore would be there, waiting for them. In taking his sister, they had made an implacable enemy, unleashing on themselves a nightmare that would never end as long as they drew breath.

Don't miss the next installment
in the Sons of War series!